CRAIGLOCKHA...

David Toulmi...

Blown Seed

Pan Books London and Sydney

7

The first edition of *Blown Seed*
was published with the assistance of
the Scottish Arts Council

First published 1976 by Paul Harris Publishing
This edition published 1978 by Pan Books Ltd,
Cavaye Place, London, SW10 9PG
© David Toulmin 1976
ISBN 0 330 25287 9
Printed and bound in Great Britain by
Richard Clay (The Chaucer Press) Ltd, Bungay, Suffolk

Part One

Folk in the Bogside would tell you that the MacKinnons came to Lachbeg with the railway; that Radnoch MacKinnon came off the train at Leary Station while the Irish navvies were still working on the line. They had heard their grandfathers talking about it, they said: how Radnoch MacKinnon came down from Duff House in Banffshire as coachman for the Laird at Lachbeg; and how he had married the head cook, Joyce McCombie, and the two of them leased the farm of Bogmyrtle, on the Laird's estate, with some help from the Laird, they said, because Radnoch was a great piper and the Laird wouldn't let him out of his hearing. From that day on, mostly on a summer evening, when the sky was clear and the wind was quiet, you could hear a MacKinnon playing the bagpipes at the gable of the house at Bogmyrtle; and when Radnoch died his son Craig took it up, him being a piper for the Queen's Volunteers at Leary Hall, by the station yonder. Craig was still alive, but it was his son Riach who did the piping nowadays, him with the wooden leg, and the MacKinnons had piped for two generations of the Farquhar Lairds of Lachbeg. Craig MacKinnon had piped the old Laird to his family vault on the estate, and most likely when the time came Riach MacKinnon would do the same for the present Laird, who was imbecilic, they said, and not likely to live much longer.

Bogmyrtle farm lay in the shadow of the Mattock Hill, directly under the white stone deer on its slopes: where he sniffed the wine breeze of the heather in his shapely nostrils, his great antlers spiked out on the peat slopes, gazing down with a fine disdain on the folk in the howe; watching their trauchle in field or moss, cutting their peat or forking hay, with the scent of honey in the clover. The antlered deer survived their short lives like a great sphinx, rejoicing in their births and marriages and mourning at their deaths,

7

while he surveyed their funeral processions to the old kirkyard at Lachbeg, where you could read the names of most
of the folk who had lived in the howe, carved out on the old
leaning gravestones. The MacKinnon stone wasn't as old as
some of them, and it still stood upright among its fellows,
but what with Radnoch and Joyce, and the bairns of Rachel,
and her miscarriages, the grave was tramping full, and the
MacKinnons would have to buy new ground and set up
another stone at the next death in their family.

From the day that a bairn first remembered seeing the
deer on the slopes of the Mattock, to the day of his death,
the deer would still be there. During his short life a Mac-
Kinnon would take a few danders up the hill, mostly on a
Sunday afternoon, to clear away some of the weeds that
covered the white quartz stones of the deer, and from there
he would get a deer's eye view of Bogmyrtle and the howe,
the woods of Lachbeg and the Myreloch, where the sea had
made an angry bite on the coast. But nobody in the howe
could tell you why the deer was there, or to what purpose.
He was just part of the hill and had always been there for all
they knew; and you might as well ask why the sun was in the
sky, or the moon for that matter: you left that to the gentry
and the folks that understood books, no need to clutter your
brain with stite like that.

On misty days you couldn't see the deer at all, but you
could hear the foghorn on the Battery Head, far out on the
coast, the graveyard of many a sailing ship, wrecked on the
serrated rocks that spurred the shore like the teeth of a saw
blade. Between the rocks and the bented shore was a fine
stretch of sand and gritted shell, where the white-topped
waves had dashed the buckies to tiny particles on the rocks,
and at low tide the farmers of the Bogside would load it into
their carts as grit for their poultry to put shells on their eggs.
They would coup a load at the gable of the steading, and
when the hens weren't scraping amongst it the bairns would
play there, ploughing and drilling with their little hands in
the soft smooth sand.

Sometimes in the autumn the wind shook the skirts of the
hill, where all summer the tall willow-herb and the thistle

8

burr stood in the sun, a red and purple patchwork on the hemline of the Mattock, reaching down to Lachbeg and the white cotton flowers on the moors. Now the soft wind carried the seed over the parks, tiny motes in the sunhaze, each one in its parachute of lightest down, blown seed in the wind, showering over the crofts and farms like snow in summer, sprouting in a year or two where folk scythed and hoed to keep their crops clean.

The railway that came to the Bogside still ran in its deep cuttings round the shoulder of the Mattock Hill, emerging on to steep embankments just under Bogmyrtle, where it crossed the road on an iron bridge towards Leary Station, silhouetted at night against the sky, the hot cinders from the funnel streaming over its back, the long row of lighted carriages gliding smoothly behind in the darkness. In day-time, when the school bairns saw a train coming they ran to hear the rumble of it under the bridge: the longer the train the longer the rumble, especially if it were a goods train, like thunder in their ears. When the boys among them grew up that same train took them to hear the thunder of their lives on the bloody fields of Flanders, while the girls waited in vain for their return and wept at their passing. When a horseman was on the road with a pair of carts he would stop if he saw a train coming, afraid to be caught under the bridge and a train rumbling overhead, for if you wanted to fleg a gelding take him under the iron brig at Leary and wait for a train, and most likely the beast would go frantic. A braw place to train them for the cavalry and the thunder of guns when the war came. But for all that, the trains had brought prosperity to the farmers of the Bogside, carting away their grain and potatoes and bringing back fertilizer; taking their cattle and sheep to market and their wives to Brochan and Aberdeen, a place they had never seen in their lives before.

Brochan was the busy fishing port on the eastern shoulder of the country, where the roughest seas converge on beach and rock and the lighthouse sends his beam of light across the stormy waters. Long trains were loaded with herring in the summer, threshing out of Brochan for the south in high spirits, until they reached the slopes of the Mattock, where the engines had a sore trauchle, hoasting their way up past Bogmyrtle, the hot cinders sometimes setting fire to the heather on the skirts of the hill, until they reached Stronach, the little village on the elbow of the Mattock, where the line levels out and the train moves freely. But the passenger trains came down from the Mattock at tremendous speed, braking hard at Leary Station, where the farmers' gigs were waiting for their wives and visitors; but if you were a Mac-Kinnon most likely you would walk the mile and a half back from the station to Bogmyrtle, just under the cloven hoofs of the antlered deer.

Further down the coast was Scotstoun, another fishing port with brave fishermen who wore jerseys or ganzies that didn't have buttons to get stuck in their nets, and folk called them the Blue Mogganers from the leggings they wore at the whale fishing back in the days of the sailing ships. But the folk of Lachbeg didn't go much to Scotstoun, because it was a roundabout way with the train and a long weary road with a horse-cart.

In the second year of their marriage, a son was born to Radnoch MacKinnon and Joyce McCombie and they called him Craig. When Craig was just over twenty his father was killed in a fall from a horse-cart, when he broke his back and lay in his bed three days writhing in agony, the doctor unable to help him, until the pain numbed his brain and brought on a stroke that killed him. Craig took on the farm for his mother and worked Bogmyrtle in the pride of his youth; ploughing, sowing, hoeing and harvesting, while his mother did the kitchen work and milked the kye and fed the hens. Young Craig was the last of the MacKinnons to wear a kilt – not the tartan of his clan but that of the Gordons – when he spent the summer evenings with the militia at Leary Hall, in full Highland dress; and sometimes he played the pipes at the kitchen gable, while the Laird cocked his lugs from the turrets of Lachbeg.

But Joyce McCombie had not been born to slavery, and she had worked too long with the gentry to go about in rags and live the life of a tink like most farm wives in the Bogside. Joyce liked to dress herself and take the train to Brochan, where she bought her best clothes and sometimes had her picture taken in the newfangled photographic studios that had opened in the toon for the wives of the wealthy herring-curers. It was all the fashion to have your likeness taken when the cameras first came in, something that was re-served for the gentry in the days of the portrait painter; but nowadays it was quicker and much cheaper to have it done with a camera in black and white. You just sat in a fancy chair and watched the 'birdie's eye', while the photo-grapher stood behind his tripod in the middle of the floor, a black stole over his head, and when he flashed a light in his hand you were 'taken', quick as bottled lightning.

So Joyce engaged a serving quine for all the menial chores at Bogmyrtle, feeding the swine and scrubbing the floors and such like, while Joyce did the cooking and the washing and the darning and the sewing, and went to chapel at Lachbeg on the Sundays that young Craig was free to drive her down in the gig; not that he would wait for her, but would come back later, for it wasn't a chance to miss with the servant quine.

Rachael Bissett was the name of the quine Joyce Mc-Combie had engaged to help her in the kitchen, and some-times she helped Craig in the byres; a quine who could turn her hand to anything, and Joyce was satisfied that she had the best of the bargain. But she was too much of a tempta-tion for young Craig, and it is a wonder that a woman of Joyce's understanding didn't have more sense. Her son was the envy of the district, especially when he wore the High-land garb, and could have gotten almost any quine he wanted, but he had been content to flirt with them and have his fun at leisure. But Rachael's peat-brown eyes aroused his passion, the rasp-lip smile and the pearly gleam of her teeth, the smooth touch of her cheeks, the bronze gold of her hair, and the thin waist of her, and her fine legs when he got a glimpse of them, sometimes when she pulled up her stockings unaware of his presence – it was all too much for the hot-blooded Craig, for he dearly liked the serving quine, even from her first days on the place. Within months he had kissed her and fondled her breasts and her thighs, and on the days that his mother went to Brochan or the chapel he had his way with the quine in the straw of the barn. For a long time they kept their love a secret, courting in the moonlight in Lachbeg Woods, clear starry nights when Craig was supposed to be at the drill hall and Rachael at home with her folks. When Joyce discovered their lust she was furious: the day she caught them kissing in the byre, when she shut herself in the ben-room and sulked for the rest of the day.

Joyce tried to keep the lovers apart: kept the quine inside at nights when her son was free from the fields; and when there was folk in the house she sent the quine to the steading, like she was one of the nowt beasts, treating her like an outcast, threatening to sack her, until it angered her son. Craig went outside and found his lass weeping in the turnip shed, an unwanted creature his mother had sent to pick the sprouts off the tatties, while Joyce entertained her chapel-going friends in the ben-room. But it fair turned the young Craig against his mother, especially when his lass told him she was carrying his child.

When Rachael's bairn began to show, Joyce tried to get rid of her. She was the daughter of a small crofter on the Lachbeg estate, and maybe Joyce had someone higher up in mind as a wife for her son, perhaps the daughter of one of her chapel friends. But being a widow Joyce couldn't work the place without her son, and he had made it plain that he wouldn't stay on the place unless he had Rachael Bissett to share his bed; that he would even elope with her, come to that. Craig had thought that his lass being with a bairn would make a difference; that his mother would relent and let them marry – but he was mistaken, and the lass went home to her ain folk to have her child. Joyce was a deeply religious woman and she deplored the marriage on principle. Intercourse before marriage she felt was a vile sin. In later years she never forgave her son and Rachael Bissett for the way they had deceived her, lusting in the barn behind her back, though butter wouldn't melt on their cheeks in broad daylight. And Rachael never forgave Joyce for letting her have her first child out of wedlock, consenting to their marriage after the birth, on Craig's final threat of leaving Bogmyrtle.

So Rachael Bissett became mistress of Bogmyrtle. She had been one of a large family of crofting folk and had had to look for a job at an early age. Joyce rued the day she had fee-ed the quine, but to please her son and work the place she had to put up with the young wife and her bairn. But Rachael was a go-ahead young woman who soon showed Joyce she wasn't born to be a servant, at least not for long. Things hadn't gone her way for a start, but when she became mistress it wasn't long before she made an impression; no longer an outcast quine of the tattie hoose, but mistress of the farm kitchen, frowning on Joyce at every turn, though she never ventured into Joyce's ben-room. Nowadays Joyce was the servant, milking the kye when Rachael had her bairns and making a diet for Craig, and it gave Rachael an excuse for putting up with her mother-in-law.

The MacKinnons were chapel folk, and though Rachael had been married quietly into the family, rather slyly you might say, by the Registrar in Brochan, behind the backs of the clergy, she now joined the flock on a Sunday. Joyce would keep the bairn, little Helen yonder, that had been born before their marriage, while Rachael rigged herself for the gig with Craig, and the pair of them went clopping down to Lachbeg Chapel, thick with its trees and gravestones by the lakeside. There was a parish kirk at Leary for the Presbyterian folk and back at Bogmyrtle Joyce could hear the bells of both of them clanging in the distance.

Rachael was a rare figure of a woman, hand picked you might say from the common ranks of womanhood; not a lady by any means, or in the sense that Joyce was a lady of some refinement, but she had a physical grace about her that outshone her rough manners, and unless you spoke to Rachael, when her broad Scots tongue gave her away, you would have sworn she was one of the gentry. Since she had her bairn Rachael had reached a fine maturity; no longer a slip of a quine but a full-breasted woman, her waist held tight in whalebone corsets with a slight bustle behind, and what with her flowered hat and spotted veil she was fair a picture as she walked with Craig to the chapel door. The neighbour billies looked at her shyly, lads like Knockieben and Sauchieburn yonder, nodding to Craig in passing, thinking maybe they couldn't blame him for marrying his servant quine after all. But their wives eyed Rachael without a smile, clutching their bibles tightly in their black gloved hands, for their sympathies were all with Joyce, and they scorned this little runt who had trysted Craig Mac-Kinnon away from his mother.

But Rachael never heeded them, though her fine nostrils moved slightly with her deeper breathing, something you noticed when she was angered or emotionally upset, while she smiled sweetly to the minister, her thin lips curving beautifully over her white even teeth that she polished with a wet finger dipped in the soot from the back of the chimney. Her skin was soft and peach, that would tempt a man to bite her, and since her marriage to Craig she had combed out her straggly hair and brushed it with a shining stroke. When she was a servant it straggled all over her face and got in her eyes when she washed the dishes. Joyce got a strand of it in the oatcakes and riled at her for it. Now that Rachael was mistress at Bogmyrtle her hair was in a thick plait and wound round her head like a bronze tiara, so that you could see her ears, with the tiny gold dabs in the lobes, that she had had pierced in Brochan; and you could see the nape of her shapely neck, with a few downy hairs on it, and even these had character, and showed she was not to be trifled with.

But in spite of everything Joyce MacKinnon took fondly to her little grand-daughter, and the child ran to Joyce when Rachael scolded her. Helen slept with her grandmother in the ben-room, and Joyce's fondness for the bairn replaced some of the love she had lost on her son. When Joyce looked on the sweet innocent face of the bairn she forgave the fornication of the parents, or tried to forget it; desiring only to live quietly in the bosom of a growing family circle, increased by the years in Rachael's fertile womb.

Rachael had her own personal troubles common to young womanhood, and she didn't have much time or opportunity to annoy herself about the past. In giving herself to Craig MacKinnon, Rachael had shouldered a lusty yoke. He was a man not easily satisfied with a woman, and what with his bairns and Rachael's miscarriages he nearly tore the guts out of his wife. In later years it widened her pelvis and made her slightly bow-legged, an appearance which strengthened rather than diminished her look of authority, and her shrewish acumen for getting things done. Each new child that was born to Rachael in the box-bed, after it had been washed and dressed, Helen picked it up and ran through with the bairn to the ben-room, where Joyce was sometimes abed even now, and she reached out for the infant and took it in her arms fondly, a bairn of her own son and Rachael Bissett, born in honest wedlock, and she blessed it and handed the child back to Helen. 'They're nae bairns,' Joyce said to Helen, 'but wee angels, come tae bide in hell.' Rachael began to wonder if there was some truth in this, especially when Riach her second son had his right leg crushed by a cartwheel while he was still at school. Riach's leg had to be sawn off at the hip, leaving a short stump, on which he crawled for a time on the kitchen floor, a sore trial to Rachael until he could manage a crutch and ventured into the farm close.

In her last years Joyce developed diabetes and Rachael fed her on boiled turnips and kale and cabbage brose, or a hare or a rabbit that Craig had shot in the parks. Not that Rachael could really be blamed for this, for she was sore pressed to feed her growing family and her hard-working man, never mind a gluttonous old woman in the ben-room. But Joyce's appetite became a weapon in Rachael's hands, to indulge her ill humour, to gorge or fast her victim as the mood suited her, and she used it with devilish malignity. For Joyce it became a wound that gnawed and fretted her soul to dementia; a helpless dotard in her senility. Rachael locked her in the ben-room, sometimes without a fire, where she lay on her brass-topped bedstead and soiled herself on the sheets. When Joyce complained of her diet Rachael pulled her to the floor by the hair and kicked her bedsores. The bairns spat upon her and threw breadcrusts into the room, while she scrambled for them on the floor, slipping about in her own urine. The bairns went into raptures over her gluttony, gloated over her enfeebled ravishment, while Joyce devoured whatever they threw at her.

When Joyce cried for food Rachael sometimes sent Helen to thrash her, maybe out of spite because Helen was her favourite. Helen told Joyce to scream, to make it sound real, while Helen thumped at the pillows and her own bare hips. Joyce understood and cried out 'Mercy mercy,' in a hoarse pitiful screech that Rachael heard from the kitchen. 'Skelp 'er up!' Rachael cried, while the bairns in the passage skirled with laughter.

On the days that Craig and Rachael went away with the shelt and gig old Joyce was somewhat relieved of her suffering. Helen was able to give her grandmother a treat. She sent her brothers and sisters to the byres, carrying Riach with them, and when she had the house to herself she kindled a fire and tidied up Joyce's room. She washed her granny's face and her bed-sores and dusted them with powder from Rachael's press in the box-bed, clean and soothing for Joyce. Helen combed and brushed Joyce's grey hair, changed and washed her stinking bedclothes and put a clean warm gown on her frail body. She made oatmeal brose and fed them to Joyce with cream from the milk house, skimmed from the wide brown earthenware basins on the blue flagstone shelves. She cut a slice from the cheese kebbock, crumbling with mites, stole some quarters of oat-breid and placed them under Joyce's pillow. When evening approached she lit the paraffin lamp and pulled down the blind, then sat a while by the bedside, reading aloud to Joyce from the big family bible on her knees.

Before Joyce fell asleep, she said, 'God bless ye, lassie, and may the warld use ye weel!'

When Helen tiptoed out of the room she found some of

the bairns in the passage, where they had been spying on her, what she had been up to with their grandmother. 'We'll tell on ye,' they said, and Helen got a skelpin' from Rachael on her return.

But sometimes the bairns could be bribed to silence with a good supper: then they were on her side and things weren't so bad. She could tell them ghost stories and frighten them into submission.

On such a day as this, when Helen sat reading the Bible, Joyce said to her, 'Sin lies at your father's door!' So Helen laid the Bible aside and got a pail of warm water and soap and scrubbed the stone step at the back kitchen door, because nobody used the front door, and while she was about it her parents returned in the gig.

'What are ye at, quine?' her mother asked. 'I scrubbed the back doorstep juist this mornin'.'

Helen looked up innocently, from where she knelt by the kitchen door. In one hand she still held the dripping scrubber, with the other she put her black hair back from her eyes and forehead.

'Granny said that sin lies at oor father's door, so I got soap and watter tae wash it off!'

Rachael's eyes embered at her words and she raised her fists in the air. Her fine nostrils moved quickly as her breath came faster in her rage. 'Did ye her that, Daw?' she asked, standing up in the gig, so that the tartan rug fell off her knees. Craig's face blazed in anger and he jumped out of the gig without opening the door. He picked up the pail of dirty water Helen had been using, strode over her kneeling body and dashed into the kitchen.

He came upon his mother in the front passage, searching for food when her door was unlocked. He took one wild look at her decrepit body and threw the pail of water over her. 'That'll teach ye nae tae slander us on yer death-bed!' he cried, and ran out of the house.

Joyce screamed, while the cold shock of the water took her breath away. She staggered and swayed and reached out for support, clinging to the grandfather clock. The brown filthy water ran through her hair and over her face, dripping from her nightgown on to her bare chilled feet. She clung harder to the tall clock, until it swung with her weight and fell on top of her, where she lay senseless in a pool of sewage, urinating as she fell.

Rachael was avenged in this last outburst. Years ago, in this same kitchen, when she and Craig returned from their honeymoon, Joyce had sniffed and tossed her head high, clashed the door and walked along the passage to her room, leaving a neighbour woman who rose politely to greet the newlyweds. Craig had been in Highland dress, wearing the tartan of the Gordons, with sporran and plaid, because he was one of the Queen's volunteers at the time, a piper in the local band, with silver buckles on his shoes and a dirk at his sturdy knee. Rachael blushed beside him in her frills and lace, a white flounced dress with a miniature locket fastened at her throat, a present from Craig on their honeymoon, with small gold earrings in her pierced lobes, a pleasant and lovely bride if Joyce had welcomed her as a daughter. But Joyce rose from her easy chair and sniffed the air like it were poisoned and walked ben the hoose.

Now at last Rachael felt that haughty sniff could be forgiven. The vengeance of the years lay in that crumpled heap on the wet floor of the passage. There was even a glimmer of pity in her ice-clear eyes as she watched Helen and the bairns carry Joyce back to her room. Even Craig, her only son, had been turned against his dying mother; Rachael's cup was full, she was satisfied.

'Vengeance is mine, saith the Lord, I will repay.' But the ways of the Lord were a trifle slow for Rachael MacKinnon. He needed a bit of prodding, like most ordinary men, to get things done. She still went to chapel occasionally and was on speaking terms with God; but sometimes things had to be done behind a man's back, and maybe God was no exception. At least she knew a lot of evil things that were done on this earth and God seemed to turn a blind eye to them.

But at last Joyce was left in peace. She got clean bedding and new curtains on her window; she had a peat fire most of the day and her diet was improved, and her door was left open so that neighbours and visitors could see Joyce if they wished, though few of them bothered, and took Rachael's word for it that she was wrong in the head.

Eventually the family doctor was called and he saw things as they should be. Doctor Mundy had seen Rachael through most of her pregnancies but had never been called to Joyce since he came to the parish. All he could say to Rachael in the kitchen was: 'Poor woman, she's dying of natural causes: diabetes we call it, Mrs MacKinnon, and there's no cure; mostly it's the drinking diabetes you know – too much sugar in the blood – but she's got the eating kind. I've never seen it before but her sight is affected and most likely she'll go into a coma before the end.'

'She's got an awful appetite,' Rachael ventured.

'I'm sure she has,' said doctor Mundy, 'but don't hunger the old woman: there's no point in it; give her what she wants!'

On the morning that Joyce died Helen heard a deep sigh in the byre. She was milking the black horned cow, the one that Rachael said was a daughter of the devil, when she heard a great human sigh coming from the rafters. Yet Rachael didn't hear it where she was baking in the kitchen, just along the passage from Joyce. Maybe she couldn't hear it for the thumping of her knuckles on the oat-meal dough; for the scrape of her knife on the girdle, where it hung from a crook on the swye.

But Helen heard it under the rafters of the old tiled byre. She didn't wait for a second warning but dropped her pail and ran to the house.

'Granny's dyin' Ma,' she whispered, breathlessly, 'I heard her sechin' in the byre.'

Rachael stared at her in surprise, nothing further from her mind than old Joyce in the ben-room. 'Ach, awa' wi' ye, quine,' she cried, 'ye're aye seein' things in the cloods and hearin' things in the wind; it's what she's taught ye has filled yer heid wi' dumfoonery.'

'I tell ye, Ma, she's dyin'. I juist ken.'

Rachael looked at her daughter, and saw conviction in her eyes.

'Ye're a young witch. Yer Daw could skelp ye for the wye ye look at him sometimes.'

He skelped her whatever way she looked at him. It made no difference.

Rachael dropped her breid roller on the table and went ben the hoose. Helen followed and watched her mother bend over Joyce to listen for her breathing. It was laboured and unsteady, with a slight rasping in her bosom, what Rachael would have called 'the death hurle'. Her limbs were cold to Rachael's touch and her pulse feeble and erratic.

'Run, quine, and get your Daw,' Rachael ordered.

Helen ran to where her father was scything grass by the roadside. 'Granny's dyin', Daw,' she panted, 'come quick.' And they both hurried back to the house.

Craig was just in time to see his mother heave her last hoarse forlorn breath. While he bent over her she reached out a thin careworn hand and laid it on his sleeve. A half-choked token of farewell or forgiveness gurgled in her throat, never quite reaching her lips, her eyes moving under closed lids, searching the dark for her son. The touch of her feeble hand was a heavy blow to Craig, rending his soul with remorse and pity. He hurried off on his bicycle for Doctor Mundy, hiding his secret tears from Rachael and his family.

Helen had been eighteen when her grandmother died. Now she was twenty-one. She had laboured in her father's fields and sweated in his byres; doing a man's work to save him paying wages. She had done everything but drilling and ploughing, which Craig did himself with Meg and Bell, and when he wasn't using them Helen would saddle Meg and drive home turnips she had pulled in the rain the day before. In the early hours of spring mornings she gathered weeds and stones from the harrowed furrows, a mantle of white frost still on the ground, awaiting the warmth of the rising sun. She had gone to school with cow dung caked on her shoes and with chaff in her tousled hair, because she never had time to rig herself, and the bairns of gentler folk jeered at her untidiness. While they were still in bed she was up milking the kye and mucking out the byre, with scarcely time left to take her breakfast. Things were worse when Rachael had a bairn, but now that they were growing up a bit Helen felt that her father could manage without her on the farm. She wanted to get away from it all for a while, to see a little of the outside world, a world that came to her only when she went to the shop or Leary Post Office, when folk spoke to her on the news of the day, and sometimes of far-off places she knew nothing about. During the Boer War her father had sent her for a paper every day, and she had learned how to read it. It was the best of her education, besides an occasional visit to Aberdeen with her father on the bicycle.

And there had been her affair with young Murdoch the gamekeeper. Murdoch had been a fine lad for her and she hated her father for chasing him off. He had been game-keeper to the Laird but apparently not good enough to suit Craig MacKinnon. Maybe the Laird's son could have taken away Craig's finest slave but not the gamekeeper. But Helen felt that he would have been the same with any young cheil who tried to make love to her. Craig had threatened Murdoch with an axe when he found him with Helen in the stackyard, and since then he had kept a double-barrelled gun behind the back kitchen door to scare him off. Already he had fired two shots over the steading when he suspected Helen had a tryst with Murdoch. Her lover had gone abroad in great distress, to Canada, leaving a letter for Helen at the Post Office. Ah well, no use going after Murdoch. She had little chance of finding him, with the few shillings she possessed in the world, though she still kept his letter under her pillow.

Much of Rachael's malevolence had died with old Joyce but she still had a sharp edge to her tongue, even for Craig at times, though she feared his temper and usually gave in to his moods. The long years of work and child-bearing had subdued Rachael's haughty spirit, though she still angered at her daughters; but less so with Helen since she grew to womanhood. It seemed that Rachael had a grudge against her own sex, whether beast or human, and when she could find no fault with her quines she ran to the byre and lashed the cows with a stick; never the bullocks, but always on the calf-bearing, milk-giving cows; on creatures almost like herself she sought to relieve her spite.

When Rachael milked the cows they gave their milk in fear, not with relief and satisfaction. When she opened the byre door they were chewing the cud and relaxed; but when they glanced round and saw Rachael they stopped chewing and began to fidget, dreading her wicked little fingers on their big warm teats. When she sat down on her stool and began to tug and squeeze at the teats they stood with their hind legs straddled, ears back on their necks and their noses against the white-washed wall, their big liquid eyes alert and watching, afraid almost to switch a tail, lest Rachael got it in the eye, when she would get up in a fit of temper and thump their backs with the sharp edge of her stool. When Craig tied up the cows he sometimes petted and fondled them in complacent mood, but Rachael's presence soon put an end to that, as if the thought of it made her jealous. Their purpose in life was to rear calves and give milk so that she could churn butter and make cheese, and if Craig wasn't around she soon let them know it.

But Rachael never laid hands on a bullock, and suffered the lazy brutes to lie down in peace, to grow sleek and fat for the butcher's knife; maybe she thought it a shame to harass their short sacrificial lives, martyred for carnivorous humanity.

But woe betide the poor mares in the stable, and especially poor Meg, because she was nearest the door. A horse Rachael could abide, but not a mare, and Craig never knew it. Now that old Joyce had gone she turned her spite on the dumb helpless beasts, tied or chained to their stalls and entirely at her mercy. Even at noon, while Craig, newly fed, was asleep in his chair, she would have a sly poke at his mares with a long-handled fork from the stable door; sharp smarting jabs on the hips that made them prance and kick, and they got no peace to munch their hay. She was afraid to go into the stable and she had a bairn posted at the kitchen door, ready to warn her if Craig should awake. And Heaven help a bairn if it told anything, especially if it were a quine, for Rachael would have her by the hair and throw her on the floor, kicking the bare hips of the creature if she didn't get up again fast. So Craig would yoke his mares, content that they were fed and rested, while many a day the poor bitches got little peace to eat their dinner. And heaven help the mares on a day that Craig was away at the marts; not always, of course, but if Craig had offended Rachael or she had a tantrum over something, she would take it out on the mares. But she was careful not to mark them with pinpricks of blood; rather tormented them with persistent little jabs till she had them snorting and frantic, when she would replace the fork behind the stable door and return to her kitchen, her anger gone now that the score had been settled. But God help even Rachael if Craig had found her out, for he had a feeling for beasts over humans sometimes.

Helen had good reason to remember it, though since she grew to womanhood her father hadn't raised his hand to her, just glowered at her with his piercing stare till she learned to stare him back, long enough to give him the fidgets and cry out, 'Dinna glower at me like that, quine!' And sometimes she would be glowering at him unawares, her mind far away at the time, maybe thinking of running away after Murdoch or something, when he would hide his face with the newspaper, or she came to her senses again. 'Aye dreamin', quine,' he would quip at her, 'it's time ye woke up noo that ye're a woman body.' It's just what she had in mind herself, though she didn't say as much; time that she got out about to see what ither folk were doing, time to look for a lad and have some fun, but she would speak to her mither about it first. Surely she must be eating herself out of home and it was a wonder that Craig had kept her so long under his roof. But now that Hamish and Riach were nearly grown men maybe he would let her go. She would think about it seriously and one of these days she would be going.

The morning of departure came at last. Courage came with the dawn; with the first grey light that gave an outline to the Mattock Hill, lying there so quiet like a great beast in a park, its head stretched out on its forelegs and the curve of its back against the morning sky, watching over the sleeping howe and its kirn of folk, now yawning and raxing them-selves for the chauve of another day; the sun rising out of the sea like a great red ball, his fingernails of light filtering over the dewy landscape, colouring the fields and the trees with his mellow touch, soft and rich against the livening sky above the Mattock, where the farming folk could see that he meant well for the day, with not a folded cloud on his frown-ing brow, but a bright smile that lit up the hay parks and the mantling green of the turnip shaws, wet with sparkling dew, and a breath of wind that swung gently on the corn stalks. Soon you would hear the knack of wooden cartwheels and the whistle of a horseman on the brae, the mewing of gulls over from the sea and the Myreloch, the croak of the Hoodie crow and the crooning of pigeons deep in Lachbeg Woods.

Helen sat on her bed in the attic, scarcely able to contain herself, waiting for morning long before it came, bringing forth the day she was to leave her father's household, the day that would change the whole course of her so far inno-cent life. She fingered the letter in her bodice. Perhaps it had decided her in making up her mind. She could read it again now that it was light.

'Dearest,' she read, 'Your father is a savage heathen; to reason with such a man is out of the question. Your brothers and sisters are only half civilized and not fit to mix with decent people. You are an angel in hell and do not belong amongst them. Why do you stay in such a hole? Run away, dearest love, before it is too late. See what the rest of the world is like. By the time you read this I will be far away, as I said would happen. When I cannot have you I must be out of your reach forever. I shall be in Canada, seeking my fortune. I send my love as always and it breaks my heart to think that you can never be mine. Yours Always, With Kisses, Murdoch.'

She crumpled the letter in her hand and sighed deeply for what might have been. She would have to burn it before Craig or her mother got hold of it. She laid the letter in the empty grate and kindled it with a match, watching the flames turning it into a black whorl, then to flakes and ashes, until nothing was left of her affair with Murdoch the gamekeeper; and she still blamed her father for spoiling the one romance in her life.

She got up from the bed and made faces at herself in the mirror over the dressing-table. She had small heart for fun but some little devil prodded her to laugh at herself, to stick her tongue out in the mirror, to pug her pretty nose, to wiggle her fingers at her ears; then she sat down on the bed again, giggling at herself. What a little fool she was, but she had to put on a brave face for the day; more than likely she would need it before the morning was over. Her father would be bitter about her leaving, and she hoped her mother had told him of her intentions. She had got round her mother but her father might be difficult. But even though he refused to let her go she would run away. It made no difference now, her mind was made up, but she would rather have his blessing than his curses.

She pulled her little bandbox from under the bed and tried to dress herself from its limited contents. A straw hat, a skirt and blouse, black woollen stockings, shoes with buckles, bloomers and vest and petticoat, a shabby tweed checked coat and faded suede gloves. She looked a bit gawky in the mirror, especially with the straw hat, but her eyes were as bright and blue as the morning sky outside her window. She would wash in the big brown basin downstairs. Maybe one of her sisters would rinse her long black hair with cold water, before she took it under her hat and stuck in the pins.

Swifts and sandmartins were darting over the garden, snapping an insect meal in the first heat of the sun. Out at the back she could hear the gobble of the bubblie-jock, the crowing of cocks, the cackle of the geese, even the grunt of the old sow, awaiting her breakfast from Rachael. But she wouldn't work today, not a stroke; she didn't care any more and she was too excited even to think of breakfast. She was surprised at her own eagerness to be away, at her own courage, and the thoughts seemed to tumble out of her mind like apples from a barrel. She should have run away years ago.

Helen took a last nervous look round her bedroom. God knows when she would be back; maybe not long, but she had no way of knowing. She would remember the wallpaper pattern with its strange flowers, the pictures on the wall, the brass knobs on the bed, the patchwork quilt she had helped her mother to make, the firescreen with its little coloured pictures of all the animals in *The Jungle Book*; the view of the garden from her storm window, rich with the smell of onions and flowers when she opened a sash. Downstairs she could hear the commotion in the kitchen. Her father had come in from the stable and the family were at breakfast. She closed the bedroom door and went down the stair with wobbly knees, a little handbag on her elbow, grasping the rail. The grandfather clock was striking eight in the passage, but it had never kept the time since it fell on grandma. The wag-at-the-wa' clock in the kitchen was more reliable if you wanted to catch a train at Leary Station. When she opened the passage door the air was rich with the smell of porridge and strong tea.

Her brothers and sisters were crowded round the table and they all looked up at her when she entered. Craig was at his brose and porter at the head of the table, nearest the fire, the youngest bairn on his knee, Little Janet, supping out of his bowl with a long wooden spoon. Like all the others she was barely weaned of her mother's milk when she knew the taste of porter and ale. Hamish, the eldest son, was at the top of the wooden deas, next his father, then Moira, Nora, Nancy and Kirsteen, seated round the table, and at the end nearest Helen was Riach, her crippled brother. Rachael seldom sat down to breakfast but snatched a morsel, standing in the middle of the floor, watching over the others, always on her feet; and maybe that was why she was as slim as any of her growing daughters, all nervous energy and never getting time to grow fat.

'So ye're leavin' us, quine,' Craig said, staring at his daughter in the passage door.

'Aye, I'm gaun tae the toon, Daw. The quine in the

26

post-office says I could get a job there in a fish-curer's hoose.'

'It's a wonder that I hinna heard o' this afore, quine; ye've been affa sleekit aboot it. What's wrang wi' yer life here? Ye get yer keep, don't ye? and a shillin' or twa tae spend. What mair wad ye hae? Wad ye like me tae feed ye wi' a spoon, like the bairn here?'

'No, Daw,' and Helen's lip quivered with her answer, tense and nervous under her father's stare.

'What ails ye than? Speak up when ye've got the chance.'

'It's nothing, Daw. It's juist that I want tae see ither folk; I'm tired o' bidin at hame and I'd like a change.'

'Is it the gamekeeper ye're after noo?' Craig asked his daughter. 'Is that what's annoyin' ye quine?'

'No, honestly, Daw, it's nae that.'

'Let the lassie go, Daw,' Rachael interposed, 'we'll manage withoot 'er, noo that the ithers are grown up. She canna bide here a' her days onywye; she's a woman noo, wi' a' her life in front o' her. We canna treat 'er like she was still a bairn. I've been thinkin' aboot it, Daw.'

Craig pushed his bowl aside, for he had just finished his brose, and he laid the bairn on the floor. 'Losh preserves, woman,' says he, mockingly, looking at his wife, 'so ye've been thinkin', have ye? Weel weel, the wardle's surely comin' tae an end. And when did ye turn sae gentle? It's nae mony years since ye had the quine by the hair o' the heid, ruggin' 'er tae the fleer.'

Rachael said nothing to this and there was silence for a time, save for the clatter of plates and spoons and the stirring of tea. Craig was looking at his eldest daughter as if he had never seen her before, still standing by the passage door, a stranger almost in her own home; almost afraid to speak unless she was spoken to. 'Poor bitch,' he thought, 'I never thocht she had grown up sae fast.' He secretly felt like going over to her and taking her in his oxter; his ain quine, and he had been that sair trauchled bringing up the others he had almost forgotten that she was his ain flesh and bleed. Now that she was bent on leaving them he felt for her, now that she was a woman and going out to face the world alone, and God knows she was ill equipped for it.

'A' richt, quine,' he said at last, 'ye can go; but dinna come runnin' back here greetin' and say that the warld has ill used ye.'

'I wunna, Daw. I'll get a job. Ye'll see!'

'I hope so than. Sit doon tae yer breakfast. Ye canna face the warld on an empty stammick – and mither, see that the bitch has some siller in her purse; I dinna want a dother o' mine tae be beggin' frae ither folk.'

'She'll get siller, Daw,' said Rachael, making a place for Helen at the breakfast table, for she too was beginning to feel for her first bairn going out to face the wicked world, though she knew fine it was time for her to go.

Helen had little stomach for breakfast but she did her best in her excitement. It hadn't been so bad after all and she felt encouraged. Perhaps she had her mother to thank for it, and it was better than running away on her own. It didn't matter what the others thought. They could jeer if they liked. She had her mother's blessing and that was enough.

She said good-bye to them all at the corner of the milk-house, where she held her straw hat in the wind and clutched tightly at her little handbag. She looked back when she was well down the road. They were still at the head of the avenue, all except her father, all waving, Riach's crutch highest of all, with his cap on top of it. Wild geese were cackling in the sky, breaking their flight above the Myre-loch, where they had come for the mating season.

When Helen reached Leary Station she bought a third-class ticket to Scotstoun and waited. The train came hissing into the station and slowed gently to a halt, panting out his white breath across the fields, while Helen got into a compartment with a fishwife who had a creel between her knees. Helen had seen her at Bogmyrtle, but not for a long time, and she said she was off to Stronach to sell yellow haddock for the day. As the coaches eased away smoothly from the platform Helen felt the merest twinge of homesickness, for in all her drab and narrow life she had scarcely been out of the parish, and never alone. The train climbed round the shoulder of the Mattock Hill, where she got her last glimpse of Bogmyrtle, the smoke rising gently from the kitchen chimney, the deer lying on the hill like a great white skeleton, until the train entered a cutting and hid it all from view.

The fishwife got off at Stronach and Helen had the compartment to herself. A strange new hope was pulsing in her heart and she could scarcely keep her seat. She got up and looked at the pictures under the luggage racks – far away places she had never heard of – while the train lurched and swayed and swished under bridges. She sat down again and the music of the carriage wheels soothed her thoughts. Ah well, even though she had to tramp the street she had enough money to pay her fare home again, and maybe buy a bite of dinner. She could make it a holiday and pretend it was her day off, even though her brothers and sisters should laugh at her when she returned.

But her spirits rose with the adventure of the journey, the speed of the train, the changing scenery, the folk at the stations, until her thoughts became a whirl of expectation, with no room left for the sadness of her past life. It was as if she was being born anew, rocked into a world of which she had no understanding. Bridges and farms and meadows and trees flashed past her window at such a speed she got up from her seat again, opened the window with the leather strap and gazed out at the spires of Scotstoun, high above the town, with the grey wrinkled sea behind them, the herring boats coming into harbour with their catches, their funnels smoking and the white gulls overhead, rounding the lighthouse pier and heading for the town.

The train went gliding into the station over a maze of rail joints, smooth and steady, under the glass roof in a hissing cloud of steam, where the engine stopped with the slightest jolt, clanging the buffers between the carriages. Helen got out in a dither of excitement, in a press of people, handed over her rail ticket and made for the exit. She followed the horse-cabs from the station. They went spanking along the High Street into the town. There were no shops or offices for a long way down the street, but on each side were the grandest houses and the loveliest gardens Helen had ever seen: rich red, white and yellow roses round their varnished, glass-panelled doors, blue and white clematis clinging to the red granite walls, lashings of powder-blue hydrangeas, smooth green lawns, gnomes and urns on the doorsteps, brimming with nasturtium and lobelia, with blue and yellow pansies on the borders; not a flower but Helen could name it, and it was enough to make her father pluck his moustache in envy, had he seen such a show. Surely, Helen thought, the townspeople must be awfully rich to live in such mansions: perhaps the well-to-do fish-curing families the girl in the post-office had told her about.

Two men were digging in one of the gardens and Helen asked them the way to the Servants' Registry Office. The men stopped their spadework and stared at her for a moment, no doubt sizing her up as a quine new in from the country, looking for a job in the toon. They were young men; one fat and jovial, the other earnest and thin. The stout one said, 'Oh aye, but you've a good bit tae go, lass. This is the posh end o' the toon; the workin' quarters are awa' near the centre o' the place, and that's whar the office is that ye're lookin for. It's the third openin' on yer richt, aboot half-wye doon Kirkburn Street – isn't it Audie?' he asked his companion.

Audie nodded his egg-shaped head and blinked his small blue eyes. 'Aye, it's Kirkburn Street,' he said, and wiped his nose on the palm of his hand.

The stout fellow looked hard at Helen, no doubt taken with her sparkling blue eyes and country cream complexion, her small elfin figure in the doll's dress, her shapely ankles in the black stockings and the wide flared sun hat. 'Ye'll be frae the countrie, are ye lass?' he asked her.

Helen blushed under his gaze, the tint of the rose in her cheeks. 'Oh aye, I'm frae the country, and I'm lookin' for a job in the toon.'

'Oh ye'll get a job a' richt,' the man said, with a bit twinkle in his eye.

Helen became a little bolder and asked what they were doing.

'Oh,' said the fellow, 'we work for the Toon Cooncil and we're delvin the Provost's gairden.'

Helen didn't know about the Provost nor what his function was and she thought the fellow was trying to make fun of her, so she didn't wait to be taunted. 'Well, ta-ta,' she cried and padded down the pavement on her flat heels, 'but thanks for directing me.'

She knew they were watching her; indeed she felt everybody's eyes on her band-box attire and awkward country manner, like a dairymaid on the rampage.

She found the Registry Office with a brass plate on the door and walked in. A woman was knitting by the fire, but when Helen entered she got up from her wicker basket and came to the counter.

'Well, lass,' she ventured, 'can I help ye?'

'Mebbe ye can. I would like a job as a domestic at one o' the big hooses in the toon.'

'Ye're frae the countrie than?'

'Aye.'

'Any references?'

'No.'

'Ah well, what's yer name?'

'Helen MacKinnon.'

'And your age?'

'Twenty-one.'

'And your address?'

'I've nae address in the toon. If I dinna get a job the day I'll juist hae tae gang hame again.'

'And where's that?'

'Och, nearly twenty mile awa'. Ye wadna ken the place onywye.'

'But I could write to you later, if I found a job suitable for you.'

'Oh I see. Ah well it's Bogmyrtle Farm, Leary, by the Bogside, that would find me.'

'So you are a farmer's daughter than?'

'Aye,' Helen confessed, as if it was something to be ashamed of.

'Well now, what would a farmer's daughter be looking for a job here for? I would have thought that a fine-looking lass like you would be looking for a farmer's son and a farm of your own.'

'It's nae like that in the country,' Helen explained; 'sometimes ye never see anybody for months – unless it be a passing ragman.'

'But didn't you go to the dances? Sometimes you can meet a fellow that way.'

'No, I've never been to a dance in my life; my father wouldn't let me.'

'Oh dear. Well it's none of my business really and I'm getting too personal. I'm sorry, lass. I just wondered. We get all sorts in here, you know, and we have to be careful. Anyway, you just try the gentry with that for a recommendation: tell them you are a farmer's daughter; that should make them listen.'

She copied out five addresses from her ledger and gave them to Helen, charging her a shilling deposit for entering her name on the Employment Register.

But the wives of the gentry were not impressed, and those that were interested had already found a servant. After three protracted interviews and a lot of walking Helen found herself in a weary state, disconsolate and hungry; for not one of the mistresses had offered her a cup of tea. She went back to the Registry Office, tired and dejected, with little enthusiasm for another search. But the woman encouraged her and gave her one more address, on the High Street, a fish-curer's family, and urged her to try it; even made her a cup of tea in her own little teapot by the office fire, with a buttered roll from her bag.

When Helen banged the big brass knocker on the polished door on the High Street her heart was thumping in her throat. But this time it was Lady Luck herself who opened the door for her and Helen found herself with her first mistress.

She got a meal and admission to her bedroom that very night, so she didn't have to catch the last train home. But first she went back to the Registry Office to pay her other shilling, and to thank the lady for finding her a job. Her wages were a pound a month and free board and laundry and a Sunday off once a fortnight. She would have to buy some new clothes when she had the money but her mistress supplied all working overalls.

Daisy May was kitchenmaid and shared a room with Helen. She had far more experience of housework than Helen and was an excellent cook, ranking higher than Helen in the domestic scale, though in most households the housemaid would be a higher position than the kitchen wench. But Helen couldn't have managed Daisy's work and was content in her secondary role in a mode of life that was completely new to her, even taking Daisy's advice on the duties of the household. On her first night in the Durward household there wasn't much talking done. Helen was rather tired and fell asleep quickly, leaving Daisy talking to herself in the upstairs bedroom. But Helen's slumbers weren't entirely dreamless, for she dreamed of two men that were pulling out all the beautiful flowers in the Provost's garden and throwing them on the pavement, then they dug up all his new potatoes and pelted them at passers-by on the street, and one of them hit her on the head and knocked her hat all askew, so that she woke up laughing, sitting up in bed, holding on to a hat that wasn't there.

In the weeks that followed, Helen felt homesick, though she had little time to think about it. The work wasn't hard but she had much to learn, and it was all such a change from the byre and field work she had been accustomed to. Her mother's housework was crude in comparison, and nothing she could have learned at home would have been much use to her now. She had to learn polite manners, especially when guests were in the house, and how to conduct herself properly while serving them, and as the Durwards entertained quite a lot she soon had her hands full. But Daisy was a great help, and so was the Mistress, and between them they soon had Helen opening the front door to visitors with

such courtesy and politeness you would have thought sh
had done nothing else in her lifetime. Daisy had shown he
how to do her hair, thick and black to her shoulders when i
was down, but now done up in a bun like her mother's; an
what with the white cap and apron over her dark blue dress
white starched collar and cuffs, the fine shape of her legs i
the black worsted stockings, and the sweet smile of welcom
when she opened the front door – no wonder her fathe
hardly knew his own daughter that day when he banged o
the knocker.

It was about a month after Helen left home that her fathe
called, just to see that they weren't ill-using his quine, as h
put it, though Helen had already written to Rachael, giving
her all the details. But there he stood on the doorstep, dressed
in his best Kersey Tweed, with a white dickey over his shir
and a striped tie that Rachael had fixed for him, because he
was such a fumbler with his collar studs and usually los
them under the deas or the box-bed. When Helen saw him
standing there she ran to his oxter, felt his strong hand on
her shoulders clasping her close to him in the first fatherly
embrace she had ever known. All the homesickness she
thought she had overcome in the last fortnight now flooded
back on her in a surge of emotion, and while he patted her
back she felt the hot tears welling into her eyes. There was
the old familiar smell of mothballs in his suit, whisky and
tobacco in his breath, and she fingered the amber stone that
always hung from his watch-chain. In that brief moment of
reunion Helen felt the smell of honeysuckle in the hedges of
home, the tang of sharn and peat reek, and she wanted to
run back into the thick of it; what with a father's love like
this she would never have left it, and she clung to him for a
brief space like a bee in a flower.

Meg stood by the kerbside, the long cart behind her, and
on it a brand-new bicycle Craig had bought to take her
home at weekends. Helen freed herself and ran to Meg and
buried her face in her breast, forgetful of her fine clothes,
hungry for the scent of hay and harness blacking, stable
dung and urine. Craig unloaded the bike, a lovely model
with stainless steel rims on the wheels and flashing spokes

when you spun them, cords on the back mudguard to protect her dress, a gearcase over the chain, a leather saddle
with a small toolbag on the back, a carrier for parcels and
chrome handlebars tipped with black celluloid. Helen was
afraid to set it against the stone wall for fear of scratching it,
but just then Mrs Durward appeared and said she could
take it through the garden to a shed at the back. Craig was
invited inside for a dram and a cup of tea, his big red moustache sweeping over the dainty china cup and saucer Daisy
was instructed to serve him with. He cracked with the
mistress about fishing and farming, and she told him she was
well pleased with Helen. He lit his pipe on leaving, filling
the grand house with the strong smell of black twist, familiar
to Helen since her girlhood.

When Daisy wasn't out with her lad she shared her
leisure with Helen. In the summer evenings they went for
long walks in the town and suburbs, sometimes arm in arm,
until the sun had set behind the steeples and the sky was all
rose-pink, when they returned to number seventeen on the
High Street. Daisy pointed out the homes of some of the
grand families she had worked for, with a brief sketch of
their behaviour and foibles; of the masters who kissed her
on the sly, and the sons of some of them who had their hands
up her clothes at every opportunity. It wasn't for the want
of temptation, she said, that she had kept her virginity till
the right lad came along. Oh aye, she could look after herself among the gentry, she said, for they were no more to be
trusted than the poorer folk; even less, for if you had a
bairn they would give you money to keep your mouth shut
about it.

On one of these evening strolls the girls came upon a side
street where people were gathered; music was playing and
people were dancing. Helen thought later that Daisy took
her there on purpose, though she never cared to ask. There
was laughter and hooching as the dancers waved their arms
and pranced around in jubilant circles. A quadrille was in
progress, and men and girls were hooked in each other's
arms and skipping around in time to the music. There was
another shrill 'Hooch!' and the couples changed partners

and skipped around in the other direction, their free hand
in the air, the long skirts of the girls swirling this way and
that, sometimes swung off their feet by the more exuberant
males.

Helen had never seen such a sight and it filled her young
heart with a warm glow. She stood arm in arm with Daisy
and watched and smiled and listened, until the music had
her tapping her foot in exultation. A crowd of spectators was
gathered round the door of the nearest house, and the girls
had to squeeze forward to see where the music was coming
from. Now they got a glimpse of a gramophone horn,
striped green and white, like a huge paraffin filler, facing
towards them, so that they were looking down its throat.
Helen had never seen or heard a gramophone before and
she was amazed at where the music was coming from. Two
men sat on the doorstep, one selecting records from a cardboard box, the other placing them on the machine and
winding the spring handle. They were young men, one
rather broad and clean shaven, the other thin and narrow
shouldered, with a small brown moustache.

The music stopped suddenly and the dancers fell out for a
breather. The clean-shaven gentleman put forward a record
and his companion placed it on the turntable, fixed a new
needle in the sound-head and started up the gramophone.
This time it was a Scottische on melodeon, with fiddle and
piano, and the dancers changed their pattern and began
another mad caper. The stoutish fellow now waved and
shouted encouragement to the dancers, but the other was
silent and thoughtful. He sat with his cheek on his hand and
tapped his foot to the music; a dedicated listener, content
with the thoughts it gave him, without physical reaction.
Then he wiped his nose on the palm of his hand and Helen
remembered him. She recognized them both. These were
the two men who had shown her the way on the first day she
came to the town; the men in her dreams who were throwing flowers in the street and pelting folk with potatoes. An
odd pair, to be sure, and Helen wondered what they would
be up to next time in her dreams.

'Who are they?' Helen asked, pulling Daisy's arm

and pointing at the men on the doorstep.

'Wha? Them?' Daisy giggled. 'Oh ye'll get tae ken them well enough yet if ye like.' Then she spoke low in Helen's ear, 'One o' them's my lad!'

'Your lad?' Helen queried, fair astounded. 'Which ane?'

Daisy gave her a jab in the ribs with her elbow, 'The fat ane, ye silly; d'ye think I'd hae that sullen dreep wi' the moustache? He's a good soul, Audie, but he's nae for me.'

'Audie what?' Helen asked.

'Audie Foubister, and he bides wi' his mither and step-father up in Toddlebrae yonder, nearly oot in the countrie.'

Daisy was for saying more but the lamp-lighter appeared and they had to move away from the lamp-post. He fixed a giant match to the thin end of a long pole and thrust it upwards inside the glass frame, scratched the match on the ironwork and set the mantle alight.

'You quines lookin' for a lad?' he cracked.

'Mind yer ain business, Leerie,' Daisy told him, and her face spread into a giggle in the white glow of the street lamp. Leerie winked at them and moved on to the next lamp standard.

The sky was turning to dark velvet, sprinkled with twinkling stars. Lights appeared in the windows along the street. Folks who had been listening to the music went inside and closed their doors. The crowd began to thin as the air grew colder. A policeman came swaggering up the street with a thumb in his breast pocket, while he pushed young-sters off the pavement with his free hand. 'This can't go on all night, ye know. Folks have got to sleep; decent folk anyway. Come on now, break it up!'

He stopped and stared down at Bill Smith and Audie in the doorway, folding his arms as he spoke. 'Well now, what have we here? A new fangled barrel-organ that plays itsel' eh? But ye'll hae tae shove off wi' yer hurdy-gurdy or I'll be takin' yez for a nicht's lodgin's in the Toonhoose. I dinna ken what the warld's comin' till.'

The bobby moved on down the pavement and the girls were left alone with the two men on the doorstep. They were dismantling the gramophone and packing the records into the cardboard box. Bill put the thin end of the horn to his mouth and blew a loud blast after the bobby. He had just gone round the corner but he reappeared, waving his fist in the distance. Bill slipped back into the lobby until he moved off again.

'Maybe he thocht it was the fog-horn, eh Audie?'

Audie didn't answer but Daisy laughed.

'Are ye comin' inside the nicht?' Bill asked her.

'No, Bill, nae the nicht; we canna, there's nae time. We've got tae be in by ten o'clock, and it's nearly that time already. Friday nicht mebbe, if we can get oot thegether.'

'Thegether, eh. Is this yer new hoosemaid than?'

'Aye,' Daisy replied, 'but she's a bit shy. I told ye she cam' frae the countrie.'

'Oh aye,' said Bill, and turned to his companion. 'Look Audie, wha's here – haven't we seen her afore somewye?'

Audie Foubister had just finished packing his box of gramophone records, the lid still in his hand when he looked up at Helen, glanced at her shyly with his small friendly eyes. 'Aye,' he said quietly, 'was she no the lass that speired the road at us when we was delvin the Provost's gairden?'

Bill looked at Helen in the gaslight. 'Isn't that richt noo, lass?'

Helen was so shy but she admitted it was her.

'So you three have met before,' Daisy intervened, showing her surprise, 'and she never let on. Well well, there's more in the countrie quines than a body would think.'

'Now now, Daisy, she was only askin' the road,' Bill said, 'and she's never seen us again till now. Aren't ye gaun tae introduce us properly?'

'Little sense in me introducin' ye tae somebody ye've seen afore,' Daisy quipped.

But Bill Smith insisted, 'At least it would gie us an excuse tae shak' hands wi' the lass; no harm in that surely.'

'A' richt,' Daisy agreed, 'but that's as far as it goes for you, Bill Smith, though Audie can please himsel'.'

Daisy introduced them and both men shook hands with Helen. 'Just the lass for you, Audie,' Bill added, 'as fresh a rose as I've seen frae the countrie for a lang time.'

Daisy gave him a challenging look but said nothing. Neither did Audie, just leaned against the lamp-post, smiling sheepishly, his hands in his trouser pockets.

'Audie's shy too,' Bill jeered, 'but no matter, Daisy, you bring Helen along on Friday nicht and auntie will mak' her welcome. What d'ye say, auntie?' he cried in at the door — 'will it be a' right for Friday night? Come and see wha Daisy has got here, auntie.'

Bill's aunt came to the door, a woman in her forties, with a plain face and dark hair mixing with grey. 'Wha is it?' she asked, staring blandly at Helen.

Bill Smith took Helen forward to meet his auntie. 'This is Miss Helen MacKinnon,' he told his aunt, 'the new house-maid that Daisy has brocht along for a lass tae Audie here. Will it be a' richt for a cup o' tea and anither gramophone concert on Friday nicht, auntie, juist by way of introduction like?'

'Mercy aye,' said auntie, 'bring the lass along, Daisy. I'm very pleased to meet you, Miss MacKinnon. You're welcome here at ony time, though Audie's here or no. Never mind Bill there, he's a teasin' brute.'

Helen blushed and smiled and she felt grand being called 'Miss MacKinnon'; nobody had ever called her that in her life before and she felt like one of the gentry.

'Three's bad company onywye,' Bill concluded, 'and four would be better.'

Audie Foubister smiled and said nothing, yet he was thinking plenty, and a bit excited when he shook hands with Helen on parting. He felt that she had a strong grip for a quine, warmer and firmer than his own.

The girls walked back to the mansion house on the High Street. They sipped their tea in the pantry and tiptoed upstairs to their bedroom. Helen went over to the storm window and closed the curtains. The moon was rising and his soft beams gilded the rooftops with a fairy glow. Ah well, maybe she had met a new lad but he was no match for Murdoch the gamekeeper. She stood at the window for a while, thinking of what might have been if her father hadn't interfered. Yet somehow she forgave him; he seemed so much kinder to her now since she had left home; different somehow, and she liked him better as a father than she had ever done before.

'What are ye dreamin' on?' Daisy asked. 'Come on to bed.'

There were two or three more gramophone concerts at the home of Bill's aunt, and then Helen began walking out with Audie Foubister. The four of them met at the corner of Prince Street and then Bill Smith and Daisy walked off, leaving Helen alone with Audie. She didn't seem to have much choice in the matter. The only alternative was to walk off alone, and there didn't seem to be much point in that either, so they had a word or two of greeting, like: 'It's been a fine day', or 'I'm glad the rain's aff!' and then sauntered off down the pavement. They didn't go hand in hand, or even side by side, but single file, Helen walking first and Audie following her, like a friendly puppy. Two or three times she looked round but he was still there, so she decided to wait on him. But no sooner were they abreast than he fell behind again, walking with his hands behind his back, watching Helen like he was her bodyguard. Helen looked in the shop-windows to let him catch up, then loitered behind to see what he looked like. She thought that the man should lead the way, or walk by her side, even take her arm, and they could be like other couples. Daisy and Bill were fools to think they could pawn her off with such a simpleton. She was a bit gawky herself but maybe not as stupid as they thought, even though she did come from the country.

But such a strange fellow Audie seemed at first that Helen thought he must be married with a wife hidden away somewhere. He was thirtyish but looked older, and by the look of the suit he was wearing it seemed to have come out of a pawnshop. His trousers were baggy and crumpled at the ankles; his jacket was much too long and the pocket lids were dog-eared, his cap too small and barely covered his head, the shabby tie he wore little wider than a shoelace. He was pensive and absorbed in she knew not what and seemed to get in everybody's way. Sometimes he wiped his nose on the palm of his hand, a gimmick that Helen tried herself and nearly sprained her wrist. She watched herself in a shop-window and it was so funny she could hardly stop giggling. It was a wonder she thought that he didn't have a pug nose. But he didn't. Indeed it was one of the finest features of his face and his moustache suited it marvellously. There was no fault in his face at all; in fact he was quite good-looking, and he had clear blue eyes, rather small perhaps, like a baby's eyes almost, innocent looking eyes that appealed to the mother-love in a woman. His teeth were strong and even when he smiled, which wasn't often, and his chin was rather handsome, determined looking, in a dogged sort of way, and seemed to add a certain dignity to the rest of his face. He looked as if he could be very smart too if he liked, but he didn't seem to try, or didn't want to. It was the way he was shaken up that played hell with the man. He couldn't dress himself properly, that was the trouble, and maybe nobody took the trouble to help him.

But for all his faults, Helen MacKinnon still walked out with Audie Foubister. And as they walked and talked she learned something of his background; of the harsh farm life that had beaten him into the ground almost, and of how he had tried to escape it in the town, though things weren't much better there either and he would go back to the country now that he had had a taste of town life. This was something Helen understood and shared with him. After this she felt that she couldn't disown him; they were birds of a feather ... perhaps two wanton seeds blown together by the adverse winds of circumstance. After all there was no one else Helen could turn to for companionship. Without him she was lonely, even homesick, and he seemed to want her company. Bill and Daisy May were now engaged to be married and left them more than ever on their own to-gether. But as Audie talked and Helen listened she could see that he needed her strength and confidence far more than she needed him.

It was a kind of pity that Helen felt for this strange quiet man; a sort of compassion that took hold of her in his company. He seemed so helpless, so dependent on others, on anyone who would take an interest in him. He appealed to the best that was in her, all the help she could give. She wanted to see him smile. He seldom smiled, yet he was quite entrancing when he did. He was serious about everything, miserable almost. She wanted to comfort him, buck him up and make a man of him. He lacked the vigour of her father and brothers, something she liked to see in other men. But if Helen had been afraid for her chastity she had nothing to fear from Audie Foubister. He hadn't even kissed her or held her hand, and he was what some women would have called a perfect gentleman as far as sex was concerned.

Audie told Helen he had been brought up by his grandmother in the village of Nedderton yonder, and he had worked on the farms till she died. Since then he had lived with his mother and step-father in the toon and worked as a council labourer. He had been born illegitimately while his mother was in farm service, but the bachelor farmer who was Audie's father wouldn't marry her and she was forced to go back to her parents when he was born. Audie's mother eventually married a ship's carpenter, Joseph Barbour by name, and they had two sons and two daughters. Audie took his mother's name, which was Foubister, her maiden name before she married. The Barbour family lived in a tenement flat up in Toddlebrae, a swell flat out in the suburbs among the gentry, and Audie invited Helen to come and see them sometime. He was a bit of an outcast, Helen thought; like herself but worse, having a step-family, and it was something more they had in common.

Audie complained bitterly about his treatment from the Barbour family. Frank and Herbert, who were his half-brothers, weren't so bad; but his half-sisters, Doris and Susan Barbour, left him in no doubt that he wasn't wanted in the house.

'They even grudge me soap tae wash ma face,' Audie complained, 'and they watch every morsel I put in ma mooth. I pay them twelve bob a week for ma board, nearly half ma wages, yet they treat me like dirt. Digs are nae easy got or I'd shift the morn. If it werena for my dig money that pays their rent they'd throw me oot. They're a bigsy lot, I tell ye, far above the likes o' me!'

There was no doubt the Barbour quines despised Audie. They resented him in their closely knit family circle; an incomer they could well do without. But his mother still had her feelings for him and the rascal farmer who fathered him, up in the Reisk yonder, his spitting image, God rest his soul, and a pity Audie hadn't his gumption or he'd have that MacKinnon quine bairned by now. Old Joseph Barbour was a gentleman as far as Audie was concerned and always respected his wife's feelings for his stepson. The only time he threw it back at her was when she ragged him for drinking, for Joseph liked a dram, especially on a Saturday – when he turned his back on his wife to count out his pay, and maybe kept her a bit short on the housekeeping money, making her more dependent than ever on Audie's board money.

Maybe coming into the family in manhood was against Audie; living with his grandmother out in Nedderton yonder he had hardly ever seen the Barbours when he was a bairn.

'Audie has a big stomach,' Susan pouted to Helen later on, when they were better acquainted, 'and we shall be glad to get rid of him.'

'Narra minded bitches,' Audie retorted when Helen told him, 'a day's wark wad do them a lot o' good. They quines have never worked in their lives and ma stepfather spoils them. If it wasna for ma poor auld mither washin' claes tae the gentry they could never afford to bide at hame.'

Audie had never seen his real father, except from an old photograph his mother used to treasure, but left it with his grandmother when she married Joseph Barbour. He had been a big broad-shouldered man with a beard – Robin Gay they called him – a typical farming cheil of his day, and the photograph showed him standing bareheaded and short-cropped in a local studio, cross-legged, and his left hand clutching the narrow lapel of his thick coarse tweed jacket, a tie at his neck and a watch-chain across his waistcoat, his right hand leaning on the back of a rustic chair with lions' heads for arm-rests. Audie had taken after his mother, thin as a rake and narrow shouldered; even spoke in the same hurried stammering way, repeating some of his words and crying out 'eh what?' as soon as Helen had begun to tell him something, as if he hadn't the patience to wait or she had finished. It wasn't that she spoke all that slow, and later on she noticed that he did it with everybody he spoke to, which was a bit annoying at times but you had to make allowances for folk.

Audie still had the photograph of his real father in his kist, and he had promised to show it to Helen when she came up to Toddlebrae. Somehow he felt proud to tell her of his real father, though it made him a bastard bairn really, and he still resented the way he had treated his poor mother, throwing her out when Audie was born, though he paid a little for his keep later on. But if Robin Gay had married his mother, Audie would have been a farmer's son, and now that the old man was dead most likely farmer at the Reisk, with real sisters and brothers, and none of that crowd at Toddlebrae to bully him. When Audie explained all this to Helen she was impressed and gradually identified herself more closely with Audie Foubister's twisted life, which was worse than her own when she thought of it, though she had little chance of being farmer at Bogmyrtle while Hamish was still alive, though he was her younger brother.

But surely, Audie thought, if his poor old mother was worth having a time with she was worth marrying, and he felt he would never do a thing like that with a quine like Helen MacKinnon, if ever he got the chance, and maybe he would have to tell her about his big rupture before he went that far . . . Meantime he looked shyly at the sweet flower-like face of her smiling there and blushed deeply at the thought of it.

It was Frank Barbour who first broke the news of Audie's love affair to Doris and Susan. He said he had seen Audie and a country lass at the Music Hall, coming down the stone steps arm in arm mind you, which was certainly something new with Audie, for they had never seen him with a quine in his life. Frank never thought his half-brother

44

had it in him to get a lass and he must certainly be coming out of his box. Then Herbert the baker 'the dough thumper', as Audie called his younger half-brother, had bumped into Audie and Helen coming out of the new Picturedrome on the High Street, where they had been to see Mary Pickford. Herbert ran all the way home to Toddlebrae to tell his sisters. 'And a right bonnie quine she is,' he gasped out, 'I wadna mind havin' my shoes under her little bed I can tell ye! She's as good-lookin' as Mary Pickford ony day, and juist aboot her size too – or Lillian Gish either,' he added, 'a real film star I tell ye. Gish what a dish,' he sang out, waltzing over to the washstand to wash the flour from his whiskers.

So Helen had become a subject of great speculation in the Barbour household, especially with Doris and Susan. To think that Audie had a girl of any sort amused them considerably, but when someone told them she was a farmer's daughter they were dumbfounded.

'A farmer's daughter! Just think of it,' cried Doris, as she sat one evening darning a sock for Audie. 'A farmer's daughter, and him only a servant! What will become of us all? I suppose in a short time her folks will be coming to see us in a phaeton or governess cart, or maybe in one o' these new-fangled contraptions they call an automobile!' And she bit into the worsted thread with her sharp white teeth.

'But she's a worker too,' said Susan, 'a servant in the toon.'

'Aye, Su, but it's juist a pastime, 'cause there's nae a job for her at hame: a wye tae broaden her education. It's nae that the MacKinnons are hard up or onything like that.'

Susan stood tiptoe with her duster to squash a fly on the wall. 'Oh aye,' she mused, 'Audie will hardly look at us after this; he'll be lookin' down his nose at his poor half-sisters. I tell ye, Doris, we will be the Cinderellas of this little pantomime!'

'And they say she's affa bonnie,' Doris sighed. 'Frank was fair smitten wi' her looks.' And Doris looked at her own chubby face in the glass of the sideboard.

'It's what she sees in poor Audie that puzzles me,' said

Susan. 'Maybe if he had a new suit he wadna look sae bad. That suit he's wearin' just now, the grey one – well, maybe her father wouldn't even put it on his scarecrow!'

'Think shame, Susan, that we should let our poor half-brother be so humiliated – I think that is the right word – humiliated, to be seen courting in a suit like that. We must do something about it, sister: Audie must have a new suit, new boots or shoes; a coat, gloves, maybe spats and a hat, then it won't be our fault if we don't have farming relations in the family. Audie might think on us later on, in fact, if we did our best for him now.'

'Weel weel,' Susan laughed, 'I think I see oor Audie in spats, and ye'll never get him to wear a hat. You've enough ado getting him to change his fule sark at the week-ends!'

'Aye, true enough, Audie can be real thrawn at times, but he'll do it for the sake o' his lass. Mind you, this quine might change oor Audie completely.'

'Well, she has something ado,' Susan asserted, 'for I don't think she'll change oor Audie in a lifetime.'

'But Susan, its nae a chance tae miss. A farmer's daughter. Can't ye see what that means? And if we get Audie spruced up he may lead us all to clover; a land flowing with milk and honey.'

'And what about the expense?'

'Never fear, Su. Audie has money in the bank. Mother says he has. And if we can get mother roon tae oor wye o' thinkin' she'll get Audie tae open his purse strings. After all, it wad be for his own good.'

Susan sighed. 'Maybe this Helen MacKinnon might have a brother that would suit me fine.'

'Aye, or me, Susan.'

'Aye, or you, Doris. Audie could be good bait for us yet.'

'And we'll have to invite them up for high tea sometime.'

They did eventually, but in the meantime the house-proud sisters turned their suburban foppery to good effect as far as Audie was concerned. They had him measured for a new suit and had it tailored to the latest cut in fashion. They had him buy new boots with eye-slit lacing, a new shirt and a coat, until he looked the most debonair gentleman in the burgh. He rebelled at the spats, however, and the very idea of a hat frightened him, even a straw hat or boater that were all the fashion in the toon. Gloves were also out but he consented to a rather flashy dam-brod cap of small black and white squares, with a hoop or 'spangie' inside to keep it flat on his head; anything reasonable to impress his lass, and he paid out what money was necessary to make himself respectable.

When Audie went out in the evening to meet his 'country lass', as they called her, his half-sisters combed his hair and brushed his new suit; even went down on their knees to polish his boots. Doris embroidered a silk handkerchief (for exhibition in his breast pocket only – not to blow his nose in) and Susan went out to the back garden for a rose or a carnation for his buttonhole, with a dab of her best perfume under the lapels of his coat. Doris gave him a spare hankie and warned him not to wipe his nose on the palm of his hand either.

Audie was charmed out of all suspicion that his half-sisters could have any other motive than to please him in their recent fit of servitude. He couldn't see through their stinking pride nor their fur coat and no drawers underneath attitude to life. After all, his money had been well spent and he didn't care. It was enough that his going about with a lass had impressed them, and he felt a little burst of pride at the thought of it, an infection almost from his half-sisters. Never in all his dreary life had he known such flattery. Now he was charmed and delighted out of all remembrance of his former existence. Frank and Herbert now treated him with courtesy and a new respect, as if he were a full brother, with a little jibe about his good-looking lass thrown in for good measure, which Audie regarded as a compliment and took it in equally good humour. Even his step-father asked him round to the Whaler Inn for a pint of bitter and introduced him as his son to some of his cronies, something the old man had never done in his life before.

Bill Smith and Daisy May were getting married shortly and they had asked Audie and Helen as best man and bridesmaid. They had been shy at first but after some coaxing from Bill Smith they accepted the invitation and Audie thought his expenditure had served a double purpose.

Audie was really happy for the first time in his life. His heart was light and his step was sprightly when he walked out of the tenement on Toddlebrae to keep his evening trysts with Helen. Doris and Susan were watching him from behind the window curtains, giggling at the success of their venture, yet forced to admit that Audie gave justice to his new attire, and wore it like a gentleman, and that a hat and cane would have made him a real dandy.

Helen was waiting at the corner of Prince Street, and when she saw Audie coming down the pavement she could hardly believe it was the same man.

'How do ye like ma new suit?' Audie asked blandly, well aware that he had made an impression.

A smile lit up Helen's face, like the sun in a flower garden. She had a new dress herself and a floral hat but she was no match for Audie; such a change from the town tramp, if he didn't wipe his nose on the palm of his hand to spoil it.

But he didn't, and Helen laughed, almost clapping her hands at the sight of him. 'But tell me,' she asked, 'did ye do all this just for me, Audie?'

'Well it was they bitches put me up to it,' Audie said, blushing under her admiring eyes, 'they rigged me out like this. I suppose it was tae please ye though and I hope ye're nae angry.'

'Angry, heavens no, but it reminds me o' a story I once heard about a laird who dressed himsel' in rags tae rescue a poor orphan lassie he wanted tae marry, but when she saw him later on, dressed in his kilt and a' his finery, she wad hae nothing more tae do wi' him.'

'But surely . . .' Audie stammered, 'I was only tryin' tae please ye.'

'No no, Audie, naething like that. I'm glad tae see ye dressed up. It was good of yer sisters tae dress ye up. Surely they canna be sae bad as ye say they are.'

Helen was sharper than Audie but still she couldn't see the deception behind the motive to please her. She was unaware of the image she had created in the minds of the half-sisters; of their visions of grandeur and the riches of farming life. How could she when she had never seen such riches or such grandeur? Such things were for the Lairds, not for their humble tenant farmers. Helen knew nothing but poverty and the grind of ceaseless work and struggle in the unrewarding fields, with just enough to keep the spirit alive at the end of the day. How could Helen know what the sisters thought? Surely they were in for a shock.

'They want ye tae come tae the hoose some nicht,' Audie said quietly, reassured by her smile.

'The bitches?' she asked, her fine teeth uncovered by her smiling lips.

'Aye, ye'll see them in their high-heeled shoes, flappin' their dusters roon yer lugs, like ye was a flea on a wa'. And ye'll hear them talk, polite like the gentry, as if they were better than you or me.'

'Maybe I'm no match for them, Audie, the "Bitches" I mean.'

'Ye're better than them ony day. Ye're the bonniest woman I've ever seen.'

And Audie looked Helen straight in the face with his small clear blue eyes, like the eyes of a baby in the first light of understanding. He had uttered his first endearing compliment and it made Helen blush more than she had expected.

Helen had saved enough to buy a new costume, dark brown corded material with a pleated skirt, a new blouse, hat and shoes, so that when Audie took her to Toddlebrae she felt quite presentable. She was looking better too than when she first came in from the country, maybe because she had an easier time and better food, though the Barbours would never believe it. If she had missed the sunshine and the fresh air the want of them hadn't done her any harm. Moreover she had cycled home every fortnight on her new bike and the exercise had braced her figure in womanly proportions.

But she had never seen a home so spick and span as the flat at Toddlebrae; even her own mistress could hardly equal it. She was reminded of the shining caravans of the

gypsies when they camped in the woods at Lachbeg, every
thing glittering bright and clear and not a speck of dir
anywhere. No matter when Helen went up with Audie t
Toddlebrae the girls were always dusting and polishing
They dusted a chair before Helen sat down on it and the
polished the door knobs while she was still in the house.

'Hoose pride!' Audie said of his half-sisters. 'A body i
aboot as bad aff as a flea bidin' in a hoose like that. Ye cann
licht naewye but they're efter ye wi' a duster!'

Audie took Helen up to his bedroom and showed her hi
chaumer kist and the photograph of his father as he had
promised. He was just like Craig, Helen thought, except fo
the beard, and maybe a bit older. Doris and Susan wer
giggling when the couple came downstairs and Helen fel
sure they were being mocked and made fun of. Most likely
they were thinking of something else and Helen thought she
knew what it was. After all it was a bit embarrassing when
Audie invited her up to his bedroom.

Now besides his gramophone and his double-cased lever
watch, and his passion for steam engines, Audie had one
other great solace in his life, namely his bicycle. It was his
pride and joy and he spent hours on it with a duster on
Sundays, almost as bad as his half-sisters, until he had it
shining like a new pin. On Helen's Sunday off they went for
long rides together in the country, spinning along between
the hawthorn hedges, among the green fields and the bird
song and Audie had contentment in his heart beyond his
wildest dreams. And that new record he had just bought for
his gramophone: 'A Bicycle Built for Two', he was whistling
it all the time.

With Helen beside him Audie was a new man altogether.
Just think of what she had done for him already: all the
menfolk who formerly ignored him now beaming over him
with their broadest smiles, no doubt some of them a bit
envious of his 'countrie lass', and his high-minded half-
sisters down on their knees polishing his boots. My but it was
grand! And just wait until he got to know the MacKinnons,
and could talk to Helen's father – then he would show them

all what he was worth. He felt a little twinge of sadness that his poor old grandmother hadn't lived to see this splendid day in his manhood. She would have liked that, poor soul.

'I dinna ken what will happen tae Audie when I wear awa.' That was what the old body had said: but now Audie had somebody better and bonnier than his old grandmother to look after him. Indeed, Audie thought, things were just beginning to happen in his drab life.

'Audie has certainly changed,' Susan had said to Doris, 'such a difference that Helen quine has made to him. I wouldn't have believed it possible.'

'Aye, Su, but mother was just tellin' me this mornin' that Audie is leavin' us.'

'Leavin' us,' Susan gasped, stunned with surprise.

'Aye, Susan, efter all we've done for him. That's gratitude for ye. I'll bet this bitch of a quine has put him up to it. He's taken a job on a fairm, drivin' a pair of horses; says he wants tae save money tae get married, getting free board on the fairm and such like.'

'Married – did you say they were getting married?'

'Aye, but not yet, Susan.'

'But there's been no word of an engagement.'

'No no, not yet, Su, but Audie has been telling mother his intentions. He tells her everything.'

'There wouldn't be anything wrong would there now?' Susan contemplated, leaning on her sweeping brush.

'Na, Susan, oor Audie wadna ken the wye tae do onything wrong. And remember, he's got that big rupture mother used to tell us aboot, and how Audie would never get near a woman with it to have a family. Mother used to worry about it because he wouldn't go near a doctor to have it sorted; something his grandmother neglected to see about when he was a bairn and mother felt responsible for it.'

'But maybe that's just mother's idea,' Susan suggested. 'There must be thousands of married men with ruptures and they still have families.'

'Aye, but mother said that Audie had a special big one; that his privates were as large as a teapot.'

51

'Mother must have seen them then?' Susan wondered.

'You don't have to,' Doris said. 'You can see them bulging his trousers if you watch.'

Susan laughed out loud. 'I'm not in the habit of watching where men's trousers are bulging, and there could be another reason for it you know.'

'It's not a hobby of mine either,' Doris laughed, 'but it could be an amusing one, come to think of it.'

'But I don't think Audie's rupture ever bothers him, and you never hear him complaining. I'm sure mother exaggerates these things, like she does everything else.'

'All the same,' Doris said, 'that MacKinnon quine could be buying herself a pig in a poke with oor Audie.'

'Well that's up to her to find out,' Susan laughed, 'and I'm sure I'm not going to be the one to advise her; you can please yourself.'

'Not me, nor mother either, come to that I suppose.'

'Of course not, Doris, and don't you be saying anything about it to upset mother. Never trouble trouble till trouble troubles you, that's what I say.'

'I won't say anything to mother, don't you fret,' and Doris switched the subject to the question of money. 'But surely the MacKinnons would put by the wedding – if there is one; Audie wouldn't have to worry about that.'

'Aye, sis, that's true; it's mostly the bride's folk does that, though I can't see how our drunken father could manage it – if ever he gets the chance. But maybe the MacKinnons are nae sae well off as we thought they were; there's a big family of them and a lot of sisters to be married.'

'But we'll miss Audie's board money,' Doris concluded. 'Maybe we'll be worse off than we was before, after Audie leaves us, I mean.'

But Audie was ignorant of their claik and never concerned himself about a rupture that had never bothered him. He was as keen on a woman as the next man, just a bit shy, and he never had the courage to go that far with any woman; never had the chance, and he wasn't going to spoil his affair with a fine lass like Helen MacKinnon to prove anything, if there was anything to prove. All good things in their time, Audie thought, and his chief concern in the meantime was to get to know the MacKinnons, to meet Helen's folks and get acquainted, then maybe he would think of marriage and the other things that went with it.

As for Helen herself – well, the world had not 'ill used her', as her father feared it would. If she went home with Audie someday she wouldn't be on her hands and knees, begging her father to take her back. Maybe he thought she would come home with a bairn in her wime, like he had done with Rachael her mother. But Helen was still a virgin, and maybe determined to remain one till she was married, like her grandmother had taught her. Audie had never touched her, or even suggested anything improper; a perfect gentleman he was in that respect and not like some of the men that Daisy May had told her about. All the same Helen knew that her brothers and sisters would laugh at Audie, just as they would take the raise of any lad she brought home from the toon; but especially Audie with his genteel ways and peculiar little habits – they just hadn't the manners for anything else, nor had they seen much of life to know anything different from their primitive, childish, old-fashioned ways at Bogmyrtle.

Finally, after giving the subject a lot of thought, and discussing it with Daisy May, Helen decided that Audie Foubister should meet the MacKinnons. Coming from such a grand family, and accustomed to all the finery of town life, she began to wonder what Audie would think of her folks, or what he would tell his own people concerning them. Indeed it was Helen's turn to feel embarrassed, even inferior, and she felt a twinge of self reproach when she shyly invited her sweetheart out to Bogmyrtle.

'Foo wad ye like tae come oot tae Bogmyrtle tae see my folk?' she asked.

'Oh fine,' Audie said, 'I was juist wanderin' when ye was goin' tae speir.'

'We could go on oor bicycles on Sunday, if it's a fine day,' Helen suggested.

Audie agreed but made one small condition: 'We wunna hae tae bide late 'cause I have tae get oot tae the fairm afore it's dark. I dinna like runnin' a bike in the dark.'

'Are ye fear't in the dark, Audie?'

Audie fidgeted in his new suit and so far forgot himself as to wipe his nose on the palm of his hand. 'Weel,' he said, 'I dinna like scutterin' aboot wi' they oil lamps in the dark; I'm fair lost when they blaw oot.'

'My folks call them "Bibblie Willies",' Helen joked, trying to prepare him for some of the banter awaiting him.

Audie smiled rather sadly. ' "Bibblie Willies", ' he mused, 'I've heard them called that afore.' Then he added: 'But we could leave the toon early in the mornin' and be hame afore dark.'

Helen agreed, and she wrote and told her mother they were coming, if it was a fine day, and would arrive sometime in the forenoon.

Audie spent the whole of Saturday evening polishing his bicycle for the Sunday run, looking forward eagerly to meeting Helen's people, thinking it would sort of break the ice with her parents when the day came to ask Helen for his wife.

Rachael read Helen's letter and handed it to Craig: 'It's frae Helen,' she said, 'she's bringing her lad oot frae the toon on Sunday.'

'So I see,' said Craig, 'I can read, woman. But she micht hae lookit for something better than juist a workin' body . . . a toon's lad at that!'

Rachael took the tongs and rearranged the peats on the fire. She was pregnant again and it took much of the pith out of her actions. She sighed and hoped it would be their last bairn, though God knows they had been careful enough and still it had happened. The change of life would come and she hoped that would stop it. But Craig was rough with a woman and his lust had taken the sting out of Rachael's temper, subduing her high spirits to the common level. Ah well, it would be over before her eldest daughter could have a bairn; that much she knew from the look of her quine when she came home at weekends. She would like to be

inished having bairns before she became a grandmother.
There hadn't been any word of marriage so she hoped that
her quine would be better placed than she herself had been.
She wouldn't like the quine to come crawling to Craig's
door with a bastard bairn in her wime.

'Maybe we have oorsel's tae blame, Daw, that the quine
hasna gotten somebody better than a workin' body. We kept
her sae lang at hame workin' for naething that the lassie
never got much of a chance tae look for a lad. Maybe it's the
best she could do in service.'

'Ye did a' richt yersel' in service, woman.'

'Aye, but I had tae suffer first, and I wadna like ma ain
quine tae be in the same fix. Ye wadna lat her get the gamekeeper but surely ye canna interfere wi' the lassie a second
time. And there wasna much wrang wi' the gamekeeper
onywye; this time ye'll maybe hae tae pocket yer pride.'

'Ach, woman, she's nae a bairn noo. She can look efter
hersel'. Maybe she juist took the first lad she clapped eyes on
in the toon. But she's a fairmer's dother, woman, and I
thocht she micht get somebody better than a scaffie.'

'He's nae a street sweeper; he worked wi' the Toon
Cooncil, and he works on a fairm noo.'

'Ah weel, that's nae sae bad, woman; maybe we'll put 'im
in a place somewye. We'll see what's in the breet, if it's
mair than the spoon puts in.'

Rachael was first to see her daughter with her young man
enter between the hedges at the head of the avenue. They
dismounted from their bicycles and Audie was removing the
clips from his trousers before walking down to the farmyard.
Everyone peered through the kitchen window, trying to get
a glimpse of the lovers through the gaps in the privet hedge.
All except Craig, who kept his armchair, content to catch a
glimpse of them as they passed his gable window.

Rachael gave her final orders to the family: 'Now you
bairns behave yersel's (though some of them were men and
women), I dinna want tae hear impudence frae ony o' ye,
understand! And Daw: nae spittin' on the fleer.' She then
eyed herself in the overmantel, tucking the tufts of greying

hair under her white dust cap, lifted her breasts an
smoothed her apron as she went to the back door to meet he
guests.

'Ye wad think the Prince o' Wales was comin',' Riac
joked to anyone who cared to listen, as soon as his mother
back was turned. 'I suppose a body could hardly risk lattir
a fart sae lang as he's in the hoose!'

Riach's remark triggered off a chorus of waiting laughter
a ribald explosion that reverberated to the back kitche
door. Audie heard it outside and he blushed like a cockscom
in his jam-jar collar. Even the turkey cock gobbled his dis
pleasure and the pigeons flapped up to the barn roof. Flos
the collie had her big sandy paws on Audie's waistcoat an
was like to bite off the huge amber stone that dangled fror
his watchchain. The couple had just laid their bicycle
against the harled wall of the milk-house when Rachael ra
outside and shook hands with Audie.

'Ye've gotten a fine day,' she glimmered, kissing Helen o
the cheek, 'just put your bicycles in the gig-shed and com
awa' doon the step intae the kitchie.'

Audie removed his diced cap and followed Rachael int
the smoky gloom of the kitchen, cool and quiet under th
trees despite its crowded atmosphere. Helen introduce
Audie to her father, who got up from his armchair and shoo
hands with the shy stranger. The ring of faces confrontin
Audie were bursting with mirth. At any moment ther
might be another explosion of derisive laughter. It hung i
the air like a bubble on a pinprick, and the slightest excus
would burst it. But Audie braved it, and as he clasped eac
warm hand in turn their faces relaxed in friendly concer
for the stranger.

Hamish and Riach were seated behind the table, on th
long wooden deas, their backs to the window, Hamis
nearest his father at the head of the table. That must b
Riach at the end of the deas, Audie thought, from wha
Helen had told him, for there was his crutch propped agains
the wall behind him, his wooden leg sprawled across th
stone floor.

Riach spat on his palm when he shook hands with Audie

'Aye, ye're a gie toff though,' he winced, out of the corner of his small twisted mouth. And Audie got such a grip from Hamish as nearly pulled him across the table, and he almost set his other hand on the butter print to save himself. Moira and Nancy were leaning against the door jamb to the front passage and Nora and Kirsteen were lurching over the end of the dresser. Audie made a rough count of the ring of peering faces and reached about eight or nine, including little Janet, who was seated on a stool at the fireside, a big rag doll in her lap.

The long wooden table had been scrubbed until the grain in the wood was ribbed on its surface, coverless but set for tea, a fly-cup for the visitors before dinner, to refresh them after their long tiring journey out from the toon as Rachael said. A huge kettle hung from the crook on the black swey over the peat fire, and when it came to the boil Rachael made tea in a red enamelled teapot. The arch over the fireplace was whitewashed, as were the stone binks at the sides, and a black polished brander covered the ash-pit on the floor. Audie was seated on a hard chair between the kitchen press and the box-bed, where he stared up at the wag-at-the-wall clock in the corner by the fireplace, with its long brass chains and leaden weights nearly touching the floor, with cherubim figures carved on its coloured face. Rachael gave Audie a cup of hot strong tea in his lap, with a home-baked scone and strawberry jam. 'Do ye take milk?' she asked. Audie said 'Aye', and Rachael poured a suppie cream from the stoup into his cup, because none of the family ever took milk in their tea. Audie became less self-conscious under Rachael's care, and while he sipped the tea his eyes wandered round the old farm kitchen: from the great oak beams across the low roof, slung with salted bacon, curing in the peat smoke, to the green distempered walls hung with brown wooden racks filled with blue willow-patterned dinner plates; the recess under the dresser with pots and pans, some of them brass for holding berries, the shelves overhead laden with crockery, ashets and tureens and heavy soup plates. Lanterns were hanging from hooks in a beam and a long-handled churn stood in Riach's corner, the whole kitchen compact, crowded, warm and lively.

Helen went to the front passage to hang up her coat and hat, removing the long steel pins that held it in place in the wind, then stuck them back in the hat. Daisy May had done up her hair in the morning, one thick plait that was rolled on top of her head, showing her ears at the sides, enhancing her womanhood, while her white embroidered blouse, tight-fitting tunic and long sweeping skirt aroused the interest of her sisters. They tried on her coat and hat, sticking the long pins in their hair and admiring themselves in the overmantel. Though her sisters were younger they were taller than Helen, looking down on her almost, as they turned her round and round, admiring her dark blue costume. 'It's fine, though,' Moira said, and smiled through her sunny hair, where it swung over her face like a veil.

Rachael bent over the fire again with the long-handled tongs, collecting the peat embers into the centre of the grate, then broke some fresh peat over her knee and stacked it round the little blue flames, the white scented smoke rising into the overhanging chimney. 'Ye maun be tired,' she said to Audie, chattering on about the long run out from the toon, mostly for want of something to say. 'But the drop tea will refresh ye. I never learned the bike masel' but Daw runs a bike sometimes. When we baith want tae get aboot we tak' the gig. Craig has a fine shelt for the gig.'

After tea most of the MacKinnons went outside to their various jobs, tending the cattle and the vegetable plots and carrying water for the flower gardens.

Audie and Helen now moved over to the deas, next to Craig, where he had remained at the gable window.

'Naebody's gaun tae the chapel the day,' Craig said, 'the flooers are a' wiltin' in the drouth and we'll need abody tae carry watter.'

'He's juist haverin', Audie,' Rachael said, giving Audie his name for the first time; 'never heed'im; naebody here gangs tae the chapel nooadays . . . we're a' heathens.'

Somebody giggled in the passage. 'Moira – Nora,' Rachael cried, 'go and mak' the beds and nae stand there sniggerin'. They're bitches, that quines,' she added aside to Audie. 'They think they might be missin' something.'

Audie said nothing. Inwardly he thought the quines were exciting and grand, though maybe not quite so well faced as Helen, except perhaps for Kirsteen, with the long gold hair. 'I've fairly picked the best ane,' Audie assured himself.

Craig sucked away quietly at his pipe and plied Audie with questions about the ways of farming in his neighbourhood. 'The crops are comin' on grand,' he puffed, 'in spite o' the dry weather, and I believe the hairst will be fairly early.'

'Quines,' Rachael cried again through the passage door, 'stop that gigglin'. Come and pare the tatties, I've got the broth ready.'

After dinner Audie produced a packet of cigarettes and offered it to Hamish and Riach. They each took a fag and Audie fitted one for himself in a mouthpiece to protect his moustache. He never inhaled, but smoked his fag in a holder, like a pipe. Craig fixed a glowing peat cinder with the tongs. He held it out for Audie to light up, then passed it over to his sons behind the table. They pressed their fag-ends to the glowing ember and handed back the tongs to their father. Craig held the hot cinder over his pipe and drew on the amber mouthpiece while the blue smoke spiralled into the kitchen roof.

Rachael finished her dinner on Little Janet's stool at the fireside. She never had time to eat while the others were at the table, so now she had her share while the quines washed the dishes.

After dinner Craig put on his bonnet and took Audie for a canny stroll across the parks. The stirks were lolling about like kittens in the sun, their heads flat on the grass and their legs stretched out, some of them getting up and raxing themselves, their long tails twisted over their backs. Meg and Bell were on the brae, as fine a pair of mares as Audie had seen for a long time, nickering at their approach. The corn was unsheathing and still green, wilting almost in the drowsy sunshine, thirsting for a shower of rain. The turnips too were parched but closing between the drills, awaiting moisture to swell the bulbs. The potato crop was in flower, mauve, white and purple for the different varieties, and where the flower had gone green plums were forming on the shaws. The hay was stacked in a corner of the field, the second crop now ankle deep in red luscious clover, an autumn bite for the cattle when the summer pasture was on the wane. Audie wandered over the parks with Craig, mildly excited at the prospect of having such a father-in-law, and marrying the daughter of a man who was the equal of the farmer he worked for. Audie wasn't all that keen on farming but the idea was worth thinking about. Meanwhile he tried to be interested, listening to Craig most of the time but with little to say in reply. His boyhood interests were just across the road from Bogmyrtle, where the railway embankment curved round from the hill, sweeping towards Leary Station. Audie felt he could have thrown his cap in the air if an engine had come plunging round the bend. But it was Sunday and the line was dead, except for the humming of the telephone wires and the smell of hot tar that came up from the sleepers. The brown shadow of the Mattock Hill frowned over all, with the antlered deer on its shoulder, like a monolithic skeleton sprawled in the sun. Over to the north the dark green shade of Lachbeg Woods with the white castle in the centre, and nearer the coast the white splatch of water known as the Myreloch.

Back at the steading Craig took Audie round the vegetable plots and the flower gardens, where some of the quines were weeding on their knees, sheltered by the privet and cupress hedges, while others carried water from the spootie and the Kelpie Burn, which ran through the farm and drove the water wheel on threshing days. Huge vegetable marrows were ripening under the gooseberry bushes, now heavy with their fruit, while blackcurrants hung in clusters from their leafy greenery, and there were long rows of raspberry canes and beds of strawberries. Plum and apple trees abounded, besides quince and flowering shrubs, though Audie didn't know one from the other.

'We wad be glad tae hear the whaups skirlin',' Craig

remarked, 'owre frae the Myreloch; it micht bring a suppy rain.'

The glass-houses glimmered in the hot sun. Inside, the air was humid with the tang of compost and growing plants, a hot exotic fragrance from the multifarious display of palm fronds and cacti. Long rows of pot plants frothed over the wooden shelves, a luxuriant galaxy of summer blooms, gay and rich with colour, with red tomatoes at the windows and green vines against the stone walls. There were hot water pipes under the trestles, fed from a boiler and firebox at the door. The fire was out and the pipes were cold but Audie was sweating profusely.

Craig described the various flowers, their peculiarities and their commercial value. He sold a lot of pot plants and cut flowers in Brochan, besides fruit and vegetables, and his interest in the business was yielding considerable profit. Audie daubed his warm brow with his white embroidered hankie and pretended as much enthusiasm as he could muster in the circumstances. But he was greatly relieved when Helen came dashing through the blue hydrangeas and told them that supper was on the table.

On her way back to the house Helen leaned over the sty for a word with the breeding sow, grunting over a shovel of coal Rachael had thrown in to grind her teeth on. When Audie looked over the dyke he said he'd never seen the likes before and Helen laughed at his ignorance.

Audie got the affront of his life after supper when he asked the whereabouts of the lavatory.

There was an immediate explosion of hilarious laughter.

'A lavatory!' Riach jeered, 'never heard o' sic a thing. What's a lavatory?'

Audie flushed to the roots of his hair, his ears red as the wattles on a growing cockerel.

'Weel, a water-closet than,' he ventured.

'A water-closet!' Riach yelled, and nearly fell off the deas.

There was another wild chorus of guffaws and the girls

squealed with laughter. When this had subsided Audie had another try. 'Some folks call it an earth-closet and sometimes a latrine.'

'A latrine!' Hamish shrieked, 'and wha the hell wad put earth in the closet?'

He gave Riach a thud on the back and both sat convulsed in laughter. A cloud of dust rose from Riach's jacket until he spluttered and half choked and water ran from his eyes.

Helen sat in a corner, demure and blushing, scarce daring to glance at her lover, where he stood in the middle of the floor. She had expected something of the kind would happen, but they had all been so well-behaved during the day she had almost forgotten their ill manners; never dreaming that Audie would find himself in such a delicate situation.

Even Craig was amused and puzzled, wondering how far the thing would go, or how long Audie could thole it.

Audie made a last ditch effort to ease his discomfort: 'A PRIVY THAN!' he shouted, amid the rising laughter.

When this subsided Hamish let off an enormous fart, like the arse of his breeks was torn, and lept over Riach, clean out of the deas, linked arms with Audie and birrelled him round the floor in a mocking waltz, fair roaring with laughter, while Rachael ran for a paper and lit it at the fire and chased them round the floor, the flame at the arse of Hamish's trousers to burn up the smell. The laughter now turned to shrieks and yells and Craig couldn't restrain himself, until Audie broke loose and made for the door in a huff. He was the stoic supreme but this all but broke him. Rachael threw the burning paper in the fire and made after Audie and brought him back to the kitchen. The house was quiet again and she spoke in his ear, while he bent down slightly to listen. 'There's nae a lavatory, Audie. We juist a' bare oor bums tae the weather and the neighbours on the sharn midden at the back o' the steadin'. But if ye want tae be oo to' sicht ye can go under the water wheel.'

'Aye, juist the thing,' cried Hamish, where he leaned against the dresser; 'juist the thing, and we'll open the sluice gate on 'im.'

Another cataclysm of laughter.

'Ye'll do nae sic thing,' Craig cried at last, 'let the man alane!'

This silenced everybody but it couldn't take Audie out of his present predicament.

The youngsters now eyed him in subdued amusement, wondering what he was going to do in the circumstances.

Audie was dumbfounded. He had merely meant to be polite. Living in the town he had become accustomed to plumbing and sanitation, and though there were no field lavatories on the farms there was usually one in the farmhouse, especially for visitors. He knew well enough what Rachael meant; he had worked on the farms long enough to understand her perfectly, but coming from a woman the information had shocked his little soul.

'But some fairms have lavatories,' he persisted, 'some have ane above the mill-race for their workers.'

'That's a good idea, Audie,' Rachael said, 'and we'll keep it in mind!' She was going to add, 'For your wedding', but thought better of it: poor Audie had been offended enough for one day; though secretly she made up her mind she would talk to Daw about it.

Audie had to comply with Rachael's instructions. Personal discomfort impelled him. He made for the back door, well aware that almost the entire household would be after him. He was a bit wary of the mill-wheel, much as he would have preferred its seclusion. So he chose the dung midden, fortunately well down at this time of year, while at others it can be well above the dykes; so he had some seclusion, though conscious all the time that he was being watched from every hole and bore in byre, stable and barn, and even from the skylight up in the corn loft.

'We'll hae tae leave early,' Audie reminded everybody, timid and blushing when he returned to the kitchen. 'We've a lang road tae go and I dinna like cyclin' in the dark.'

'He's fear't that his Bibblie Willie blaws oot,' cried Riach, trying to set the ball rolling again.

But nobody took any notice.

The youngsters followed the couple to the head of the avenue, giggling and sniggering behind, while Rachael walked with her arms folded beside Helen. 'How are ye, Mammie?' Helen asked tenderly, looking at her mother in the evening light. 'Och I'm a' richt,' Rachael said quietly, 'I've a whilie tae go yet. Maybe ye'll be married or that time.'

'I hardly think so,' Helen whispered, and if Audie heard them he never heeded, pushing his bike and talking to Craig.

When the couple got on their bicycles the youngsters all began wiping their noses on the palms of their hands, some of them on both hands, one at a time, fair dancing with laughter, even Little Janet in her pig-tails, and Riach with his crutch high in the air, his cap on the end of it, a rousing send off from the top of the brae.

To have angered Audie would have delighted the Mac-Kinnons. But they were beginning to realize that this would be difficult, and some of them already had a silent respect for this strange timid little man.

Henceforth he always arrived at Bogmyrtle around break-fast time and departed in the early evening, just when more conventional wooers would be putting in an appearance. The MacKinnons were highly amused at this for a time but they had to get used to it. They had to accept him and eventually they left him to his wiles with their sister. At least he was good to her and they felt she was safe in his care.

Audie was glad of it. He thought his patience with the rascals was well rewarded, with Helen as the special prize.

But moonlight romancin' and huggin' in the dark was out of the question with Audie Foubister. He went to bed early whatever was afoot and rose with the lark on the morrow.

Helen was still a virgin. Never even been kissed since the gamekeeper did it, except for a wee peck on the cheek from Audie with his moustache.

Eventually Audie Foubister made up his mind to ask Craig MacKinnon for his daughter in marriage. He chose his time carefully, staying for the night at Bogmyrtle, when none of the younger scallywags would be at hand to snigger behind his back. They had all gone to bed, while he and Helen still sat by the peat fire in the kitchen, talking to Craig and Rachael in the box-bed, Craig lying at the front, Rachael at his back.

Conversation became difficult and eyelids began to droop. The slow deliberate 'tick-tock tick-tock' of the great wag-at-the-wa' clock measured out the lasting minutes in drowsy monotony. The giant minute hand slipped forward nearly an eighth of an inch with every other beat of its iron heart, while one of the brass chains lowered its leaden weight a fraction nearer the floor, the other rising accordingly, an endless see-saw with eternity.

Craig began to yawn. Maybe he had been wrong, but he thought Audie had something on his mind. Helen gave Audie a nudge and at last he got up and went to the bedside. Rachael rose up on her elbow at his approach and Audie nearly choked on his words. She had never seen such a meek and humble man but she never doubted his sincerity. He wouldn't be her choice of a man but her daughter could please herself; if she was happy with Audie that was all that mattered and Rachael wasn't going to interfere. Maybe she would get more of her own way with a man like this; not like Craig with his headstrong, stubborn ways.

'Helen and me was thinkin' on gettin' merrite: what dae ye say tae that, man?'

Even the clock seemed to wait for the reply; the great hammer of destiny poised, waiting, listening, a moment pregnant with fate.

Craig raised himself to speak, leaning on his elbow. 'Aye man,' says he, 'I was half-expectin' that, and I've nae objections, Audie man. She's been a good dother tae me and a grand worker; in fact the place hasna been the same since she left and gaed intae the toon. But tak' her, Audie man, and be good tae her and dinna keep the purse yersel; gie her fair play wi' the bawbees.'

Rachael piped up from his back and added, 'And get up first in the mornin', Audie, and light the fire; maybe gie the quine a drap tea in her bed.'

Helen thought it was more than she had ever been

accustomed to but she said nothing. Everything was being arranged for her.

Audie splayed out his hands almost in supplication. 'I'll do the best I can for her; and richt glad I am tae get 'er, Craig man. I hardly ken what tae say tae thank ye baith.'

'Say nae mair aboot it, Audie. Ye're an honest cheil and nae a bad soul at that. And I'll put by yer weddin', every penny o't, so ye needna worry yersel aboot siller; leave that tae me.'

Rachael chirped up again from the back of the bed: 'And maybe some day, Audie, we'll put ye in a fairm o' yer ain, once ye've got mair experience. Foo wad ye like that Audie?'

Audie was astounded. He had never dreamt of such a thing; not that he could remember anyway. What would his folk have to say about that? Especially his half-sisters. Funny that Helen had never mentioned it. For a brief moment Audie sunned his heart in the warm smiles of fortune. He just couldn't believe his good luck. Him a farmer. Then panic siezed him and he shied at the responsibility.

'I'm hardly fit for that, man,' he said to Craig, half smiling at his own confession, 'I hinna the experience tae manage a place masel'.'

'Weel weel,' said Craig, 'We'll say nae mair aboot it juist noo. We'll see foo ye get on. We have oor ain twa loons tae think on as weel, so we'll leave it at that in the meantime.'

Audie was so much taken out of himself he could hardly keep his head on the pillow. A strange elation came into his mind, filling his thoughts with a gladness he had never known before, joy and sleep battling for supremacy. He was bedded with Hamish upstairs, over the room where old Joyce had endured so much. But Audie knew nothing of Joyce and her suffering. The old house was silent and kept its secrets, but for the quiet bustling of his beloved, while she barred the back kitchen door and came upstairs to her old bedroom, sleeping with her sisters. Audie thought not of the past nor pried into the future but went to sleep suddenly in a daze. He didn't even hear the owl that hooted in the plane tree when Helen blew out her candle.

*

The wedding was planned for December, a month later than Bill Smith and Daisy May, when Audie and Helen would be Best Man and Bridesmaid respectively. But in autumn there was talk of postponement. Rachael was so near the menopause that her pregnancy was threatening her sanity; draining her bloodstream, the doctor said, and that there wasn't enough oxygen reaching her brain, causing her to have giddy spells and hallucinations. But of course doctors told you things they didn't even believe themselves, but they had to say something to pretend they knew what they were talking about. But Rachael defied them and regained her equilibrium, like the wiry vixen that she was, so the banns were called for the wedding and the invitations went out as arranged.

Up on Toddlebrae in Scotstoun preparations for the wedding were carried out free from hindrance. But it had come sooner than Susan Barbour had expected it and the news caught her unawares.

'Audie has fair surprised us, mither,' Susan remarked when the invitation cards came in, 'Imagine oor Audie makin' a match like that; he's done better than ony o' the rest o' us are likely tae manage.'

'Ye dinna hae tae imagine it, lassie,' her mother replied, 'it's real I tell ye. Audie has beaten the lot o' ye this time, and ye dinna gie him much credit for it either. It'll cost ye a bonnie penny tae rig yersel's oot for a fairmer's weddin', and besides that ye'll hae tae gie the lassie a decent present.'

'It's hardly fair that we should hae tae pay for all this oorsel's,' Susan retorted, 'Audie should hae tae open his purse for us.'

'Dinna be daft, Susan,' her mother replied, defending her prodigal son, 'Audie will have enough ado wi' himsel'; for one thing he'll hae a hoose tae furnish.'

Doris swatted the last surviving fly of the season. 'Aye, that's another thing,' she said, 'oor Audie is getting a dowry with her Ladyship, which is mair than oor father will ever manage for us.' And she swanked about the house in mocking derision.

'Nae doot the lassie has worked well for her dowry,' and

Mrs Barbour looked at her daughters almost in disdain. 'That's mair than I can say for you two idle bitches; ye wad hae yer poor auld mither oot scrubbin' fleers and washin' claes tae ither folk tae save yer ain selfish skins.'

But Doris had the last word. 'I'll bet Audie won't have to furnish his house; her ladyship's father will furnish it for them – and for nothing.'

The wedding ceremony was conducted in Joyce's death-chamber, and most of the nearest relations on both sides were present. The room was crowded and the younger members of the family stood in the front passage, right along to the grandfather clock by the front door. Joseph Barbour was there, buttonholed and smiling, with his spruce little wife and his gaudy daughters, besides Audie's step-brothers Frank and Herbert, and a hantle of other folk too numerous to mention.

Now there was nothing remarkable about Joyce's bedroom: it was merely the ben-room of an old Scottish farmhouse; a square apartment with a stucco ceiling and papered walls, a marble fireplace in the gable and panelled wooden shutters on the windows. Most of the furnishings had been removed to make room for the wedding ceremony, including the old brass bedstead where Joyce had died. A polished dining-room table remained in the middle of the linoleumed floor, which the minister was to use for his bible and marriage certificates, besides three high-backed chairs with their horsehair seats under the table leaf. A fire had been lit in the grate and Joyce's tongs and poker of bronze still lay inside the steel fender, a shovel and brass coal-scuttle by the wall skirting board. Floor-length curtains of heavy green material hung by the window, suspended from thick wooden rings on a brass rod, the lower sash raised so that a fresh cool breeze entered the room, dispelling any smell of damp or mustiness that might have gathered over the years. There were several pictures on the walls, mostly photograph enlargements of the MacKinnons in heavy wooden frames, including Craig and Rachael on their wedding day, but the one over the fireplace caught most folks' attention as soon as they entered the room. It was an enlarged portrait of old Joyce in a gilt frame, photographed in a studio on one of her rare trips to Brochan, in the days when she was still a healthy woman. It was a good likeness, clear and distinct for its day, black and white in sharp contrast, blending a strength of character and personality worthy of an artist's hand. Joyce looked like a typical Victorian lady, seated on a high-backed chair with carved arm-rests, her hands in her lap, and what with her beehive hair style in side-combs and flowing dress, laced at the neck and wrists, with tight-fitting bodice, she looked a picture of regal majesty: the way Helen always liked to remember her, before she became the ravenous senile scavenger for breadcrusts on the floor, the victim of Rachael's lunatic treatment. Standing beside Joyce in the picture was a little girl about three years old, with her hair in ringlets and her hand on her grandmother's knee, a shy timid smile on her sweet little face – Helen's face, now a full-grown woman on her wedding day.

But whatever way you looked at Joyce her eyes were upon you, all around the room, clear luminous eyes with a soft pleasant stare that followed you everywhere. No matter where the guests stood each one felt that Joyce was looking at them and watching all the proceedings. She saw her son Craig MacKinnon bring his daughter through from Riach's closet, arm in arm, and give her away to the solemn faced Audie Foubister. She watched the minister pronounce his blessing on the betrothed couple; saw Audie put the golden ring on Helen's finger, saw her blush and smile faintly, the smile of a virgin, pure as the driven snow for the bridal bed. As Joyce had taught her so had she lived, with maybe the gentle Audie to thank for it; for better or for worse, as the minister said. And while Frank Barbour and Moira MacKinnon signed their names in the marriage register Joyce's eye was upon them, and she watched the parents on both sides do likewise.

There was hand-shaking all round and some kissing of the bride, Frank and Herbert Barbour determined not to miss their chance though they had little experience; and then bride and groom left the room, followed by the guests, and went over the close to the barn, where everything had been prepared for the reception. The cobwebs had been brushed from the old mill and the walls were newly whitewashed, gleaming in the light of the stable lanterns that hung from the roof beams. The mill was garlanded with flowers picked by Kirsteen from the glass-houses: winter flowering begonias, azaleas, primulas, gloxinia, cyclamen and hyachinths; sprigs of fir and yellow jasmine were pinned to the walls, with little pots of flowering cacti in every niche that could be found. Berried holly hung in the corners and mistletoe in the centre of the roof, where any damsel caught there might be kissed as you please.

Long wooden planks were set up on trestles, where the guests could sit at the tables, three or four of them, the length of the barn, borrowed from the joiner at Leary, who was something of a fiddler forbye, and was a guest of honour to provide music for the dancing, besides a lad from Knockieben who played the melodeon. The table was laden with roast beef laced with bacon from the kitchen rafters; chicken that had been thrappled and plucked by Helen's sisters and roasted by Rachael on the peat fire, besides dumpling and trifle, wine and whisky, with a giant iced cake towering over all.

When the minister had said grace Nora and Nancy did the carving, while Kirsteen carried the laden plates round to the guests, the huge dinner plates from the kitchen racks, blue and Willow-patterned that were mostly used to feed the men at the threshing mills. Moira kept her seat because she was the bridesmaid, with Frank Barbour beside her, feeling like the Laird of Cockpen, while Sherran Beg that was her lad sat with Hamish further down the table. After the general feasting the minister held up his hand for silence, while Helen and Audie got up on their feet to cut their cake, Audie with his hand over Helen's on the knife handle, pressing hard through the ice until the slice fell away on the trenchard. Helen was blushing when she sat down and there was a mild clapping of hands and drinking of toasts on their behalf, and then her sisters carried a morsel of cake to each of the guests, to be eaten with their port wine, while the remainder of the cake was carried to the farmhouse. The minister said a few words before leaving and then the tables and forms were dismantled to clear the floor for dancing. The vricht from Leary got scraping on his fiddle, high up under his chin, and the lad from Knockieben played his melodeon over his knee, a thing nearly as big as a blacksmith's bellows but a better tone. Another billie got knacking with a pair of horn spoons and one with a comb at his mouth, while Riach played the pipe chanter, and they kicked up such a din that the nowt beasts were howling from the byres. But it kept the hooching dancers in a constant whirl, Doris Barbour and Hamish MacKinnon going at it like Cutty Sark, while Frank and Herbert were linking at it with the MacKinnon quines, first one and then the other, till some of them were light-headed, not to mention neighbours and relations that gave them a bit birl, and a kiss under the mistletoe, till the poor quines were fagged out and Nora ended up on the sack lifter, too drunk even to stand. Even Little Janet had her share of dancing, her pigtails out and her fine hair shimmering on her shoulders, caught in the light of the lanterns, a little doll woman in her long cotton dress. For Ladies' Choice she took Old Joseph Barbour, for drunk though he was he could fair dance, his jacket off and his white sark sleeves rolled up to his elbows.

Helen and Audie had never learned to dance, and no wonder, you thought, when you remembered the way they were brought up, trauchled with wark and never mixing with other folk, so they just stood idly by and watched the others, pleased in a way to be the cause of all their hilarity. Some lads prigged sair with Helen to get her on the floor, half drunk some of them and yearning for the feel of her against their lusting bodies. But she shyly refused them, saying she couldn't dance a step, though some of the lads were determined to teach her. Moira MacKinnon came over for Audie, determined to have him on the floor, pulling at his jacket till she nearly had it torn, but he stood his ground and said 'Eh what, woman, but I canna dance!' So Moira grabbed the first male she could get hold of for the next mad Scottische.

It was a great spree for old Joseph Barbour, for he drank the barley bree till he could scarcely stand, and he held forth to Craig in such praise of his farm that Craig was almost convinced that the rascal meant it.

Rachael went early to the farmhouse, her head sore with the noise and the fumes of drink and tobacco smoke, her nerves on edge at the chauve of the bairn within her. She sat by the kitchen fire, listening to the music coming across the close, and Nancy or Kirsteen came at times to comfort her; then Mrs Barbour, and the two of them had a right good claik about folk and having bairns till well after midnight.

Helen took some of the folk to see her presents, carrying a lamp through to Riach's closet, where the gifts were stacked on a table. She had worn a two-piece suit for her wedding, royal blue serge with a thin stripe, and a white silk blouse of ruffled lace. For going away she had a wide-brimmed floral hat with pins and a broad band round it that went down her back; a half-veil to the tip of her nose, and even high-heeled shoes, in the style of Susan Barbour. Craig had paid for all of it, and he had given her a gold brooch in the shape of a wish-bone that glittered at her throat. She looked a radiant bride, blushing like a rose at the dawn of matrimony.

'Tak' a drink, man,' Craig said to Audie, 'ye look like a ghost at yer ain funeral.'

'Eh what!' Audie stammered, taken by surprise, 'juist a wee drappie than,' while Craig fetched a glass and bottle. 'I dinna want tae get drunk and us gaun awa' amon strangers.'

The couple were to spend the first night of their honeymoon at Knockieben, who was a close neighbour of Craig, and on the morning they would catch the first train at Leary station for Aberdeen, to see the sights. Audie had never been to the Silver City and was fair looking forward to seeing the trains. Helen had cycled to Aberdeen with her father when she was a young quine but had never been there since she grew up.

But now the shelts and ponies were led out of the byres and sheds and hitched to the phaetons and gigs in the farm close. Candle lanterns were kindled and most folk got muffled up for the journey home, all except the Barbours and a few others who had to stay the night and catch a morning train.

Some slept in the spare bedroom under the staircase, adjoining Riach's closet, while Joseph Barbour and his wife rigged the brass bed for themselves in Joyce's room, Frank and Herbert sleeping on the floor. The wind rose during the night and the old man was disturbed by a tapping noise behind Joyce's picture, as if she were stamping her foot in disdain at the whole affair. His sons blamed the drink and said they slept grand and hadn't heard a thing. But Joseph was sober in the morning and when he rose to dress he went over and had a closer look at Joyce in her picture. 'Damned nice-lookin' woman,' he mused, 'and the quinie too. But of course it could hae been a bird in the lum or a rat ahin the lathin' sticks.' 'You old fool, talking to yourself again,' his wife taunted while she spread up the beds.

Whatever it was, Joseph never mentioned it to the MacKinnons. He supped his porridge with a flourish and spent a long time shaving at the mirror in the porch, remarking to Craig in passing about that fine new lavatory he had erected over the millrace.

Craig drove the Barbours down to the station in the springcart, besides some of Rachael's folk that were ready to go. He waited till the train came in to see them off, maybe hoping to catch a glimpse of his daughter, if they had slept in, but he was disappointed for they were off with an earlier train, and knowing Audie he should have had more sense, for Audie wouldn't have missed it for the world.

It was the only time the Barbours and the MacKinnons really mixed. As things turned out they never made much of it together, living in different worlds almost, Joseph with his town ways and always dressed while Craig could never get the smell of sharn out of his nose. They were such a contrast you never would have thought their blood would mix in the creation of new life. Joseph went back to his carpentry and the pubs and his post-card albums and never came again to Bogmyrtle. Frank Barbour tried it once, fair lovesick over the ravishing Moira, but the MacKinnons plied him with such devilry that he never came again. Even Rachael in her pregnancy stuck out her tongue behind his back and Hamish carried his bicycle to the topmost pinnacle of a haystack.

To win a MacKinnon quine was not as easy as Frank Barbour had imagined it would be.

'What has Audie got that I dinna hae?' he asked his mother.

'I dinna ken,' she said, 'ye're his half-brither, unless it be patience. Audie has great patience. He wad put up wi' onything frae the MacKinnons tae get what he wanted; onything, even bein' made a fool of, and I can only hope it has been worth his while.'

For several months after their wedding Audie and Helen lived in the upstairs bedroom at Bogmyrtle. Audie cycled from his work at the weekends to his bride. It was only a temporary arrangement until the May Term when Audie could get a cottar house on the farms. During this time they purchased some bits of furniture, which was stored in the barn, in preparation for the day when the young pair could have a home of their own.

Craig presented his daughter with a magnificent mahogany sideboard, the likes of which he didn't possess even in his own farmhouse. A splendid dining-room table and four polished chairs were added to this dowry, and in appreciation of such generous treatment Audie worked a whole fortnight to Craig without wages. He became real friendly with the old tyrant, and bye and bye he was honoured with a seat next to him on the deas, a favour which had always been accorded to Hamish, as the oldest son of the household, until he got a job in a granary store in Brochan.

Rachael had her last bairn. Meston they called him, another young Craig MacKinnon to the very lips, and a sorry time Rachael had over it and nearly lost her reason. She was glad of Helen about the house at the time, for what with all the outdoor work in the spring, and the normal chores of house and dairy, Moira and Nancy could hardly cope.

The teuchats' storm was fierce that year, driving sleet and a stinging wind that sent the birds in droves to the sheltering firwoods. Then came the Gab o' May, cold and driech and bitter, withering the newly sprung corn and starving the beasts newly out in the parks. White frost mantled the grass fields and blighted the potato leaves emerging on the drills. On the day of the cottar market Audie put on his big coat and caught the train at Leary for Brochan. Doon in the Broadgate he would maybe get a fee, where the farmers gathered on mart days, besides paying their accounts to the tradesmen, seedsmen and implement dealers. Farmers were on the lookout for servants they hoped would be capable and trustworthy, and the working cheils for a better place than the one they would be leaving, though mostly they were disappointed and found that the grass was no better over the dyke though it looked a bit greener.

When Audie was away Craig took the size of him with Helen, trying to belittle her man in the might of his own brawn and muscle. 'Jod, lass,' says he, 'Audie will hae tae stuff his breeks wi' straw and put on twa jackets afore ony fairmer cheil will look at 'im, he's sic a sober crater.'

Helen flushed in anger at her father's taunt. She thought of Murdoch the gamekeeper, a fine strappin' cheil that her father had despised. But for him and his high-mindedness Murdoch might have been her man. Her father had changed his tune since then but it was too late in the day to be mended. Audie had that big hernia, which she didn't know about until their wedding night, so that he couldn't get near her; and a fumbler besides, scarcely knowing where to put it to give her pleasure, going all to pieces in his excitement and messing the sheets between her hips. She knew so little about sex that she wasn't even prepared for that; heaven knows what the woman had thought next day when she went to make the bed. Her wedding night had been a disappointment, lacking fulfilment, without the joy she had expected; thanks to her grandmother's teaching and the Stool of Repentance, now she would have to repent on it for the rest of her life, for the opposite reason from that intended. Nor had she married in haste; it was just that they had been too shy to do something they should have done, or tried to do, before they were married. Now it couldn't be helped and it was a shame to blame poor Audie, she herself was just as bashful.

It was this swarthy brute in front of her who was to blame, or partly so, though he hadn't made the same mistake himself with her mother. But now he would taunt her on Audie's weakness, or so she imagined.

'He wad mak' a fine Auntie Sally at a bairns' school picnic.' Craig had his final jibe at his daughter and she looked at him with her cold stare; a stare that brought back all the guilt of ill-using his mother and badgering his family. Helen continued to glower, pinning him to the wall of his own conscience. He turned a bit white in the face and wavered, blinked his eyes feebly and left the kitchen.

He had his wiles with her mother, still in bed with little Meston, with no sense of balance when she stood up and depressed almost to melancholy, not half the woman she was. He hadn't spared her mother in bed and now he would laugh at Audie because he couldn't do the same. But maybe he only guessed? How could he know what happened that night at Knockieben? Surely the woman hadn't told them; no, it was hardly likely. Perhaps it was just mere chance that her father had caught her in her weakest moment, pouring salt in a wound he didn't know existed.

Despite all this Audie went to the fee-ing market and got a job as a stockman with old Toby Mathers of Millbrae. Audie didn't even need a reference, old Toby took one look at Audie's honest face and engaged him on the spot at twenty pounds for the year, plus coal, meal, milk, potatoes and a free house and garden, besides the liberty to keep hens, which was a fair average existence for the cottar just before the Kaiser's War.

Of course Craig was delighted, even though Audie had far exceeded his expectations in the feeing market. When Audie came home with the news of his good fortune Craig set the whisky bottle on the table. 'Dammit, man,' says he, slapping his son-in-law on the back, 'dammit, man, we'll hae a drink on't. Yer nae a bad breet man. I ocht tae think

hame o' masel' – ach man, never mind what I say, haud
yot yer gless and I'll fill 'er up wi' the best.'

He also poured a wee glass for Helen and she put a drop
of water in it to wash down the lump in her throat, and
when it made her eyes water it excused the tears that were
forming there. Whether they were sad tears or glad she
wasn't sure but she was proud for Audie and the way he had
taken the conceit out of her father. If Audie wasn't man
enough for him then she would back him up; maybe make
a man of him yet; a good man, for Audie was everything
else a woman would want him to be. Ah well, Craig had
very nearly apologized: she knew what he meant, with his
dram.

So Helen and Audie had a home of their own at last; not
much of a home but what might be called a hovel, a clay
biggin' with a thatched roof, not unlike the Burns's Cottage
in Ayrshire, but that it had two tenants, chimney-pots on
the gables, and the earthen floors had been replaced with
cement. The foreman and his family lived in one end of the
cottage and Helen and Audie moved into the other, the
end with the gable facing the roadway. On the day of the
Term, Craig yoked Meg into the long-cart and led her
round to the barn door. Audie gave him a hand and the
two of them carried the furniture out of the barn and
loaded it on to the cart and Craig put a rope over it. He
took the load down to Millbrae, Helen and Audie going on
before with their bicycles.

When Craig arrived with Meg they carried the furniture
into the house, the sideboard, table and polished chairs
through to the ben-room, the best end of the cottage; the
dresser, table and odd chairs to the kitchen, besides a washstand, crockery and dishes, pots and pans. The kitchen
recess formed a built-in box-bed, so there was no need to
buy one, and Rachel had given Helen all the bedding she
needed to cover it. Helen made tea for her father before he
left and he was as kind and understanding as ever she'd seen
him and talking to Audie man to man, like Audie was his
own son almost, and surely Helen thought he must have
found a new pride in his son-in-law. Helen gave Meg a

piece at the door, some oatcakes from the little girnal Racheal had given her to hold the oatmeal. Then Craig lit his pipe and got up on the empty cart, clicking his tongue to Meg, and as the great wooden cart rumbled out of the close he waved to Helen and Audie standing in the cottage door.

Audie had planted the garden beforehand and the tattie shaws were just beginning to show above the ground. Helen had a wander round the place and then went inside to tidy the house. Audie went up to the farm for the milk, where he had a bit news with the foreman about the ways of the place and the work that had to be done. Drew Strachan had been the foreman at Millbrae for a good many years and knew all the outs and ins of the place and the ways of old Toby Mathers that was farmer, and he gave Audie a few broad hints on what he liked and disliked about a man and his work, and Audie felt he would fit in fine and that he would be happy at Millbrae.

There was talk of war in the papers and folk speaking about it but Helen didn't pay much attention. She was more concerned about the loss of her periods, for with all his fumbling and ignorance of woman Audie had nicked her. She just couldn't believe it at first, but as time wore on and she grew sick in the mornings there was no doubt about it. Not that she'd had any fun out of it either but there it was. When she told Audie about it he said 'Eh what?' before she got spoken, so she had to tell him again. 'So I've managed it efter a', wuman,' says he, and almost danced in his glee. Then he fussed and fretted over her and stroked her hair and called her his 'bonnie wee crater', till she was embarrassed and pushed him aside with a little laugh of annoyance. But he was a different man for weeks and the equal of any of them; no need to take the size of him now, and if anyone tried it Audie would take him a chap on the chin. It would fair give his half-sisters something to think about, or even his half-brothers; and if it was a loon he got he would call it after Craig, just to humour the brute, and keep the right side of him, and maybe help him to get into a fairm later on. But this bludy war would spoil everything and he might be called up. Why the hell did they have to fecht with the Germans when everything was going fine for folk?

Helen went often on her bicycle to Bogmyrtle, but she never mentioned her condition to Rachael, just let it show, and when her mother noticed it she took Helen in her oxter and kissed her fair cheeks, something she had never done in her life before, and a moist tear came to Helen's eyes in her mother's arms. Helen had never realized her mother was such a mere handful, her thin girlish shoulders so easy to clasp and hold, her waist like a quine at courting, her hair grey at the roots that once was bronze and shining as the sun on new ploughed lea. Frail and worn her mother seemed since she had her last bairn, but now she could stand without Helen's aid, without leaning on folk with her arm; and she was less depressed, the old light coming back into her eyes, like a glint of morning after rain. Helen let her go and picked up her wee brother from her mother's skirt. Meston had her father's corn blonde hair and sky blue eyes and he put his finger in her mouth and smiled at her as if she was a stranger. He wouldn't be much older than her own child and yet he would be uncle Meston, and Helen smiled at the thought.

So the war came and the foreman's son next door was one of the first to go. He was a Territorial and was drafted to France in support of the first Expeditionary Force. He was killed at Mons and Helen was talking to his mother at the door on the day that she got the fatal telegram. Mrs Strachan almost fainted when she read it. 'Oh my poor loon,' she cried, 'I'm heart sorry for my loon.' Then she asked Helen if she would go and show the telegram to her man at the ploo, 'cause she hadna the stomach for it herself. So Helen took the telegram and ran to the stubble park where Drew Strachan was ploughing with his mares, Love and Blossom, with a swarm of screaming white gulls behind him on the glistening furrows. Helen, big with her bairn, ran till she was out of breath, her long skirts swirling about her, and the kittiewakes took fright at the sight of her and rose from the field, screaming high overhead. When Drew heard the commotion among the gulls he glanced over his

shoulder, and when he saw a woman come panting up th
rigs he stopped his pair and twined the reins on a shaft of th
plough. When she came nearer Helen could see a smile o
Drew's sun-browned face, even a twinkle of mischief in hi
eye, for Helen was but a quine to Drew Strachan, to teas
and banter with, for he had daughters of his own about he
age, fee-ed and looking for lads. Death was as yet a strange
from the Kaiser's war; Helen was one of his first messenger
and Drew was not aware of her urgency.

Helen gave him the telegram, and as he read it the smil
left his face. It was as if she had stuck a knife in his briest fo
the wound went deep in his heart. He sank down on th
stilts of his plough with great tears in his eyes. Helen put he
hand on his shoulder, as if to comfort him, and she felt hi
body heave in a convulsion of grief. When she left Drew sh
felt a hot knife in her side, a wound that made her gasp
for breath and hold her belly. Drew still sat on his ploug
his head in his hands, his mares in a droop, as if they share
his sorrow. To Helen he was in a whirl; the world was up
side down, the stibble park in a spin, the trees and sky in a
haze, and she fell on her knees and grasped the stubble. Th
world kept turning and she tore out the stubble by the roots
the hot knife twisting in her side. Drew lifted her up and se
her on her feet, saying you've run too fast quine for the stat
you're in, his own tears dried away at the sight of her, whit
in the face and her hands in a tremble. It's the doctor sh
would be needing, he thought, and he'd come home with
her. She said nae tae bother, that she was all right now
only a spell and she'd manage. But Drew said he woulc
come home anyway and maybe console his wife; the mares
would wait.

Audie had arranged with his mother to come and look after
Helen when the time came for having her bairn, so they sen
her a telegram and she came with the train that day. Dr Rae
came out from Brochan with his hooded car and said it was
a false alarm, but he put Helen to bed and told Mrs
Barbour to let him know when the labour started. Helen had
pains in the night and they sent for the doctor in the morning. Helen was in labour all that day and the next night,

and on the morning of the second day Dr Rae put her under chloroform. Her bairn was born in the box-bed in the kitchen, a wee girl that had nearly been the death of her, but for the skill of the doctor and her own iron constitution. But she came round again when it was all past; sick and weak and her lips cracked and dry and a pain in her insides when she moved, a dull blunted pain where the hot knife had carved something out of her. Turning her head on the soft feather pillow she could see the sunlit window and the lace screen she had fixed across the sash in the spring. Her geraniums were in flower, violet and pink and white against the glass; beyond were the green fields and bird song. Then she remembered Drew at the plough and the son whose pain was over and the young life at her side. She was sad and she was glad and a soft warm tear tickled a little as it ran down her cheek. It ran into the corner of her mouth and she felt the salt of it on her cracked lips. From the corner of her eye she watched her mother-in-law pottering about at the fireplace. How like Audie she looked from behind: slim and round-shouldered, and with such a machine-like industry in her thin active elbows, like a spider at a web on dewy mornings. Helen turned to look at her bairn but the nails hurt where she lay on her cross of pain. This time she cried out and the tears came full force. The older woman looked at her, the black kettle in her hand, then laid it down and went to the bedside. 'Aye quine, have a good greet,' she said, 'and I hope ye're feelin' better efter yer lang sleep.'

For all that Helen knew of her mother-in-law it was as if she had spoken to her for the first time. She wasn't unlike her own mother, but taller, with a sharp wrinkled face and bad teeth. 'It's a wee dother ye've got,' she said, and lifted up the doll like figure in the white shawl from the mother's side. 'She's still asleep but you can look at her; she's got blue eyes like yersel' and dark hair, and a sair trauchle you had over it too.'

Helen looked at her bairn and smiled in spite of her pain. All she could say was: 'We'll hae tae call ye Granny now Mrs Barbour.'

'And why wad ye nae. Sure I'll be proud o' my grand daughter.'

So Granny replaced the child in the bed and made te and took it over to the bed on a tray. She placed the tray o a chair and poured some tea into the saucer, then she pu her arm under Helen's head and raised her up gently putting the saucer to Helen's lips. 'That's it noo,' she cooed refilling the saucer and repeating the dose; 'juist you drin it doon, but dinna move yersel' much 'cause ye'll be sair. ken what it is lass; I've come through it all mysel' lass afor yer day, but the first time seems tae be the warst. Maybe shouldna tell ye but the doctor said it was your life or th bairn's at one time, but how glad he was when he manage tae save ye baith. Ye was singin' aboot Jesus when ye wa under the chloryform, and the doctor had tae skelp lif intae the bairn and dip 'er in a tub o' cauld watter tae ge the crater tae greet.'

Helen flushed hot and sweaty. She felt she would fain under the strain. But at last the woman desisted and sa down on a chair 'tae pare the tatties for the man's denner' she said.

Audie came in for dinner at noon and stood bonnet i hand in the middle of the floor. He looked vaguely at hi wife in the box-bed, then at his mother, lost for speech o who to speak to. 'Weel, wuman,' he ventured at last addressing his wife, 'Are ye a' richt noo?'

'Nae sae bad,' Helen said.

'And what like is the quinie?' Audie enquired.

'She's a' richt,' Helen assured him. 'Ye'll see her shortly G'wa and tak' yer denner afore it gets cauld.'

Audie sat down to his broth at the table by the window blowing on every spoonful as he raised it to his mouth from the plate. His mother went to the bedside and tried to coax his wife with a plateful of hot broth, talking all the time to one or other of the parents.

Audie mumbled away until he fell asleep on his chair. His mother woke him with a cup of tea, and when he had finished he smoked a cigarette in his holder, blowing the smoke up the chimney. When he rose to go he went over the box-bed. He stroked his wife's smooth black hair with his rough hand and murmured, 'Ye're a bonnie crater hough, aye are ye, ma bonnie wee wifie!'

This irritated Helen. She felt hot and embarrassed in ont of his mother and tried to push him away.

Audie looked at the pink puckered face of his little aughter, swaddled in the white shawl at her mother's ack. 'And what are ye gaun tae call the crater?' he asked. Ye ken we never made up oor minds aboot that.'

Helen looked at him with her blue eyes clearing after the ain, like morning skies after rain, then said simply, 'Ruth.'

'Ruth, wuman!' Audie exclaimed, full of surprise, and as about to wipe his nose but checked himself.

'Aye, Ruth,' Helen repeated, 'It's a bible name and I ancy it. My grandmother used to read her story to me and I ked to think of her in the harvest fields.'

'A fine hame-ower name,' Mrs Barbour interposed. 'I ke the soone o't.'

Audie didn't seem so sure. Maybe he felt that Rachael ounded better, but one of them was enough in the family. Then there was Sarah and Rebekah and Mary, not that Audie knew much about the Bible, but this much he emembered from his schooldays. 'Gin it had been a loon,' ae concluded, 'I micht hae called him Samson.' And with hat he put on his bonnet and strode manfully out of the cottage.

'Some Samson,' Helen thought, 'and him such a wee nite.' But she didn't say anything aloud in front of his nother.

Helen was up and about in a fortnight and Mrs Barbour leparted for her home at Toddlebrae in Scotstoun. Audie promised to send her a sack of oatmeal out of his perquisites when old Craig went to town for the flower show.

Helen bought a white bamboo pram to show off Ruth to the neighbours. She even wheeled her up the Laird's avenue at Lachbeg House, past the 'Private' sign at the lodge gate. She met the old laird in the grounds with a walking stick, clad in kilt and tunic and a Glengarry bonnet on his head. But he wasn't interested in Ruth; never even looked into the

pram, but raised his stick at Helen and told her to 'keep to
the King's Highway!' But Helen never heeded him and
walked on round the big house and returned at her leisure
half expecting the laird would set the dog on her, but no
and when she returned to the lodge he was gone.

Craig and Rachel came down from Bogmyrtle in the gig
to see their first grandchild. Rachael had a cape about her
shoulders, her hands in a brown fur muff. Craig had maybe
expected a loon and didn't say very much, though Rachael
told Helen later that he had made a wooden cart and horse
that wouldn't be much use for a quine, and that she would
have to give it to Meston. Rachael took off her hat and veil
to look at her granddaughter in the bamboo pram, then
pushed a half-crown piece into her tightly closed little fist,
already full of wool from plucking at her shawl.

'She's gaun tae be a thrifty wifie,' Rachael teased, 'look
at the wye she grips the siller.'

Some weeks later the minister came to the hovel and
sprinkled a few drops of Holy Water on Ruth's baldy head
while Helen held her in the shawl. The Reverend Shand
pronounced her name 'Ruth Foubister' and read a few
words from the Bible in the bye going.

But the noise of the war grew louder and more and more
young cheils were called away from the plough. If you went
to Brochan or Scotstoun they were swarming with young
men in khaki. The trains were full of them, soldiers on
leave and recruits for training; long lists of killed and missing
in the papers and terrible stories of the fighting in France.
Helen's sisters were working as Land Girls and Doris and
Susan Barbour were in munitions in England. Rachael had
grave fears for Hamish being called up and the man that
Moira had married was already in the thick of it. Helen had
to tuck up her own skirts and gather corn in the hairst parks,
little Ruth running beside her, and sometimes Mrs Barbour
would come out from Scotstoun to watch the bairn.

Audie got his call-up papers but was deferred because of
his job at Millbrae, fattening nowt for beef to feed the troops
and maybe help to beat the German submarine blockade.
Audie was glad of this because he was afraid of the war and

didn't want to fight the Germans. But he had to join the local defence volunteers, 'The Buttermilk Sodgers', as folk called them, for home defence, training in the hall at Leary and going on manoeuvres at the weekends in his spare time; not that Audie had much of that, what with pulling turnips and all his hard work in the byres at Millbrae, but he was thankful to be left at home with his 'Bonnie wee wifie', come what may.

Now it is a fact that Audie Foubister, whatever his short-comings and weaknesses (and God knows we all have these) but despite his faults he had a tidy mind; washed every night and combed his hair, shaved twice a week with a cut-throat razor (which had a Hamburg ring about it when you flicked it with your thumbnail) or so he said, at the risk of sounding pro-German in his praise of their cutlers' precision; trimmed his moustache regularly, manicured his nails with a pen-knife; in fact he did everything short of taking a bath, which would have meant taking in one of Helen's wooden wash-tubs – but despite all this respectability and his regard for punctuality, working to a strict time-table between the byres and turnip field – in spite of all this Audie Foubister was hopelessly unfit for military training. He was awkward with his equipment, clumsy on parade, slothful and untidy in the King's uniform. It would have been a sad day for Britain, indeed for the world, and a great triumph for the Kaiser, if Audie Foubister had been the standard prototype of the personnel of His Majesty's forces.

But Helen MacKinnon was the woman behind the man behind the gun in the Foubister platoon. She did everything for Audie Foubister: she cleaned and oiled his rifle after firing practice, using a pull-through on the barrel; she blacked his boots, polished his buttons and leather-work, packed his kit, got down on her knees and rolled his khaki puttees around his thin legs, buttoned up his tunic and slung his rifle over his sloping shoulders; she even took his rusty bayonet and thrust it in and out of a sod dyke and scoured it with fine sand until it shone like a shaft of sunlight, the thought of Doris and Susan in her work.

'Go to the gless noo,' Helen would say, when she had

Audie rigged out for a fortnight under canvas, 'and let's see how you salute the sergeant major.' Audie saluted himself in the shaving mirror and thought himself real smart in his khaki tunic with its shining brass buttons, each with a tiny crown embossed on its glittering surface. 'Och ye'll do ye gipe,' Helen would say, 'but dinna tell the ither lads that I dressed ye up or they'll think ye are a Granny's John.'

'Oh na,' Audie mused, 'I wunna tell 'em, wuman.' And then he would give her a wee peck on the cheek with his puckered lips, enough to tickle her soft skin with his short moustache, and then swagger to the door with his heavy pack, where he had to bend down to get the muzzle of his rifle under the low lintel. Then he would hop-skip-and-leap from the back step of his bicycle on to the saddle scrambling for the pedals with his dangling feet, precariously balanced on the road with his awkward burden.

It would have been easier to get on his bicycle in the ordinary way, with one foot on the pedal and throw the other leg over the saddle; but Audie always seemed to have to do everything the most difficult and awkward way, like getting on from the back-step, as if he were mounting a horse over the tail.

'Ta ta!' Helen cried, as she waved to him down the road. And little Ruth cried 'Ta ta, Daddy!' and held on to her mother's soft flannel skirts. But Audie daren't look round lest he fall off and hold up the manoeuvres.

So Audie was highly complimented by his officers for being so smart and sprightly in the King's uniform, and was commended for the polish and lustre of his equipment and the neatness of his kit, parading him in front of the squad as an example of what they should look like after a spell of square-bashing. 'Splendid,' said the CO, with his cane under his arm, as Audie sprang to attention. 'Splendid, keep it up Foubister!'

But Audie couldn't keep it up, and after a week in camp his ineptitude for the army became a glaring monstrosity, even as a Buttermilk Sodger. Then it was that Audie had to ask the other men to fasten his straps and fix the hooks at the neck of his tunic. He couldn't even roll his puttees and had to get somebody else to do it for him, otherwise he had them into a piece of rope around his legs. When Audie was on target practice it was every man for himself; lying with his belly on the grass, his eye on the sights of his rifle, it was anybody's guess where the bullet would go. When he dropped a grenade in the trench the platoon had to scatter, but fortunately he had forgotten to pull the safety pin. The CO was astounded at Audie's fumbling inefficiency, but to save face in front of his men he had to keep his trap shut. 'One born every day,' he mumbled under his breath, whacking his leg with his stick, 'yet he could have fooled me!'

On Sunday morning the CO and everybody else had the answer to his question: the woman behind the man behind the gun in the Foubister corner of the army; for there stood Helen at the gate, just got off her bicycle, asking after the welfare of her soldier husband. All eyes were fixed on the Florence Nightingale of the moment, and some thought it was the angel from Mons, until she produced fags for Audie and sugar for his tea. Audie looked cold and miserable and neglected without her comforting hand; but she soon had him spruced up again and fit for parade with the best of them, and if anyone ever said she would never make a man of Audie Foubister they might be wrong at that.

But now that the secret of Audie's spit and polish was revealed to the troops he ran the risk of becoming a laughing stock, especially when he lost his temper over the packet of Player's cigarettes he got from his wife – his hands numbed with cold, so that he couldn't open it, fumbling at the packet – so he tore it to bits and threw it in the mud and danced on it with his feet, almost weeping over it in his rage, like a bairn with a broken toy. Some thought his wife should have seen him at this: like a spoiled brat that didn't get his own way; a bloody shame after the way she had pampered him on the field. As soon as her back was turned Audie had gone to pieces. Fortunately for Audie most of his companions were married men like himself and wished they had the same attention.

'Lucky bugger,' said Jock MacFarlane, who was foreman

at Mucklecrag, over the dyke from Audie's place, 'I think I see my auld bitch comin' here wi' fags!'

'Aye,' said another, 'and damned nice-lookin' too. After a fortnicht amon you buggers the sicht o' her nearly sprung ma spaver buttons.'

Hamish MacKinnon was called up at last, exempted till now because his brother Riach had a wooden leg. Hamish had given up his granary job and worked with his father since the war started. Craig was furious and cursed Lord Kitchener and General Foch for bleeding the country to death. He had felt snug in the belief that the exemption would continue, but now that the clamour for flesh and bone had come to his own front door Craig was defiant. Why should his only fit son be called up while others were allowed to go free: lads like Audie Foubister that played tin sodgers and hid behind the skirts of their wives? Why, he cried, should farmers' sons have to go and face hellfire while their servants stayed at home in comfort? He had one son a cripple and they would take away the other; his daughters in the Land Army and munitions – how the hell was he going to manage the place? But he would take the law into his own hands and Audie would go first to the firing line. He had stuck his bayonet into sacks of straw long enough and it was time that Audie gutted a live Hun. Craig got fell drunk in his anger and was determined to get out his spite on poor Audie Foubister, the most likely victim, his own son-in-law, his daughter Helen the wife whose skirts sheltered Audie.

Hamish suggested they give Audie a thrashing, so the three of them, mad with drink, Craig, Hamish and Riach, jumped on their bikes for Millbrae, determined to knock the daylights out of poor Audie Foubister, who up till now had actually been doing more for his country than any of them, even as a Buttermilk Sodger, giving up all his spare time on military training, besides his wark in the fields. If the Germans did come over Audie could at least fire a gun at them; he knew how to handle a rifle (and a hand grenade by now) and he was in uniform. It was Hamish who had been slinking behind his mother's skirts till now, and the only thing that Riach could muster was his crutch; a shame to say it but he should have stayed at home with his poor demented mother, who was heartbroken over Hamish going away, and had cried to them over the hedge to come back and leave poor Audie alone, for Helen's sake and the bairn. But Riach never heeded, and jumped on his bike with the others, pedalling with one foot, a strap over his toes, his crutch lying along the bar like a rifle.

So the three of them lays hands on Audie and rips the buttons off his tunic, for he was just back from parade, and Riach with his crutch raised like to pound him over the head. They took Audie out of the house and had him reeling in the close, Craig holding him by the sark till he nearly choked, asking why the hell he should be exempted while poor Hamish there would have to go to the front? Helen tore at her father's coat, trying to pull him away and free Audie before he had him choked. The Strachans next door were all outside to see what the commotion was about, though they were afraid to interfere. The MacKinnons had a reputation for violence and devilment and folk gave them a wide berth, especially when they were the worse for drink. Hamish stood aside, perhaps when he saw Audie in uniform, but he did nothing to stop his father from choking him, while Riach hopped around on one leg, trying to get a smack at Audie with his crutch, but afraid that he might hit his father.

Helen could make nothing of Craig, he was too big and powerful for her feeble hands. Craig had Audie on the ground, his knee on his chest, his hands at Audie's throat, choking the life out of him, foam at his mouth, near his last gasp, yet shielding him, unaware, from Riach's crutch. Helen ran to the house, in terror it seemed, but in a few moments a shot rang out that brought the MacKinnons to their senses. Helen had loaded Audie's rifle and fired a shot in the air. Craig released his hold on Audie's throat, Riach lowered his crutch, Hamish stared at the cottage door, straight into the barrel of Helen's rifle, where she stood in the door, the gun wavering slightly but her face in deadly earnest. The next shot was for them and they knew Helen.

She would pull the trigger. Drew Strachan was half-way down the close to intervene but the shot stopped him in his tracks, frozen to the wall like a statue, surprised and shocked. The MacKinnons all got on their bicycles and set sail for Bogmyrtle, never even saying good-bye, and Riach waving his crutch in the air, defiantly, like a rifle.

Audie got up from the dust and shook himself and went towards his wife and took the rifle out of her hand, still warm from the shot and heavy it seemed for her slender grasp. Helen sat down on the doorstep, sobbing, not so much because of what had happened, but because it was maybe the last she would see of Hamish; a sad way to see him off to the front, with a rifle in his back, held by his own sister, as if she were driving him there. Hamish wasn't always like that and she would have liked to put her arms round his neck and kiss him good-bye; she had never intended it like this. Ruth was crying from her crib and the cat was in Helen's lap waiting to be stroked, her tail straight up and tickling Helen's neck, forcing her to smile in spite of everything. Drew Strachan came to the door and she explained what had happened and he blamed the drink. In his noble eyes she was a real heroine sitting there on the doorstep, her long skirts reaching to her toes and the evening sun in her hair, a wayward tear glistening on her cheek, and Drew Strachan would have felt proud of such a daughter. Audie gathered up his buttons and went inside with the rifle, Helen following him to quieten Ruth; to look at Audie's swollen throat and to sew on his buttons again.

It was a sad day at Bogmyrtle when Hamish rigged himself for Aldershot, where he would be trained to fight the Germans. He was in his best suit of blue serge and a grey tie, a wide heather-mixture cap on his head and a waterproof over his arm in case it rained. The poor devil had never been from home in his life before, never further than Brochan or Aberdeen, and the thought of going all the way to England by train shook his very bowels and sickened him with fear. He put on a brave face in front of his mother but the thought of gunfire nearly made him cry, especially when he looked at Kirsteen and little Janet, all that was left at home of his sisters, and Meston on his rocking-horse, little knowing what it was all about, staring with his wide eyes at his big brother all dressed up and smelling of mothballs.

Helen never came to see him off; maybe she was afraid after what had happened. But maybe he would get embarkation leave before he left for the front, after his training at Aldershot, when he would go down to Millbrae and make it up with his sister. Hamish had other things on his mind as well: that quine he was going with, Muriel Spark, who worked in the Emporium at Leary. His mother disliked her but welcomed her to the house because she supplied them with things that were scarce: like sugar and treacle that couldn't be got at any price, stealing them from the shop to supply Rachael, hoping to get her son in return. But Rachael was jealous of any quine who would take away her finest son, so she despised her when Hamish was not aside and tried to put her off. Hamish wasn't all that caring for the quine, but he promised to write to her and Rachael would forward his letters.

Riach drove them to Leary Station in the spring-cart, Hamish and his father and mother, who would accompany him to Aberdeen to join a troop train for the south. Rachael wore her costume of grey serge texture, with a fox tail about her neck, fastened with a small chain over her shoulder. She cried when they cordoned off her son in Aberdeen like a pet stirk among strange cattle, she thought, away to be slaughtered; and she went into hysterics and clung to the railings, refusing to leave without her Hamish. She cried after his scared white face when the officers hustled him along the platform to the waiting carriage, crowded with soldiers, out of her sight for ever, she thought, and fainted at the prospect. She crumpled down in a heap, her white hands in her lap, bloodless from their grasp of the railings, her once fine bronze hair grey as peat ash, her closed eyes oozing tears of sorrow. Craig lifted her up tenderly and carried her to the station buffet, where they revived her with strong tea, but sobbing for her son as soon as it came into her mind again. Craig got her into the home train, her tears dried and her face composed among strangers, for the first time sharing their sorrows, no doubt with heavier hearts than her own. It took some of the conceit out of Rachael's heart, thinking of her son pounding forth on the south train, and all those other sons whose fathers and mothers and sweethearts and wives were sitting around her now, perhaps as ready to shed a tear at the first blink of weakness.

The hairst came round again and Helen was back in the corn fields, Ruth three years old and following the carts to the stackyard. Helen was with another bairn to Audie, in spite of his hernia, but as yet hardly showing, and she could still work in the fields cheerfully. She was working on a croft at the time, across the parks from Millbrae, Fergie Duncan's place, in the Clatterin' Howe, stooking the sheaves on the sun-hazed stubble. Old Fergie was on the binder seat, and when the twine got entangled in the machinery he couldn't get off to unravel it. He cried to Helen and she crawled under the binder to get at the twine. The horses were hungry for the corn ears and reached forward to get it while the old man filled his pipe. When they had eaten all about them they took a step forward and moved the big driving wheel under the binder. Helen was lying in front of it, trying to unravel the twine, and she couldn't get out of the way quick enough, so the great ponderous wheel went over her midriff and crushed the young life within her. They took her home in a cart and she nearly bled to death or the doctor came. He took the bairn from her and threw it on the fire, a bundle of bleeding membrane that had scarcely taken shape, and was soon incinerated. Mrs Barbour came out of Scotstoun again to nurse Helen, and it was several weeks before she was on her feet again, worse than having a real bairn.

But that wasn't the last of Fergie Duncan, for old and stiff though he was he managed to get into bed with his housekeeper, a woman young enough to be his daughter. His wife had been dead for years and his family up and scattered, though you would have thought with his asthma reliever and his Buffalo Bill novels he had enough ado in the evenings without molesting his housekeeper, unless it was to keep him warm on winter nights. But the old scoundrel went too far with the woman, and when she had his bairn he threw her out, bairn and all, maybe to keep his family quiet. But it was bleak November and the woman had nowhere to go, nowhere but the barns and whindykes, until she remembered Helen Foubister, the woman who had worked in the hairst time in the Clatterin' Howe; the woman who had lost her own bairn under the binder.

Helen saw her from the window, a woman in black coming across the snow, making for the cottage door at Millbrae. She rapped at the door in the howling wind and when Helen opened it she saw this woman with snow beads in her hair, her teeth chattering in the cold, her skin wrinkled and pinched with hunger, a little bairn in her oxter, raw and blue with starvation, and she asked Helen if she would take her in for the night. She sat on a chair by the fire and tried to give the infant suck from her breast, but the creature was past nourishment and merely puckered its face in a greet. The woman herself was a ravenous animal and ate like a beast, and all the time cursing the man who had fathered her ill-gotten bairn, but maybe with the scarcity of young men she had opened her legs too willingly. Helen stripped the bairn of its rags and washed it in warm water, with Sunlight soap and a drop of lysol. Its little backside was raw from exposure, but Helen soothed it with powder and dressed the infant in one of Ruth's baby gowns. Ruth had been playing in the press, with the empty tins of Cherry Blossom boot polish, because she so admired the flowers on the lids. But this was something new to her and she came to her mother's side, fair taken with the little bairn, a wee angel in its beauty, a baby girl that Ruth could fondle like a doll.

Next day the housekeeper went to the Inspector of the Poor, who listened to her story, and she came back and stayed with Helen and Audie until she got another place. Helen got the doctor and tried to feed the baby on Benger's Food, but it had little appetite and began to fade. A fortnight later it died of Pneumonia, and the undertaker stretched it out in a little white coffin frilled with lace, like a wax doll on the room table, so sweet and dainty in her white shroud. Every hour of the day Ruth asked through to see her little friend, this little angel so beautiful in death, like marble in the moonlight, and she longed to stand on tiptoe and touch her cold cheek.

The Inspector of the Poor called at Millbrae, talked to Helen and the two of them went through to look at the bairn, Ruth behind them, standing tiptoe by the coffin's rim, admiring her friend. Next day the undertaker returned and put the lid on the coffin with screws, while Helen held Ruth between her skirted knees in the kitchen, her fingers in her mouth, weeping over the bairn. In the afternoon Audie and Drew Strachan dressed themselves and took the white coffin on their shoulders to the green churchyard at Lachbeg.

But Helen grew homesick for Bogmyrtle and her ain folk; in spite of everything blood was thicker than water as they say, for never a word had she heard from them since Hamish went to France. Her mother had written to say that Hamish never got embarkation leave, but was drafted out to the fighting after only six weeks' training. So it had come to that: this war's gluttony for young men's lives and souls; this great monster from the minds of men who lived on their bodies, devouring their flesh and drinking their precious blood in horrible extravagance.

It wasn't only the men that were called up but the horses as well, and Craig was afraid for Meg or Bell being taken away for the cavalry, what with they knickerbockered officers searching for horses among the farmers of the Bog-side. And if a beast suited them you couldn't say nay; you were paid for the animal and away he went, far worse than taking the poor brute under the railway brig at Leary.

There were seaplanes landing on the Myreloch and zeppelins in the sky, watching for German submarines that were sinking our cargo ships in the North Sea. The zeppelins came from a lair at Lenabo, in the hinterland of Longside, and the folk called them 'The Lenabo Soos', sailing across the sky like sausages, with a basket slung underneath their bellies for the engines and the air-crew. Drew Strachan hated the brutes when they purred low over the fields and frightened his mares at the ploo, when they would neigh and shie and kick over the traces. He didn't mind the crews throwing kisses to the land girls, that was but natural, but watch out if they threw out a slop pail in the wind. There were German zeppelins as well, much bigger than ours, but they flew over London mostly with their deadly bombs and you hardly ever saw them up here. All the same folk had to be wary and darken their windows at night and whitewash the glass on their bicycle lamps and motor cars.

There was even talk of covering up the deer on the Mattock Hill, because the Military said he could be a land-mark for the German zeppelins and their deadly bombs, looking for Lenabo; or he could be a guide for the German U-boats in the North Sea, taking their bearings from the white deer on the hillside. German spies had been every-where before the war, dressed up as wandering minstrels and performing in the towns and villages all over the country, and all the time taking photographs and making notes and spying out the land.

It was into January 1918 and Helen had no letters from her brother at the front. And still no word from Bogmyrtle, not even a line on the sly from her mother's hand, for Helen felt sure her father had forbidden Rachael to write. But Helen couldn't stand this isolation much longer: it made her feel an outcast from her ain folk, a creature to be despised and shunned – pointing a gun at her own kith and kin; threatening to shoot her own flesh and blood, frightening her own people, no wonder they hadn't come back. What if that gun had gone off in her hands and killed one of them? Maybe her own father? Even poor Hamish who was so far away now and in constant danger? Or Riach, her crippled brother? She only meant to scare them off, not to threaten; but the safety catch was off and she had already sent one bullet spinning over their heads. Now she felt guilty and afraid; a would-be murderess. She had never fired a gun before in her life and the recoil of the rifle had nearly knocked her over. That one shot was in desperation; to protect her man against her drunken family. But would they trust her again as a sister? Surely Hamish was still alive or they would have told her.

Helen told Audie she was going to Bogmyrtle. Would he keep the bairn? Oh aye, wuman, he would watch the quine; but better tak' care on the road this dark nicht, though it was fine and the stars shinin'. But will yer folks let ye in, wuman? Maybe they'd be feart she had a gun and bar the door in her face. My God! Helen thought, if poor Audie imagined this maybe her fears were justified.

She left a hot-water pig in Ruth's crib, wrapped in her little nightgown, so that Audie wouldn't have much trouble putting her to bed; the rag-doll on her pillow, her usual bowl of gruel on the bink by the fire. Audie said that after he'd washed he would play the gramophone and that would keep the bairn amused. She liked the music and stood by the horn listening most of the time. Helen made sure that the blackout was secure on the window and had Audie bar the door when she went out. She struck a match and lighted her gas lamp, though it wasn't much help with a whitened glass, barely lit the road, but the bobby would run her in if he caught her without it.

She went through the Clatterin' Howe, where she always had to walk up the steep brae, pushing her bicycle by the handlebars. Folk said it was called the Clatterin' Howe because at night-time you sometimes heard the clatter of horse hoofs, supposed to be pulling a hearse over the brae, where a tinker quine was ravished and murdered long back, and you could just see the outline of the hearse in the dark from the lettered stone by the roadside that marked the evil spot. But Helen had gone through the Howe so many times in the dark, on her way to Bogmyrtle, and had never seen or heard anything unnatural, that she scarcely gave the story a thought, or if she did at all she mostly put it down to somebody's imagination; another ghost story, and that things like that were all in the mind.

But somehow tonight she remembered the story and a vague silence dogged her footsteps. The faint halo from her lamp gave shadows to the whins and broom that grew by the roadside: weird, wind-blown shapes that might conceal a body with ill-intent, leaping out upon her from the dyke. But it was from behind she was suspicious; something or somebody was following her, she felt sure of it; something sinister, but she was afraid to turn her head. There was no sound of footsteps in the whispering wind, only her own, and when she stopped there was silence. But she was aware of a presence; she was not alone, and in a moment of defiance she turned her bicycle and shone the feeble light down the brae. But there was nothing, nothing but the silent winking of the stars and the brooding darkness. She passed the lettered stone and bravely stared up the brae, where the rim of the road was outlined in the blackness, but nothing else.

But the presence persisted, and she daren't look sideways, for she heard the rustle of clothes, like the swish of a heavy cloak, now caught up with her and bearing into the night; a priest-like figure robed to the ground and blacker than the night, without footsteps, without visual movement, silhouetted in the gas light against the sky, with sloping shoulders, its hands clasped in front, like a minister in prayer, a rigid figure now ahead of her, aloof and silent, passing into the night. It might have been a woman, Helen wasn't sure, and as it poised on the rim of night a tremendous flash swallowed it from sight. Helen waited for the thunder, terrified, but it never came, only a dead silence that was even more terrifying; and with her aching eyes she stared into the night, half blinded by the flash. She stood on the brae and hung on her bicycle, praying to God there wouldn't be another flash, and that the thunder wouldn't come; that it was only fireflaucht or winter lightning that folk said was harmless, though she had never seen it so close.

Helen was almost on her knees with fear, her hair bristling at the roots, her lips dry and her heart throbbing at her throat; her body trembling, her mind almost devoid of thought, except for turning back. But no, she was a Mac-Kinnon and she wasn't afraid, and she goaded her footsteps up the haunted hill. What she had seen wasn't of this world, she was sure of that, and when she reached the spot where it had disappeared there was nothing; so she jumped on her bike and pedalled into the night.

Helen reached the joiner's shop and felt safer, then past the lake and into the woods of Lachbeg, dark and eerie in their solitude, where every moment she felt that the apparition would reappear by her side. Could it be that Hamish would be killed? Was it a premonition of his death in the trenches, that he would be swallowed by shell-fire going 'over the top' as some folk called it, in 'no man's land'? Some people got warnings about these things though Helen couldn't remember the name for it. Her mither had always called her a witch and maybe she was one of these people . . . clairvoyant, that was the name for it, though she could never say that she was ever in league with the devil.

When Helen came out of the woods a train was leaving Leary Station, the steam from the funnel like a comet in the night, lighted by the fire in the engine's belly, hoasting its sparks into the darkness; a comforting noise to Helen, an assurance that she was still in a world of reality, among human earthly folk.

Bogmyrtle lay snug in its nest of hedges, high beech and elm trees, hushed in the shadow of the Mattock Hill, and there was the smell of peat smoke, the spice of turnip shaw, the tang of cow dung – the blinded lights from the crofts friendly pin-pricks in the alien night.

Helen heard the rush of water from the mill-race, drowning her footsteps as she got off her bicycle at the gable, blowing out her lamp. There was a streak of light under the kye byre door, where her mither would be milking, and maybe she could reach it before the dog barked. Rachael would smooth the path for her with her father, if it was needed, and with Riach too for that matter.

She knew the shape of every cobblestone in the close, the feel of them under her foot, larger as she approached the streak of light under the byre door. It was in this same byre she heard the sigh of her grandmother on the morning she died. The thought came to her as she twisted the door hasp, and as she opened it the wood scraped slightly on the cobblestones. Little Janet stood on the greep, her hands at her back, her huge shadow on the whitewashed wall from the lantern before her. Some of the beasts rose and stretched themselves and made their water in the channel. Janet was startled at her sister's sudden appearance and Rachael rose up from a cow with her pail of milk. 'My God, quine,' she gasped, 'what brings ye here?'

Rachael laid down her pail and took her eldest quine in her bosom, reading the thoughts in her anxious face and clapping her back with her hand. 'No, quine, Hamish hasn't been killed but he's been gassed at the front, just a whiff, the letter said, and he wouldn't be home over it. I had meant to write and tell you, Helen quine, but we just got the letter yesterday. No, Daw wasn't angry: He rues the day he fell out on Audie and he doesn't blame you for firing the shot. Forget about it, quine; it's over and done with. Your father is quieter these days and he was worried about you, quine. He'll be glad to see you. He has a lot on his mind nowadays, what with Hamish at the war and your sisters away and him slaved with wark. Och never mind Riach. I'll soon put him in his place. An how's the bairn? Oh that's fine. Your sisters are fine but Moira's man has been sorely wounded at Pashendale (as Rachael would say it). He's back in hospital in England, Rippon I think they called the place, and Moira has gone down there to be near her man. Come on in, quine, afore yer father suppers the horse.'

'But I saw a ghost in the Clatterin' Howe, mither, like a minister body or a nun in a lang black shroud and sloping shoulders with its hands clasped in front and went sliding past in the dark without any sound or movement in its feet, and as it went over the brae a great flash swallowed it up but there was no thunder. It must have been fireflaucht and I prayed there wouldna be anither flash for it blinded me. Oh, mither, I was scared and I thocht it was the chaplain come to tell us Hamish had been swallowed up in shell-fire; maybe a warnin' that he would be killed shortly.'

By now they were over the close, hard by the kitchen door, Rachael with the warm lantern under her apron, Floss growling from the lobby step. 'Ach, quine, you was always seein' things naebody else could see, ferlies in the quiles and faces in the sky, like a witch ye was, quine.'

They were in by and the door closed. Craig had taken off

his spectacles and lowered his paper with its long columns of war dead. He was only too glad to see his quine back and there was no bitterness in his voice. Riach was sulky but he thawed out in time. Kirsteen was at the shop. 'It's a wonder you didn't meet her, quine. No, she's no feared in the dark. We think she has a lad, so why should she be feared? Aye, Meston was in bed, sleepin' in the closet.'

Rachael sieved the milk and washed the pails and basins. Kirsteen came home with her hair like ripe corn on her shoulders, her blue eyes shining out of the night with dew on the lashes. Helen had seen the day when Rachael would have pulled her to the floor with hair like that, in the passion of her youth, like she had done with her sisters on the slightest provocation. But her sisters had black hair and Kirsteen was the golden favourite of her parents, fortunate that she was born later in their life and spoiled a bit in their maturing years. 'I hope you've got the brown sugar, quine,' Rachael was saying, while she emptied Kirsteen's bag on the table, 'We've never seen the white sugar since that Muriel quine left the shop, and she's never looked back here since that nicht she fell aff her bicycle. God knows what Hamish will think.'

Helen had her usual seat by the press door, at the end of the box-bed, where she got a cup of tea in her lap, with a pinch of carbonate of soda to give a stronger brew in these days of scarcity. Tea was over and everybody had left the table, all except Riach at the far end of the deas and Craig in his armchair by the gable window, both of them smoking, and the reek as thick you could have stirred it with a stick.

Then it happened: a tremendous crash that came through the window and shattered the paraffin lamp on the table; a huge stone that just missed Craig, bounced off the table and rolled on the floor, leaving the place in darkness, but for the flicker of the peat fire and a cold draught from the broken window.

Surprise and shock seemed to freeze everybody where they sat or stood, while the broken lamp kindled the paraffin spilled on the table. Helen gathered her thoughts quickly and sprang from her chair. She picked up a rug from the floor and smothered the fire on the table, covering up the cups and saucers and broken dishes, while Kirsteen lit a byre lantern on the dresser.

Craig leapt out of his chair and made for the door, the dog and Kirsteen and Little Janet at his heels, Riach hopping on his crutch, round to the gable window where the stone came from, while Rachael and Helen peered through the empty sash. But there was nothing there but the whisper of green ivy leaves against the stone wall. Craig's chair was anent the window and the stone had missed his head by inches. He said he felt the whizz of it with the bursting glass, and who ever threw it must have known where he sat; somebody who had been in the house and bore him a grudge, or had seen him through a chink in the blind, now torn with the force of the stone.

But who would want to injure Craig MacKinnon? He could think of two or three he had offended in his time, but nothing so serious as would drive them to this sort of revenge. Poor Audie Foubister had more reason than any of them, but Helen was here and he was at hame with the bairn. But whoever threw the stone had vanished into the night, regardless of having injured anyone.

Kirsteen swept up the broken glass and the stone was passed round from hand to hand, each one trying to guess the weight of it, and Little Janet had to hold it in both hands lest she drop it on her toes, then reached up and placed it on the dresser.

Helen was for getting the police but Craig and Rachael wouldn't hear of it. Craig said they didn't want to become the claik of Lachbeg, for it would likely get in the papers if Helen went to the bobby. He would move the dog's kennel to the gable and nobody would get near the place with Floss on guard. But Helen was determined to report it at Lachbeg on her way home; even though the bobby was bedded she would knock him up.

'But wouldn't you be feared to go home in the dark, quine?' Rachael asked. 'Couldn't you bide till morning? Audie would watch the bairn.' But Helen argued it would still be dark in the morning when Audie went to the byre at six o'clock – and who would watch the bairn then if she wasn't home? No, she wasn't feared, and when Craig went out to supper his horse she went with him and set sail on her bike, while they all gathered at the gable window to cry her off, and Floss ran off in front, barking at her gas light.

It was still very dark, with a blanket over the stars, and pitch black in Lachbeg woods, with a hooting of owls deep in the trees. Helen met not a motor car nor a motor-bike, nor anyone else on a push-bike, and the last friendly train had long since left Leary Station for the night. But maybe she would catch the bobby yet, just beyond the lake and the joiner's shop.

She was now anent the lake, quiet and deep and mysterious, with its smell of dead leaves and the croaking of frogs. She wasn't cycling fast, nor with any thought of urgency, just ambling along with her thoughts on the happenings of the evening, thinking maybe that if she had gone to Bogmyrtle in daylight things would have been different. She wouldn't have seen the ghost anyway; and she would get a carrier for Ruth on the bicycle and go during the day.

Then something sprang out from the roadside and grabbed Helen from her bicycle, somebody quick and powerful that gave her no time to think, but had her on the ground in a moment and the wheels of the upturned bike spinning in the darkness, the gas lamp out and a man breathing over her, his hand on her mouth and his arms a vice grip, dragging her towards the lake. In vain she tried to kick and scream and bit his fingers but he was too strong for her. She was helpless in his powerful grasp, paralysed like a fly in a spider's web.

The man was breathing heavily and he spoke in gasps: 'I've been waitin for ye,' he said, 'and I'm goin' tae drown ye in the lake for what yer folk did to my sister, Muriel Spark. It was all right so long as she was stealing things from the shop for yer mither, but when yer brither was called up and the shop folk found her out for stealing, and she couldn't get any more sugar and treacle yer mither didna want her ony mair; so they stretched a rope across the road on a dark night and tripped her off her bicycle. She got such a clite that she took hoosemaid's knee and galloping consumption, and now it has gone to her brain and she's raving mad: mad about yer brither Hamish, and they have taken her away to the lunatic asylum in the Black Maria, like she was a criminal, with only weeks to live . . .'

Helen shook her head vigorously, biting the fingers at her mouth, until she could speak or mumble. 'So you're Meldrum Spark,' she gasped, 'Muriel's brither, come tae tak' revenge on me, an innocent body!'

'Aye,' the man retorted, never relaxing his grip, 'but ye wunna live tae tell the tale, 'cause I'm gaun tae droon ye in the lake . . .'

'But it has naething tae do wi' me,' Helen blustered through his fingers; 'it's the first I've heard of it and it won't do ye ony good tae drown me.'

'A life for a life,' the angry man spat out, tightening his grip on her body, while she kicked and struggled to be free, biting his hands and butting his breast with her head, knocking her hat askew and loosening her hair. She was free to the wrists but still he held her, spinning around in his grasp, twisting her body this way and that, while she kicked his shins in the mud of the lake. She tried to pull the man's hands towards her mouth but she couldn't, so she lowered her head and bit him deeply, crunching into the veins on the back of his hand.

'You little MacKinnon bitch,' he cried out in his pain, and spun her round against a tree, her wrists by her side, his knee between her legs, his chin against hers, spitting the words into her face. 'I tried tae get yer father wi' a stone through the windae, but when I ken't you were there I said I'd get my spite oot on you on the road hame, 'cause I ken whaur ye bide. But it's yer mither that loads the gun, nae yer father, and the bairns fires it – if ye ken what I mean? . . . and if ye could call them bairns, for they are auld enough and sud know better. One o' yer sisters was home on leave at the time, I dinna ken which ane, but some o' them put the tow across the road, tied it tae a post and held the ither end in the hedge, then ran oot o' sicht when the lass fell aff her bike. Muriel couldna see wha it was in the darkness. She went back tae the hoose and they werna there, but cam' in later, efter they had taken doon the tow, innocent lookin' as tame mice, and supposed tae be supperin' the kye. Yer mither was washin' my sister's knee wi' warm watter and lysol, but they a' denied kennin' onything aboot it, though Muriel was sure it was them that put the tow across the road. But never a letter did yer mither give Muriel from Hamish and it broke the lassie's he'rt.'

'You should have gone tae the bobby,' Helen said, almost rubbing noses with the man; 'juist like I was goin' the nicht tae report ye.'

'I wasna here at the time,' he said, 'I was in the army.' He was calmer now, but still angry, the bitten hand at her throat, warm blood trickling down his wrist. 'When I cam' hame Muriel wadna hear of it, so I took the law intae my ain hands, determined tae have revenge.'

He tightened his grip on her throat, crushing her Adam's apple into her windpipe, until she could hardly breathe, gasping out the words, defiant in her helplessness. 'Then have yer revenge, Meldrum Spark,' she cried, 'choke me if ye like; drown me in the lake and ye'll have me on yer conscience for the rest o' yer life. Ye'll see my ghost here every night ye pass the lake, juist as I saw yer sister's ghost the nicht in the Clatterin' Howe. I thocht it was a man I met withoot feet, a priestly body in a lang frock-coat that went glidin' by me in the night; but noo I ken it was a woman . . . yer sister, Meldrum, in her shroud. I thocht at first it was ma brither killed in France, but noo I ken it was yer sister . . . she maun be deid, Meldrum Spark!'

She choked out the words and the hand at her throat was relaxed. The man stared at Helen against the tree; the feel of his eyes upon her, his face outlined in the dark against the sky.

'You're a witch, quine,' he said, 'and I would be cursed for life if I killed ye. My sister could well be dead, though I havena heard of it yet.'

'But you will, Meldrum Spark; you mark my words. But go ahead and strangle me. Drown me in the lake if you like. I defy ye, Meldrum Spark. I defy ye . . .'

She tried to wriggle free but he still held her, and she squirmed feebly in his tightening grasp. She had cowed him with her ghost story but he wouldn't let her go.

'I havena the guts tae kill ye, quine. And besides, ye are the best o' the MacKinnons. Why should ye pay for their ill deeds? It wad do me little good tae murder ye!'

He came closer to her by the tree. She could feel the bulge of her breasts against his waistcoat, his warm lips against her mouth, a soft tender kiss that gave her no desire to struggle; the sort of kiss she often hungered for but Audie couldn't give.

Maybe he would ravish her, this stranger in the night she had never seen before; scarcely knew he existed. If he tried it she wasn't fit to resist. He was too strong for her; her wrists aching now in his iron grip. She could cry for help now but who would hear her? She could kick and bite, she could . . .

But the man was gentle now, soothing in his approach, and when he released her hands he put his arms round her waist, her thin girlish waist, drawing her towards him, kissing her twitching face, her warm beating neck, her mouth, all over her face, while his penis rose steadily against her hips. She could feel it in the right spot and her heart pounded at the thought of it. She took his kisses and returned them, without any will to resist, her arms now about his neck, holding him, her hot dry lips hungry for more. He undid his trouser flap and pushed against her, the hard warm feel of it against her belly, soft and yielding to his pressure. Both his hands were at her elastic, pulling down her knickers, lifting up her skirt around her waist, the sweet smell of him exciting her. In a moment he was in, the hot strength of him thrusting deep, bringing her to helpless ecstasy, her kisses hot with desire, yielding herself to his rhythmic stroke, joy in every movement, hoping it would last, and the final tilt that sent the hot sperm spinning into her womb, making her gasp with pleasure, overwhelming her in the joy of her own orgasm that the thrust had brought her. She was smiling and limp in the aftermath, trembling in his arms, her hat still askew and her hair about her face,

while he still held her to his pounding heart-beat, brea
fast in her embrace. An owl went 'Too-whit, too-whoo,
whit too-whoo!' from the far side of the lake, breakin
silence with sudden alarm. Helen broke away sudd
pulling up her knickers, a sense of shame seizing her
skirt falling around her knees, warm and heavy in the f
it. The man fastened his trousers, an urgency in his m
ments and a feeling of guilt in his mind, but smiling st
the memory of it.

It was the first intercourse Helen had ever enjoyed t
utmost satisfaction, and the thrill of it burned like
unquenchable fire that made her hunger for more. Meld
took her hand gently and led her to the road, the t
crackling sharply under their feet, while Helen straight
her hat, her black gloves still on her hands, then lifted
skirt and pulled up her garters. They stood together in
open a moment and Meldrum picked up her bicycle
the side of the road. 'Are ye mad at me, Helen N
Kinnon?' he asked. 'No,' she said and held the bike w
he struck a match and kindled her gas lamp. 'Not much
light,' he joked, 'more like a brass tack in a blackbi
arse,' and they both laughed at the thought. 'Well, I've
my revenge,' he added quietly, just above a whisper, in
silky voice that Helen noticed, 'and I hope I hav
nicked you, quine!' He kissed her over the handlebars,
holding the bike, and she just stood there, all his for
taking it seemed, had he wanted more. 'Och it doe
matter,' she said at last, getting on to her bike, 'it
worth it!'

'I'll maybe see you again some day,' Meldrum ca
after her, pushing her into the darkness, loth to let her
'Some day maybe,' she called back, and went pelting al
the road.

The bobby's house was in darkness and Helen ne
troubled him. She went sailing through the Clatterin' H
exhilarated, with no thought of fear, humming to hersel
the joy of a new experience. Such a pity she hadn't m
more sure of seeing him again, this stranger in the night v
had thrown the stone at her father, and the sudden thou

brought her back to reality. Ah well but she wouldn't think about it now to spoil her moment of bliss; there would be plenty of time for that later. Then she remembered that she should have shown her light in his face to see what he looked like. His joke about the brass tack made her laugh a second time, and maybe it wouldn't have done much good. But she wouldn't forget his voice, that wonderful voice; especially after his anger had gone and he spoke gently, so warm and silky and crept all over you with feeling – she would remember it anywhere if she heard it again.

Millbrae was in darkness, the little cottage a blur in the night. She blew out her lamp and put her bicycle in the shed, then knocked hard on the door to waken Audie. He came to the door in his long woollen drawers, walking on his heels on the cold stone floor, mumbling to himself while he pulled out the wooden bar. Helen was as fresh as a newly plucked flower, the smell of the night wind still about her, her eyes shining in the light as she turned up the wick of the paraffin lamp on the table.

'Ye're affa late, wuman,' Audie mumbled, after barring the door again, hardly looking to see what the stars looked like, glad to get back to his warm bed. 'There's a cup of tea for ye on the bink,' he added, and was soon fast asleep again, little Ruth at the foot of the bed, a doll still in her oxter.

Helen would tell him in the morning that everything was still all right at Bogmyrtle; but no mention of the ghost or the stone at the window or her affair with Meldrum Spark. His kisses still lingered on her rasp-coloured lips, kindling a hunger inside her that poor Audie and his fumbling could never satisfy.

Helen was anxious about her periods for a month or two and when nothing happened she felt relieved. It had been a great thrill but she had never seen Meldrum Spark again to give it another trial. Since that night in Lachbeg Woods his name had been all over the parish, caught as a deserter and likely to be shot, and that was why he had never gone to the police about his sister. His name had been in the papers and he must have been in hiding when he threw the stone through her father's window. But Helen was too involved to mention his name at Bogmyrtle, far less tell the story of Muriel's death, or Meldrum's version of it, or how he had taken his 'revenge' on her in Lachbeg Woods. According to the papers Muriel Spark had died on the very day that Helen had seen the apparition in the Clatterin' Howe, so it was no idle tale she had told Meldrum, nor was he likely to forget in his short life, if he was to face a firing squad. Poor devil, Helen thought.

Helen had mentioned to her family that Muriel Spark had died in the asylum, and Rachael said she had seen it in the papers, and had often wondered why she had never come back after that evening when she had hurt her knee. So it was possible that her mither had nothing on her conscience concerning Muriel Spark; that she knew nothing of what her wound had led to, and thought little of the prank that caused it, beyond writing to Hamish telling him that his lass had died; perhaps destroying the letters Hamish had sent her, if Meldrum's story was true. But Helen hadn't the nerve to ask her mither about the letters, for after all it was really none of her business, and she didn't want to get too much involved, in view of what had happened between herself and Meldrum. And who was she to sit in judgment on her family? Or to scar their minds with Meldrum's belief, if it was really true? Craig would be furious if he heard such a tale. Not that her silence in any way remitted their guilt, but she wasn't going to outlaw herself a second time by bringing a storm on their heads. Craig had merely said that he was thankful she had changed her mind that night and hadn't gone to the bobby; after all the window had been repaired and nothing had happened since.

Spring and summer passed and the war still rumbled on, with hardly a young man left on the farms nowadays, apart from a few Conscientious Objectors, mostly Englishmen who refused to kill their fellow men at any price, and would rather face a firing squad than fight with the army. Helen got a basket for Ruth on the bicycle and went to Bogmyrtle in the daytime. Ruth was getting bigger and played Hoosies with Little Janet while Helen helped with the hairst or worked with her mither in the kitchen. Not that she was afraid to go to Bogmyrtle in the evenings, especially if there had been any hope of meeting Meldrum Spark again, for in spite of everything Helen still hungered for the man, believed she was secretly in love with him, and would surrender herself a second time if ever she got the chance. But it wasn't just lust, she thought, or arse love as some folks called it, but something more respectable, something higher and cleaner, something of the soul and mind; even heavenly, something she had never felt before for any man, not even for Audie, poor soul.

Poor Frank Barbour was killed in the autumn, Audie's half-brother, blown to bits by a shell apparently and not even a brass button left to send home to his mother. Helen was heart-sorry for her mother-in-law, and she had been so engrossed with her own family troubles she forgot all about poor Frank being in the army. Between the half-brothers Frank had been Audie's favourite, more so than Herbert, who had been discharged from the army on medical grounds. When Helen got a letter from Mrs Barbour, telling her to break it gently to Audie, poor Audie broke down and cried for his half-brother, and Helen pitied him and wiped the tears from his eyes with a damp cloth and washed his face and sent him off to work again. What would Audie do without her, Helen sometimes wondered, if ever she took it in her head to run off with another man, a lad like Meldrum Spark, who could thrill her to the core of her being; while Audie with his feeble efforts merely upset her. Yet he could be spiteful at times and said the fault was hers; that she'd never been clean since she lost that bairn under the binder. Helen knew herself this was a damned lie for she was as clean as the next woman, and would have gone to a doctor if she wasn't. She flew into a temper about this and threw taunts at Audie about his big hernia, telling him he was too big a coward to do anything about it, and they had hellova rows about this and stopped speaking for days. The evenings were torture for Helen; sheer boredom, with never a word spoken, while Audie spent the time manicuring his nails and washing his feet, and Helen felt like telling him he should wash the other bit too, but was afraid of his temper, for he could be vile at times, and it would only start another fight in front of the bairn, and Ruth was beginning to take notice, playing with her dolls or knitting a 'Cattie's Tail' with old worsted on a pirn, using an old darning needle that was blunt enough not to do her any harm if she stabbed herself. But sometimes Helen couldn't stand it any longer; this isolation with the bairn and a man who couldn't even cuddle her properly, or give her one passionate kiss. So Helen would sulk with the pair of them and put on her hat and coat and clash the door and be off on her bike to Bogmyrtle and the peat reek; ghosts or wild men couldn't scare her, nor the graveyard at Lachbeg when she passed it in the dark. She almost prayed for Meldrum to spring out at her from every bush, to crush her in his great arms, to overwhelm her again with the surge of his whole being. But he could be dead by now for all she knew, for the army had small mercy for deserters. Kirsteen said he came from Stronach, the little village on the far shoulder of the Mattock Hill, little better than tinks she said, and that Meldrum used to hawk the country with heather besoms when he couldn't get a job, though he was sometimes quite nice when he called at Bogmyrtle with his box. Oh aye she'd seen him there since Helen was married, with all manner of things to sell, like brooches and rings and tie-pins, pirns of thread and needles, shaving soap and scent, bootlaces and buttons, all manner of things; and his box had a fine smell with the stuff he carried in it. But why should you be interested in a lad like Meldrum Spark when you're married, Helen? Och never mind, Kirsteen quine, can't a body ask about somebody else but you have them eloping with them or something. Mind your own damned business. And though Kirsteen was a bold hussy in a way, she was shy of taking the rag of Helen; her big sister that had worked in the toon and had seen a bit more of life than she would ever do at Bogmyrtle. Indeed Kirsteen secretly admired Helen for going off on her own and getting a man for herself like that and she wished she had the nerve sometime to try it herself. Oh, Audie maybe wasn't much of a catch but there must be something in him when he'd made a bairn, and Kirsteen wouldn't mind having a bairn to anyone if they gave her the chance.

One day at noon Audie walked into the little kitchen and said, 'The war's feenished, wuman!' Helen asked who had won and he replied, 'Oor folk, of course!' seemingly confident of a British victory.

He hung his bonnet on the back of his chair and sat down to dinner, ruffling Ruth's curls playfully, for she was already seated on her high-chair, with a white bib on her breast.

'I wonder what will happen tae the Kaiser noo?' Audie mused. 'Will he still be sittin' in his Imperial Palace twistin' 'es mouser and layin' forth aboot bein' King o' a' Europe and the Breetish Empire?' And Audie stroked his own brown fusker (much too short for waxing) in mock imitation of the much exalted Kaiser Wilhelm II of Germany, current arch enemy of the world.

'Na,' Helen said, sitting opposite, at the other end of the table, the bairn between them. 'He'll nae be sittin' in his Berlin Palace; the papers say he has fled tae Holland for safety, for fear that his ain folk tear 'im tae bits in the streets. He has caused a lot o' sair he'rts wi' his pride and ambition and all the world must surely hate 'im.'

Audie couldn't read the papers, so he was obliged to Helen for any news of the war forthcoming from that quarter.

But Helen was more concerned about her brother Hamish than she was for the wicked Kaiser, and she could spare a thought too for poor Frank Barbour, who would never come back. Audie seemed to read her thoughts for he said, 'Yer brither will be hame again, wuman. He's been lucky compared wi' some; he hasna gotten a scrat!'

'No, but he was gassed,' Helen reminded him, 'and I'm sorry for poor Frank Barbour.'

'Oh aye, it's a pity,' Audie said, blowing on a spoonful of broth, and now somewhat hardened to the loss of his half-brother. He cleared his throat, maybe to check a tear that was welling in his eye, while Helen pretended not to notice and wiped Ruth's chin with the corner of her bib.

Maybe just to change the subject Audie ladled himself another plate of broth and said, 'Aye, wuman, but it's a pity too that yon quine Muriel Spark died 'cause Hamish might hae married 'er when he got hame.'

Helen thought it better not to say anything more about that, but Audie wasn't finished, and maybe out of a little spite for the MacKinnons, he added, 'But your folk are bein' blamed for that wuman, or so I've heard on the sly; that they stretched a wire across the road in the dark tae trip the lassie aff her bicycle – nae wonder somebody tried tae kill auld Craig!'

So Audie knew all about it and said nothing till now; and the rope had now become a wire to trip up Muriel Spark.

'Who told ye all this?' Helen demanded, hardly noticing that even Ruth was listening, her spoon poised half-way to her little rose-bud mouth.

'Och I juist heard it at the thrashin' mull, some lads newsin' and they didna ken I was married to a MacKinnon – so I cocked my lugs and harkened.'

Helen wondered just how much more he knew, and she was thankful that there had been no mention so far of Meldrum Spark.

'But there's nae proof that the accident caused her death,' Helen ventured, rather hotly, now rising in defence of her kith and kin. 'No proof at all, and my father's not to blame. He had nothing to do with it.'

'Well, you could hardly call it an accident, wuman, and grown men and weemin ocht tae hae mair sense. And it was worse afore the war, they say, when the MacKinnons were a' at hame: And how they took Tom Stag's red letter-box from the end o' his fairm road and stuck it up in the middle o' a ploo'ed park and the postie couldna find it in the mornin'. Syne they opened auld Slater's gates and let oot his nowt on the road and it took him a whole day tae find them. And they sent a parcel of horse dirt tae the gairdener's folk at Lachbeg, through the post mind ye, and they could hardly open it for the smell.'

These were trifles that Audie mentioned and they had their funny side, besides other tricks her brother and sisters got up to, like putting sods on people's lums and taking the wheels off their carts and running them down a brae. But there were more serious things she remembered, like poor Cranna Morgan in his sanatorium in his mother's garden just before the war, when Hamish and Nora had swung it round and round in the moonlight till the poor creature cried out in his torment. Dying of consumption he was and light-headed with the spinning and begging for mercy till his mother came out and scared them off. Nora was fee-ed at Cairnielug at the time and after Cranna died she couldna get sleep in her bed for a young man pulling down her bed-clothes. It was Cranna's ghost taking its revenge at the foot of her bed and Nora was demented, for every time she pulled the blankets up the young man hauled them down again. Nora lay naked and cold half the night until she lit the lamp and the young man disappeared. But when she screwed down the lamp and happed herself with the blankets and tried to sleep he came back again and soon had her tirred, staring at her with empty eye sockets and hollow cheeks and the bones sticking out of his body. On the second night Nora ran down the stair and rapped on the door of the closet where her mistress slept, and the woman said it would just be the nightmare and she could sleep with the lamp burning. On the third night Nora left the lamp burning by her bedside, hoping to defy the ghost, but after midnight she woke up cold, the blankets all at the foot of her bed, and a skeleton standing there gasping for breath, in the full glow of the lamplight. Nora sprang from the bed in her nightgown, grabbed her slippers and flew down the stair and out of the farmhouse and on to her bicycle and never looked back to Cairnielug, riding full tilt for Millbrae, her nearest refuge in the dark night, banging on the door with her stickit nieves to waken Helen.

Helen was big with Ruth at the time but she knew her sister's voice at the door and let her in. All in a muddle she was and her hair over her face, and Helen set her down on a chair where she bibbled and grat and confessed her guilt with Cranna Morgan. Audie had snored through it all and perhaps knew little about it, though he did speir why Nora was in the room bed in the morning and the lamp still burning, and Helen lied that her bicycle had punctured and Audie never questioned her story. When daylight came Helen gave her sister breakfast and some clothes and sent her home for she wouldn't go near her place again. But her confession of guilt laid Cranna's ghost and he never bothered the quine again.

Helen herself was not without her faults, for when she was working in the hairst parks she came home one night to Millbrae in the dark and listened at the cottage window, 'cause she heard the bairn crying. Audie and his mither were at a great hub-bub, getting on about Helen spoiling the bairn and giving Ruth too much of her own way. Audie's mither was supposed to be looking after Ruth and the bairn was determined to have her father's watch, a double-cased lever with jewels, Audie's most prized possession, more important even than his gramophone. Ruth had found the watch under her father's pillow when granny put her in the box-bed, Audie's resting place for his watch, and she wouldn't give it up: howled murder when they tried to take it away from her, and wouldn't go to sleep without the ticking watch in her hand or at her lug. Audie and his mither were going at the howling bairn and were determined she shouldn't have her father's priceless watch. 'She shant have it! She shant have it!' Mrs Barbour was crying, while Audie screeched out with 'It's a skelpin' she's needin'.' Helen heard it all at the window and she took a spite at Audie and his interfering mither, even though she knew it was wrong to give the bairn the watch. So Helen went to the garden for clods and pelted the window with sods and earth, until she had Audie and his mither fair terrified and afraid to open the door. Audie was afraid to go outside lest he got his nose bashed, because they were blaming the MacKinnons. After a while, when Helen had washed her hands in the dewy grass, and had knocked gently on the window, in her usual way, they opened the door suspiciously to let her in, explaining that somebody had clodded the window and they were afraid. Helen went to the box-bed and took up the bairn and gave Audie back his watch, thinking the pair of them were a bit henny-hearted and easily scared by a poor land girl, a MacKinnon at that, for they were all tarred with the same brush you might say.

'A penny for yer thochts, wuman?' Audie asked, and it brought Helen out of her reverie.

'Oh I was juist thinking about yer poor mither, 'cause she won't have much to rejoice about though the war is finished.'

Audie finished his broth and pushed the plate aside. He took two cakes of oatbreid from the trencher and set them up before the fire, then crumbled them into a bowl of milk, added a little spice and supped them with a spoon.

Ruth got down from her chair to have her breid warmed at the hot bars like her pa, so he half toasted an extra cake and she had her melk and breid with him at the table, though he had to watch her with the salt and pepper. Not that Audie had all that time for the bairn and she ran to her mither in times of stress.

Audie took a red hankie with white spots from his jacket pocket and wiped his moustache. 'That'll be the end o' the volunteers onywye, and ye wunna hae tae scoor ma baynet in the sod dyke again, wuman.'

'No, thank heaven for that,' Helen agreed, 'nor tie yer puttees either, ye gipe; and it will be the end o' the blackoots as weel, and the whitewash on the bicycle lamps.'

Audie put a fag in his holder and lit it with a twist of paper at the fire, well away from his moustache, and blew the smoke up the chimney. He looked at Ruth finishing her melk and breid, and said, 'Ye spilled the skimmed melk the day, ma bonnie quinie!'

'Aye, she spilled a suppie,' Helen said. 'She's just hardly big enough to carry it yet, though she's determined tae try it.'

'It's nae far frae the fairm though,' Audie said, 'but I think she fell when she came over the dyke.'

Ruth looked from one to the other, her little hand cupped over her spoon, her eyes bright with excitement. 'Tell dad about the ring, mam,' she said.

'Aye, she picked up a richt bonnie ring on the ploughed park,' and Helen went over to the dresser for a gold ring set with sparkling stones and dropped it in Audie's palm. 'Must have belonged to one of the Laird's daughters,' she said; 'it was covered with earth when Ruth brought it home but I washed it in soap and water.'

'Aye, a richt bonnie ring,' Audie remarked, 'nae wonder she spilled the melk; she had been in a gie hurry hame tae show ye a thing like that.'

Helen took back the ring and slipped it on her finger beside her marriage ring.

'What are ye gaun tae do with it?' Audie asked.

'Keep it,' Helen said, 'the quine may want it hersel' one day when she gets married. Meanwhile I'll wear it like an engagement ring, something I never got from you!'

Audie blew out his fag-holder into the fire and fell asleep in his chair till nearly yoking time.

When Hamish MacKinnon came home from the war he brought with him the brass nose-cone of a German shell, fired at him he said from an enemy artillery post, and landed at his feet, steaming hot. It now stood on the wooden dresser at Bogmyrtle, a war trophy that Craig took great pride in showing the neighbours, swinging it up and down in his hand, as if he was trying to guess the weight of it, and then dropping it into a neighbour's palm, telling him to mind his toes and asking how he would have liked to get a clout on the back of the head with a thing like that? 'caus that was what our Hamish had to put up with and he had been lucky, poor soul.

Hamish also brought home a brass slide with five rifle cartridge-shells that he gave to Helen on his first visit to Millbrae. Helen thought the world of them and set them up on the mantelshelf in front of the pendulum clock, like five miniature organ pipes, complete with copper tips, and they matched the brass mounting that was tacked on to the shelf. Every now and then she dusted and polished them and replaced them fondly on the mantelpiece: 'a keepsake', she called them, just to show that her brother had been at the war.

Hamish also brought home a hirst of French post-cards of

naked women, which he kept locked in his kist, and he told a hantle of stories about the brave Ghurka soldiers he served with, of how they had cut off the ears of the Germans they had killed in their night raids on enemy lines, and sometimes a whole head, and rolled them in a bloody parcel and slept on it for a pillow. Hamish seemed none the worse of his gassing and he seldom mentioned his lass, though he told Helen he had been to see her grave at Stronach. She had stopped writing, he said, and never seemed to suspect that his mither had kept his letters from the quine. He wasn't going to work at home again, he said, and took a fee at Wolfhill, a place not far from Millbrae, and used to cry in by Helen on his way home on his bike, sometimes with a dram for Audie and a sweetie for Ruth. Helen asked if he ever heard of Meldrum Spark, but Hamish said no, but most likely he would still be in the jile, if he hadn't been shot for deserting.

But Hamish wasn't long at Wolfhill or he was feared to go home in the dark, because he said a woman was chasing him in her bare feet, skelping on behind him and he heard the slap of her feet on the road, especially if it was raining. When he got off his bike and turned his light on her she disappeared; but when he got on his bicycle again she came on at the trot, only yards behind and gasping for breath, and when he glanced over his shoulder he saw the white shape of her in the darkness. She always appeared at the Mogget croft, where Hamish sometimes made his trysts with Muriel before the war, and the woman followed him nearly to Wolfhill, but never crossed the water of Gorth; once over the bridge the woman left him, but was waiting for him again the next dark night he came by the Mogget croft.

Hamish was like a frightened bairn when he told Helen the story, and he said it scared him more than anything he had seen in the war. He thought it was the ghost of Muriel Spark he said, and wondered why the poor quine would be haunting him. So Helen put on her hat and coat and walked with Hamish her brother until he was clear of the Mogget croft, and saw him on his bike in the dark, his gas lamp burning bright, and he never looked round for fear he saw the woman, nor listened for the sound of her footsteps. Helen walked back alone, and she knelt and prayed at the Mogget croft that Muriel Spark would leave her brother in peace, and henceforth Hamish never saw her ghost again.

It was in the spring of the next year that old Toby Mathers died, farmer of Millbrae, and because his only son had been killed in the war his daughter Isobel took over the farm. Audie had gone up in the morning as usual to sort his nowt, but he had to go to the farm kitchen for his lanterns, because the kitchiedeem had filled and cleaned them the night before. But the quine had slept in and Audie had to rap on the back door to waken her, and when she came down with her wick lamp they found the old man lying stone cold on the kitchen floor. Isobel was a woman in her middle twenties, and you would have thought she would be hardened to the sight of death by that time, her mother having died some years back, but when the maid brought her down the stair she fainted at the sight of her father lying on the floor. Audie had to oxter the woman to keep her from falling, and the quine ran for smelling salts, and held the bottle under Isobel's nose, and when she came to in Audie's arms he was a new man in her sight, and he became a great favourite with the new mistress of Millbrae. It was after the funeral that Audie noticed it, when Isobel got over the shock of losing her father, and then he saw there was a change in her, maybe because she was mistress now, he wasn't sure, but instead of going to Drew Strachan about the wark, as her father had done, she went to Audie, and she aught to have had more sense, Audie thought, because Drew Strachan was the grieve. Audie had been six years in her father's service, looking after the cattle, besides doing the garden at Millbrae; and even swept the farmhouse chimneys, but he wasn't at all keen on having charge of the place.

But Drew Strachan took offence, and said he wasn't going to work under Petticoat Government, as he called it, and gave in his notice and left at the May Term. Isobel saw her chance and thought she was doing Audie a favour by asking him for grieve, but he refused and she was sore taken aback, and she said she would have to advertise in the papers. But Isobel Mathers had about as much idea of what a working man should look like as she had about a work horse, which was precious little, and didn't ask half the awkward questions her father would have speired at a man, just to see what was in him, so that when the lads came by in answer to her advert in the papers Isobel had no idea which one to choose. She might as well have lined them up in the close and said, 'Eetle-ottle black bottle, eetle ottle oot,' pointing with her finger, until only one man was left for her. But when Long Dod Watt came down from Stepping Stones and said he had been in a croft Isobel was fair impressed, and maybe she was a bit taken with the gangling breet besides, and he told her as many lies about his misfortune in the place, and nothing about his own laziness, that she fee-ed him as the new foreman to Millbrae without a single reference. So when the farming billies round about Millbrae heard about Long Dod of Stepping Stones taking on the job for Isobel they said, 'Hach, that's what ye get with Petticoat Government.'

So the Watts moved in next door to Helen at the May Term; Long Dod that had been like John Grumlie in the song and sent his wife to chauve and work on the croft while he sottered at the kitchen sink washing pishen hippens and fule sarks till he was fair scunnered making bairns and had his wife wear the breeks. And the wife was right glad of the change, they said, because Long Dod had her nicked every year, like a breeding sow; but when she donned the breeks and did the wark outside he was content to lie on his hip and let her chauve, while he pared the tatties and washed the dishes and got the bairns off to school. Syne the cheil thought he had got the worst of the deal, but the wife wadna swap, and the two of them sat down in a sotter that would have scunnered a tink, and beasts died and crops failed and they ran into debt and fell behind with the rent, until the Laird summoned them out of Stepping Stones and they had to cottar for a living.

So the Watts came to Millbrae and all that remained from their crofting days was the bits of furniture that hadn't been poined to pay their debt and half-a-dozen bedraggled looking hens and a tame goose. And the goose waddled in and out of the kitchen any time it pleased, until it had a beaten path from the door to the fireplace, picking up crumbs from under the table, and then came down the close with the bairns to see them off for school. Dolly Watt was the eldest quine, long legged like her father but sweet and freckled in the face, with long red hair down her back, thick as a sheltie's tail, and she rocked the cradle with the youngest Watt bairn, till the goose stretched its long neck under the rocker, and then flapped all over the kitchen floor in its death throes. And Dolly got such a skelping from her mother for killing the pet goose that she stammered for years in her speech, which was a pity, folk said, because the poor quine couldn't help it. But she took Ruth by the hand on her first day at Leary school, a long tiring day for Ruth, away from her dolls and cattie's tails, even though she had a new school bag of fine-smelling leather and cheese and bread and ginger cake to eat in the school porch at dinner time. Even Rachael had given her a varnished wooden case for her slate pencils, with blue forget-me-nots on the sliding lid, and Miss Drone, the teacher, gave her a new slate with a wooden frame to scribble on.

And so the weeks and months passed at Millbrae and the sun was on the ripe corn again, with red poppies at the gates. Ruth pulled them in handfuls and took them home to Helen, and Helen put them in water in a little vase in the window, and they were 'Poppies of Flanders' she said, but Ruth never knew what she meant. Ruth now slept alone in the ben-room, even in the dark, with no sense of fear or a memory of the little marble corpse that had been so brief a friend. Her childhood memories were short and her consciousness was only of the present. On the sunny mornings at the weekends she lay in bed a long time looking at the two framed pictures on the wall that Helen had gotten as prints in The People's Journal. They hung each side of the polished mahogany sideboard with the bevelled mirror where Ruth could look at herself if she stood on the padded stool. It wasn't a warm and friendly room, because there was seldom a fire in the grate, except when Audie swept the kitchen chimney; so it was rather quiet and distant and treated you like a stranger, and the people in the pictures kept looking at you whichever way you turned, as if you were disturbing their privacy. Some of the people in the pictures were dead, but they were still alive in that little room, watching your every movement with their silent eyes. But there were pictures of Grandad MacKinnon in his kilt and sporran, a tartan plaid upon his shoulder, a tight-fitting tunic, topped stockings, a dirk at his knee and buckles on his shoes, and sitting beside him was Grandma Rachael, looking very young and sweet, with her hair done up in a tiara and a white flounced dress to her feet, cuffs on mutton-chop sleeves and a ruffled waist. Then there was uncle Hamish in his khaki tunic when he went away to the big war; and aunts Moira, Nancy, Nora and Kirsteen, bright and happy in their summer dresses; and on the sideboard were some photographs of the Barbours, but not so many, because Mama wasn't interested so much in them, though Grandad and Grandma Barbour stood inside a gold fretted frame and glowered about them like total strangers.

But it was the coloured pictures that intrigued Ruth, one with a nurse in snow-white uniform and a cap to match, with a red cross upon her breast, kneeling over a wounded soldier in a pool of blood, her arm supporting him round the shoulders and a small bottle in her free hand, like a bottle of lysol or medicine, Ruth thought, while red shells were bursting in the blue sky and there were shattered buildings in the background. The caption under the picture said, 'The Real Angel of Mons', and after a year at school Ruth could spell it out and read it aloud, though she wasn't quite sure what it meant. When she asked Helen she said that so many poor soldiers had been killed at the terrible battle of Mons that an angel appeared and tried to stop them, but that the wicked Germans took no notice and the killing went on. The King was in the other picture, very smart and upright he was in khaki uniform with ribbons and medals on his breast and a high peaked cap, a leather belt about his waist and a sword scabbard hanging by his leg. The

King was pinning medals on a row of brave soldiers all standing erect in khaki, and the one nearest the King was saluting. Under this picture was printed, 'King George V and the VC Heroes', and Ruth was a much bigger girl or she understood the meaning of that one; though Helen told her the soldiers were getting a prize from the King for being so very brave fighting the Germans. No, uncle Hamish wasn't one of the soldiers, though he looked a bit like the one on the left who didn't have a moustache.

On the Sunday morning, when Helen went through to the room, Ruth was on her usual perch, looking at the pictures, her elbow on the sideboard, her cheek resting on her hand, like The Boy Titian, staring up wide-eyed at 'The Real Angel of Mons'. The room needed airing, for there was damp on the walls, you could see it on the wall-paper, bulging under the pattern of wildflowers, so Helen raised the lower sash of the window and took Ruth's hand to the kitchen. 'Your dad is going to sweep the kitchen lum this morning,' she told Ruth, 'so I'll kindle a fire in the room to boil the kettle, then you'll get your breakfast and you can watch your father up on the thatch.'

Breakfast was usually porridge or a boiled egg. Today it would be a boiled egg, because the room grate wasn't big enough to take the porridge pot. 'No, Ruth, we canna light the kitchen fire, because the soot would burn when your dad sweeps the lum, and it might set fire to the hoose.'

After breakfast Helen dressed Ruth, and Audie went up to the farm with his empty milk flaggon and brought back a ladder and the tackle for sweeping the chimney: a long rope with heather besoms tied to it here and there and a weight at the end. While he was away Helen took all the ornaments from the chimney-shelf, including the pendulum clock and the five cartridge shells she got from uncle Hamish. She draped a sack over the fireplace, tacked to the mantelshelf, then covered all the furniture with sacking and closed the doors; and all the time Ruth watching her and getting more scared.

Audie climbed the ladder with the rope on his shoulder, up the thatch to the coping, then crawled along like a cat to the chimney-stock, where he straddled the stonework and lowered the rope and besoms down the chimney, working them up and down to brush off the soot, and the noise in the lum was like thunder and frightened Ruth. She had to get outside to watch her dad, content to peep at her mother through the slightly opened door.

Helen kept watch by the fireplace, peeping behind the sack to see if the weight was down, and when she heard the rumble of it above the range she ran outside and cried up to Audie on the roof, 'It's like the devil's foundry in there,' she cried, her hand at her mouth to carry the sound, 'and the wecht's doon, so you'd better haul it up again for fear ye smash the oven.'

'Aye, the Hammers o' Hell, wuman,' Audie cried on the wind, 'but I wunna brak' yer range. The soot maun be a' doon noo!'

So the awful rumbling ceased and Audie came down the ladder and coiled up his rope, smearing Ruth's soft cheeks with a sooty hand in the bye going, and Helen swore at him for blackening the bairn.

Ruth plucked up courage to go inside again, even though Helen had told her that the Black Devil was behind the sack, with horns on his head and a long tail and cows' feet, maybe just to get the bairn out of the way, because she carried the soot all over the stone floor on her little shoes. Ruth thought it would be Santa Claus, because they always cleaned the chimney for him before Christmas, when she hung her long stocking under the mantelshelf. Last year she got a doll's cradle and blankets, snakes and ladders and sweeties, black-sugar straps and a sherbet bag; but Helen telling her about the devil behind the sack somewhat changed her idea of Santa Claus, sowing the first seeds of doubt in her mind.

When Helen took away the sack Ruth ran outside, for fear she saw the devil in the huge heap of soot in the fireplace, high as the grate with its iron bars. Helen shovelled the soot into the orra pail and carried it outside to the kailyard, where she spread it out on the earth and around the rhubarb stumps.

Audie was in great demand for sweeping chimneys and he had a flair for heights that frightened bigger men, less sure of their footing on the greasy slates, and it gave him a chance of looking down his nose at lads who looked down on him at ground level, more ways than one; so he took great pride in his chimney-sweeping round about Millbrae. Audie was quite the Jackanape up there on a chimney-head, high as the trees, watching the heavies on the grun, glowering up at him while he pulled on the rope, muttering to himself, 'Aye, ma mannies, this is a job that ye wadna care tae tackle though, na faith ye, there's nane o' ye has the heid for this racket; ye wadna like tae think yer wee pooper was sae far aff the grun, and I dinna ken what wad happen if ye took the skitters at this hicht, ma bonnie mannies!'

When Audie came home with his rope on a Sunday morning he wore a smile of triumph, like he had just hanged his worst enemy, a merry twinkle in his eye and his breath reeking of whisky; not that Audie was a boozer, but he never refused the odd nip. What with his black face and toothy smile, pale lips and his eyes all whites, blinking with mischief, he would chase Helen round the kitchen table with his sooty hands, trying to get a clacht on her clothing, till she was nearly light-headed and out of breath, when he would stop suddenly and fumble in his trouser pocket, and out came two florins, which he would display gleefully, one in each sooty palm, the fee that some grateful farmer's wife had given him for his pains. He gave one florin to Helen and the other to Ruth, and Ruth would reach up to the dresser and drop it into her porcelain bank, a miniature replica of 'The Turra Coo', with a slot in her back for the pennies. She got the little white cow from auntie Moira, her that was married to Sherran Begg: the only trouble was that she had to empty it with a butter knife, through the slot, sliding the pennies down the blade when she held the cow upside down.

During Ruth's second summer at school she went to the annual picnic on the links at Brochan, close by the railway line, where a little engine pulled the coaches backwards and the fisher wives waved from the carriage windows. About half-a-dozen farmers washed and painted their carts for the occasion, and the horsemen polished and beetled their harness, and shook their back-chains in a sack with a burning peat, till they shone like silver snakes, and plaited and rolled their horses' manes with coloured raffia, and tied up their tails in a bun like Miss Drone did her hair, with coloured streamers from the saddle-bow to the tall spikes on the hames, and rosettes and martingales on the straps and buckles. Wooden harvest frames were fitted on to the carts and matted all round with straw rapes for the bairns to sit on. Even uncle Riach had a cart, with Meg all donned up to the nines, and a sack of hay in the cart, besides Riach's crutch, and his bagpipes in a little black wooden case, because Mr Jack, the dominie, had asked him to play for the bairns on the bents.

Mr Jack and Miss Drone and Miss Florence rode on the carts with the pupils, and the last cart was loaded with milk in cans, and baskets filled with home-baked scones and bannocks, jars of rasp and strawberry jam, prints of butter, oat-cakes and cheese, mugs and teaspoons, though every bairn was supposed to bring his or her own cup for tea. They were also supposed to bring a few pennies to spend at the little shoppie on the promenade, mostly on liquorice straps, sherbet bags, Battleaxe treacola, Fred's Candy, Lucky Tatties or a candy apple. Also on the last cart was the effigy of Aunt Sally, a sort of glorified female scarecrow, stuffed with straw and nailed to a post, and penny prizes would be awarded to the bairns who could break one of the clay pipes stuck in her mouth, and a stock of old golf balls were provided as ammunition.

It was the first time Ruth had seen the sea, the big green waves rolling up the sands and splitting into white at her feet, the froth and bubbles swirling all around her, then running back and gathering again for another splash on the beach. Uncle Riach came hirpling over the dunes on his crutch and held out a sixpence for Ruth, and when she took it he seized her little palm and rubbed it against his stubbly chin, until the tickle made her laugh and dance and he had to let her go. Riach's crutch went deep in the sand, but it anchored him for a crack at Aunt Sally, and he broke one of her clay pipes, but when Miss Drone offered him the penny prize he refused it. Meg was tethered to a cart-wheel, eating hay out of the sack, and seeing Riach had a wooden leg one of the other lads came round with a pail of water and offered her a drink.

Riach took his pipes out of the wooden case and put the tartan bag under his oxter, squeezing it with his elbow until it squiled like a pig, blowing out his cheeks on the mouthpiece, his fingers waltzing on the chanter, the ribbons from the ivory drones flying over his shoulder, while the skirl of 'Heilan' Laddie' mingled with the cries of the gulls and the swish of the waves on the shingle, Riach leaning against the cart and the bairns crowding round to hear him play, little Ruth proudest of all because he was her uncle.

Mr Jack ladled the milk into the bairns' cups while Miss Drone spread the scones and bannocks with jam and Miss Florence carried round the baskets. Ruth was shy with strangers, even with the bigger quines not in her class, so that Miss Drone had to coax her into the races: the sack race, the spoon race, the three-legged race; and the bigger loons and quines got a penny from Mr Jack if they could leap-frog clean over his back. About four o'clock in the afternoon the farmers yoked their horses and everybody got back into the carts and headed home for the schoolhouse, dropping children off at their homes by the wayside, their mothers waiting for them in the evening sun by their cottage doors.

It was during the school holidays, just before hairst, that Audie and Helen dressed themselves and cycled into Scotstoun to see the Barbours. Audie had been several times to Bogmyrtle, and was on speaking terms again with old Craig MacKinnon, so now it was Helen's turn to go to Audie's folk, to humour Audie if nothing else, for he felt that his mother and stepfather were just as important in his family relationships as the MacKinnons, and a damned sight more respectable, he would say, if you had questioned him on the subject.

Audie was all dressed up in his Sunday best, with a watch-chain on his waistcoat and a new bonnet with a hoop inside, and clips in his trouser legs to keep them away from the cycle chain. Helen was in her costume suit, with a hat and half-veil, just over her eyes; clip-on earrings she had got from her sister Nora, and she wore the gaudy ring Ruth had found on the ploughing. She was a well-faced woman at any time, but dressed up like this the men folk gave her a second look, and Long Dod Watt next door fair glowered at her when he went by with his pails for water; her long skirts swirling about her shapely thighs and the swell of her breasts under her open necked blouse.

Audie took the two bicycles out of the coalshed and pumped up the tyres, then wheeled them over to the kitchen door, so that Helen could feel if they were hard enough, for Audie never had confidence in his own judgement. Ruth ran inside for the red velvet cushion, which Audie tied on to the bar of his bike, because she was getting too big for Helen's basket, and two loops of string hung down as stirrups for her little feet. Audie lifted her up and seated her sideways, though sometimes she wanted to sit stride-legs, like a loon, to ease her doup, for it was a long way to Scotstoun and Ruth wearied on the journey. But she always forgot her weariness and looked forward to the next trip with renewed excitement, eager to be off in the morning sun. Her father jumped on behind her from the back step, while Helen locked the door and hid the key in the thatch, then got on her bike, which had cords over the back wheel to keep her skirts out of the spokes.

The Barbours still lived up on Toddlebrae, grand as ever, and when Ruth got off her father's bicycle she was cramped stiff and could hardly stand, her backside numb and her legs all pins and needles, so that she could hardly climb the stone steps at the back, clinging to the iron railing with her mittened hand, staring at the chimney pots and roof-tops when she reached the second landing, a height that frightened her when she looked through the bars. But it was awfully grand inside, just as Helen had told her it would be, still as spick and span as ever, even though Doris was married and away and Susan was left on her own. Herbert was in his undervest, shaving at the washstand behind the door, his face smeared with white fine-smelling soap, while he whetted his razor on a brown leather strap. Herbert had been discharged from the army on medical grounds and was still thumping dough at Sangster's bakery in the High Street. Poor Frank's photograph stood on the sideboard, dressed in khaki, and though Ruth stared at it from time to time she had no idea who he really was, or that he had been her half-uncle.

Ruth stood by her mother's chair and bit her lip shyly, watching her grandmother laying the table for dinner, first with a white embroidered cloth with laced patterns all over it; then she laid out the plates, fancy plates with flowers on the rims, then knives and forks and spoons were laid between the plates, and a great glass vase of bronze and gold chrysanthemums was placed in the middle. When everybody was seated at table granddad Barbour said grace, like the morning prayer at school, then grandmother fixed a white cloth round Ruth's neck, lest she should spill her soup, and everybody behaved so perfectly that the bairn felt uneasy, afraid to open her mouth except to put the spoon in. But she was hungry and the soup was good; piping hot, so that she had to blow on her spoon, and there was boiled beef afterwards, with tatties and vegetables and mustard and sauce, then custard and fruit jelly and tea and shortbread. It was a grand dinner, Ruth thought, and she felt much better after it, and liked granny better, though she didn't have a doll or a toy in the house for Ruth to play with, even though she was an only grandchild. Oh she sottered over Ruth for a bit, but on the whole she hadn't much time for bairns and liked to keep them in their place, which was mostly at the foot of the table or out of sight, and they should never be heard unless spoken to and should never speak at all when their elders were talking.

Most of the afternoon, while the big folk blethered, Ruth stood before the fire with her little hands behind her back, staring at the dance of the flames in the grate, peering through the fireguard at the polished irons on the steel fender, gleaming in the warm firelight; then up at the mantelshelf, hung with pale green tapestry, frilled at the edges, and crowded with ornaments and two white porcelain dogs staring down at her with eyes like amber beads and gold chains about their necks. There was a marble clock in the middle, with strange figures that Ruth couldn't read, and pillars at the side of it like a small Grecian temple. Above all was a painting of Napoleon after Waterloo, where the great general stood bare-headed amidst the carnage of battle, his arm inside his greatcoat, his eyes on the ground, the last of his cavalry fleeing in the distance and the living pillaging the dead. The picture absorbed Ruth for nearly an hour, staring up at it with her wide blue eyes and the long dark lashes that swept them like a sleeping doll. And the fine sturdy knees of her, dimpled deeply at the back when her stockings were down, long black worsted stockings that Helen had knitted, held up with elastic garters under her knee-length skirt, blue with kilted pleats and a white blouse of spun cotton. A young growing quine beginning to take stock of her elders, watching their every move in the by going and listening to the tittle-tattle of their conversation.

But there was little for Ruth at Toddlebrae, nothing but respectability, which she didn't understand, and the fear of making a mess, so that she asked Helen to take her to the loo, where the rush of water frightened her when Helen pulled the chain. Ruth had much rather been at Bogmyrtle, where she could play at hoosies with Little Janet, gathering all the broken lames and china that Rachael had thrown out of the house; broken plates and cups and saucers in lovely floral patterns, all the colours you could imagine, that the quines used as crockery, with orange boxes for cupboards and their dolls cradled in an old shoe. Even Meston had a gird to run about with and he wasn't above giving Ruth a shoud on his rocking horse. And there was the rabbits and the pigs and the hens, the cats and the pigeons, and even Floss gave you a paw if you asked properly, or snapped a crust of bread when you threw it up in the air.

Uncle Herbert didn't smoke, you could see that, but uncle Riach did, and gave you his cigarette cards, with all those lovely pictures on them, and so did uncle Hamish if you asked him.

Ruth was just about wearied to death with all their chatter, and not even a cat to stroke or a book to look at, when old Joseph Barbour noticed the child's dejection and took her on his knee and showed her his wonderful post-card album. Oh but this was different, grandfather Mac-Kinnon never took you on his knee, only Little Janet had that privilege, even though she was your auntie and not much bigger than you. But it was wonderful sitting on granddad Barbour's knee, looking at all those lovely post-cards with the tartan edges, pictures of all the different places, great cities like Venice and Paris and London, even though you had no idea where these places were, because Miss Drone hadn't shown you on the map yet; the big canvas map that hung on the classroom wall. And all those lovely animals from the zoos and menageries, some of them in colour and those fine ladies in their lovely dresses, page after page as granddad turned them over; and you had the good sense never to touch them, apart from pointing with your finger, you just looked and looked and asked questions.

But you were too heavy for granddad's knee, for you were a bigger quine than he thought, and he let you slide down on your feet, where you stood between his legs watching all the on go; grandma making tea and Helen and Susan newsing and uncle Herbert and your father going at it hammer and tongs. Then granddad let you listen to his watch ticking, a big one like your dad's that he kept in his waistcoat pocket, tethered with a long silver chain, and when he lit his fancy pipe he let you blow out his match, and the smell of the smoke was sweet enough to swallow. It was cosy and warm and you didn't want to move, but now the big folks had finished their tea with the fancy cakes and it was your turn, so you sat down with granddad at the table and had your tea and then Helen put on your coat and a scarf about your head and you had to get down the back stairs again, just when you was beginning to like it, and your father set you on the bar again and jumped on after you and you waved good-bye to the Barbours as you sped down the Toddlebrae out of the town.

Long Dod Watt couldn't manage the oil-engine at Millbrae. Isobel Mathers began to see his shortcomings before he had been long in her service, especially on threshing days when he couldn't get the engine started. Audie knew all about the engine. He had watched Drew Strachan starting the thing for six years, and had sometimes started it himself when Drew was off work, but it wasn't his regular job and he didn't want to interfere, just stood by and watched while Long Dod fumbled and peched and spat and swore and couldn't get a hoast out of it – or if he did it was a back-fire and the fly-wheels spun the wrong way. He either had the blow lamp too hot or too low to time an explosion in the piston chamber. Isobel got concerned one day and came running over the close in her long frock to the engine hoose to see what was wrong. The kitchiedeem gave the men a hand in the barn on threshing days, forking up sheaves to Long Dod on the feeding bench, while Audie as cattleman took away the threshed straw from the shakers at the tail end of the mill, stacking it against the back wall of the barn. Isobel wondered why the quine was always so late in coming back to her housework, maybe thinking she was having a rumble-tumble in the straw with Audie or Long Dod, though she had little cause to worry in that respect – yet she wondered what could be hindering the quine.

Now as ill luck would have it, on the day that Isobel was in the greasy engine-hoose with her long frock Dod Watt got the engine started first crank, barking away with a steady chook-chook – chook-chook, and the great flywheels spinning smoothly, when Isobel's frock got tangled with the axle, dragging her ever nearer the murderous wheels, while she skirled in fear and Long Dod stood dumbfounded, for he couldn't remember how to stop the engine. The axle-rod ripped away the skirt part of Isobel's fancy frock, and then her pink petticoat, stripping her to the knickers, and soon would have mangled her to death or disablement, for it was strong material and wouldn't let go, but for Audie's swift action in stopping the engine. He had saved the life of his mistress while Long Dod stood abashed and scared to the roots of his hair. Isobel was angry and frightened, embarrassed and ashamed; standing there in front of the men, trembling in her bloomers, all mixed up in her feelings, while the kitchiedeem glowered in at the door. Isobel called Long Dod all the ill-names under the sun, or all the ones she could think of in her anger, hardly leaving him with the character of a mongrel dog, with a swear word thrown in here and there, the kind of language you'd never expect to hear from the likes of Isobel Mathers, the genteel mistress of Millbrae, her that bought and sold most of her own cattle at the marts, and was on speaking terms with most of the gentry, and even with the Laird himself; and if she hadn't gotten a lad folk would tell you it hadn't been for the want of trying. But here was Isobel, standing there in front of the men in her half frock and knickers, with long stockings up to her shapely thighs, and fancy garters holding them up, like a half plucked hen escaped from the knacker's yard, ranting and waving her arms, while Long Dod and Audie stared at her up and down, until she ran to the house to cover her nakedness.

But Isobel was grateful to Audie for saving her life. After she had come to herself again and got over her fright she dressed herself in a different frock and went over to the byre when the lanterns were lit and thanked Audie for his pains. She had a fine smell of scent about her, Audie thought, maybe because she didn't like the smell of the byre, and a braw chain about her neck, and little gold rings that dangled under her ears, her hair done up like cart wheels on the sides of her head. She told Audie that henceforth he would have charge of the engine, no matter what Long Dod said (though she called him Mr Watt to Audie) after all she was the mistress about the place and if Long Dod didn't like it that way he could leave. She admitted that a bargain was a bargain and that a body should hold by it, but Long Dod wasn't capable of the work he had taken in hand and she wasn't going to stand for it any longer. The one thing she forgot was to offer Audie a pound or two more to his wages for the extra work involved, but Audie insisted that she tell Long Dod herself about the new arrangements.

For a whole year after this Audie enjoyed the sunshine of Isobel's smile, the waft of her perfume and the glint of her beads, her hair all dolled up like a princess and even high heels on her shoes, out with cups of tea and home-made shortbread on the sly, treating Audie like a Lord while Long Dod chauved and slaved in the neep park in his wall-tams, over the queets in dubs, the rain pelting down, driving home neeps for Audie's nowt. Many a time he never spoke to Audie, fair mad with jealousy, just mucked out his stable at evening and fed his horses, then grabbed his milk flaggon from the kitchie door and through the park to the cottar house with his long strides, a spring in his foot that made him look taller than he was, walking on his toes almost, while Audie followed him like a wounded dog, never a word between them.

But Audie never heeded him; what with Isobel on his side he didn't have to, though he knew fine what was irking Long Dod. Audie never had it so good in his life before; running the place almost and nobody giving him orders at yoking time, his own master you might say, though he never abused the privilege, and he had been as long at Millbrae he knew the run of the place and the things that had to be done in season, like fencing in spring and cleaning out watering places before the cattle went out to grass from the byres. He still dug the garden for Isobel and planted all her tatties and vegetables, cleaned out her poultry houses and swept her chimneys while she stood over him with her trays of shortbread and cups of sweetened tea, her love-sick smile cloying at his insides, and the scent of her nearly charming Audie out of his wits. Audie was full of praise for his mistress, until Helen began to wonder if there was anything between them, a little smart of jealousy arousing her suspicion, until she snapped at Audie and he learned to praise in silence. In the years to come Audie was to remember Isobel as the one real Goddess in his drab life, under whose wings he could have sheltered for life, safe in her protection from the wicked world: far too wicked for the gentle, unsuspecting Audie, with his little outbursts of childish temper that proved his undoing, but was no real match for the scheming nature of his fellow man.

Audie might have known something was in the wind when Long Dod started speaking to him again, coy and sly as any fox, but Audie was always anxious to be friends and never saw any harm in anybody. People liked Audie for his condescending ways, though they mostly called it 'obliging ways', and Long Dod wasn't slow to butter him up to suit his purpose. He had a subtle brain, the lad, and for a long time he had been quietly scheming how to put Audie out of favour with his mistress. First he thought that a story about him taking up with her would have most effect, depending on who he told it to, but thought it might back-fire and harm himself. Back-fire gave him the idea and he thought of the engine, now Audie's pride and joy; the very weapon that had enthroned Audie could now be used to unsaddle him. What's more, no need to tell the story to anybody but Audie himself, and Audie would believe it without question. Long Dod was sure of it if he was any judge at all of human nature.

So Long Dod whispered in Audie's ear that he had heard that his mistress was complaining to folk out by, that he was using too much paraffin for his engine and causing a lot of expense, besides spending far too much time polishing the thing, when he should be in the neep park or doing something more useful about the place, like draining and ditching and the like. Now Audie knew himself that he spent a lot of time cleaning and polishing his engine, just as he did with his own bicycle, and he took as much care of Isobel's engine as he did of his own watch or his gramophone. Audie knew this was true, but thought he was only doing his duty, after the mess Long Dod had left it in, and remembering the sparkle in Isobel's eye after he had cleaned it up, polishing all the clear parts that were going to rust, besides gathering up all the greasy sacks that were lying about and spreading sand on the floor in case of fire. Audie never suspected that his mistress was grudging him the time to look after her own or that she thought he would be better employed in the neep park helping Dod Watt, or biggin' up dykes between the fields. As for grudging the paraffin, Audie was real surprised, chewing it over for days in his mind and sometimes in his bed at night, tossing and turning at the thought of it, until Helen asked what ailed him, because Audie had never missed an hour of sleep since she had known him, and always rose in the morning refreshed for the day. Even in the darkest days of the war Audie had never missed a snore, and now here he was tumbling about in the bed like a sow at the pigging, and springing up with a shout and a start that frightened Helen. So Audie told Helen Long Dod's story, and that maybe his time wouldn't be long at Millbrae, seeing his mistress was tiring of him and was so ill to please. But even Helen never suspected Long Dod's treachery and said she thought Isobel had a damned cheek to say that about her man after he had served her so long and faithfully. So, with Helen fanning the flame that Dod Watt kindled, Audie worked himself into one of his childish tantrums and flew at his mistress like a snarling dog and fair disgraced himself in her high regard for him. Poor Audie, better that he had never risen that day, throwing away his privileges in a passionate outburst, snapping at the hand that fed him, stamping and cursing like one demented, swearing at the offended Isobel, who was shocked and surprised to hear it. Yet she denied his story and refused to have any part in it, beyond having it out with Long Dod where it came from. But Audie was so worked up he never waited for this but gave up his job on the instant, shouting at Isobel that he would be leaving at the May Term and she could get any bugger she pleased to work her engine.

So that was that, and after Audie had it out with his mistress he went ranting down to his thatched cottage and sprang into the little kitchen like a wild bear, telling Helen to 'pack the crockery, wuman, we'll be leavin' at the Term,' barking it out like a distempered dog, then turned on his heel and left, clashing the door behind him.

Helen was stunned for a moment and sat down to think about it, little Ruth at her knee, for it was a Saturday and she was not at school. After all, it had been their home for nearly eight years and she would miss the little cottage with its garden out front and hen-run at the back, and she looked round the small kitchen with its memories that came crowding back, even to the birth of Ruth; and to give it all up so suddenly, just like that. But maybe Audie was justified, for he had gotten little thanks for his honest work over all these years, and she thought less of Isobel for her ingratitude, and for saying such things about her man.

The following weekend Helen got busy with the crockery, packing it into boxes she had gotten from the grocery van. Ruth gave her a hand, dusting all the ornaments while her mother wrapped them in newspapers and packed them into the wooden boxes. Ruth was clearing the mantelshelf, standing on the fender to reach for the knick-knacks when a flip of her duster brought down the five cartridge shells Helen had gotten from Hamish when he came from the war. The cartridges fell out of their slide and clattered on to the steel fender Ruth was standing on, two of them detonating on the sharp edge of the ironwork. There was a terrific bang, while one of the bullets went through the roof and the other pierced the lobby door. Helen got the fright of her life and the bells rang in her ears while her nostrils filled with the acrid smell of cordite and gun-powder. Apart from the sudden scare, Ruth was too young to understand the danger, and her ignorance saved her from fear. She could have been shot through the belly or any place, because the bullets exploded between her legs. Helen took her in her oxter and hugged her close, thankful to God that her quine had been spared, for either of them could have suffered death on the instant. Helen examined the hole in the lobby door, and from where she stood at the moment of the explosion she hadn't been far from the path of the bullet. Ruth pointed at the hole in the roof and Helen picked up the two spent shells from the kitchen floor. She searched under the furniture for the three remaining cartridges, still live in their brass slide, and she bundled the lot in a duster and laid them safely away in one of the drawers of the dresser.

Helen never knew the cartridges were loaded, never

dreamed of such a thing; she thought they were merely empty shells that Hamish had given her as an ornament, perhaps to remind her that he had been in the war. But he should have had more sense than to leave her with loaded cartridges that could have killed any of them. What if they had fallen in the fire and exploded? Then she thought it was maybe Hamish's way of taking revenge for that shot she had fired over their heads to save Audie. But surely he would have forgotten about that by this time, or at least forgiven the incident. After all, it was done in self defence. So that very night Helen set off on her bicycle to Bogmyrtle to have it out with Hamish for trying to kill her and the bairn.

But she didn't see Hamish, for he was now working in a grain store in Brochan, and Rachael said he wouldn't be home or the Sunday morning, 'cause he was biding in digs, and most likely would be out having a drink for the evening; but she would tell him about the cartridges as soon as he got back.

So Hamish went down to Millbrae on the Sunday afternoon and took the powder out of the three remaining cartridges with his pen-knife. But he swore to Helen that he thought they were empty and harmless, and said he would never have left them with her if he had known they were still loaded. After he had pacified Helen and got his tea, he gave Audie a fag to put in his mouthpiece and speired gin he had gotten a job? Audie said he hadn't, not yet anyway; so Hamish said he had heard that Candy Birnie of Sauchieburn was looking for a cattleman, and because it was getting gie near the Term maybe Audie should try it.

On the Monday night Audie did just that, and went hop-step-and-leap over his saddle on to his push-bike, bound for Sauchieburn. Audie never asked Isobel for a reference and Candy Birnie fee-ed him without it, just asked him some questions about his wark; like how many nowt he looked after and how long he had been at Millbrae? When Audie told him eight years come the Term he was well satisfied and said it was a reference in itself. Audie told him the truth why he was leaving, putting all the blame on Isobel and never mentioning Dod Watt, because even yet Audie never suspected him. Candy Birnie gave Audie a fair wage and the usual amenities and said he would send two horse-carts for his furniture on the Term Day, and that if he liked Audie could go in by and have a look at the cottar house on his way home.

Audie never looked in by the cottar house because he wanted to be home before dark, but he told Helen it was close by the main road and had a slated roof and that Ruth wouldn't have far to go to the school because it was just down the brae from the farm. Helen said she knew the place fine but never thought she would bide there sometime and that it was just about two miles from her father's place. Audie said he hadn't been inside the house yet to see what it was like, because he didn't want to bother the woman so late in the evening; but maybe she would take him inside to see the rooms another time: some evening when he went back to plant a few tatties in the gairden. In any case he assured Helen that she wouldn't 'think lang', at Sauchie-burn, what with all that motor traffic going past the door.

On the eve of the flitting it rained. Helen had everything packed and the floors scrubbed out, the pictures down from the walls and the curtains from the windows. The iron bedstead with the brass knobs had been dismantled in the room and laid against the wall, the blankets and sheets folded and bundled into Audie's chaumer kist and meal girnal. The bedding had also been removed from the box bed and laid out on the floor as a shakie-doon, where Audie and Helen slept the night, with Ruth at their feet ready to jump at the first cock-crow, or the sound of horses hooves in the morning. The fireside had been cleaned for the last time and the ash removed. A few kindlers to boil the kettle in the morning was all that was required. Everything had been packed but the tea caddy, a few cups, a teaspoon, a butterknife and a jar of jam. Sugar could be spooned out of a paper bag and the loaf and biscuits were in a tin. Audie had even buried Napoleon deep in the gairden for the last time, which was the cottar's way of saying he had emptied the privy pail in a deep hole, and covered it up with earth so that the new tenant couldn't say they weren't respectable

When morning came it was still raining, streaming down from the thatch and running into puddles in the close. Two horse-carts arrived out of the cold grey mist at Millbrae, two mighty Clydesdales with the smell of polished harness about them and harvest frames on the carts, a bundle of straw to pack the furniture, old sacks and ropes. Everything was carried out in the rain and Audie handed up chairs and the iron bed-ends to the foreman on the cart, who was biding on at Sauchieburn and wouldn't have to flit this Term. It took both of them to lift the heavier stuff on to the carts, the massive mahogany sideboard, the dresser and the chest of drawers, the wardrobe and the gate-legged table, Audie's kist and the meal girnal. Helen carried out pots and pans and crammed them into every space she could find among the furniture, and all the time nagging at the foreman about the placing of this and that on the carts; and the man could see that she wore the breeks, and he wouldn't have stood half so much from his own wife.

'My pot flooers are in the washtubs,' she cried up to the man, 'put them on the back of the second cairt; if ye put them on the first cairt the second horse will eat them.' Her face was wet with the rain and it hung about her hair in liquid beads of morning silver.

The man said, 'Oh aye, gin he has a fancy for geraniums,' but felt like telling Helen it wasn't the first flitting he'd done and that he knew his job fine without her telling him.

The hens had been fastened into coops the night before, bedraggled and miserable looking, with an egg or two rolling about their dirty feet, seeing there wasn't a nest to lay in. The cat had a small coop all to herself, where she crouched with large scared eyes, ready to spring for freedom at the first opportunity.

'The hens wad scare the second horse if ye put them on the first cairt,' Helen cried to the foreman, while Audie twisted the rain out of his cap.

'Oh aye,' the foreman said, trying to humour her, 'he's fear't at his ain shadow as it is. He wunna see his shadaw the day, for want o' the sun, but I suppose he wad be scared tae death o' a clockin' hen. Gweed kens what'll happen gin we

meet ane o' Jammie Salter's traction engines – Lord help ye
furniture, lass; it wad a' be knocked tae bits.'

Long Dod's wife came running down the close with a
towel over her head, splashing through the rain in unlaced
shoes. She put a sixpence in Ruth's little palm and said that
would be something for her Turra Coo bank.

'Ta ta,' she cried, 'Ta ta, Mrs Foubister, ye're gettin' a
terrible day tae flit. Ta ta,' she cried again, this time to
Audie, who bore her no ill-will, no more than Helen did,
for she had been good enough as a neighbour. The woman
closed the towel over her face again and ran up the close
splashing through the muddy pools.

When everything had been loaded and roped on to the
carts the foreman and Audie took a horse each by the rein
and walked beside the carts. It was too wet and cold to sit
on the carts so Helen walked behind with Ruth by the hand.
Her little face was chilled blue with the cold and her shoes
sapped through. By the time the flitting reached Sauchieburn everything was soaked; the chaff mattresses sodden,
the bread in the baskets all gone to sops. But the foreman's
wife had lit a fire in the empty house and Ruth stood by it
and warmed her hands and steamed herself dry. When all
the furniture had been carried inside Audie had to go to the
farm steading for four sacks of dry chaff to fill the mattresses,
and he had to yoke a horse-cart to drive them down to the
house. The rain ceased in the evening and a red sky closed
the day. A lorry driver stopped for water to put in his
radiator and he left a fry of kippers. Audie thought this was
great, for you never got kippers at Millbrae, and the house
smelled strongly of frying kippers for tea. Ruth had to get
on a chair to climb on to the new-filled chaff bed, and they
all slept together again for there was no box-bed at Sauchieburn.

Next morning the sun shone out of a clean washed sky
and the slopes of the Mattock Hill came barren out of the
mist. You couldn't see the Mattock Hill from Millbrae, but
here at Sauchieburn it rose sharp and clear against the
dappled sky, the white deer on its shoulder of bleached
stones with antlers spiked out on the purple heather. You

could even see the blue thread of peat smoke rising from the chimneys at Bogmyrtle, the red barn roofs in a smudge of green trees, the parks rising to the hill in a gentle slope. The surrounding country was flat and dotted with farmsteads and belts of trees, with a glimmer of sea on the far bents at the Myreloch.

Audie had the day off before he started work at Sauchieburn, so after they had set the furniture in order Helen suggested they go into Brochan with the train and buy a new bed, one of those with the brass rails and knobs that were all the fashion nowadays. Next day, when the new bed arrived with the carrier, Helen set it up in the ben-room, with wooden blocks under the wheel-castors to save the linoleum, and a new quilt over it she had bought in the toon. Here she now slept with Ruth, while Audie slept alone in the kitchen, making the excuse that Ruth was afraid to sleep in the new room herself and that she was getting too big to sleep at their feet. If Audie suspected her proper reason he didn't say anything, but it was the beginnings of their estrangement, a cold stab for Audie that was ill to cope with in his new surroundings; a coldness that deepened with the weeks and months, punctuated with embittered quarrels and bickering, until Audie learned to bear in silence, to endure with patience, where his little outbursts of temper were of no avail. This was something too big for him; something he never really understood from Helen's point of view, except that it made him feel useless and inferior, only half a man. His big rupture was to blame for it, like a huge teapot with a little spout, so that he couldn't get near Helen and it put her off. Yet he was afraid to have anything done about it and it gave him no physical pain. It was something his mother or his granny should have seen about when he was a bairn; something he had grown up with and got accustomed to; not until he married did he find it an encumbrance, and now it embarrassed him beyond endurance. Maybe in time he would have to pluck up courage and do something about it, if it wasn't too late. But would Helen give him time to make up his mind about it before it wrecked their marriage. It looked like she had taken the first step already, sleeping with Ruth in the ben-room. She had called him a coward as it was and he knew he was scared to death of doctors: the very thought of seeing a doctor worried him and stuck in his mind like a burr. He had never had a doctor in his conscious memory and he would put up with purgatory rather than have a tooth pulled. Helen said that if he was a woman having a bairn he would have to face things, and so they argued on . . .

Ruth went to the little school at Rashiehowe, about a mile from Sauchieburn, where the MacKinnon bairns also got their schooling, and Meston and Little Janet called in by for her every morning. Helen had to buy books for her as they were all different from what they had been at Leary school. But there was coup-the-ladle over the quarry rail, and when the bigger loons and quines would let them play, Ruth and Janet got a tilt on the board. They also went in search of tadpoles in the Sauchie Burn, just under the farm, where the water was slow and deeper and covered with chickweed. It was better if you got the frogs' eggs, of course – floating in jelly, little black dots like sago pudding – for then you could watch the eggs grow tails and hatch into tadpoles that darted through the chickweed in your jar. But it was too late in the season for this, and Ruth was content to scoop up a few tadpoles in her jar that she took home and set them on the window-sill facing the sun. She gave them fresh water every second day and a sprig of chickweed from the ditch. During the summer she watched the tadpoles grow legs and turn into frogs, and one by one she had to topple them back into the Sauchie Burn. At the weekends Ruth took her mother's bicycle out of the back shed and learned herself to run it on the turnpike, just managing to reach the saddle when free-wheeling, the tips of her toes on the pedals.

Several times Ruth had been to church at Newpirn, about two miles from Sauchieburn, the big house where God lived without a fireplace, and He must be terribly cold, Ruth thought, and He only had visitors on a Sunday, and He rang a bell on the roof to let everybody know when to come and see Him. Her dad was all dressed up on these occasions, with his best suit out of the wardrobe with the mirror on the door, besides his Sunday boots with the eyelet lacing and a white hankie in his breast pocket, his hair brushed flat and shining under his cap. Mother was also dressed up to the nines with her veil and gloves on her hands and carried a Bible and always took a long time to dress; and Ruth and her father could hardly wait for her at the door to get it locked. Ruth was also dolled up and had her hair washed and fixed with slides and a pink ribbon, besides her best frock and a new coat and shoes that were fastened with a button-hook. All three walked the two miles to Newpirn in case they creased their fine clothes on the bicycles, but sometimes Ruth went hop-step-and-leap in front of her parents, or hopped on one leg and kicked a pebble, like playing at 'Beddies', until Helen called her back for spoiling her shoes.

When they got to the church everybody sat very quiet and an organ played sweet music, though Ruth could never quite make out where it was coming from, because she couldn't see anybody playing, so she thought it must be the angels playing their harps and maybe you wasn't supposed to see them. God didn't have pictures on the walls but had them painted on the windows, so that the sun lighted them up from outside, beautifully coloured pictures of saints and shepherds with lambs on green hills, even better than 'The Real Angel Of Mons', that now hung on the room wall at Sauchieburn. The minister appeared in a black frock and went up the steps where a man shut him into a pen, where he sat down almost out of sight, then stood up again and told everybody to pray. When this was done and everybody was coughing, Ruth asked her mother if that was God?

'No, you silly, that was the minister,' Helen told her.

'Then where's God?' Ruth asked in a whisper; 'Where does He bide?'

'Up in the sky,' Helen answered her, rather sharply, and told her to be quiet.

Eveybody was now standing up and singing loudly with open Bibles in their hands and it seemed to Ruth that all the big folk were back at school again, and she wondered if any of them would get the strap from the minister, like Mr Jack used to strap the big boys at Leary when they did anything wrong. But nobody got the strap and everybody sat down again and the minister told a long story about a boy called David who killed a wicked giant with a stone in a sling, and Ruth thought it was the best story she had heard since she was with Miss Drone at Leary. Poor Miss Drone, but she was not to be seen in God's house with the big windows; maybe it was too cold for her without a fireplace, because Miss Drone always liked a good fire in the grate at Leary school.

When everybody had stopped coughing and clearing their throats again the minister said, 'Next Sunday being Palm Sunday, we hope there will be a large attendance, when children of the chirch will be baptized at both ends . . . of the chirch!' There was more singing and Ruth's bum was beginning to get sore on the hard seat and she wanted to stand all the time until Helen pulled her down. On the way home Ruth was searching the sky and asking why they hadn't seen God? Helen said He was invisible: that He was a spirit and you couldn't see Him, though He could see you and you had to be very good not to offend Him.

Then Ruth remembered the other churches she had seen, especially in Brochan where there were quite a few, with huge spires on their roofs; and she wondered how God could have so many grand houses, or how He could be in them all at the same time; always on Sundays, and you never heard of Him during the week, except when somebody swore about Him or the teacher mentioned Him at school. It was all so very puzzling that Ruth was home before she realized it, trying to solve the problems of God. She remembered it all through the hot dinner, blowing on the spoon like her father, and even when Helen took off her fine claes and hung them in the wardrobe again, besides her own and father's, though she left the ribbon in Ruth's hair when she went outside to skip with the girl next door, who hadn't been to church looking for God.

As Audie had said, Helen's new home had a slated roof and stood close by the main road from Brochan to Aberdeen, where the motor lorries with solid tyres went tearing by the windows, loaded with herring in barrels for the south markets. The two cottages were shaped like the letter L, and Helen and Audie lived in the front part, while the foreman and his family occupied the tail-end of the letter, furthest from the road. Their doors opened on to the backyard, in two halves, like the doors of a farm stable, and fastened with a sneck. Out back were the coalsheds and the two privies, one for each cottar, dry lavvies with a pail, an ashpit between them, a hen-run and clothes green for each and a kailyard, while the Sauchie Burn ran under the road and splashed along in front of the foreman's windows, with boor-trees and willows leaning over the banks. Both cottars carried thier water from a pump at the roadside.

Being so much nearer Bogmyrtle Helen went more often to see her folks than she did at Millbrae. It was like old times for her and she felt like a young quine again, but with a new freedom − free from her father's old tyranny − and could come and go as she pleased. Two of her sisters were at home again, Nancy and Nora, helping Kirsteen in the vegetable plots; for Craig had extended his acreage and had ploughed in part of a field to grow more. He had a daily round with the springcart in Brochan, where Riach sold fruit and vegetables to the fisher wives, while Kirsteen sold the flowers, cut or potted, whichever they wanted. It was a thriving business and kept all the MacKinnons busy, what with attending to the greenhouses; and the ordinary farm work always to hand, summer and winter.

So Helen was back in the fold at Bogmyrtle, where the evenings were pleasant in the company of her family, a sort of escape from the boredom of cottar life, alone every day in the house since Ruth went to school. Sometimes Moira was at Bogmyrtle with her man, Sherran Begg, him that was wounded at Passchendaele; half libbed he was and had one of his testicles taken away, but none the worse for it and had managed to make three or four bairns with Moira in as many years; cousins to Ruth but not a bit like her and far less refined. Sherran Begg worked as an undertaker in Brochan, and just after the war he had worked half the night making coffins for all the folk who had died of the 'flu. Audie never liked him because he was further in with old Craig than he was, bragging and blowing about his work and the things he could do, while Audie sat quiet as a mouse listening to his blab. But Sherran could sing brawly and recite poetry, and he kept the house lively and liked a laugh and a feel at the quines, while Audie would have fallen asleep, fagged out from his work in the byres and the neep park.

Nora and Nancy had lads too, and Kirsteen had several, so there was sometimes quite a gathering in the old farmhouse, especially when Hamish came home from his digs on his motor bike, with a quine on the back pillion; Cora Swapp they called her, and he seemed to have forgotten all about Muriel Spark. Cora's widowed mother had a bit croft over the road from Bogmyrtle, near the Mattock Hill, and it was rumoured that if Hamish married her Cora, he would most likely get the croft when the old woman died, or maybe sooner than that if he could put up with the two of them in the same house. Craig had promised all the help he could give, and would set him up with a two-wheeled lorry and a shelt in the vegetable trade, for there was room for both of them in Brochan, he said.

Audie could snore in his chair if he liked nowadays when Helen went to Bogmyrtle, because Ruth could play the gramophone herself in the evenings. She had developed a strong taste for Harry Lauder and Jock Lorrimer, the two Scottish comedians with their lilting songs, besides Peter Wyper on the melodion and Scott Skinner on the fiddle; and from time to time Helen bought her a new record when she went to Brochan to keep her amused.

Helen arrived at Bogmyrtle one Saturday evening just before dark, when who should be standing in the close but Meldrum Spark, holding a shelt by the bridle, while her father lifted its fetlocks and walked around sizing up the animal, and Hamish and Riach stood smoking their fags and nodding their heads in low voiced conversation. Helen stared at Meldrum with her wide clear eyes as she laid her bicycle against the milkhouse wall. Was it possible, Helen wondered, that this was the man who had tried to kill her father with a stone, or at least to maim him, and that what some of them had done to his sister had justified his attempt at such revenge; a vengeance he had once tried on herself, with remarkable consequences, because she had fallen in love with him. But none of them knew her secret, none but Meldrum himself; and if anyone had forgiven anything surely it was him. He was in the camp of his enemies, or so it seemed to Helen, yet perfectly at his ease in their midst; trying to sell her father a shelt, and by the looks of Craig's approval he was likely to succeed. Even though the whole parish whispered of what the MacKinnons did to Muriel Spark, most likely the MacKinnons would be the last to hear of it. Even Hamish never suspected it and Helen never told him. Yet Helen only had to step forward and point at Meldrum Spark as the man who threw the stone through the window to set them at each other's throats, and devil take the shelt. The thought crossed Helen's mind but she never entertained it; rather sought the glance of her lover as he stood there clapping the shelt, stroking his hand over the velvet gloss of its coat, the first time she had ever seen him in the full light of day. Was it possible that she had fallen in love with a man in the dark? without ever seeing his face? – remembering only the thrust of his penis and the thrill it gave her? No no, that couldn't be, for now in the full light of heaven she could see she was not disappointed: He was everything she had hoped for or imagined he would be: big strong and handsome, and a heart-melting smile about him that fair cloyed at your insides – smiling across at her now, while she smiled back, coy as a maiden, her heart all a-flutter at the sight of him. Helen could hardly believe that this man had been a deserter, for he looked the bravest man she had ever seen, and his very presence at Bogmyrtle strengthened her belief. Anyway, the army officers hadn't shot him for it and she was thankful for that. Maybe he was just out of prison and trying to sell his mither's shelt? – and then he would skidaddle with the money.

Helen didn't like the look of the shelt anyway: it had a

white ring in one of its eyes and its ears lay flat on its head
like it had an ill-temper, but was sturdy and well-bred for
all that, and apparently her father was pleased with it. He
knew more about horses than she would ever learn and her
minor criticism would count for nothing though she
mentioned it. Her father would soon put her in her place if
she interfered, yet instinct told her she didn't like the shelt
and that no good would come of its purchase. Anyway she
was too late, for Meldrum took a half-bottle of whisky from
his hip pocket, whipped out the cork and handed the bottle
to Craig. Apparently the deal had been completed and they
were sealing it with a dram. The old man ran the whisky
down his throat and handed back the bottle, wiping his
moustache. Hamish then had a swig and handed the bottle
to Riach, who tilted it up in his twisted mouth, gurgling
down the contents. Then all three burst out laughing when
Meldrum offered the bottle to Helen. Timidly she came over
the close and took it out of his hand, drank one mouthful and
handed it back, merely to share in their celebration, though
the stuff nearly made her splutter. But she laughed in the
sunshine of the moment, her blue eyes sparkling and her
moist red lips wimpling over her white even teeth in a
friendly smile; the feminine smile that gladdens the heart of
brooding man. Meldrum took the last swig from the bottle
with her eyes upon him, searching his face for some response;
a strong face, harsh almost in its manliness, yet gentle and
reassuring, his big brown eyes honest and restful, his black
hair thick and curly over his ears and the back of his neck.
Helen glanced at the shelt and turned and left the menfolk,
to join her sisters at the kitchen door, Nancy and Nora,
crying everyone in for tea.

It was salt herring and peel-an'-ate tatties for supper, and
Rachael had a big steaming pot in the middle of the stone
floor, where everyone helped themselves to a herring on a
saucer, and a tattie from another pot on the ash brander,
tatties still with their skins on and with a special flavour,
and you skinned them yourself and ate them with your
boiled herring. Then it was oatcakes and home-made
cheese, scones and honey, and strong milkless tea to wash it

down. After supper the quines got busy on the dish-washing behind the kitchen door and the men enjoyed their fags and friendly banter. Sherran Begg wasn't there to sing that night and Riach wasn't in the mood for the pipes, so it was story-telling; and Meldrum took a penny from his pocket and passed it round the kitchen, first to Helen and then all the rest of the family, each one explaining to the other, 'This is the house that Jack built!' When the penny came back to Meldrum he passed it round again, with 'This is the malt that lay in the house that Jack built,' and the third time as 'This is the sack that held the malt that lay in the house that Jack built,' until you had the whole story to recite from memory, line by line, repeating the whole recitation every time the penny came round, until you had the whole story by heart:

'This is the Priest all shaven and shorn,
Who married the man all tattered and torn,
Unto the maiden all forlorn,
Who milked the cow with the crunkled horn,
That tossed the dog all over the barn,
That killed the cat,
That worried the rat,
That gnawed the string,
That tied the sack,
That held the malt,
That lay in the house that Jack built!'

Then came the story of the gamekeeper who had a dog, a rabbit and a cabbage, and he had to cross the river in a small boat, in which there was room for only one of them at a time, and you had to state in which order he made the crossing. Some tried the dog first, but Meldrum explained that if he did this the rabbit would eat the cabbage while he was away. Another tried the cabbage first, but again Meldrum said that while the gamekeeper was away with the cabbage the dog would make short work of the rabbit. Little Janet was clever and she would try the rabbit first, so there would be no fear of the dog eating the cabbage while the gamekeeper was away with the rabbit. 'Very good,' Meldrum said, 'and what next?' – because no matter what you took over the next trip one would eat the other on the opposite bank, while you went back for the third article. Either the dog would eat the rabbit you had brought over the first time, or the rabbit would eat the cabbage while you went back for the dog. So there seemed no way the gamekeeper could transport his game in safety, without loss; but what Meldrum hadn't told them was that he could take something back with him in the empty boat, which nobody had thought about, and it turned out that the gamekeeper was cleverer than any of them, because he took the rabbit over first and went back for the cabbage, then took the rabbit back over the river again and left it on the first bank, while he fetched the dog, then made a final crossing for the rabbit a second time, thus never leaving the dog alone with the rabbit or the rabbit with the cabbage.

Meldrum was full of these conundrums and all manner of card tricks, flipping cards from mid-air and down his sleeve faster than you could watch, and no matter which card you drew from the pack he could always tell the number of it, King, Queen, Knave or Joker. Then every-body joined in playing 'Old Maid', all except Craig, who sat mostly behind his newspaper, and Rachael contented herself looking over their shoulders. Now there was only one loser in 'Old Maid', which applied to either sex, and you was sent to the back of the kitchen door, where you stood with your hands over your ears, your face to the wall, while the victors whispered among themselves in selecting a partner for you in marriage, chosen from the whole parish; and it might be an old hag of the moors, or the tinker with his pack, even the Laird himself or the fairest lass in the Bogside. The conspirators chose the four Kings from the pack, or the four Queens, depending on the sex of the loser, and these were placed face downwards on the table, each one a different person known to the players. When their final decision was complete the culprit behind the door was called back to the table, where he or she had to decide what to do with each individual of the four cards on the table. You could do anything you liked with any three of the characters: burn them at the stake, drown them in the lake or whip them with barbed wire and pour salt in the wounds, even go to bed with them; but one you had to marry, choose blindly how you liked; and you weren't given the identity of the character until you had passed sentence. So you could sleep with the tink and dine and wine with the hag or drown the fair maiden; and lucky you were if you picked the right partner. But there was great fun anticipating what the loser would do with each individual character, and noting his or her reaction when the identity of their choice was revealed.

It so happened that Helen lost at 'Old Maid', and they sent her to the back of the door and Rachael watched that she didn't look or listen to what was going on at the table. Now you could stamp a card for any person present, which made it all the more fun, and Nora and Kirsteen chose Meldrum as a character for Helen, and as Meldrum didn't object the decision was unanimous. When Helen was called to the table she did frightful things to three of the characters; one of them she would stick his head in a rabbits' hole on his knees and drive a post between his legs, and when it turned out to be old Craig there was tremendous laughter, and the old man even crumpled his newspaper to join in it, though he said in fun that he thought his oldest quine would think more of him than that, and of course he knew the Blind Man's Buff of the game. Helen said she would tar and feather the Laird and put Audie in a barrel and roll him down the Mattock Hill. The irony of it: luck, fun or fate, call it what you like; but Helen was left with only one choice to marry, and that was Meldrum Spark. And there the laughter ends and our story really begins.

Part Two

The night was dark and a thin drizzle of mist seeped in the wind. Nearing midnight the folk began to depart, mostly in pairs, or twos and threes, disappearing into the darkness. Now it was Helen's turn, while she buttoned up her coat and put on her gloves, adjusted her hat and stuck the pins in it, and pushed her hair under the rim. Meldrum Spark set a match to her cycle lamp at the door, meaning to accompany her to the head of the avenue, and they walked out about together when they had said good-bye to the MacKinnon folk around the kitchen door.

But Meldrum Spark walked further than the end of the farm road with Helen MacKinnon, in fact she never got on her bike, and he walked the two miles with her all the way to her cottage door at Sauchieburn. They walked in darkness, save for the flutter of light from the cycle lamp, which showed them the verge of the road. They talked in whispers, each heart thumping with excitement in the presence of the other, anticipation and desire in their thoughts, until Meldrum put his hand over the lamp glass and kissed Helen in the darkness, a soft gentle kiss that she half expected and willingly gave. But that was all, and they talked of Meldrum's disgrace in the army, of his Court Martial and sentence to be shot by a firing-squad; a sentence later commuted to imprisonment, then acquittal after the war and his final discharge: all of which he disclosed shamelessly, and Helen could think what she liked of him; he merely wanted to be honest with her. After the war he had tried to make a living as a pedlar, and now things had got so bad he had been forced to sell his mither's shelt to pay their debts. He had the money in his pocket now, just as he had got it from Helen's father, and he said he would hand it over to his mother in the morning.

Helen wanted to know what he was going to do now, and

he said he didn't know. Why didn't he take a fee? Surely there were plenty of jobs for single men on the farms. He said he had never worked on the farms, and didn't know anything about the work, though he might try a navvy job on the railways, or breaking stones for road-making, but there wasn't much going in that line when so many other ex-service men were looking for work. Most likely he would just go back to hawking, but without the shelt and cart, and he would have to make do with a box on his bicycle, filled with all the knick-knacks that country folk would buy. Sometimes his mother had gone with him on the cart, collecting rags and selling dishes, but he would have to give up that side of the business now, and as his mother hadn't been so well lately, and not fit to stand up to the cold country journeys it didn't really matter.

The easy drawl of his quiet voice fascinated Helen, like a great cat purring in her lap, ready to spring at her in a frenzy of passion, quickening her pulses at the thought of it; holding her breath when he stopped on the road to listen to some ferlie, like a bird in the hedge or a weasel in the dyke, while the fine mist clung to them and the darkness shut them out from the prying world.

Meldrum Spark fought hard with himself, subduing the desire that rose within him, wary of how he would be received a second time, and determined to await better acquaintance. But his heart thumped in his throat in Helen's presence, and he was tempted to take the bike away from her and have it standing up by the roadside. But as each impulse seized him he thrust it aside with an iron will, determined to show her he could be a gentleman when he liked, and that he wasn't given to ravishing helpless women in the dark at every opportunity. Whatever his shortcomings he wanted to impress her with his good intentions, and maybe he would get his way with her later on. Helen was content to let him please himself, submitting to his kisses on the way, and the final embrace at her cottage door, with a promise to see her again. Maybe he would call with his box, he said, and maybe he could sell Audie a stick of shaving soap or a pair of bootlaces – assuring himself in silence that in this way he might get a foot in the door of the Foubister household, and a bit of fun in the by-going. A bit of flirtation was what he had in mind, surely there could be no harm in that with a MacKinnon quine, even though she was married, and when he had had his fling he would clear off to pastures new, and other cows that he fancied.

There were other times that Meldrum Spark saw Helen home, other times that he kissed her. Sometimes she made an excuse to Audie that she was going to Bogmyrtle, and then ran outside to the arms of her waiting lover. Eventually he came to the door with his wares in broad daylight, one day at noon when Audie was at his dinner. With cap in hand he found his way into the kitchen, where Helen beckoned him from behind the door, where Audie couldn't see, and he unslung his box from his shoulder and sat down on a hard chair by the fire. Helen pretended never to have seen him before, while the supposed stranger opened his box and displayed his trifles for sale. Audie was accustomed to the occasional pedlar in the house and thought nothing of it; indeed if it wasn't for the pedlars a body could hardly get a collar stud or a tie-pin or a shaving brush: shops were few and far between and your visits to the toon were mostly at the Terms or an odd holiday, so Audie was real interested in Meldrum's box, and he took keenly to the smell of moth balls and scented soap that came out of it when Meldrum opened the lid. He was greatly taken with the cut-throat razors that Meldrum showed him, each one stamped and engraved on the steel blade, made in Hamburg or Sheffield, and Meldrum pulled a hair out of his head and showed how it could be split with a flick of one of these open razors. Audie took the razor in his own hand, opened it and twitched the end of the blade with his thumb nail, so that he could hear the ring of it, then closed it again and slid it back in its case. So Audie had to have a new razor: 'Faith, wuman, ye ken the one I've got is finished, won't take the edge on the strop any more, and I've had it ground several times at Danny the Barber's in Brochan. Aye, I'll have one of your razors, lad, and a stick o' shavin' soap, that fine smellin' kind, and a pair o' bootlaces forbye. See what money ye've got, wuman; Twal and saxpence ye said for the razor, but ye'd let me have it for saven and saxpence?' Meldrum nodded agreement. 'Faith but that's a bargain. Ye're aye cryin' aboot safety preens, wuman, and there's hardly a kaim in the hoose, and ye could get a ribbon for Ruthie's hair.' Helen thought that Audie was going to buy the contents of Meldrum's box, and had to remind him that she wasn't made of money, while she went to the dresser drawer for her little black purse and paid Meldrum the money for what Audie wanted. He also fancied a scissors to cut Ruth's hair, even though he couldn't do it himself, but Helen had to tell him he would get that another time, and Meldrum assured him he would be back again some other day he was in the district. Audie then insisted that Meldrum get a plate of soup and a cup of tea with him before he left for work. After the soup and the tea Meldrum produced a packet of Woodbines and offered one to Audie, who fixed it in his mouthpiece from the mantelshelf and blew the smoke across the dinner table. Then it was time for him to go, and he went and got the flaggon for the milk from the washstand behind the door, while Meldrum shouldered his box and made off with him for the farm, in the hope of selling something to the farm wife, both saying 'Cheerio' to Helen where she stood, with her arms folded, in the kitchen door, the cat purring round her legs, the hens pecking in the close.

Now it was always a problem with Audie finding someone to cut his hair, and when Meldrum told him he was a dab hand at the job Audie insisted he should call some evening with his box and give him a haircut, any time he was passing with his bicycle; it wouldn't take long and maybe he would give the lassie's hair a snip in the bygoing, though the wife mostly did it hersel', though she wasn't much of a hand at it.

So the next time Meldrum called in by at Sauchieburn it was in the early evening, while it was still daylight; just in the passing, he said, and he had a new record with him for Audie's gramophone. No, he didn't want anything for it; it was just a present, he said, seeing he got his dinner and that, and while he snipped at Audie's brown hair with comb and scissors Ruth played it over on the gramophone, two fine Scots comedy songs by Jock Lorrimer, an up-and-coming comedian who was beginning to rival Harry Lauder in popularity. Next time Meldrum called he had a sleeping doll for Ruth, a wax beauty dressed in lace in a frilled box that won her over as soon as the doll opened its fringed blue eyes when she set it upright on the kitchen table. But Meldrum never brought a present for Helen, nor showed any interest in her while he was in the house, nor did Audie suspect that any interest existed. And Meldrum wouldn't have cut Helen's hair even though Audie had suggested it, for he would have considered it a sacrilege to touch it with anything other than loving fingers, the long black folds that fell to her waist when she let it down over her shoulders, a sable curtain that hid her face when she tilted her head to the sweep of the comb.

Meldrum developed such a respect for Audie, even friendship, that he hated deceiving him; indeed he would have given up his love for Helen and left the little household in peace, but that Helen encouraged him, enticed him, and wouldn't let him be. He said he felt ashamed to take advantage of such a simple soul as Audie: one of God's own bairns, he said, and it was like taking something away from a blind man. One night in the moonlight he begged Helen to give him up and he wouldn't come again, and she broke down in his arms and cried in the lithe of a whin bush. Her heart would break, she sobbed, if he left her now, for he had all her love and all her body, as much as she could offer to any man. But how long could it last? Meldrum argued. And there was little Ruth to consider – what would happen to her? Helen had no answer for this but she couldn't give him up. Couldn't they just go on as they were, seeing each other on the sly? Maybe no harm would come of it and nobody would be any the wiser. So Meldrum saw her home to the cottage door again, kissing her while the moon was behind a cloud, while Audie snored in the kitchen bed and Ruth slept in the ben-room, the doll in her oxter, and always wakening up when her mother came in from the cold. Two or three times she had slept with her father, especially when she woke up and her mother not in bed, but she couldn't stand the snoring and ran back to the ben-room and covered her head with the blankets.

But after three or four months of fervent intercourse Helen was pregnant. No longer would it be possible to keep their love a secret, though they had plotted and planned to make it so. Audie wasn't such a fool but he would know he wasn't the father, for he hadn't slept with his wife since he came to Sauchieburn. Several times he had tried her for intercourse, in spite of his hernia, but she had denied him and went to bed with Ruth in the ben-room. So Audie had to be content with masturbation, dreaming of her womanhood in the darkness of his lonely existence, or some other creature of his imagination, while the hot sperm sprang from his loins, all gone to waste on a dream. He sighed and fell asleep till morning, awakening with a sad thought in his mind that something was amiss in his life.

Audie never had an alarm clock, but always awakened at the appointed hour, lit the lamp and sat on the edge of the bed a minute, bewildered like, and scratched his head, wondering what it was all about. He pulled on his drawers and lit the fire and set the kettle on to boil for his brose. He put on the rest of his clothes and fastened his bootlaces, taking the lamp from the table and setting it on the floor to let him see, getting down on one knee and then the other to tie his laces and the wall-tams around his knees. He set the lamp on the table again and when the kettle came to the boil he made the tea, then mixed the oatmeal with a pinch of salt and pepper in a bowl and poured in the boiling water to make brose, not too much or too little, but just the right amount for supping, so that the cream floated on top, with a spoonful of sugar or treacle for sweetening. Helen had set aside a bowl of milk for him the night before and he skimmed the cream from it in the morning, then supped his brose quietly while the cat purred at his feet or clawed at his knee, her long tail in the air, reminding him to leave a little of his brose milk for her in a saucer by the lobby door, where she lapped it up with her pink tongue, like a little hinged spoon in her whiskered mouth.

There was a time when Audie took a cup of tea to his wife when she slept in the boxbed at Millbrae, just as Rachael had asked him to do when he sought her daughter's hand in marriage, but since they came to Sauchieburn and she slept in the ben-room he never looked near her, just drank his own tea in silence and chewed his slice of treacled loaf and threw a crumb to the cat, the only real friend he had in the world these days. Helen never looked ben to see if he were alive or dead, though she sometimes heard him scraping in the grate with the poker, or talking to himself or the cat, but she just took Ruth in her oxter and fell asleep again. And many a morning as Audie sat there smoking a fag in his holder he remembered Isobel, his old Mistress at Millbrae; how good she had been to him and gave him some pride in himself and his job, and he regretted that vile morning he had lost his temper and threw up his little cottage. And as he pieced the ends together he could see how Long Dod Watt had deceived him with his idle tales, and he wondered if Helen would have changed so much had he not listened to him and stayed far away from Sauchieburn, which was so much nearer the MacKinnon place and Helen living there till all hours of the morning and hardly ever at home. Ah well, there was no use greeting over spilled milk, as his grandmother used to say, so he swung into his jacket, blew out the lamp and set out the cat before him, and with a somewhat comfortless heart he trudged up the road to the smudge of trees in the darkness, sometimes in the rain, where the farm stood, mostly with a light in the stable windows, where the foreman from next door had already been feeding and mucking out his horses.

Helen and her lover tried to plan what was to be done to meet the new situation. Walking up the road arm in arm, whispering in the darkness, Helen said they would have to take Ruth into their confidence; no need to tell her everything, about a new baby and all that, she was too young to understand anyway, but she would have to get used to Meldrum's company, to see if she would accept him, otherwise she might stick to Audie and Helen said she couldn't bear that. Elopement was what they had in mind, round about the May Term, when Audie would have to leave the house, for it wasn't likely the farmer would give him the chance to stay on without a respectable wife, especially when the scandal broke and he found out what had happened. So the next evening that Helen went to Bogmyrtle she took Ruth along with her, walking all the way and staying until it was quite dark, when Rachael accompanied them to the head of the avenue, never suspecting that Meldrum Spark was lurking in the shadows down the road.

Nowadays when Helen went home her father was always deeply engrossed in his newspaper, reading all about the Bywaters and Edith Thompson Case, the young couple who fell in love and murdered the husband to get him out of the way. Helen had read about it herself and sometimes compared herself with the luckless Edith Thompson, but hoping that she would fare better in the end, for after all they hadn't murdered Audie. But in another respect Helen was in a worse position than Edith Thompson, for she was with child to her lover, a desperate thought rankling with despair. But they would never dream of doing away with Audie. Meldrum would never consider it, and he told her so when they discussed the Bywaters and Edith Thompson murder trial. Her father spoke gravely of the case that was taking up so much space in the newspapers, though it was grand reading, he said, and gave a body something to think about, and some feelings besides, depending where your sympathies lay. Mr Thompson was dead, as Craig reasoned, and didn't need sympathy any more; but think of that young couple in the death cell, with little chance of a reprieve, waiting to be hanged; their lives ended when they could have had a life of sorts together if they hadn't gone in for murder. God, that was the last straw, Craig thought, and he felt sorry for the woman and thought that she shouldn't be hanged. Surely they didn't have to hang them both for the same crime, especially when it was her lover who actually murdered Thompson: a life for a life was enough, Craig thought, and that the wife should get off with life imprisonment. But na na, Rachael said, she should hang as weel; nae doot she had put it into the young man to kill her husband, which made her worse than her lover; and Rachael's sympathies clearly lay with Bywaters, no doubt with a mother's view of the circumstances.

What the MacKinnons didn't know was that a similar tangle was brooding in their own family, and but for the timely warning of the Bywaters and Edith Thompson the case might have taken a similar course. Now they had seen the bloody writing on the wall. But if they hadn't seen it in their desperate case they might have been tempted to more drastic measures, though of course Helen never allowed her mind to dwell on such a thought.

Meldrum had suggested abortion, adding that he knew a woman in Brochan who could do it with a button-hook, and for a few shillings. But Helen said she wouldn't dirty herself with abortion; that the bairn she had lost under the binder was enough of that. Nothing doing: she would rather take her chance with natural birth; so Meldrum said no more about it.

Meldrum was waiting for her on the way home, stepping out from the lithe of a whin bush without any warning on little Ruth, though Helen was well prepared for him. Out of his pocket he took a mouth-organ in a little cardboard case and bent down and gave it to Ruth, while she stared up at his face in the darkness. She took it out of the box and the tissue paper and blew on the reeds, stuffing the packing into her coat pocket, while she blew and sucked on the notes, trying to form a tune as she walked behind her elders. Nothing was explained to her and she asked no questions: she was so completely absorbed in the instrument Meldrum had given her. She could hear some of their whispering in the wind but the noise of her mouth-organ practice drowned most of it. She had seen Meldrum before but didn't seem to concern herself why he was here with her mother, any more than she would have asked why her father was here at this time of night. Tomorrow was Saturday and she could play her mouth-organ all day if she liked, and perhaps manage to capture some of the tunes she heard on the gramophone. Meldrum couldn't have given her a better distraction, for she took not the slightest notice of him, and his only instruction was not to tell her daddy where she got it, but to say mummy bought it the other day when she was in Brochan.

Suddenly her elders stopped on the road, and Meldrum said, 'How did Audie Foubister manage to get his hands on a lass like you?'

'I dinna ken,' Helen answered. 'It was a kind o' pity I felt for Audie; nae real love, as I feel for you Meldrum. I didna ken onything aboot men at that time. I was brocht up on wark and ignorance and never saw much o' the world or I was twenty-one. I never got time to think until I was married and then it was too late.'

'And then you got too much time to think, eh!' Meldrum spoke in his usual husky whispers that were raptures in Helen's ears, and she squeezed his ribs where her hand went round his middle.

They walked on again while Ruth pursed her small lips over the tin face of the mouth-organ.

Meldrum was speaking again, raising his voice this time, and it wasn't exactly the language of an army deserter. 'Men have waded through blood and braved fire and water for a woman like yourself, quine; fought and died for them – songs and poetry and great ballads have been written about it, and mony times they didna get their woman, for they were crossed by fate. But Audie gets a woman like you just 'cause he's a dreep. A' he has tae do is stand and look miserable at a street corner and one of Heaven's finest angels is sent down to comfort him.'

They were hooked arm in arm and Helen said, 'But he's one o' God's bairns, why shouldn't he have an angel tae comfort him?'

'He had,' Meldrum replied, 'but now I've stolen her. You are my stolen angel. The Deil is aye guid tae his ain and I'll have ye yet!'

She was soft and warm with her head against his shoulder and Meldrum squeezed her fondly. They stopped on the road and she held up her face for his kiss, like a flower opening to the sunlight. He twisted his eager mouth into hers with an impassioned softness that brought her nearly to ecstasy, a compulsion she had no desire to resist. She stood on her toes and lifted her heels out of her shoes. Her arms went round his neck and the movement lifted her hemline above her knees, dimpled at the backs.

'You are my Bonnie Prince Charlie,' she whispered, between the kisses, and her sweet breath was incense to Meldrum Spark.

'And you are my Flora MacDonald,' he said, 'and you will hide and shelter me from Audie Foubister, and all those wicked folk who are watching us, until the time comes when we shall run away.'

'But where will we go, Meldrum?' Helen asked.

'Ye'll see, lass. I'll tak' ye places ye've never dreamed on; I'll show ye things ye've never thocht on. Audie's nae a bad breet but he doesna deserve a woman like you.'

They walked on again and Meldrum drivelled into song: 'Come Under My Plaidie The Nicht's Gaun Tae Fa'', and 'Will Ye Gang Tae The Heilan's Wi' Me?' And Ruth blew and blew on her mouth-organ, trying to catch the refrain.

'Damned but she's gettin' a tune on that thing efter a',' Meldrum said, catching her lilt in the night breeze, as if he had forgotten that the bairn existed, being so much absorbed in her more beautiful mother

'And tae think there was a time when ye tried tae drown me in the lake at Lachbeg,' Helen teased, squeezing Meldrum close in the darkness. – 'Wad ye still want tae drown me Meldrum Spark?'

'No quine,' he returned (for he seldom called her Helen) 'I wadna want tae hairm a hair on yer precious heid; nor lay an angry hand on yer saft and tender skin. But wasn't it strange the wye we met quine? And wha wad hae thocht it wad turn oot this wye, us bein' sae friendly like and sae much in love; after sic hate, for there was a time when I hated the MacKinnons for ill-usin' my poor sister – and you my jewel have been the reward for my pains. If I'd drowned ye that nicht in Lachbeg wuds I'd been juist as weel tae jump in the lake masell!'

'But I hope ye dinna hold that as a grudge against me?' Helen enquired, with concern in her voice, speaking louder in the night breeze – 'Your sister I mean.'

'No quine. You are more to me than ony sister could ever be!'

'And ye dinna worry aboot it?'

'No. The only thing I worry aboot nooadays is you my angel; in case I might lose ye!'

They were nearing the cottage at Sauchieburn and Helen told Ruth to put away her mouth-organ. 'Put it back in its box and dinna blow on it again tonight,' she ordered, 'leave it till morning.' And she tip-toed towards the cottage door.

She opened it gently, without a creak, and went softly into the kitchen. Audie was snoring in the box-bed and the fire had died in the grate. Nothing ever disturbed his slumbers and he slept in blissful ignorance of the wickedness of the world about him, peaceful as a child. Helen went through to the bedroom and lit the paraffin lamp and pulled down the blind, a signal for Meldrum to come inside, and he took Ruth by the hand, his finger on his mouth, sushing her to be quiet, while the cat mewed at the door when Meldrum closed it.

Ruth was eager to see her new mouth-organ in the lamp-light, the picture on the red box, a man with a feather in his hat and a bugle in his mouth, and a horn by his side, like Robin Hood in her school books, blowing an 'Echo' in the mountains, and she pondered it deeply while Helen peeled off her clothes, the frock over her head, Ruth holding the mouth-organ in one hand and then the other while Helen drew out her long sleeves. She stood in her dark blue knickers without any embarrassment, and when Helen put on her nightgown she wriggled them off and went to the orra-pail behind the door, then slipped quietly into the cold bed, the mouth-organ under her pillow.

Ruth fell asleep quickly, while her elders were bedding down beside her, but she awoke soon afterwards with the shaking of the bed and the amorous sighs of her elders. For a long time they fondled each other rapturously, and the bed shook violently with the intensity of their intercourse, spending themselves at last in gasps of prolonged pleasure, Meldrum firing his life's substance into the face of posterity. After all, bare skin in bed was better than having it fully clothed behind a whin bush by the roadside.

Next day Ruth played her father's gramophone in the kitchen and practised on her mouth-organ, trying to pick up the fiddle tunes of James Scott Skinner and Mackenzie Murdoch, while her mother and Meldrum locked themselves in the ben-room for more intercourse. Audie was at work all day in the byres and turnip field, except for a two-hour break at noon for dinner. Meldrum was locked in the room himself and the only evidence of his presence was the smell of cigarette smoke. Helen had never smoked but nowadays she kept a packet of Woodbines on the kitchen dresser to allay suspicion. Now and then she took a drag at a fag and Audie remarked about the candle burning at both ends and maybe he would have to stop. He smoked very little himself, and only when he was at rest at home, never at his work; and maybe he thought it was the smell of his own morning fag still about the house. But he was easily deceived, and if he had questioned Helen about the smell of cigarette smoke in the house she would have lied that her brother Hamish had been in by for his tea, or even Riach, and it was a wonder Audie hadn't seen them from the turnip shed. And Audie would have wiped his nose on the palm of his hand and taken a heavy drag on his mouth-piece and blown the smoke right across the kitchen, at the same time shaking his head sadly and remarking that a body never sees anything up at that place, nothing but nowt and neeps and pigs and sharn and dubs, and you might say he was missing the charm of his old mistress and the flower-like smell of her perfume.

While Audie was in the house Meldrum lay quietly in bed or cowered in a corner away from the window and the light. He had to keep out of sight of the loons playing next door, flashing past the window after a football, or romping in the garden in front of the house, and he stifled a sneeze or resisted a cough with enduring patience. Ruth was forbidden to mention him to anyone, least of all to her father, with the threat of terrible punishment from Helen if she did, like all the stars falling from heaven and the world coming to an end.

Ruth remembered that time at Millbrae when Craig and her grandmother came down in the gig to say goodbye to Audie and her mother because it was prophesied in the newspapers that the world was coming to an end. It was just before Ruth went to school, and she remembered it fine, because Rachael gave her a string of beads for her birthday (in fear of never seeing the child again); and Grandad Craig explained that a great comet was approaching the earth, and that if the merest tip of its mighty tail should as much as brush the world it would go on fire and everybody would be burned to death. Some people were afraid they would be roasted in their beds and stayed up all night watching for the comet. But it was a false alarm and everybody was relieved when the next day passed and nothing happened and nobody had even seen the comet with the naked eye. But the story gave some credibility to Helen's prediction that the stars might fall upon the earth if Ruth told anything she knew about her mother and Meldrum Spark. The end of the world will come 'like a thief in the night', Helen said, because it was written in the Bible like that.

So Ruth looked upon her father as a sort of intruder in the house to be treated with indifference. Meldrum Spark was her new daddy. Audie had such little time for the bairn she never really noticed much difference, except that Meldrum took her on his knee more often than Audie did, and sometimes kissed her cheeks or gave her 'beardy' with his stubbly chin, which made her squeak and giggle, and he could do all manner of things with a scissors and paper, like cutting out lace patterns for her doll dresses, and told her stories in the room while Helen was making the supper in the kitchen; wonderful stories about Lords and Ladies and castles, and tramps and horses, and played all manner of games with her, like draughts and snakes and ladders, so that Ruth had more and more time for Meldrum and less and less for Audie.

But for her pregnancy, Helen's deception with Meldrum Spark might have gone on indefinitely, or ended in a harmless flirtation when Meldrum tired of her. For weeks on end he was never in the house and everything was normal, honestly going his country rounds with his chattels and making a few shillings from the farm and cottar wives, flirting with most of them in the by-going, and flattering them besides with tales of their beauty; how this bangle would enhance a pretty wrist or those earrings would just be ravishing in such lobes as those, and the lonely, sometimes love-starved jades, living away at the back of beyond, where the sight of a handsome stranger like Meldrum Spark was like a new star in the sky, they were only too glad and too willing to be taken in by the music of that silky voice that had so enthralled Helen MacKinnon. She wasn't the first nor was she likely to be the last he had taken to the barn, blowing his nose in their knickers so to speak, and gave the poor quines a thrill they weren't likely to forget for the rest of their humdrum lives. A ring for the finger, a slide for the hair, a brooch, a string of beads, lipstick, face cream, baby powder – Meldrum had the lot and the gift of the gab to sell them.

Sometimes he made a deal with the stable lads, supplying them with shaving soap and the newly fashioned safety-razor blades in exchange for their horse hair, cut from the tails or manes of their plough horses. The only thing unusual about Meldrum's absence from the Foubister household was Helen's eagerness for his return; her tantrums and lack of patience when his return was delayed, snapping at Audie and biting at Ruth like a cat with its tail in a door jamb, tormenting herself with jealousies of the farm wives and kitchiedeems her lover would be charming at the cottage doors. What Helen didn't know was that Meldrum had a passion for most women, but especially for married women, and the fact that they were mostly unobtainable seemed to provide a challenge for his ego he couldn't resist, or tried very little to subdue; and Helen was merely an attachment where his favours had succeeded, thanks to Helen's infatuation and Audie's unsuspecting nature. He very seldom drank, which was something in his favour, unless he was with the MacKinnons, or others that encouraged him, and but for his fag smoking he might have kept going with his hawking, for apart from the odd present for his intended victims his needs were cheap and small. His honesty was more genuine than Helen deserved, for had she had her way she would have kept him in the ben-room always, a prisoner from the cottar wives that she hated, zealously paying for his keep out of Audie's hard-earned wages. But Meldrum would have none of it, and after a night of her pleasures, he set off with his box on his shoulder as soon as the coast was clear.

While Audie was at work and Ruth at school Meldrum would call with his box and be off again before the wife next door took much notice, maybe even selling her a card of buttons or a reel of thread to soothe her suspicion, but Helen would know when to take the bar out of the door once Audie was snoring, and sneak her lover through to the ben-room. And once more Ruth would be wakened to the shaking of the bed while her elders subdued their passions with a great expenditure of physical energy. They whispered far into the night, until Audie stopped snoring, then dead silence till morning and the first cock-crow.

Ruth had been taught to cough or clear her throat in imitation of Meldrum, just in case he forgot and made a mistake, and Helen took to smoking again, while Audie bustled in the kitchen getting his breakfast ready. When he stamped out of the house and clashed the door everybody breathed more freely. Meldrum gave Ruth a Jew's harp for being such a good girl, sitting up there in bed with her long curls while he lay with her mother in his oxter. Helen rose and made a ham-and-eggs breakfast for Meldrum, because he couldn't stomach brose, he said, though he sometimes took porridge. Ruth got an early breakfast for school, then Meldrum was off with his pack or his box before daylight, kissing both of them before leaving, the smell of morning fresh in the air, like the world was young again, while Ruth strummed her Jew's harp in the doorway.

Audie might have noticed that his otherwise demure wife,

his 'bonnie wee crater', as he used to call her, was now occasionally cock-a-hoop, with his supper on the table waiting and a cheery fire in the grate, the lamp glass cleaned and shining brightly, the crockery dusted and the bed-rails polished, newly baked oatcakes on the trencher, besides some scones and bannocks. These were the nights that her lover was expected to call, and it was well for Audie not to be fooled enough to spoil her good humour by asking for intercourse. But if Meldrum was absent for a long time she slipped back again to her slobbery, something she never used to do before, whatever her faults; for she had always been a spick-and-span wife, with Audie's meals ready on the table and everything right for his comfort, even though they weren't always on speaking terms. Now she didn't seem to care any more, and you might say a whore would look after a brothel better than she cared for her home, and even her window flowers were beginning to droop for want of water. Ruth was feeling the pinch and her hair crawling with lice that made her scratch occasionally, and her underclothes were sometimes dirty. When Meldrum stayed for a day or two in the cottage, which he sometimes did, the dishes were piled high in the wash basin and the ashes remained in the grate. Ruth was late for school and Audie had to be content with a brose dinner and a blibber of tea for supper, which wasn't enough for a working man and made him crabbed and irritated and miserable, snapping everybody's nose off, from the farmer to little Ruth, and he began to find himself out of favour where before he had been welcomed with a cheery smile.

Meldrum couldn't face Audie any more and he had stopped calling while he was in the house. Shame or guilt or embarrassment held him back; perhaps even fear of the little man he had wronged. It seemed a wise enough thing to do but his absence aroused Audie's suspicions, especially when the Jew's harp appeared, and Audie knew Helen had never been away to buy it. Ruth sat strumming it in the evening between her homework lessons and Audie snatched it from between her teeth. 'Whaur did ye get that thing?' he demanded, staring at his daughter like an angry bull over a gate. But Ruth was between two fires and she held her tongue, remembering that if she told anything the world would grow dark at noon next day and the stars would rain like fire from the sky, killing all her friends at school and even her beloved teacher; though she never dared tell them of her fears. She stared at the floor in mute silence, while her father stormed and danced in his anger, one of the childish outbursts that overwhelmed him like a sudden storm from the hills. He tore the stang out of the trump and trampled them underfoot, demanding once more where it came from. Helen was unprepared for this one and she couldn't think of an answer. His acceptance of the mouth-organ without question had made her over-confident and she had forgotten the Jew's harp completely. She was even afraid of Audie's sudden burst of temper and what he might do to her in her present state. She was caught off guard and as tongue-tied as her daughter. Ruth stared up at his writhing face, afraid to open her mouth, when the slash of his hand caught her across the cheek, an accursed blow that almost tore his daughter out of his heart. He lamented immediately and took her in his oxter and fussed over her and said it didn't matter about the trump or where it came from. But Ruth ran to her mither and buried her face in her apron, where she sobbed out her little heart in silence, afraid that if she spoke a word the stars would fall, and many a night thereafter she awoke in terror when she had been dreaming of the falling stars.

Helen held her close to the little heart-beat that had lately awakened in her belly, like a little pulse you could put your finger on but could never find it; and Ruth stood sobbing against her solar plexus, Helen's hand behind her head, holding her close, while Audie almost cried in his agony of heart, pleading from his soul for the little woman who had gone out of his life, beseeching her with his sad little eyes; and in the next minute rejecting her, despising this whore who had taken her place at his respectable table and denied him his rights in bed.

Meldrum wasn't in the house, but for once Audie couldn't sleep for the thought of it. To think that sometimes you lay in the box-bed masturbating while that bastard was having his way with your wife in the ben-room, just through the partition, yet she wouldn't let you put a hand on her yourself. Maybe you was partly to blame with that big rupture of yours and the poor bitch had maybe been driven to something of the kind. But with a tink of all people, for Meldrum was little better than a respectable hawker, and not very respectable at that when you came to think of it, taking up with a married woman beneath your very nose. Now he wasn't fooled any more by the hustlings in the ben-room and the smell of fag smoking. By morning Audie was in a towering rage and talked to himself all through breakfast. He was for breaking down the ben-room door but thought better of it. He couldn't be sure that Meldrum was in there, and after last night he didn't want to frighten little Ruth again. Maybe she had been on his side until he hit her, and now that had spoiled it. And if he took a cup of tea to Helen most likely she wouldn't let him into the room, or if she did he might throw it in her face for the way she was treating him. It was enough to send a poor man to the mad asylum, but you would just clash the door and curse the evil day you was born and cry aloud to the stars in your agony of mind.

Matt Yule, the foreman from next door, had just gone up the road in the darkness, back from his breakfast to kaim his pair of horses: a man that had a good sonsie wife to stir his porridge and set it before him with a bowl of milk, still in her nightgown and her loose hair hanging down her back; a woman that pulled off his boots when he was wracked with backache, or maybe his trousers when he was frisky and wanted something else. So here was a man who had little to complain about, except for a large family that his wife had borne him, and as he swaggered up the road he heard Audie crying on the wind and waited to let him catch up to hear what he had to say. He was a swarthy cheil, Matt Yule, with the smell of horseflesh about him and the reek of his pipe, waiting in the hedge for Audie, for they had been good enough friends the eight months they had been together at Sauchieburn, since that wet Term Day when

Matt had flitted Audie from Millbrae with the horse-carts.

Audie was panting when he came up, not knowing of Matt's presence in the hedge, the smell of his pipe away on the wind, where he waited there friendly like, with no evil thought in his mind. When Audie was anent the foreman he cried out to High Heaven and the winking stars that jewel the gates, and he cursed Meldrum Spark to Hell and its torments, and Matt Yule got such a start that he sprang out of the hedge after Audie, passing some remark about being on his high horse this morning, or that he had gotten out of bed on the wrong side. But Audie was so much surprised at the sight of Yule in the darkness, his thoughts all fuddled and bewildered, what with worry and the want of sleep, that he mistook the foreman's greeting for a taunt, a jibe at the sad affairs of his little household, which he imagined was on everybody's tongue; but which Yule honestly knew very little about, and concerned himself less, though he had heard the odd rumour. It was mostly in Audie's mind, and what with the sudden embarrassment of being overheard talking to himself at this early hour, and recalling the things he was saying, a sudden temper seized Audie and he struck the foreman a stinging blow in the face, knocking his pipe clean out of his mouth. So the foreman thought tit-for-tat and took a swipe at Audie and split his eyebrow. And now Audie laid on at him, blow for blow with the foreman, giving all he meant for Meldrum had he broken down the room door. This friendly innocent man, who might have been his ally against the common wife-thief, now the target for all the malice that Audie had meant for Meldrum. And Yule was amazed at the tenacity of his little neighbour, wondering what ill he had done him to deserve this; the fury behind his blows, the persistence of his onslaught, brave and game as a tormented bantam cock, though he managed to overpower him in the end. And Audie gave no explanation, just gave his face a dabble in the cold water of the horse-trough to wash off the blood, then into the byre breathless, his heart pounding, his brain in a turmoil, scraping out the troughs for the morning feed. Yule was dumbfounded, while he cracked spunks and scraped in the hedge for his pipe, then into the stable with a swollen lip, determined not to speak to Audie again until he spoke first.

Audie came home at noon with a black eye and he and Helen had a hell of a row. Helen was in tears in the end and went and hid herself for shame in the ben-room, kneeling beside the bed and sobbing her heart out, her bed of sin. She cried as much for Audie as for herself, for Ruth and for the little life within her, even for Meldrum . . . and at the thought of him she got up and sat on the bed and dried her tears, in spite of the tragedy of their lives. But this first real discovery of their love affair brought a taste of the bitter tears it would bring them; the shame and the sorrow and the shattering of their little household, and the gossip of evil tongues. But now it was too late to turn back and she would have to live with her shame and face the consequences.

The foreman got another job and left between the Terms for shame, unable to face Audie every day with such a fox in his hen-run. Candy Birnie fee-ed a single man to take his place and the house next door stood empty, leaving the coast clear for Meldrum to come and go as he pleased, with no one to spy at the windows. But he brought no more presents for the family and kept out of sight or sound of Audie, hiding behind Helen's skirts from a man half his size, a brave little man who, given half a chance, would have fought till he dropped to overpower the cad who had ruined his home life. But now with the world and fate against him he was beginning to lose heart, fighting a losing battle for a woman he couldn't hold.

But now Meldrum came right out in the open and visited the cottage in broad daylight, where Helen was always waiting for him with a kiss and open arms. He even took Audie's bicycle out of the coalshed and set Ruth in front of him on the bar, sitting on the red velvet cushion, getting on behind her on the back-step, just as her father did, though he was merely apeing him, and Helen got on her own bike, and the three of them set off for Brochan, while Audie watched them from the turnip shed, where he was feeding his nowt.

Audie came home tired and hungry to a supperless table and a black fire, so he kindled a blaze in the grate and made brose for himself from the oatmeal girnal. By the time they came home he was in bed, tired out and sleepy and dead to the world, and in no fit state to stay up for them. All three crept in quietly as usual and barred the door, and the bed was soon in motion again with Meldrum's idle lustfulness.

Next morning Helen was awakened by the rattle of the bedroom door. Audie was shaking it and several times he threw his weight against it but it wouldn't budge. 'Is that Devil in there?' he cried out, his voice a screech of temper, and Helen heard his breathing in the passage. She jumped out of bed in her nightgown and said she would come out if he left the door and went back to the kitchen. He argued a while but then retreated and said she could come out, that he wouldn't harm her. Helen opened the door cautiously and squeezed herself into the passage, while Meldrum pushed Ruth out of bed to lock the door from the inside, afraid that Audie would rush Helen and get into the room. Audie did thrust Helen back along the lobby, where she stood like a human cross, her white arms across the door jambs, defying Audie to open it.

'There's nobody in there,' she lied; 'naebody but the bairn, and I think ye've scared her enough withoot mair!' Inside the room Ruth stared at Meldrum but he sushed her to silence. The dart went straight to Audie's heart and he relented and moved away from the door, back along the passage to the kitchen, mumbling as he went and Helen behind him. He ceased to shout at her and merely stared at her with his pinhead eyes.

Helen lit the fire and soon had the kettle boiling for his brose. It was the first time she had ever done that for him in her life and the thought of it amused him. After all those years of cold lonely mornings it had happened, and there she was pouring the boiling water into his brose bowl. 'Canny wuman,' he said, 'that'll do, ye dinna want tae drown them,' for he didn't like thin brose. Helen made the tea and they both had a cup together, Helen on a chair at the fire, her bare feet on the cold fender, her rich black hair straggled over her back, staring into the coal flames. Audie smoked his usual fag and stared at her in silence, at the old nightgown with the big roses she had worn for years at Millbrae. His own wife and his own predicament and again his little heart went out to her. He saw himself as only half a man again, and his eyes softened with welling tears. He wanted to lay his hand on her little round shoulder and assure her that all would be forgiven. That if she gives up this man he will go to a doctor and have his rupture sorted and be like other men; that he will shift to another place where nobody knows them and they can all live happily as before. Have patience, lass, and all will be well. But all these words were in his mind and never found a voice. Somehow he couldn't get them out for the lump in his throat, so he quietly threw on his jacket and left the cottage, closing the door softly behind him.

From that day on Audie gave up the fight, resigning himself to whatever lay before him. And he didn't have long to wait for further torment. It came late one evening with a visit from Helen's brothers, Hamish and Riach MacKinnon on a motor bike, Hamish driving and Riach riding pillion, both the worse of drink, celebrating the occasion of Riach's new artificial leg, and the fact that he could now walk without a crutch, and he had left the thing at home. He went swaggering into the house without any help and sat down on a chair, a bottle of whisky sticking out of his coat pocket. It was a cork leg, he bragged, not an old-fashioned wooden one, and he could bend it at the knee and have it under him like a real leg. No more sprawling it over the kitchen floor to trip folk up. Hamish went along the lobby, apparently looking for Meldrum Spark, but he was disappointed, for when he opened the room door there was nobody there. Helen went after him and he questioned her but she had nothing to say, though it showed that her brothers knew of his presence. Audie was already in bed when they arrived and happily snoring, so they had a quiet drink not to waken him and Helen was persuaded to take a glass. Hamish told Helen they had something else to celebrate, for he was to marry Cora Swapp in the summer and move into her mother's croft, and that the shelt Meldrum had sold them would come in damned handy for carting the vegetables. Things were looking up at Bogmyrtle, he said, and Kirsteen was likely to marry a lad that had a big garage in Brochan; and he sold Hamish that big motor bike standing outside for next to nothing, and maybe the next thing you'd hear of would be the folk at Bogmyrtle getting a motor car. And hadn't Helen heard that Nora was getting married to a big farmer down in England, where she had worked as a land girl, that the cheil had written to her and then came up all the way in the train to Leary station to see her, and asked her to be his wife, and she's going away shortly. And then Riach piped up with his story about Sherran Begg getting up a joiner's business on his own, with some little help from old Craig; that he was tired making coffins all the time and there wasn't enough people dying anyway to give him a job. Everybody was getting on but you and Audie, Hamish told Helen, and that it was time they woke him up to give him a drop of whisky that would put some life into the man.

Without Meldrum in the house for devilment it had to be Audie, but Hamish suddenly thought of something quite different from what they had intended ... All the week Helen had been giving Ruth lessons on the drop-head sewing machine, now that her legs were long enough to reach the pedals, making dolls' dresses from odd strips of cloth, and even now Ruth was cutting out patterns in gay colours from a fashion catalogue that had come through the post. Hamish spied his little niece at this employment and went over to look at her handiwork, the glass of whisky in his hand and swaggering a bit as he went. The sewing machine was open to view, and so were Audie's working trousers that were lying on the mat in front of the bed. Hamish set his glass on the table and picked up the trousers, removed the braces and pushed Ruth out of the chair in front of the machine. He then sat down himself and spread the trousers on the sewing board, whispering to Riach to come over and give him some assistance, and between them they got the thick trouser legs under the needle, first one and then the other, and stitched them right up the centre and across the waist, the machine running smoothly and silently, the thick soft material muffling the sound of the shuttle, and then snapped the white thread and replaced the trousers on the mat. Ruth stood and watched mystified, not fully grasping the seriousness of what they had done to her father's breeks, and afraid to protest even if she had, while her mother made no attempt to stop them. Hamish then demanded Audie's Sunday suit from the wardrobe but here Helen put her foot down and said they had done enough of devilment for one night. She got up from her chair and made strong tea and sobered them down considerably, and when Audie was wakened for his cup they gave him a strong tot of whisky. He leaned on his elbow on the edge of the bed but never noticed the stitching in his rumpled trousers. When her brothers left Helen put out the cat and barred the door as usual and went to bed and forgot all about Audie's trousers that were still lying on the mat. Maybe she meant to take the stitching out of them but the thought escaped her completely. Nor did Ruth remind her, but was so quickly asleep she never felt the hot-water bottle her mother placed at her feet.

Next morning Audie was in a frantic rage. Helen thought he would have the house down trying to get his legs into the stitched breeks. He kindled the fire, in his drawers, and threw the poker at the bedroom door. 'What's the meanin' o' this?' he stormed. 'That's yon twa bastards last nicht did this. What the hell are ye a' comin' till that ye canna leave a man alane in his ain hoose? But they'll pay for this yet, you wait and see. There's a High Power above will see tae that!'

This brought Helen forth in her nightgown again and she got to work with the scissors and took the stitches out of his trousers. Audie was nearly in tears in his rage and stamped on the cement floor with his bare feet. 'This canna go on, wuman,' he cried, 'I canna stand it ony langer. I'm leavin' at the Term and ye'll get the hoose tae yersells. I'm for nothing more tae do wi' ony o' ye, understand!' And then he put on his clothes and fumed out of the kitchen in a stifling rage, clashing the door with such a bang that the sneck nearly fell off. Ruth heard the uproar, sitting up in bed, startled.

The snowdrops had come and gone, mantling the green lawns with their white lobes, weeping their frozen tears over the sodden earth. The tiny primrose flushed in the spring breeze, spreading her radiant colours to the kiss of the sun-beams. The crocus sprang for a while, sprinkling the earth with her saffron kisses, then stood wan in the sunlight, dying in the midst of her beauty. The lilies had opened their gol-den eyes to glimpse the sun, and the daffodils had raised their silent trumpets to the glory of the morning. Tulips cupped their chaliced hands to catch the rainbow drops, and the hyacinth graced the air with her fragrance.

And so the days of the long dreary winter lengthened and brightened into spring. The rooks began to caw and flutter in great numbers over the budding tree-tops, surveying the wrecks of previous homesteads. Oyster catchers came over from the Myreloch to gossip in the turnip fields, to lay their spreckled eggs in the silliest places, in the path of the iron-spiked harrows, or to be crushed under the seed rollers. Late comers fared better, when the corn and turnips had sprung and the heavier implements had left the fields.

March hares gambolled in the parks, tame and careless of the hunter's gun, aware it seemed that a truce had been observed for their mating capers. Lapwings began to swoop and dive over the furrows, filling the crimson twilight with their cries of 'peezie-weep, peezie-weep', until it faded in the darkness and died in the cold hush of nightfall. Black-birds began to 'twee-twee', in the rosiness of morning and the tuneful lark soared into the sunlight with his cheery song. The sparrows and starlings made noisy chorus in the hedges of copper beech and on the leafless trees around the farmsteads. The meadows were sprinkled with daisies, and bluebells and cowslips clustered under the trees and along the borders of the garden paths.

But all this rejuvenation in nature meant nothing to Audie Foubister. The days were getting longer, the sun was warmer at noon, and the turnip leaves were less crisp with frost in the mornings; these things he may have noticed, and that he didn't need his smoky lanterns so long in the byres: these things were the same every year and never changed; otherwise he had far more serious things to think about. A stranger was lodging under his roof and trying to steal his wife: his 'bonnie wee crater', the solace of his life till now; and the affairs of his little household were on everybody's tongue.

Such anguish of mind as he endured might have sharpened the wits and strengthened the feelings of other men, but it seemed to have the opposite effect on Audie. He became morbid and fretful, depressed and disheartened, a prey to every rankling thought. It was the winter of his disillusionment; the end of his peace of mind. Meanwhile he sought advice from his mother and stepfather and even confided in his employer, Candy Birnie of Sauchieburn. Candy told him to see a lawyer, because he would have to move out of his cottar house at the May Term, so that he (Candy Birnie) could have it for another cattleman. Audie had been a good servant, he said, and he would have liked to keep him on for another year, but he didn't like the scandal about the place, and as he would also need a new foreman next door he would like to start with a clean slate. Audie felt like a bruised worm under the heel of a giant, but an understanding giant who removed his foot rather than crush his victim.

When Audie went to see his lawyer in Scotstoun he called in by at Toddlebrae to see his mother and stepfather. They had only heard whispers of his affairs and were rather taken aback when he told them the full story. Susan condemned Helen as a bitch and a whore and turned up her trig little nose at the very mention of her name. Helen had been a sore disappointment to all of them, to what they had expected of a farmer's daughter.

'Divorce her, Audie, and be finished with the bitch,' was Susan's advice.

'I canna afford a divorce,' Audie replied, 'and I suppose the lawyer will keep me a' richt on what tae do,' somewhat scorning her advice.

The lawyer advised Audie to remove all his furniture and belongings to safe storage, at least in the meantime, and to try and find other accommodation; to keep an open door, so to speak, and to await developments. 'You say that your wife has committed adultery with this other man, Mr Foubister – but have you got proof of this?'

'I've got the lassie tae speak for me,' Audie said, 'She sees a' that goes on in the hoose; mair than I see masell.'

'You mean she has been a witness to any intercourse you suspect has taken place?'

'Aye, she has been wi' them day and nicht, locket in the ben-room; she's bound tae ken what has been goin' on.'

'How old is your daughter, Mr Foubister?'

'She'll be eight next birthday.'

'She's too young to testify. She may not even understand. It's hardly a thing to expect from a child, especially against her mother. And what makes you think she is on your side?'

'I dinna ken.'

'I think we should leave your daughter out of this, Mr Foubister, if we possibly can. You've got to be sure about these things. The fact that your wife has been sleeping with this man is enough to go on with.'

The lawyer paused and sighed and moved the papers on the desk, checking the particulars he had taken down from Audie. 'I think I've got everything here, Mr Foubister, but there is the question of alimony. You say that because of this scandal your employer has more or less given you notice, and that you must get out of your home on the twenty-eighth day of May, because your house goes with your job.'

'Aye, it's a cottar house and I have tae get oot at the Term.'

'In other words you will lose your job and your home because of your wife's misconduct.'

'Aye, that's the wye o't, man, though I couldna put it intae words like that.'

'It's my job, Mr Foubister. Now if your wife sues for money after your separation she gets nothing until she returns to you. All transactions must be done through this office and then we shall know where we stand. But what is to be done about your daughter, Mr Foubister?'

'Oh she would be gaun tae the wife's folk I think, when the time comes. I dinna think she wad come wi me onywye.'

'Have you discussed this with your wife?'

'No, nae so far.'

'Well it would be better that way Mr Foubister, at least for the present. But come and see me again, Mr Foubister, nearer the Term; between us we may manage to iron things out for you.'

Audie had no bitterness in his thoughts; only sadness and no hope for the future. What would life be like without his 'bonnie wee crater'? It was bad enough as it was: living with her when she was only a housekeeper, or even less; but what would it be like when she was gone completely? Folk would say that he was better off without her, but now he couldn't sleep at nights for the thought of losing her. He was afraid that he might go out of his mind and do himself an injury.

But Helen hardly spoke to him nowadays, not even at mealtimes, though she still had his food on the table and made his bed and washed his fule claes. A sort of wordless battle existed between them but there was no visible bitterness; no open hostility, save that each kept their thoughts from the other. Helen even left the room door open, so that Audie could look in any time he wanted to, but he never bothered.

When Audie dressed himself and went to see his lawyer in Scotstoun he didn't tell Helen where he was going or what he was about, though no doubt she had a good idea of his intentions. Perhaps if she had helped him with his collar studs and fixed his tie, as she did before, he might have told her; but all that was changed, even to the blacking of his boots, which he now did for himself, and for such neglect he told her nothing. He had his little moments of pride and was determined to hold his head above water and show her he was more of a man than she thought, after all. But he knew her mind and that it was useless to try and change it, though the lawyer insisted that she should get one more chance.

When Audie returned from the toon he laid his cards on the table. 'Ye'll get one last chance frae me, wuman,' he said, 'a last chance tae throw that bugger oot and bide wi' me as a decent wuman. Failin' that I'm puttin' ye in a lawyer's hands until ye come tae yer senses. It's gettin' gie near the Term and we'll hae tae move, but I'll keep an open door for ye, and the quinie, at some ither hoose, and until ye come back tae me as a respectable wuman ye wunna get anither penny frae me.'

This fairly stunned Helen. There was a punch in every word he spoke and the hard facts shattered her complacency. They battered their way into her mind and brought forth a true image of herself. For the first blinding moment she saw herself as Audie saw her, as the neighbours saw her, as everybody who knew her would see her for the rest of her life: naked and sinful – a fool and a cheat and a whore. Audie had torn the veil from her temple of evil and she stood exposed to the public gaze. Where could she turn for help? Whither could she flee? She grappled for straws to floor Audie: maddened at his strength against her weakness. How much did he know? Did he guess the real truth? She couldn't tell him now. She would have to be on her knees for that and she would rather fight – rather go with Meldrum and take her chance. She was cornered and she knew it but she wanted to spit. The devil had taken her hand and she would have to go all the way with him and bear the consequences; there could be no turning back now. How could she expect Audie to father another man's bairn? A tinker's child at that? And anyway she wouldn't give him the chance.

'I'm goin' wi' Meldrum Spark,' she said, almost defiantly.

'A' richt, wuman, but ye ken the circumstances: We've tae get oot o' this hoose at the Term and I've a lorry comin' for my share o' the furniture. Ye can do what ye like wi' yer ain but we'll be finished as man and wife!'

The finality of Audie's last sentence was another blow for

Helen. '. . . finished as man and wife!' It was like a skelp in the face that awoke her from a pleasant dream. 'But what about Ruth?' she enquired.

'Oh the lawyer said I could tak' her as weel if ye hinna a decent hame for her . . .'

'I'll get a hame for her,' Helen interrupted.

'A' richt, wuman. I dinna suppose she wad come wi' me onywye, and she's better acquaint wi' your mither than she is wi' mine, if that's what ye was thinkin' on.'

Helen didn't answer but she was thankful he wasn't going to fight for their daughter. Life without Ruth would be worthless, even heartbreaking, and she was beginning to wonder if even Meldrum could compensate for that. Anyway she needn't worry, for it was better than she had hoped for.

'And if ye press for money I'll tak' ye tae court,' Audie concluded, 'and ye wunna hae a leg tae stand on.'

She scarcely had even now and she had to sit down to collect herself.

Helen had her own plans to go to Bogmyrtle. Her mother had spoken for her with her father and they had agreed to take her in for the time being and store her furniture in the barn. She explained that they would be going away to the South soon, where they weren't known, and Meldrum would find a job and a home for them. Craig and Rachael were sorely embarrassed by the whole affair and scarcely knew what had come over their Helen to make her break up her home and let Audie go in this manner. But they didn't like the idea of their quine living with the Spark folk either, little better than tinkers, and her a farmer's daughter, and all the neighbours talking about it, so that Craig could hardly face them at the marts, so they pocketed their pride and said little about it; though their sympathies lay with poor Audie and the effect it would have on his folks.

On the eve of the Term a motor lorry arrived from Scotstoun to take away Audie's furniture, and when it had been stacked on the lorry, and while the driver was making it secure with a rope, Audie opened the window in the gable and shouted into the empty kitchen. This was the window where he always used to shave on Sunday mornings, but the mirror never showed him as he looked today. His face was strained and white and his eyes mere pinheads of anxiety. His voice was almost a screech of finality: 'Weel weel, wuman,' he cried, 'so this is what it has come till eh! But mind this, ye wunna get anither penny frae me till ye come tae yer senses, mind that!' Ruth stood beside her mother in the middle of the floor but he never said good-bye; never even looked at his daughter but clashed down the window sash with a bang, wiped his nose on the palm of his hand, climbed into the cab beside the driver and was gone.

His last words were not spoken in anger but the sting of them drove the blood from Helen's cheeks. They stunned her with a sudden realization of the stark desperation of her plight, and when Ruth turned to her she hugged the bairn close against her pounding heart.

Meldrum called when darkness fell, as was his usual custom, and the sight of his tall figure, and wearing his Glengarry bonnet, restored some of Helen's confidence. He filled the house with cigarette smoke and there was some vague planning between them about what was to be done. Meldrum seemed relieved that Audie had gone so peacefully, though inwardly he had hoped that he would take Ruth with him. But apparently he couldn't have the rose unless he took the thorn also. Helen had made that plain beforehand and he had accepted it. But there was no resentment in his attitude towards Ruth; indeed he had given her more of himself in a few months than her father had done in nearly eight years.

'I think we'll go tae Angus, lass,' Meldrum mused, 'We'll go Sooth tae the berry pickin', and when that's finished we can go tae Dundee; maybe I'll get a job in a jute factory. There wadna be much difference atween handlin' rags and handlin' sacks, would there noo, lass? Och give us a kiss noo and nae look sae glum. A body wad think ye was gaun tae a funeral; surely it's nae sae bad as a' that.' He took off his Glengarry and bowed in front of her, in true Jacobite style, hoping to intrigue her with his romantic buffoonery, but with Audie's sadistic departure still fresh in her mind, and a feeling of insecurity taking his place, Helen's wasn't so easily beguiled. 'But where will we bide?' she asked.

'Och in a slum somewye; and there's aye the lodgin' hoose, though we'll have tae be doin' wi' the tent for a time or we get settled.'

A tent, she thought; great God was this the best he had to offer? Had she given up home and all its comforts for this? Folk would think she was mad. And when she looked at Ruth tears moistened her eyes.

Meldrum seemed to read her thoughts for he assured her it was a grand life and she would like it fine in the open country for a time, at least until they got settled. The bairn would miss the school for a while but she could go to the academy later on in Dundee, where she would learn a lot more than she did at a country school.

They embraced for the last time in the cottage and Meldrum bent down and kissed Ruth also, ruffling her curls and telling her to look after her mother or he came back for them at Bogmyrtle. Helen said she could take care of herself and smiled bravely for him in the gloamin', 'cause there wasn't a blind on the window and they hadn't lit the lamp, for folk seeing in. When Meldrum left, Ruth looked everywhere for the cat but couldn't find it, and Helen said it had most likely taken scare at her father's flitting and maybe wouldn't be seen again, and it was a tearful Ruth that went inside with her mother. They had a cup of cocoa together and Helen barred the door and stretched a blanket across the bedroom window, because the curtains were down here as well, and then she prepared for bed, their last night in the cottage.

Ruth was already in bed, still whimpering about the cat, while Helen was undressing in the middle of the floor. Meldrum had been gone about half an hour when someone (or some spirit) lifted the outside latch on the door. The house was eerie and extremely quiet and mother and daughter listened intently. The paraffin lamp was turned down on the table and Helen was pulling her nightgown over her head, peering at Ruth through her dishevelled hair. Both were listening for the strange presence which had entered the kitchen and opened the glass door on the pendulum clock, then closed it again, with a sharp 'click', as the spring fastener snapped into the catch. It was the same sound they always heard when Audie used to close the glass door after winding up the clock, usually on Sunday nights before he went to bed. By now Ruth was sitting up in bed, goose-pimpled, her hair stiff and cold at the roots, clutching at the blankets. Helen stilled her with a raised hand, her gown still ruffled about her midriff, until about the time a body would take to tiptoe from the kitchen clock to the outside door, when the sneck was lifted again, as if someone was leaving the house, then all was quiet.

'Did ye hear that?' Helen asked her daughter.

'Aye, I heard it, mama. Was it a ghost?'

'I dinna ken, but we'll hae a look at the kitchie.'

She turned up the lamp on the table and carried it at face level along the passage. Ruth sprang out of bed and clung to her mother's nightdress, their shadows from the lamp glare fluttering against the wall as they moved along. The door was still locked, the wooden bar in its sockets, the latch in its place, so they moved on into the kitchen.

The windows were inky black in the lamplight, where Ruth imagined that grotesque ghostly faces might be watching them from every pane. She stared at the window in the gable, half expecting that her father would open it and shout his parting words into the kitchen: 'Ye wunna get anither penny frae me, wuman, till ye come tae yer senses, mind that!' For a moment she could have sworn she saw him there, his white cold face pressed against the glass, his eyes small and frightened, his teeth chattering in the wind, his hair white like a ghost.

Ruth clung tighter to Helen's dress as she approached the clock, setting the lamp on the dresser. The clock was still ticking away in dignified secrecy, the brass pendulum swinging to and fro behind the gold figures on the glass, the black hands pointing at midnight. What strange hands had touched it? Opened the glass door and closed it again, with a snap – and to what purpose? What did the clock know?

What cold hand had touched it? Even as Helen opened the glass door the hammer struck midnight, twelve canny strokes while Helen waited, the door in her hand, then reached with her fingers under the swinging pendulum and took out her wedding ring, where she had hidden it when Meldrum asked her to take it off. She slipped the barrel ring on her marriage finger and searched for the other, the jewelled ring Ruth had picked up on the ploughed field at Millbrae, and when she held it in her palm it glistered menacingly in the lamplight. She put the ring back in the clock and closed the door, and there was the same sharp ghostly 'click' they had heard before.

They went back to bed but left the lamp burning full glow on the table. Helen had a daft idea that her lover had sneaked back to the house and tried to steal her rings from under the kitchen clock. But how could he get into the house without someone to remove the bar from inside the door? No, it was impossible and her thoughts were silly. And anyway he hadn't taken them – even if he knew where they were hid. Perhaps it was the spirit of old Joyce putting the clock back for Helen, warning her (her once darling child) that she was about to take the wrong turning; that she was leaving the straight and narrow path for the wider road to desolation. Ah well if it was, it had come too late. But she would be rid of that glittering ring tomorrow. Meldrum could pawn it or sell it and it would pay their way to the South.

Helen fell asleep on the thought and the next she knew it was broad daylight and the lamp still burning on the table. She got out of bed and woke Ruth, for they would have to dress and have breakfast before her brothers came with the long cart to take the remainder of the furniture to Bog-myrtle. Helen had asked them to come early, before the cottars who would be moving in after them and next door. Hamish and Riach arrived about nine o'clock with Meg in the long cart, Hamish sober and businesslike and smiling as he worked. Riach creaked over to Ruth on his new cork leg and pulled her hair. 'So ye're gaun awa' wi' the tink are ye?' he grimaced, rolling a fag to the corner of his small twisted mouth. But Ruth merely stared at him with her baby doll eyes, her finger in her mouth, and swung her skirt back and forth while he stood and gaped but got no answer.

During the afternoon Riach took the quine back with him to Sauchieburn with the spring-cart for the hens and the remainder of the peats, the peats her father had slaved in the moss to provide for them the previous summer. He had Meldrum's shelt in the spring-cart, loaned from Hamish, a high-stepping beauty with whites in its eyes and long ears that wiggled at every ferlie by the roadside; but he joggled along at a brisk trot and made the bairn smile, though till then Riach thought she was a sulky little bitch.

Approaching the bridge at Leary Riach saw a train coming and stopped the cart, afraid to be caught under the iron brig with Meldrum's shelt and a train going overhead. Meg or Bell could thole it but Riach wasn't sure of such a spirited beast. He stood and fidgeted while Riach held him in, flicking his ears and stamping his feet, but as the train passed on Riach loosened the reins and he moved away.

That night Ruth slept upstairs with her mother at Bogmyrtle, above the room where old Joyce died, but not a feather disturbed them, nor the scratch of a mouse.

When Helen and Ruth had been about a fortnight at Bogmyrtle Meldrum called with his pack to take them away. Craig and Riach were at work in the fields and only Nancy was in the house with her mother and Helen. Kirsteen was in Brochan with her cut flowers and Nora had gone south to marry her farmer, just as Hamish had said. She went during the fortnight Helen was at home and she'd had a big send off from Leary station, where even some of the neighbours had gone to see her away and Riach had piped her on to the train. Little Janet and Meston were at school and Ruth was playing with a ball at the gable of the steading. She saw Meldrum coming down the avenue and ran inside to tell her mother. Helen had been waiting for him and was all prepared, with most of their clothes in a raffia basket tied up with string. Her mother watched her getting ready with some concern but had little to say on the matter. There was little she or Craig could do in the circumstances: This man had broken up their daughter's home and he would have to bear the consequences. Craig had warned Rachael to hold her tongue and let events take their course, though he was pretty sure it wouldn't be long before the pair of them were back looking for somewye tae bide, though God knows what it would be like for his little grand-daughter, tramping the road like a tinker's quine, a sore affront to Craig Mac-Kinnon at mart or roup, him who always had something better in mind for his family.

Helen hadn't told her mother she was with a bairn to Meldrum Spark. She was holding off or she saw how things turned out for them. If they made a go of it in the South and things went well for them she might be proud to bear Meldrum's bairn, and wouldn't be afraid to tell them so. There was just the chance that Meldrum would get a steady job somewhere and a home for them and she wasn't going to admit defeat just yet. She had such faith in Meldrum she believed he could turn straw into gold, and she still had this ring in her purse that might be worth a fortune. So Helen put on a brave face every day she rose and surprised Rachael with her good spirits in the circumstances; and Rachael would give her head a shake in the milk-house and say to herself: 'God, it might work, wha kens!' If she guessed Helen was with a bairn she never mentioned it, and with the steel-ribbed corsets that Helen wore you would never have noticed it at this stage.

Meldrum was in high spirits when he came down the step into the kitchen, and when Rachael hinted that she hoped he knew what he was doing with her daughter he assured her that he loved the lass and would stand by her come what may; but at the same time wondering how much she knew with her bright cunning eyes and her ferret-like ways of finding things out for herself. All the same Meldrum seemed anxious to be off before old Craig and Riach came home from the parks for their mid-day meal. No need to worry about Hamish, who still worked in the grain store in Brochan, though Rachael had told Helen it likely wouldn't be long or he married Cora Swapp and moved into her mother's croft on the Mattock Hill. So Helen left without saying goodbye to her father or Riach, though Rachael convoyed them to the head of the avenue, past the cable that drove the water-mill, and the spootie that had run into the duck pond since Helen could remember, and a straw ruck held down with a harrow and an old cart wheel, though Helen couldn't think why she noticed these things. Rachael walked between them, her work soiled hands under her apron, advising and imploring but hardly knowing what to say, smiling through her tears and kissing Helen on both cheeks and hugging Ruth close to her breast.

Ruth looked back far down the road and Rachael was still standing there, waving feebly in her white headgear and no doubt brushing a tear from her cheek with the corner of her apron. Meldrum strode forward with such vigour and cheerfulness Helen was forced to swallow her tears and smile in spite of everything. Meldrum even took her raffia basket so that she could walk more freely, and her mind went back to the day when she had first left home to work in the toon, before she married Audie – poor Audie, what would he think of her now? But it all seemed such a long long time ago, like something out of a story book. The only thing that burdened Ruth was the milk flagon that Rachael had insisted on, half filling it with cream when they left.

Hawthorn blossom was scattered by the wayside, like confetti after a wedding and you might say that nature's honeymoon was over, smiling and raining by turns, but would entrance you yet with her marvels. Wild pansies peeped at them from the grass, like grounded butterflies afraid to spread their wings, and the air was scented with the musk of whin and broom, rich with golden blossom, while speeding cloud shadows swept across the fields.

They boarded the train at Leary station and went steaming round the foot of the Mattock Hill, the deer on its slopes getting smaller and smaller while Ruth watched it from a corner of the carriage. They arrived in Aberdeen in the early afternoon and Ruth nearly got lost on the bustling platform under the huge glass roof. They slept the night in a lodging house, where Ruth was awakened every hour by the ringing of bells in the church steeples, like several giants were tossing the bells over the roof-tops, one to the other, and when the clanging died down in one quarter it was taken up in another, with a change in tone and cadence, and being a country bairn Ruth wasn't accustomed to such noisy madrigals.

Next morning they breakfasted in the lodging house, and then Meldrum and Helen went to a pawn shop to sell Ruth's ring. Here Helen got her first shock when the pawn-broker offered her ten pounds for it. Ten pounds! when she had expected at least fifty pounds. A jewelled ring, set with stones, surely it was worth more than that. They argued for a while and the pawnbroker told her to take it to one of the city jewellers if she thought she would be any better, but most likely they would want to know how she came by it, in case it was stolen, and all the rest of it, so this put Helen off and she settled for the ten pounds.

The trio then went down Bridge Street, back to the railway station, Meldrum with his pack on his shoulder, Helen with the raffia basket under her arm and Ruth swinging the flagon. They boarded a train for the south, a long red train that snaked out of the station over a maze of branch lines, gliding its smooth way up Ferryhill and Nigg, with the bit ruin of St Fittick's Kirk in the valley, out by the lighthouse at Girdleness, gleaming white on the breakers in the bay. Up through the cutting they steamed and along the cliff tops by Dounies and Cove and Portlethen, the saucer-funnelled engine still gathering speed, swishing under bridges like a flash of wings, rattling over points and swinging through the stations, hooting like an owl as it tore through the open countryside. Ruth felt she was riding on a monster, and she could feel the spring of its muscles under the plush cushioned seats, the smell of its breath in the steam smoke, the thrill of its gallop in the swaying carriage, the clatter of its hoofs on the rail joints, while she looked out on the sea and the towering cliffs.

After what seemed a long time to Ruth there was a jarring of brakes and the train slowed down smoothly and stopped at Stonehaven, not that she could read the signboard properly but she heard the porter calling it out loud. There was a great banging of doors as people got off and on the carriages though no one else came into their compartment. Meldrum lowered the carriage window with the leather strap, so that Ruth could put her head out by standing on her toes. There was a great hissing of steam from the engine, panting to be off again, until the guard blew his whistle and waved a green flag; then silently, smooth as glass, the train moved off, the engine hoasting out white smoke away out ahead over Brickfield, while Meldrum lowered the window and Ruth sat down on the red cushions, smiling shyly at her mother on the opposite side.

There were several more stops: Laurencekirk, Brechin, Forfar, places Ruth had never heard of before, while she sat watching her elders with her wide blue eyes, wondering how long they were going to sit. It seemed hours to Ruth and she was beginning to feel hungry, and asked her mother for a piece, but Helen said it wouldn't be long now and to wait until they got off the train. Ruth was also sleepy, because the bells in the city steeples had kept her awake the night before. She was dozing off and almost asleep when Helen gave her a nudge to waken her. Meldrum took Helen's raffia basket down from the luggage rack and set it out with his pack in the corridor, handing the empty flagon to Ruth, while she blinked at him with sleep rimmed eyes.

The train stopped at a place called Coupar-Angus, where all three got out, Ruth's legs and feet all pins and needles and the fresh cold wind pimpling her tender skin. Still she was hungry and asked again for a piece, whereon Helen went into a baker's shop and came out with a bag of fresh smelling buns, hot rolls and biscuits, and she gave Ruth a slab of iced-gingerbread. They left the town with its lumbering horse carts and crossed the muddy Isla, over a bridge where Ruth could see red cows with long horns standing in the water. They were on the road to Blair-gowrie, Meldrum told them, the heart and pulse of the rasp-growing country, where he hoped they would all get a job pulling berries before long. Approaching Ryefield he spied an old sand quarry on the edge of a wood, a stone throw from the branch line to Blairgowrie. He went into the quarry and sat down on his pack, with mother and daughter beside him. After smoking a fag he took the flaggon from Ruth and went in search of water, telling her to gather twigs from the wood or he returned. When he came back with the water he opened up his pack and produced a small kettle, then lit a fire and boiled the water for tea, what he called 'Tinker's Tea', brewed in a tin-can over a twig fire, with a fine smell of rosin in the reek. Helen opened a tin of condensed milk, and with a teaspoonful of that and one of sugar from the raffia basket, Ruth thought it was the finest tea she had ever tasted, especially with the cream buns and currant bread Helen gave her to go with it. She was a young growing quine and the taste of food was good in her mouth, famished as she was after that long train journey and the tiring walk on the road.

The sun was shining hot now and drowning out the fire, the pale woodsmoke warm in the air, rising into the pine-trees, heavy with their cones. Ruth was revived and got up to wander round the quarry, watching the sand-martins popping into their nest holes in the steep banks, the occasional rabbit that came out to look at her, and the tartan-winged butterflies that fluttered over the yellow broom and the ragwort flowers. Under her blue waterproof she wore a pink frock with white spots, black woollen stockings, laced shoes, and on her head a bottle-green worsted bonnet Helen had knitted for her with a tassle on top, her dark brown curls hanging over her shoulders, and her soft blue eyes kindling with interest at every new wonder she looked upon. Soon a train came by, with a long string of goods waggons, their metal wheels clinking along the line, making for Blair-gowrie, Meldrum said, and when the driver spotted them in the quarry he blew the engine whistle.

Towards evening Meldrum unrolled his pack and set up a tent in the firwood, not much of a tent, but two or three waterproofs sewn together and hung over a stick between two trees and pegged out on the grass. A blanket was spread out on the ground to form a bed, with a sheet and quilts to cover them, and the folded pack was used as a pillow bolster. All three sat round the fire till nightfall, a long quiet summer evening, while the pigeons cooed in the pinewood and cattle were lowing in far-off fields. Meldrum told stories to Ruth while he sat on an oil drum and poked the fire with a stick, sending up sparks that floated and died away in the slanting sunlight. Each one disappeared in the wood for a time, Ruth a little bashful for want of a privy, then pulled up her knickers quickly, before she came in sight of Meldrum. All three crawled into the tent and it was still daylight when Ruth fell asleep, tired out with her journey, while Meldrum smoked and whispered with Helen long into the twilight.

Next morning the train driver blew his whistle again from the high embankment, while he clattered along with a row of coaches, filled with folk going to work in Coupar-Angus, Meldrum said: shop-keepers and factory workers and bairns going to school. Helen was already wide awake, listening to the singing of the birds, mostly blackbirds and skylarks, and sometimes the wail of a teuchat far out in the cornfields. Meldrum got up first and gathered sticks for the fire. Soon he had the kettle boiling, while Helen dressed Ruth and wiped her face and hands with a cloth soaked from the kettle. After breakfast Meldrum troubled himself to shave while Ruth held the mirror for him, and the end of the leather strap while he whetted his razor. He then dismantled the tent and rolled it into his pack again and stamped out the fire, then all three took the road in the direction of Blairgowrie.

They wandered as far as the Auld Brig, where the Ericht Water comes dashing under the arches, swirling over its rocky bed, all frothed and sun-sparkled in its dance to join the Isla. It seemed that Meldrum had chosen his country well, with all good intention of making some money at the berry picking during the summer. Everywhere a body looked there were fields of raspberry canes, all neatly cultivated by horse shim between the rows, carefully staked and netted against the birds, the plants now in exuberance of health and greenery, awaiting the sun and season to ripen the berries in their rich clusters of pink profusion. There were plots of gooseberries too, blackcurrants and beds of strawberries; but the rasp predominated, rivalled only by the potato crops and the wide green fields of waving corn.

But would Helen's money last out the first six weeks of early summer, until the berries ripened? Fares and food and fags had already eaten quite a hole in the £10 she got for the ring, and she had little else besides, because Audie had given her nothing of the last month's wages at Sauchieburn. A pity too that she had lost the gold wishbone she had got from her father on her wedding day; it might have fetched a bit more now in a jeweller's shop, or a goldsmith, or what ever you called them, and for all the luck it had brought her it wouldn't have mattered to be rid of it. She had lost it anyway so what was the difference.

The trio wandered back to the Wellmeadow, in the heart of Blairgowrie, the Berrypan of Scotland, where the jam kings, bankers and agents lived all around in their posh houses; where truckloads of raspberries were loaded on to the train for the jam factories in Dundee, Perth and Glasgow, besides the English markets, mostly two trains a week; and a lot of people in the town got work on the surrounding raspberry plantations. But of course the town had other connections with the farming community; like blacksmiths and implement makers, millwrights and joiners, seedsmen and granary warehouses, potato merchants and wool brokers, cattle marts and fee-ing markets, sellers of manure and sheep-dip, hand tools and so forth, though Meldrum never troubled himself about these trades, nor made any attempt to find a job in them, or even on the farms around the town; his vagrant thoughts relying mainly on the seasonal rasp, when he could be up and going again as soon as the dye was washed from his fingers.

But there he sat in the Wellmeadow, lord of all he surveyed, caring not much for anything beyond his next packet of fags . . . and while Helen had gone to get these Ruth sat beside him on the iron park bench. When Helen returned Meldrum shouldered his pack and the three of them walked out the Dunkeld road, as far as Rosemount, where they camped in the woods, and Meldrum said they could stay there until the berries ripened, with occasional sorties into Blairgowrie or Rattray for provisions, mostly fags, Helen thought, now that she knew him better.

Rosemount was a fine place for camping, Meldrum said, where you could be well out of sight in the woods, with no interference from prying passers by. But maybe he had another reason for camping there, where he could pluck rank heather from the wee bit of rough moorland around the woods, and this he made into besoms or switches and sent Ruth around the cottage doors trying to sell them, two or three under her small oxter, knocking on the cottage doors with her free hand. But never a besom did she sell, and always returned to the tent with the bundles of heather under her arm, hungry, footsore, tired and weary.

Meldrum promised her a doll when she had sold enough besoms to buy one, so she set out again, inspired by his promises. Sometimes the housewives took pity on the bairn and gave her a piece and raspberry jam, and sometimes when hunger got the better of her feelings she asked for food, something she had never done in her life before. One woman gave her a slice of bread smeared with sour butter, and hungry though she was she had to throw it away. The farm and cottar wives often asked awkward and embarrassing questions and in fear of betraying her elders Ruth had to force herself to tell lies. They wanted to know where she came from, where her parents lived, and why a nice little girl like her was galavanting the countryside selling heather besoms? They were nice besoms, the woman said, and well made but they just hadn't much use for them. And did your Daddy really make these besoms? Why didn't he make clothes-pegs instead? She might manage to sell them because they were more useful to folk. What did your Daddy do all day that he couldn't sell the besoms himself? And weren't her parents afraid she might get lost all by herself on the lonely roads? Ruth got out of answering some of these questions by simply walking away, or just by staring tongue-tied at the inquisitive women – still remembering that the stars might fall or the sun would be blacked out if she told anybody about her mother and Meldrum. But every evening when she returned to the camp with her besoms the faces of her elders grew longer and more perplexed. It was a good excuse to get her out of the way so that they could have sexual intercourse, because there wasn't much room for it in the tent at night with the bairn at their feet, so they sent her out in the daytime so that they could indulge their lust. When she tired of the besom selling, and refused to go out with any more, Meldrum soon found another errand for her so that he could have his way with Helen. He handed her the flaggon and told her to get milk at some of the farms, but gave not a penny to pay for it. Ruth had often carried the milk at Millbrae, even before she went to school, but she never had to beg for it; Isobel Mathers just saw her at the kitchen door with her flaggon and knew what she wanted. Here it was different, approaching some strange farm and tapping on the door, sometimes with a big dog growling in the close or leaping all over you and licking your face and like to knock you over before somebody came to the door. Ah well, maybe it was better than going to school, 'cause she didn't like doing sums anyway. If only the farm wives didn't ask so many questions, or if mother or Meldrum had given her money to pay for the milk, then she could have gone to any farm for the milk every second day or so. It wasn't every day she was sent for milk, but just when the flaggon was empty, or when there was no Nestle's milk in the raffia basket, and one morning when Ruth refused Meldrum gave her a stinging slap in the face. It was the first time he had hit her and she burst out crying and ran to her mother in the tent. Helen took her in her arms and hugged her and cried to Meldrum that if he hit her again he wouldn't get any more fags. Meldrum crawled into the tent and said he was sorry, it was just that they had to have some milk to drink, and for the tea, or they would all die of hunger; but Helen just hugged her quine and stared at her lover and told him he could do the begging himself for a change; after all, she said, it was what he was accustomed to, and how could he expect the bairn to do something she had never done in her life before, thanks to him and his vague promises. There was a coldness between them for a time after this, and

Meldrum walked about restlessly or sat on a big stone in a sulk, until his last fag was smoked and he had to beg Helen to let him have another shilling from the raffia basket. So they had another walk into Rattray village, where they got a further store of groceries and fags and matches for Meldrum. Back at the tent they had more Tinker's Tea and all were friends again, while the wood crackled on the fire and Meldrum told more stories in the shimmering smoke and the birds sang gaily from every brake and bush.

But things were getting serious; a whole fortnight had elapsed and the raspberries in the fields were far from ripe. It was a fine dry summer with plenty of sun and the berries should be ready for pulling early this year. That was what the south folk said in their strange tongue, but that there would be no sign of picking for a month yet at the earliest they said. A month was far too long for Helen's purse strings, and Meldrum made no attempt to find himself another job in the meantime. Maybe he could have got himself a job hoeing or haymaking with the south farmers but he never stirred himself; just sat in the sun smoking or making love to Helen in the tent when Ruth was chasing butterflies or watching the rabbits. He said he couldn't bring his trinket box and his pack as well; it was too much to carry; nor could he afford to fill it, or he would have sold knick-knacks round the doors or the berries ripened.

Just when things were getting really desperate, and Helen had changed her last pound note for eatables, and they had begun to argue about turning back, Helen saying that she wanted to go home again – then it was Meldrum had his brainwave: fishing for pearls in the river Tay; not salmon or trout or something that could be eaten, but pearls, real pearls, he said, that would make them all rich and solve all their problems. Why hadn't he thought of it before? If only they could reach the Tay, Meldrum said, all their troubles would be over, and he assured Helen that his brothers had sometimes gotten ten or twelve pounds for a single pearl; yea more, even forty pounds for a real good one, and he said that pearls were sometimes worth thousands of pounds apiece, like the one in the King's crown that was found in the river Ythan. If only they could find such a pearl they would all be rich.

Meldrum couldn't rest after this, anxious to be off in search of the Tay. Next day they were on the road again, Meldrum with his pack on his shoulder and Helen hugging her long white raffia basket. How well she guarded that raffia basket, and Meldrum had never yet managed to sneak it away from her while she slept (apart from that morning when he gave them tea in bed) and after that she slept on it as a sort of pillow; and just as well, for most likely Meldrum would have taken her money and spent it all on fags and left them with nothing to eat. Every village they passed through he was begging for another packet of gaspers as he called them, but Helen refused to spend her last few shillings on anything but essential food.

Ruth trudged on behind, swinging the inevitable flaggon among the long grass by the roadside, sometimes tired and sulky or in a tantrum and refusing to speak to either of them. But one thing Ruth was thankful for: that when Meldrum first thought of fishing for pearls in the river Tay, he picked up the bundle of heather besoms and threw them on the camp fire. With them went the promise of her doll, which she would never receive, but she was so disgusted that she didn't care any more.

Back in Blairgowrie, Meldrum went into a joiner's shop while Ruth rested with her mother on an iron seat in the Wellmeadow. Ruth was tired and her feet were blistered and Helen promised her a fine piece from the baker's shop when Meldrum came back. About an hour later he returned with a small square wooden box with a glass bottom and no lid on it. He told Helen that when you held the glass box in the water, bottom down, you could see the oysters at the bottom of the river. Helen scarcely knew what oysters were, so he explained to her that they were a sort of shellfish that lay on the river bottom, and that when they opened their purse-like shells to eat sometimes a grain of sand got washed inside the shell and hurt them, so the wee beastie surrounded the sharp grit with a sticky fluid to protect itself and reduce the pain (just like if you got a mote in your eye and couldn't get rid of it) and in course of time, because the oysters had long lives, the gummy substance grew smooth and hard as a bead about a lassie's neck, and that's what formed the pearl.

'And how do ye get the pearl out of the oyster shell?' Helen asked, 'after ye have catched it.'

'Ye dinna "catch" them, quine,' he explained, 'nae like ither fish; ye juist pick them up, and then ye prise the shell open wi' a pocket-knife or something sharp, and if there's nae a pearl in the shell ye juist throw them back in the watter.'

'And what did the box cost?' Helen enquired, beginning to show some interest in the project.

'Half-a-croon,' Meldrum replied.

'That means ye've got sixpence left oot o' the three-shillin's I gave ye.'

'Aye, but I bocht ten Woodbines and a box o' spunks, and that left me wi' a penny change.' He handed the penny to Ruth and told her to buy herself a stalk o' rock.

Ruth came off her seat for the penny and then ran down the street to a sweetie shoppie. She came back with two sticks of pink peppermint rock, sucking one between her teeth, half out of the wrapper. When she sat down on the form again her elders were still arguing about the price of the glass box.

'Ach, lass,' Meldrum laughed, trying to humour Helen, 'the glass box will mak' ye rich, lang afore the rasps are ripe; I tell ye it's the best investment ye ever made.'

Apparently assured by Meldrum's flamboyancy Helen went into a shop and squandered another florin on a few hanks of wool and knitting pins. 'After all,' she smiled, 'I maun do something while ye're at the pearl fishin'.' And though Meldrum didn't reply, maybe he guessed she would be weaving something for the coming bairn, his bairn; God help the poor woman, and for once in his life he felt truly ashamed of himself. His early promises were still in Helen's mind: 'I'll tak' ye tae places ye've never dreamed on; I'll show ye things ye've never thocht on.' Maybe the pearl fishing would be part of it, though his words were beginning to lose some of their enchantment in the glaring light of reality. The knitting was still a link with security; it anchored her thoughts and dispelled some of the hopelessness that surrounded her, though Audie's last words were still ringing in her ears: 'Ye wunna get anither penny frae me, wuman, till ye come tae yer senses!' Maybe she was beginning to realize that Meldrum wasn't the Prince Charming she had taken him for: that he was really no good at all, except that he had a way with women, and certainly no match for Audie in his wiry consistency in putting money on the table and food in their bellies.

Meldrum's hopes were high on the pearl fishing, but to reach the Tay they had to go much further afield. Helen was for turning back at the last moment but Meldrum bolstered her up in his usual persuasive manner. He soon had her swabbing her tears away and smiling again. Perhaps she was homesick for the peatsmoke and the security she had lost, or maybe the bairn in her womb was beginning to kick at her ribs.

'Nae use blubberin' and greetin', lass,' Meldrum cajoled, 'the ill's done now and canna be helped. It took the two of us to do it and you're just as much tae blame as I am.' Such was Meldrum's philosophical stock phrase to meet all present emergencies.

Before they left Blairgowrie Helen went into another shop and bought a bag of buns, a loaf of bread, tea and sugar and a jar of raspberries. She also went into the post-office at the top of Allan Street, where she stayed a long time, while Meldrum paced the square, impatient to be off again. When Helen came out of the post-office Meldrum asked why she had been so long, and she said she had written a letter telling her mother where they were and that they were all feeling fine and just waiting for the rasps to ripen . . .

'That'll mak' auld Rachael feel just fine,' Meldrum said, 'but did ye no tell her aboot the pearl fishin', quine?'

'No, I forgot,' Helen answered, 'but I will next time, if ye find a pearl.'

They left the town on the Perth road and walked under

203

the famous Beech Hedge, seventy feet high, Meldrum said, and arched over the roadway, shutting out the sun. Meldrum was heading south for the Tay, just beyond its junction with the Isla, where he said there were good oyster beds washed down by the current. He struck camp in a copse of trees just off the road, where Ruth went to bed with sore feet and her last bit of rock in her mouth, for she had saved it well since they left Blairgowrie. The owls hooted far into the night and Helen lay awake listening to them, like the crying of a baby, she said, on some far off farm.

Next morning Ruth was despatched with her flaggon for milk at the nearest farm. She was confronted by a huge growling dog at the back kitchen door. The bewhiskered farmer appeared from an outhouse and called off the dog, then asked Ruth so many awkward questions and drew her out so cunningly that she blurted out much of what she knew about her mother and Meldrum, even though she didn't understand it or what she was talking about. Then she looked at the sky and began to cry, and the farmer took her by the hand to the kitchen door and told her not to cry, that he would give her the milk.

'I kenned something was wrang, lassie,' the farmer mused slyly in his Angus brogue, 'I kenned something was wrang: yer skin's too white for a tinker's daughter, and ye're too refined like for that kinda life. Hey, Jean,' he cried to his wife, and a somewhat fat, pleasant faced woman came to the door.

The farmer took the flaggon from Ruth and gave it to his wife, going close up to her and whispering low, so that Ruth couldn't hear, and then he turned to Ruth again, raising his voice, 'Yer mither must be a bitch,' he said, almost wilting Ruth with his stare – 'a bitch tae leave yer poor faither for a tinker's life. It's a shame for your sake, lassie, if no for her ain; and think what yer faither must be puttin' up with back hame. And have ye no brithers or sisters, lassie?' he asked her.

'No,' Ruth whimpered, her sobbing somewhat subdued.

'And maybe juist as well, eh lassie. Well well, I suppose

it's none o' my business really.' Turning to his wife in the door he added, 'Put a droppie milk in the lassie's flagon, Jean, and let her be going.'

While Jean went inside to fill the flaggon the farmer stroked his fusker and looked more sternly at Ruth. 'Ye'll get yer milk, lassie,' he said, 'and for nothing; it won't cost ye a penny, but dinna show yer innocent face here again, and tell yer folks to be off my premises by noon tomorrow or I'll set the dog on them.'

Jean filled the flaggon nearly to the brim, so that Ruth couldn't run with it for fear she spilled the milk. Meldrum would be wondering what had hindered her and she would have to hurry; and maybe she wouldn't sleep for watching the stars, in case they should fall because she had told about her mother and Meldrum Spark. Or maybe it would grow dark at noon tomorrow and the world would come to an end, just when they were leaving the wood. But maybe it wasn't so bad telling a stranger and God would forgive her, for her mother had told her there was a God in the sky who watched everything you did and listened to your thoughts. God would know what she had told the farmer but Meldrum and Helen wouldn't know and she needn't tell them. She would blame it all on the dog for hindering her and tell them the farmer was going to set the dog on them tomorrow if they weren't gone by midday. She would have to tell them to be off by then anyway in case it got dark when they were leaving.

'The lousy bastard,' Meldrum exploded when Ruth revealed the farmer's threat, 'but never fret, Ruth quine, we'll be oot o' here a' richt. There's owre mony pearls in the Tay for us tae scutter here ony langer,' and he poured himself a brimming lidful of milk from the flaggon and licked his lips after it was down. 'Damned good milk though,' he mused, 'with plenty of cream on it.'

Next morning, soon after breakfast, Meldrum rolled his pack and stamped out the fire, getting ready for the road while Helen dressed Ruth and combed her hair. Ruth slept better than she had thought and had forgotten all about the shooting stars; not one had fallen, and if noon were past and God didn't put a blanket over the sun she would know He had forgiven her for telling on her mother. Soon they were on the road again, heading south for the Tay, Meldrum with his pack over his shoulder and the glass box under his arm, Helen with her raffia basket and Ruth with her half-empty flaggon, though Helen had promised her she wouldn't have to beg for milk again, and that as soon as the flaggon was empty she would throw it in the river. She would rather starve, she told Meldrum, than have her quine begging milk any more at farmers' doors.

The sun was high and bright at noon and never blinked an eyelid and Ruth knew God had forgiven her. Now she wasn't afraid any more, with God on her side, and she would say a prayer every night after this for the rest of her life (unless she was awfully tired and fell asleep in the middle of it) because God was her friend now and she would say the Lord's prayer every night in the tent, just as Miss Drone had taught her to say it at Leary school. But she would say it quiet-like to herself so that Meldrum or her mother wouldn't hear her, though God would hear her because He heard your thoughts; and she would pray for them also, that God would be kind to them, and also for her poor father, who had been left at home, for ever and ever, ah men!

Indeed the sun had scarcely blinked an eyelid that whole summer, shining every day like a hot furnace, so that the earth was warm and dry at eventide when Helen spread a ground sheet under the tent; otherwise if it had rained a lot they would have been forced to sleep in the farm barns or under a hayrick. When it rained at all it was only a few big drops from a passing thunder cloud, glistening rainbow drops that were like the tears of the angels that sorrowed for their wayfaring, for Ruth felt sure that God and his angels were watching them.

And so they slogged on, another five or six miles on the road, which seemed much further to Ruth, and she said her feet were blistered and that she wanted to take off her shoes. Meldrum said she should be going without shoes anyway at her age and that her feet would harden. He said she had been mollycoddled and her feet were soft and tender. When he was a kid he said his brothers and sisters never had shoes on their feet all summer; that his parents were poor and couldn't afford it, and they all ran barefoot every day all summer to save their shoes for winter. Ruth took off her shoes and walked on the grass to please him, cool and soothing it was until she stood on a thistle and the pain brought tears to her eyes. Meldrum relented at this and promised to stop for the night at the first suitable place. So he chose a site just off the main Perth road, after crossing the Bridge of Isla, a wood within sight of the Tay, and there they slept the night. Meldrum argued that they should have gone further south, even beyond Perth, to the river estuary, where there were good mussel beds, he said, washed down from the upper reaches of the river, where there might be a better chance of finding pearls; and even if they didn't it was much nearer Dundee, he said, and he could maybe get a job in the jute mills long before the rasps were ready for picking.

But Helen refused to go any further. Perth was at the other side of the world as far as she knew, and they were far enough from home as it was without money and very little food and their shoes wearing out, especially Ruth's, with a little hole in one of the soles she could nearly poke her finger through. Meldrum said they could take a short cut through the Sidlaw Hills to the Carse of Gowrie on the Tay estuary but Helen refused to budge. He would have to find pearls where they were or none at all for all she cared; and inwardly she had little hopes of him finding pearls anywhere, up the Tay or down.

Nobody spoke in the tent that night and there was no intercourse – even though Ruth was asleep in a twinkling at their feet, tired and worn out on the dusty roads, even forgetting to say her prayer as she had promised herself.

Usually Meldrum was a late riser, lolling in the warm tent smoking or talking to Helen till nearly noon, when the sun was too hot and the flies too lively for their long walks on the weary roads. Not so however within sight of the gleaming Tay, for almost at the first glint of the sun on the water Meldrum was on his feet, eager to try the glass box in the water, like a schoolboy with a new toy. He even had the fire going and troubled himself to shave while Helen and Ruth still slept. He treated them both to tea in bed when they awakened, when Helen opened her precious raffia basket and produced some biscuits and cheese, buns and marmalade. It was on mornings like these that Helen hungered for a plate of her mother's porridge and a bowl of fresh creamy milk, or even a boiled egg with oatcakes and home-made butter. It was nearly a month since she had enjoyed a cooked meal and the bairn in her wime craved for something more than tinker's tea and dry bread. Oh what she wouldn't give for butter and new tatties at this time of year, new dug from a cottar's garden and still with their skins on, dry and mealy with a fresh herring from a passing lorry or a fishwife with her creel. It was a time of year also that vegetables were fresh for making broth, and as she nibbled at her morsel of tasteless cheese, a poor substitute for the stuff that her mither made, she sighed for the smells and tastes of home, all the things she had thrown away for this arid paradise; this Promised Land that never materialized, but became a morass that landed her deeper and deeper in trouble.

When they were up and dressed Meldrum stamped out the fire but said he wouldn't take down the tent because it was a fine spot to stay while they were pearl fishing; fine out of sight and they only had to walk about a mile down the road and over a field to the river. He took the glass box under his arm and Helen took her knitting, Ruth her flaggon, and when Meldrum asked why she had taken it she said it was to carry the pearls in. He laughed at this and strode down the road whistling, like the birds around him that darted over the fields; sparrows, larks, starlings and swallows, searching out a breakfast for their famished youngsters. Helen and Ruth followed timidly, not too keen to go near a river so large as the mighty Tay, swollen here by the Isla, just north of the railway viaduct. Helen tried Meldrum to fish in the Isla, which was as wide as any river she had ever seen, with fine open parks on its banks, but

Meldrum wouldn't hear of it and said it had to be the Tay. He said the Tay would be the river of their deliverance from poverty, like Helen spoke about in the Bible; the river of their dreams that would solve all their problems and make them all rich and happy for the rest of their lives. The Tay would be their Jordan, Meldrum said.

Helen said nothing but sighed at his boyishness, like a loon on his first fishing trip, with no sense of responsibility beyond the present hour, and that mainly for pleasure if he could make it so. Meldrum went down the road to Cargill Church, crossing a field of rough grass near the manse to the river's edge, screened by trees and gorse from anybody watching. The dew was off the grass by now and the rabbits scuttled into burrows at their approach. Before them the broad river, swift and fearsome at eye level, the broad grassy banks lined with trees, as far in the sunhaze as the eye could see. They were now on the south side of the railway viaduct, where the trains rumbled over it to join the Highland line at Murthly, bound for Perth. High on the bank behind them the dead folk slept under the huge flat stones in Cargill kirkyard, with some higher monuments looking over the dyke, lichened with age and weather-beaten, and above it the Free Church, square as a box, with long lancet windows overlooking the river. There was a white mansion house on the opposite bank, with wide green lawns in front and a thick forest behind it. Meldrum moved further downstream, to be out of sight of these places, fearing maybe that some water-bailie would wonder what he was doing.

By now the river was a glaring liquid heliograph, where every wavelet glinted a reflection. Even so the water was ice cold, and Meldrum looked for a stretch where it wasn't too deep: where he could see the polished pebbles at the bottom, the clear water rushing over them to the deeper pools beyond; where he could use the glass box on the oyster beds. He took off his jacket, shoes and socks, and rolled his trousers above his knees, dipping a dirty foot in the water, his teeth chattering at the thought of it; then touched the bottom and stood with both feet in the river.

He tucked up his shirt-sleeves and reached for the glass box, calling for Helen to come and look into it. Helen stood back from the bank with Ruth, afraid to go near it, but Meldrum coaxed her forward to the water's edge, holding up her long skirts in the sedge, and Meldrum told her to bend down and look in the box, which he now held submerged in the water. Sure enough she could see the bottom, every pebble clear as daylight, and she dragged Ruth forward to have a peep.

'See now,' Meldrum said, when he saw a sparkle of interest in Helen's eyes, 'I told ye I'd find pearls: I've been at this game afore, ye know?'

He now rolled his trousers to his thighs and waded further in, scanning the river bottom with the glass box, while Helen took the flaggon from Ruth and threw it into the river, where the lid flew off and it quickly filled with water and sank. Meldrum was so engrossed that he scarcely heard the splash, but looked round quickly, thinking maybe it was a trout or a salmon leaping at a horse-fly. Helen walked back to the trees with Ruth, where they sat on the dry bent and watched and thought and said nothing, merely waiting or Meldrum had his fling at pearl fishing.

He was in the water a long time, wading up stream and down, searching the river bottom, now and then raising his head to make sure Helen and Ruth were still watching him. It was warm and pleasant in the sun, with only the slightest breeze that ruffled Ruth's hair across her thoughtful brow. But she soon grew restless and wandered back to the water's edge, waving to Meldrum in mid-stream. Helen was thinking deeply, her eyes on the speeding river, her thoughts far away on happier times, and a gentle tear fell on her cheek. She picked up the wool she had brought with her from the tent and wound it into a ball, Ruth holding up the hank for her with both hands in the air. Helen looped the blue worsted over her fingers on to the knitting pins, counting the loops to suit the size she required. She hoped she would get a son, though God knows what would become of him in the straits she was in, or what he would think of her when he grew up, if ever she had to tell him who his father was. She lowered her knitting at the thought of it and burst into tears, sobbing outright in her anguish of heart. She consoled herself in the thought that she still had Ruth, and even at the worst maybe Audie would take her back, if she humbled herself to ask him. She swabbed away the tears with her hankie and raised her head, where Ruth stood before her with her soft clear eyes, staring her straight in the face. In the sharpest moment of her grief Helen saw the image of Audie, watching her with all his innocence and simplicity. She seemed to look upon Ruth in a new and glaring light, as she had never seen her before; her dainty little hands behind her back, just as her father stood, her sturdy legs slightly apart, her childish eyes earnest and questioning, the pure sweet lips of her asking, 'Why are ye cryin', mammy?'

Helen reached out for her with a breaking heart and hugged her to her bosom, rocking her to and fro in her deep emotion. After all, Audie was the father of her quine, she couldn't deny that; poor fumbling Audie, and how delighted he was when he had managed it. But now she had deceived him, and in harming Audie she suddenly felt she was hurting his child also: poor little Ruth, harmless as her father was, and wringing her heart with shame and pity. Whatever came of Meldrum's bairn she didn't think she could ever feel for him as a father like she felt for Audie, the old feeling of compassion rather than love; something akin to sympathy and motherhood – something that Meldrum would never require of her – his wants were physical and robust and could only be served in bed, but she was both wife and mother to Audie. Poor little Ruth, she was his child, and she clung to her slender shoulders (Audie's shoulders) and kissed the hair blowing across her cheeks till the shout of Meldrum from the river stopped her caresses.

Meldrum stood in midstream, the dripping glass box out of the water, his other hand high above his head, an oyster shell firmly gripped in his fingers. He had found a pearl, Ruth thought, and ran towards the river, where she danced for joy while he waded towards her. Helen gathered her knitting and came forward, slowly, to give her eyes time to heal from their crying.

Meldrum laid the glass box on the bank and sprang out of the water, his great bare thighs matted with wet hair and his blue veined feet clean as the driven snow. He told Ruth to run and fetch his knife from his jacket and when she returned he prised the shell open, carefully, in case the pearl should fall out on the grass. But there was no pearl, merely the nebulae of what one day might become a pearl (if Meldrum hadn't opened the shell) a tiny blob of greyish matter near the valve or mouth of the fish. He split the dark blue shell apart with his wet fingers and examined it more carefully, then threw it back in the water. He said nothing, but snatched the glass box from the river bank and plunged in again, scarcely looking at Helen with her amber eyes still wet from weeping. God knows, she thought, the poor devil was trying his best to make her happy in his own flamboyant way, and surely no man could do more. What with two men caring for her she shouldn't have a problem at all. The thought brought a flicker of a smile to her lips as she sat down again to her knitting. Ruth spent the time gathering wild flowers, a treasured posy that she carried home to the tent and put them in an empty jam jar filled with water.

On his second day Meldrum picked up nearly a dozen oyster shells but with no better luck than the first; even worse, for there wasn't even the makings of a pearl in any of the shells he opened. Two swans were on the river with their young, sailing along with the current, the parents silent and majestic, dipping their long arched necks in the crystal water, while three or four cygnets bobbed along on the waves. A heron flapped overhead, craning towards its nest on a lone tree far on the river bank. Even as she watched Ruth saw a hawk with a tremor on his outstretched wings, hovering above the water, for a long long time it seemed, then swooped down suddenly on the bank, rising again with a mouse in its beak, winging towards the woods.

On the morning of the third day an otter sprang into the river in front of Meldrum, almost from under his feet, where perhaps it had been sleeping, and it put him off completely. He said he wouldn't like an otter's bite and didn't go in the water till nearly noon, and much further up the river. On the fourth day he took off his trousers and fished in deep water, his white shirt tail floating behind him, because he had forgotten to tuck it inside his short pants. He stared into the glass box, his lips almost touching the water, while now and then a wave lapped his face, forcing him to gasp when it caught his breath in his nostrils, spluttering for air. Still he peered down the shaft of sunlight caught in the box, scanning the river bottom like a searchlight beam, where water beetles and darting minnows were caught in the light, and the odd oyster shell that Meldrum picked up, sometimes holding his breath and submerging his head in deep water to reach it with his hand, while the undercurrent nearly swept him off his feet.

Helen brought soap from her raffia basket and washed some clothes in the river, sorely needed underclothes that hadn't been washed for weeks, until she thought of it. She soaped the garments and rubbed them between her knuckles in the water, then rinsed them out and hung them on the whins to dry, while she knitted in the sun, seated on a tartan plaid that she used in the tent as a blanket. Meldrum brought her a lapful of oyster shells to open, hoping she would bring him luck; but not one of them contained the wished-for pearl ... 'I wish to God I could find just one,' Meldrum sighed; 'just one pearl to prove to you the thing is possible!' Ruth watched on her bare knees with her little hands spread out on the grass. At the mention of God she suddenly remembered her prayers, and the position of kneeling brought her palms together, in a pose of angelic sublimity. But only for a moment, because she didn't want her elders to see her, and she remembered how Miss Drone had said you should kneel in prayer if you wanted something very much and you wanted God to listen; so this very night she would pray that Meldrum should find a pearl, just one at least when he had tried so hard, and she would pray on her knees so that God would listen. She didn't know how she would manage it without Meldrum or Helen seeing her, because they might laugh at her, but she would try it somehow, because Miss Drone had said that what you ask from God in secret He will give you openly.

But Meldrum was fed up with the pearl fishing and he sat all afternoon in a sulk, drying his clothes and smoking the last of his small hoard of rationed Woodbines. Ruth so wanted to tell him her plan to ask God to find him a pearl but she was too shy; afraid that he would mock at her and call her silly, because the only time he mentioned God at all was when he swore, and Miss Drone said this was wrong, and that God wouldn't listen to you if you took His name in vain; and that He might even punish you for it. But wait till nightfall when she could talk to God all by herself, and she would beg God to forgive Meldrum for swearing, that he didn't mean it badly anyway, and if he could only find a pearl it would make them all so happy, and even Meldrum would believe in Him forever after, because she would tell him later on that she had asked God to let him have the pearl. Miss Drone had said it was one of the greatest things you could do – to make people believe in God, so maybe tomorrow they would see a miracle.

But towards evening, with his last fag gone and hunger in his belly, quite suddenly, and without a word to anyone, Meldrum rose up and threw the glass box far into the river. Helen dropped her knitting and rose up with her great skirts billowing about her swelling waist, her hair loosened from its pins and blowing in the gentle breeze, while she watched the glass box dancing on the waves. Ruth burst out crying, and Meldrum was sore amazed at her concern for the glass box, though he never guessed her real heartache. Then all three gazed at the glass box bobbing along on the current like a tiny ship, the symbol of all their hopes and wishes gone forever; now a mere speck on the mighty river, until it disappeared completely, lost in the glare of the sun on the sparkling waters, speeding towards the sea.

That night in the tent it was decided they should return home. Helen couldn't endure the uncertainty any longer; without money or food, nor any prospect of work for Meldrum, or the likelihood of his keeping a job though he had one, and her high regard for him was finally waning. Ruth slept through all their talk and planning on an empty stomach, and with her clothes on, for there was a chill in the air from the river that night and Helen told her to keep them on. They breakfasted on water and butter biscuits, a packet that Helen had managed to save in the bottom of her raffia basket. She had one shilling left, and this she hid in her stocking, under her garter, so that the King's head was stamped out on her milk white thigh. Meldrum was desperate for a smoke and searched the raffia basket, though he wasn't slack to put his hand up her skirt also, had he thought it worth his while. 'Two pennies for five Woodbines at the nearest shoppie.' That would be enough, he said, but Helen denied him and kept the shilling to buy their last bite on the way back to Blairgowrie.

Even Meldrum had lost all enthusiasm for going on to Dundee. The disappointment of the pearl fishing and the want of a smoke had deflated him completely. As a last resort he tried Helen to pawn her wedding ring, but she refused, though she still wore it on the wrong hand. They got biscuits and a packet of five Woodbines in a small emporium by the roadside, and Meldrum put a slant on his Glengarry and asked a cottar woman for hot water and a spoonful of tea and sugar. He must have flattered her considerably, because she added milk besides, and Helen said it was the best mug of tea she had tasted for weeks, better than Meldrum's 'Tinker's Tea', she said, and ventured a vague smile, while Meldrum winked at Ruth and lit the first of his Woodbines, stubbing the spent match into the soft earth by the roadside.

Back in Blairgowrie they rested in the town square again. Helen made some excuse to go to the post-office explaining to Meldrum that when she wrote to her mother she asked her to write back to that address and she would call for the letter, presuming that they would still be in the rasp country. Meldrum waited with Ruth, seated on the same hard bench as before, his pack beside him, his Glengarry on the back of his head, staring at the horse traffic and the odd motor car circling the busy square, besides any woman body on a bicycle that showed a bit of leg. Ruth sat with her arm half across her mother's raffia basket on the seat, as if she were afraid that Meldrum would steal it.

When Helen returned she took a pound note from her mother's letter and spread it out on the seat. 'What's this then?' Meldrum asked, 'have ye robbed the bank?'

'No – ye silly ass,' Helen joked, 'but when I wrote that letter in the post-office I asked ma mither tae send us a pound note tae ease oor distress. I juist kent that yer pearl fishin' wad be a failure afore ye started, and that we wad be in trouble by this time.'

'Good for old Rachael tae send us money,' Meldrum replied sarcastically, 'but it's a pity she hadna sent us twa pound notes; or even a fiver, come tae that.'

'But it's nae easy for her tae do that,' Helen retorted. 'Daw doesna ken she's sendin' us money, and if he did he would be angry. You should be thankful for what we've got; after all, it's more than you've made in the last five weeks or so; you and yer pearl fishin' and yer tales o' grandeur and ma quine sellin' heather besoms and beggin' for milk on the roads. I've heard enough o' yer plans that come tae naething and yer promises o' better things that never happen; a' yer rosy pictures that dinna exist except in yer ain mind. If ye took an honest job o' work I might have gone on, but now I've lost faith in ye, Meldrum Spark, and yer no good to me at all.'

Helen was almost in tears by now and Meldrum again reminded her it took the two of them to play the game and that she was no angel herself sometimes – except in looks maybe, and that she had beguiled him as much as he was supposed to have fooled her. He reminded her also of the time he had begged her to let him go, because of his respect for Audie, and how she had wept in his bosom and said it would break her heart. Had she forgotten that? But the tears came faster and he relented, for he was never harsh with her and seldom lost his temper. No matter how she taunted him he was always gentle and forgiving; indeed it seemed he was sincere in his care for her but circumstances were against him. He had played a losing game from the start: no match for the stoical, indomitable little man he had stolen her from. Audie would win in the end and Meldrum knew it. The tide had turned and was now running his way. Quite soon he would have them all at his feet, begging his forgiveness and their right to live with him; even Meldrum himself would require him to father his child, and only if Audie consented would he be allowed even to see it. But how could Audie know all this? He thought he was still on the losing side, his attitude hardening to the whole affair, not knowing nor caring much how they fared, except a thought for Ruth that gnawed at his insides when he lay on his chaumer bed, the red sun of evening at the skylight, when a lonely tear would steal from his eye and wander down his cheek. But he had gotten a job again, and that was something, struggling behind a pair of horses at the Dunns' place, a fairm toon not far from Scotstoun, working as a single man, while his mother washed his clothes and sometimes put him up for the week-end.

'I doot we'll hae tae part, lass,' Meldrum was saying, 'though it breaks my heart.'

Helen knew that it wouldn't break his heart but she still felt sorry for him. He had tried to a certain extent to make her happy; to make a go of it, but he just wasn't the type to be saddled for long with a woman and a child. People were passing to and fro in the sunshine and Helen tried hard to stifle her tears. He put his arm along the back of the seat beside her and crossed his legs. Helen still had the letter in her hand and with the other she took her handkerchief and daubed away the tears from her cheeks. 'I'm goin' hame tae ma mither,' she said at last, 'though God only knows what will happen tae us after that!'

With one arm round her shoulder he placed his other hand in one of hers, where she held the raffia basket on her knees. 'I've landed ye in a sad mess, lass,' he said huskily, 'and I'm heart-sorry for ye.' She looked in his handsome face, and his brown eyes were smiling almost in gentleness, caressing her tear-stained face with all the love a woman could ever expect from a man. His voice hadn't changed: still capable of reducing her to girlhood and bidding her follow him to the ends of the earth – if it was physically possible. But for her it wasn't possible and she knew it and changed the subject.

'My mither says in her letter that Hamish has married Cora Swapp and moved into her mother's croft. They had a quiet weddin' at the Registrar's office in Brochan, just her mother and Riach and Craig and Rachael, and they had a High Tea in some hotel or other after it and that was all. And Hamish has taken your shelt with him, up to the croft at Burrowend, under the Deer on the Mattock, and he's growing vegetables tae sell in Brochan.'

'Good for him,' says Meldrum, 'but I dinna suppose I'll manage tae sell them anither shelt, nae efter what I've done tae their sister, givin' her a big belly and all that; I'll be fear't tae show ma face at Bogmyrtle again.'

Helen waited till her eyes had cleared before she went shopping, Ruth carrying the raffia basket. The pound note wouldn't pay their fares home but it would at least keep them alive. When she rose up to go Meldrum gave her a smack on the behind. 'Dinna forget ma fags, lass,' he cried after her, showing his big even teeth in a wide grin.

They slept that night in the Alyth Woods, a sad and eerie place where Helen listened half the night to a farmer's dog that howled like an infant bairn.

Next morning Meldrum took the trouble to shave, now that he had hot water again; down on his knees on the grass, while Ruth held the mirror for him. He had three days' growth of beard and squirmed under the rasp of the cut-throat razor on the hard bristle. But there was no fun in giving her beardie before he started, or swinging her in the air by a leg and arm when he had finished, as was his usual habit; things had become far too serious for that though Ruth never questioned his change of behaviour nor understood the cause of it.

And so the long journey home began, the retreat from nowhere, while the green rasps were ripening on the canes and the tinkers were gathering for the picking, their shelts tethered in the woods and quarries and the bairns playing round the smoke from their fires, their floats and spring-carts loaded with rags and dishes and their long shafts on the ground. Some of them had caravans and had come straight from Aikey Fair for the rasp gathering, while others hawked the countryside: old men with beards and rings on their fingers, women with straight black hair down their backs like schoolgirls, or plaited over their heads like tiaras, their skin browned with the sun and campfires, their eyes clear and bright when you met them with their bundles in the country lanes, some of them young with babies on their backs and the occasional grandmother smoking a clay pipe. Some of them knew Meldrum and he avoided their glances, while the women stared at Helen and little Ruth, their white skin pink with sunburn, wondering what he had to do with them. There were gypsies, tinks and hawkers, whatever you liked to call them, all awaiting the harvest of the rasp, where they would get their feet off the hard roads for a while, and then the tattie lifting in the Mearns, when they would make enough money to last them through another Scottish winter. But while the rasp ripened and the gypsies waited, Meldrum was in full retreat, he and his long-skirted woman who was a match for any of them in feature and form, but for the bairn that now forced her to take off her corsets and burn them in the campfire, a little demon that inflamed her nipples and tugged at her navel like she had never felt with Ruth, for surely it was a loon this time she was carrying for Meldrum; maybe an image of his father that would remind her of her lover for the rest of her life. But she was no match for the gypsy women in having her bairn by the roadside: compared with them she was a hothouse plant and Meldrum had to fly with her to the refuge of home and whatever cold comfort awaited her there.

Now on through Kirriemuir and up the narrow brae to Thrums out on to the road for Brechin, sticking to the main road in the hope of getting a lift from one of the motor-lorries: a long road for Ruth in her slim-soled shoes, her feet blistered on the hard surfaces, her little heart weary of walking and her hair full of dust from the lorries.

The traffic increased at Brechin but when Meldrum tried

to hail the lorry drivers for a lift none of them would stop. Helen was lagging now and Meldrum carried her raffia basket besides the pack on his back. Her heart was heavy and her legs were weary; and she heaved many a sigh and whispered many a prayer while Meldrum snored and Ruth was asleep, at night in the tent. She was a changed woman from the one who walked so sprightly to church in her dark blue hat and veil just a year before: a farmer's daughter, folk might say. And Audie had been so proud of her, showing her off to the neighbours, making it worth while going to church, just to see her rigged like that, her little hand on his arm and him in his best serge suit, waving to folk in their gigs or lifting his bonnet to the Laird or his Lady if they met them at the kirk door. Helen still wore the hat but tore off the veil weeks ago and threw it on a whin bush. Now she was a waif without a home or a husband; the black sheep who had gone astray and now sought the safety of the fold again.

The pound note still lasted and they didn't have to beg, though Brechin nearly saw the last of it for bread and groceries. By the time they reached Laurencekirk they were penniless and on to their last scraps of food. Sometimes the railway ran parallel with the road and they met a train going south, pulled by one of those saucer-funnelled locomotives that had carried them to the Promised Land in such a frantic hurry. And so on through the Mearns, rich in its brown loam and its wide green farmlands sloping to the Grampians; cattle and sheep on the pastures and the menfolk making hay, each one with his pitchfork a reminder to Helen of the man of the soil she had wronged. The cottar wives in their gardens or walking their bairns home from school, smug in their sense of home and security: something Helen had thrown to the winds and would give almost anything to recover.

They reached Stonehaven destitute, and Meldrum set up the tent by the Cowie burn. Ruth went to bed supperless; not for her the fun of the carnival across the stream on the links, though Meldrum and Helen sat for a long time on the cool grass listening to the music from the electric organ.

Next morning Meldrum made a fire of the tent when he took it down and they warmed themselves at the blaze. They stood by the roadside; homeless, penniless and without breakfast, while Meldrum thumbed a lift to Aberdeen from every passing lorry driver. But today his luck had changed, for one of them drew up and stopped. Helen and Ruth got in the driver's cab and Meldrum rode on the back, straight to Aberdeen, where they got off in the Castlegate. They made for a pawnbroker's shop in Queen Street where Helen pawned her wedding ring for a pound. This was the ring she had hidden in the pendulum clock until the night Audie left them in the cottage, the night she and Ruth heard the ghost enter the kitchen at Sauchieburn. With the money they had fish and chips in a restaurant, for by now they were famished, and they had a slice of bread and a cup of tea to wash them down. They walked up Union Street as far as Queen Victoria's statue, where she stood in her long back robes, on a pillar of polished granite, the sceptre in one hand and a great ball in the other, like a crofter wife trimming a turnip, her sonsie face composed and stern, gazing down Market Street, watching the ragged trio on their way to the railway station. Their life together was in the last hour and not a word passed between them. Helen bought tickets for herself and Ruth to Leary Station, and Meldrum accompanied them into the waiting carriage. People were passing the carriage door, looking for seats, but no one came in for the moment so he sat down on the opposite seat and held both her hands in his own. Even a child could see they still loved each other, but the world was against them. Whatever his faults, parting from Meldrum was breaking Helen's heart, but she didn't cry; she didn't want to be in tears when he left her, to carry that last picture of her for the rest of his life, so she bore up and smiled for him to the last bitter moment. He went over to her side and kissed her for the last time: not the passionate, hungry love bite of their earlier courting, when the soul is pollinated, but a tender, lingering kiss she would remember with her dying breath. He kissed Ruth also, and hugged her little form in his great arms, telling her to look after her mother for him, and when he stood up his eyes were rimmed with tears. The train was filling with people, and doors were getting a final slam. The guard went past the carriage window with the green flag under his arm; at any moment now he would blow his whistle. The engine was hissing steam, anxious to be off, the driver watching from his cabin. Meldrum was on the platform, holding Helen's arm at the open window, Ruth on tiptoe at her elbow. The final shriek of the engine whistle, and the train moved gently forward, ever so gently, slowly at first; it was the perfect parting, Helen waving from the carriage window, Meldrum throwing a final kiss from the platform, until she lost sight of him in a blur of tears.

Meldrum would find his own way in the city, afraid to show his face for some time to come in the Bogside, where their elopement was on every tongue that wagged for twal mile roon Bogmyrtle way.

Helen closed the window and sat down, and as the train clattered through the Denburn she gave way to tears. When they emerged from the tunnels Ruth was beside her and climbed into her arms: 'Dinna greet, mummy,' she pleaded, 'I'll look after ye!' After all, it was what Meldrum had asked her to do.

They were racing towards the Mattock Hill at a pounding gallop. Ruth stood tiptoe at the open carriage window, watching the rich green countryside rushing by. The hill was powdered in purple, for the heather bells were now in bloom. There were patches of green where the long-stemmed bracken grew in the shadows, and over by the Fairies' Cairn Ruth remembered that green cones would be forming on the pine trees. Lachbeg Woods were tinted with many shades of green, while here and there the bright gold laburnum swung his tassels over the Laird's dykes. Near the foot of the hill Ruth could see the thin blue peat smoke rising above the trees at Bogmyrtle.

When the train rounded the last bend Ruth could see the steel driving-rods on the engine wheels, flying like a weaver's shuttle, and the brown and cream coaches were swinging at the couplings like the vertebrae of a giant crawling centipede. The train slowed at Leary Station signal-box and Helen took down her raffia basket from the luggage rack. Now they were on the platform and Helen gave her tickets to the stationmaster at the wicket gate.

Very few others alighted, so the porter and the stationmaster had plenty of time to size them up. Soon the whole parish would know that Helen MacKinnon was home from the south, and that she was somewhat full in the breasts and round of belly, and that the clothes she wore were only fit for a tinker's wife, and not for a farmer's daughter to be seen in: least of all a MacKinnon, when her father had such conceit of himself. And that was Audie Foubister's bairn that had her hand, Craig MacKinnon's oldest grand-child, though she didn't have his corn-coloured hair, but took more after her father's people in the town yonder; a refined sort of bairn but far too innocent looking to be mixing with the MacKinnon folk, though they said at the school that the younger ones were more genteel and more like the quine herself than the older ones, and had more sense.

Craig MacKinnon's farming neighbours would be discussing the whole affair at the marts, and their wives would chew it over again among themselves at the chapel on Sunday. It would take some of the conceit out of old Craig, they thought, and maybe it was what he deserved for ill-using his Christian mother (God rest her soul) his dother going off with a tinker like Meldrum Spark, who had bairned as many women as Craig had heifers in calf, though not all of them in the Bogside, or you would have heard more about it; and most likely he was the father of the bairn in Helen MacKinnon's wime. But what about poor Audie Foubister, the breet? He would be a damned fool gin he took the bitch back again, though the cheil must have a hame and he might be right glad to have her back, bairn and all, though he wasn't its father. It was easy enough for folk to speak of what they would do with a stray wife but a different thing for the poor man body that had her. Well well, but Audie Foubister was a good servant; you only had to ask Candy Birnie of Sauchieburn about that, and he would tell you that poor Audie didn't deserve this. But the Lord moves in mysterious ways, Aye Faith, and there might be a purpose behind it all that a poor mortal body couldn't see.

So they would have a dram over it at the marts, seeing the stirks had sold so well, though not so dear as they were during the war, and it was a pity for some of them that it had to end, though some of them that hadn't folk in it wouldn't have cared how long it lasted, for they came out of it a damned sight richer than they went in. And they would swill down the blood of Christ at Communion (careful not to spill a drop on their fine clothes) like the bunch of hypocrites they were, with not a thought of His teaching in how to treat the harlot amongst them, but ready with the first stone to throw at her.

Helen and Ruth trudged up the weary road to Bog-myrtle, where the white gowans stared at them from their long slender stems and the green rowans hung in clusters from the Mountain Ash. Their path was strewn with rose petals, pink and white, a wanton mockery of promised joy. The sparrows swung gaily on the ripening corn stalks, banqueting in noisy chorus, but now swarmed off in noisy confusion. A lark sang merrily over the hayfield, but at the sight of the strangers he dropped like a stone, while the swallows swooped and dived over the scented hay swaths, heedless of human folly. As they neared Bogmyrtle Helen grew more tense; for many long nights and weary days she had dreaded this homecoming, and now it was upon her. This final rehearsal made her feel faint. So many times she had gone over it in her mind, trying to imagine what it would be like, that when the hour of fate had come she felt she couldn't face it. Would her brothers and sisters spit at her, slap her face or pull her hair out? – or would they merely ignore her with cold stares? But the spirit of old Joyce was at her elbow, whispering words of comfort in her inner ear: 'There are ninety and nine that are safe in the fold, it is the lost sheep gone astray that I have come to save.'

But even the white stone deer on the Mattock Hill seemed to sniff the air with suspicion, tilting his antlers in defiance of the intruders. The peat smoke felt repugnant, rife with resentment; while the midges rose in their myriad thousands, thirsting for the blood of the strangers.

A lone hare loped across the Buttercup Field, almost to the gate, but when he spotted Ruth he stopped, raising his long ears in sudden alarm, then scampered off as from a gunshot scare.

Meg and Bell were with the cattle on the Well pasture, plucking their evening meal from the lush meadow grass, never raising their heads, brushing the flies from their backs with their sweeping tails.

The sun gilded the Mattock Hill in a halo of flaming crimson, fingering the fleecy clouds with a Midas Touch of shimmering gold, thwarting the weary travellers with his treasures while they stood in want, awed at his splendour on a mother-of-pearl sky, a final jibe at the failure of their woeful journey. The earth lay basking in the radiance of his smile, while he spangled his gold in her lap of plenty.

Nearer the gardens there was a fragrance of carnation, gladdening their hearts with a gay caress. Wallflower scented their breath with her violet petals. Nasturtium clung to the farmhouse walls; sweet-pea flowers hung like butterflies with closed wings, all too modest in their rainbow dresses. Lupins stood like tiny minarets and coloured the gardens with their pointing fingers. Fuschias dangled on slender stems, their ruby lobes hanging like earrings in the sleepy sunshine.

It seemed to Ruth that their only friends were in the farmyard, where the water spootie that poured into the millrace showed no sign of change; still offering its crystal lavishness to the thirsting stranger. The ducks too, that gambolled in the trough, threw water on their backs from their yellow bills, like a sign of welcome.

Helen's heart was beating quickly now, and she shrank from the ordeal like a spectre would fly the dawn. All that she had tried to hide would now be dragged out in the full light of day. She suddenly felt an alien even in her father's own farmyard; alone in the world, crushed by its enormity. Her next thought was to turn and flee – but whither she knew not. And not a soul to welcome her: not even the bark of a dog or a cock crow; nothing but a brooding silence that awaited her intrusion, hanging in the air, ready to spring. Even Little Janet with a ball at the gable would have broken the ice for her.

Helen caught a glimpse of her father at the gable window, deep in his armchair and the newspaper over his head. But it was the bark of the collie dog that scattered the cats from the kitchen door and brought her mother forth in her work-a-day apron.

'Oh, my quine,' she cried, 'I'm right glad tae see ye back. The sicht o' ye near gars me greet.' She hugged Helen and kissed both her cheeks and when she bent down Ruth held up her cheek also for her lips. Big tears hung at Helen's eyelids but they refused to fall, while she clung to her mother's slender shoulders. She would have to be braver than this to face the others. Rachael seemed to sense her fears for she said: 'Never mind what Daw says, and dinna greet for ony sake; mak' them think yer brave and hearty.' And then Rachael led them down the stone step into the kitchen.

But Helen hadn't the brazen heart of a bitch and she winced under the stares that met her eyes in the gloom of the smoke-filled kitchen. She sat down wearily on a hard chair in front of the box-bed, her raffia basket on the floor, while Ruth stood beside her with her hand on the back of the chair. Nobody stirred a foot to welcome them, nor moved a lip; nobody except Rachael, who busied herself between the table and the peat fire, getting something for them to eat. 'Tak' aff yer coat and yer hat,' Rachael said, 'and I'll hang them in the passage.'

Helen took out her hat-pins and removed her hat, but shook her head when Rachael asked for her coat as well. With a woman's instinct Rachael knew what this might mean, but she said nothing and went to hang up the hat, while Ruth stood guard over the raffia basket.

It seemed that Helen couldn't have chosen a worse

evening for her homecoming. And it was no dress rehearsal but the real thing with a full cast on stage, waiting to see her ridiculed and humiliated and broken to tears. Even Hamish was there with his young wife Cora Swapp, a very good-looking woman with straight black hair bobbed all round with a fringe on her brow, and bright honest eyes that swept over Helen like a search beam. Sherran Begg was also on the deas, with Moira beside him and one of her bairns on her lap. Kirsteen sat on her lover's knee by the passage door, the garage proprietor she had met in her flower selling; maybe that was his motor car Helen had glimpsed in the close when her mother came to the door. Nancy stood behind them, the only one of the MacKinnon quines who hadn't a lad, though folk knew well enough that she wasn't a virgin. She had been jilted once or twice and maybe that was why she had more sympathy for Helen than any of her sisters. Janet and Meston sat on a stool, with Moira's bairns at their feet, playing with a pack of cards to keep them amused, until Rachael put them outside to play after Helen and Ruth arrived.

Craig awoke and lowered his newspaper and glowered across the room. When he spied Helen he seemed surprised and took off his reading glasses to see her better.

'So yer hame again, lass,' was all he said.

'Aye, I'm hame,' she ventured timidly, looking at her father with her soft earnest eyes.

'Ye'll hae seen a lot o' ferlies in yer travels in the sooth?'

Helen wasn't sure if it was a question or a statement, but she tried to answer her father politely, relying on him above all to show some understanding of her plight.

'Aye, Daw,' she answered calmly, 'I've seen a lot o' ferlies.' Her cheeks were flushed and white by turns and her heart was beating at her neck.

'Whaur's the tink?'

It was Riach who asked the question, where he sat on the end of the deas, with his cork leg stretched out purposely across the stone floor of the kitchen. He now gritted his teeth, awaiting an answer, staring at his sister with eyes like frosted glass.

Helen began to sob and dabbed her eyes with her handkerchief.

Rachael stamped her foot in front of Riach and threatened him with her fists. 'Let her be, Riach,' she cried, 'D'ye hear! Let yer sister alane. Can't ye see she's been through enough already; and that goes for the rest o' ye – let her alane!'

'Meldrum's shelt bit me yesterday,' Hamish broke in, pulling up his sleeve to display a weal on the flesh under his elbow.

'I dinna like the white ring in his eye,' Cora piped in, speaking up for her husband.

Craig took it as a sort of hint that he had made a mistake in buying it. 'He's a good shelt,' he said gruffly. 'I wadna hae bocht it had I thocht itherwise.'

Sherran Begg handed round his fag packet in an effort to stop any argument that might ensue. Whatever his faults (being a blow-bag and all that) Sherran was always the peacemaker among the MacKinnons, unless Moira blew her top, and the only way he could quieten her was in bed, with one testicle at that, and he made a brag of it when he had a dram in. Sherran with his white square face, sharp greenish eyes, toothbrush moustache, straight brown hair, parted in the middle, ears battered close to the sides of his head; stocky and alert in his movements, with a hard clear voice that could be heard above all the others in the kitchen.

Riach took a fag from Sherran's packet and stuck it in his mouth, then ordered Ruth to bring a cinder from the peat ash. 'Gie's a quile, quine,' he snapped, staring at Ruth with his mocking eyes.

Ruth went meekly over to the fire and fixed a peat ember on the tongs with both her hands and carried it round to her uncle.

But she forgot about Riach's leg stretched out by the end of the table, tripped and fell on top of him with the hot ember. Riach threw her on the floor with a thump and roared with laughter, rescued the glowing ember with his bare hand, lit his fag and threw the cinder back in the fire.

But Helen was on him like a tigress, where she picked

Ruth up from the floor, roused at last by his derision and contempt, determined to stand up for her quine at least. She stood over him with her fingers clenched, while Riach winced under her rage, trying to catch her wrists before she aimed a blow. 'I wunna hae my quine made a fool of,' Helen screamed, 'not by anyone here, and if ye dinna want me I'll clear out now and tak' my bairn with me. I'll walk the roads and sleep in barns rather than put up wi' this. Maybe I'll get more help from strangers than I'll get here!'

Helen's outburst silenced everybody and they all stared at her in surprise; amazed that she had the guts to flare up like this. But Riach now had her by the wrists, while she struggled in vain to get free, falling on top of him in her frenzy, until at last he let her go and she slid on the floor. Rachael ran to help her up and, still breathing heavily, Helen went to the passage to get her hat.

But Rachael stopped her. 'Na na, quine, we'll hae none o' that,' she cried, pushing Helen back to the kitchen and closing the passage door. 'Folk wad think we had thrown ye oot and we canna hae that.'

'Folk can think or say what they like,' Helen retorted, still defiant; 'things canna be much worse than they are onywye.'

Rachael thumped at Riach with her wicked fists until the dust flew out of his jacket, then tugged and pulled until she had him out of the deas, bending in his cork leg so that he could stand on it. 'Go and water yer flowers, Riach,' she cried, putting his cap in his hands.

He had lost his fag in the tussle and he put on his cap sulkily. 'It's hard lines,' he spat out, 'hard lines that a respectable body has tae leave his ain fireside for the sake o' a prodigal,' (though he could have called her something worse) and he looked round all the faces in the kitchen, giving his words time to sink in. 'She has disgraced the lot of us,' he continued, 'she has disgraced the MacKinnons, goin' off wi' that tink Meldrum Spark.' And with a sneering look at his white-faced sister he creaked his way out of the kitchen on his cork leg, where Janet and Meston and the grandchildren joined him at the door.

But the struggle had been too much for Helen and she fainted in Nancy's arms by the passage door. Now they all gathered round her, concerned for her safety, and they moved the table back and laid her on the deas. Nancy opened the neck of her sister's blouse, unbuttoned the coat and the skirt that held her so tightly, while Rachael ran for brandy and smelling salts to revive her.

When Helen opened her eyes again she was in bed, Ruth sleeping beside her and Nancy on a chair by the storm window. It was almost dark but she remembered her old attic, even though she couldn't see that the wallpaper had been changed in her absence. It was still a warm summer evening and she felt the sweet smell of honeysuckle that came up from the garden.

Nancy noticed that her sister was awake, and she rose from her chair and came over to her. 'Are ye a' right now?' she asked.

'Aye, Nancy, I'm fine. What came over me?'

'Ye must have fainted or something, and Hamish and Sherran carried ye up here and I took aff most o' yer claes. Mammy said she wad send for the doctor if ye didna come round shortly.'

'Oh but I'm a' richt now,' Helen said, 'I'm nae needin' a doctor. I'm juist hungry, affa hungry; I havna had ony-thing tae eat since we left Aberdeen.'

'Of course ye wad be hungry, ye didna get ony supper. But I'll go doonstairs and mak' a cup o' tae for ye. Mammy will be so pleased that ye're feelin' better. And dinna worry aboot Ruth, she got melk and a piece.'

'Thanks, Nancy, ye've been so good tae me; better than I deserve.'

'Now now, none o' that,' said Nancy, as she tripped down the narrow stair to the passage and the kitchen.

Old Craig MacKinnon had never gotten the length of buying a binder for the harvest work. Hamish and Riach had pestered him for years to get a binder and make things easier for everybody at Bogmyrtle. But he was thrawn, old Craig, and set in his ways and had a mind of his own and it wasn't easy to change him. And if you tried too hard he would flare up at you and tell you he was master and then sulk for days over it. Craig MacKinnon had never taken orders from anyone in his life and his family knew better than argue with him. He was headstrong and determined in anything he set his mind to and usually carried it out with spirit and thoroughness.

But he had a fairly strong case in carrying on with the old back-delivery reaper, for he could manage with Meg and Bell on the drag-pole, but if he got a binder (unless it was a very lightsome one) he would have to buy another horse for the hairst, or borrow one from a neighbour. And think of the precious time some of his neighbours wasted at the smiddy on a fine day with these new-fangled contraptions, and the money it cost them for repairs, compared with the old reaper that never required more than a drop of oil and a newly sharpened blade; and there was the twine to think about, at such an expense nowadays since the war, and you didn't need twine with the reaper, just a wisp of straw to bind your sheaves, and the twine wasn't good for your beasts eating the straw, and it was a wonder the creatures didn't choke on it.

Most of his neighbours had a binder or shared one, but they had a bigger acreage in crop and mostly a man's wages to pay, so that a binder was a good investment for them, whereas Craig grew more tatties and vegetables and didn't have a large corn acreage, just enough to tide the beasts over the winter and provide oat-meal for his family. Craig didn't depend on grain for a living as most of his neighbours did, but on fresh vegetables and flowers, and dammit man, you couldn't cut these with a binder. He also argued that the old-fashioned harvest provided work for his family, and kept them out of mischief, and they were tidy with a tangled crop compared with a binder. You only had to look over the dyke to see the waste on your neighbours' twisted crops, then compare it with your own that was gathered and bound and stooked by the hands of your own family. And look at the rank stubble these binders left in a lying crop, all that waste of good straw, while your old reaper

231

sheared the crop to the ground, shaved like a razor, nothing wasted at all.

So Hamish and Riach got nowhere with their father when they tried him to modernize and get a binder, though they talked it over friendly enough round the supper table, careful not to anger him. Though Hamish was older than Riach, and sat next to his father on the deas, he didn't have much authority at Bogmyrtle. Hamish had been working all these years in the grain store in Brochan, where he had been foreman in the end, until he married Cora Swapp and went to the croft at Burrowend, so he only worked spare time at Bogmyrtle, and now that he was cultivating a vegetable garden of his own he would have less time than ever to spare. Riach had been at home all his life and was now Craig's right-hand man in everything he turned his mind to.

The hairst was a bit early this year, because of the dry summer, and the crop wasn't all that heavy, so as soon as the corn was thoroughly ripe (for Craig insisted on this) Riach got his scythe out of the old gig-shed, where it hung on a rafter (out of reach of the bairns) and sharpened it with a broadstraik (lined with tough sandpaper – before the days of carborundum stone) and set off with the scythe on his shoulder for the cornfield to clear roads for the reaper. He would take Nancy with him to gather and bind the sheaves, and set them against the dykes until they were stooked with the rest of the crop.

And now you could see why it was so important for Riach to manage without his crutch, for how could he swing a scythe with a crutch under his arm? To see him on the job you could never have guessed he had an artificial leg. It was even more important to him than ploughing, because he had the stilts to lean on, but with the scythe or the hoe or the pitchfork Riach was on his own, and he had proved himself as good as the next man at any job he tried. For all his faults Riach had overcome his handicap and the neighbours admired him for his pluck with a pair of horses on one leg, and their praise gave him something to brag about.

Riach's weakness was with women, because he couldn't go to dances and get acquainted with them as Hamish did, so he was out of his element in their company and needed a dram to loosen his tongue. He was meantime content to worship from afar some of the quines he met on his vegetable round, but so far he had never managed to pluck up courage to go courting. His sisters understood Riach and his predicament, especially Nancy, who was his favourite, and had even offered to go courting for him, and wanted to ask Miss Dell of the schoolhouse to be his bride. She had dropped a few well-chosen hints to Miss Dell when she met her at the Emporium, and had invited her to go to tea and a walk through the gardens and glass-houses, and although the invitation had been accepted and performed Riach had never managed to say what was in his heart, even though Nancy had made an excuse to gather in the eggs and left him alone with Miss Dell in the potting-shed. So the match had been suspended, indefinitely it seemed, until Riach made up his mind, or could muster courage to speak for himself; or until Miss Dell found another, more forthright suitor, though she was flattered immensely being Riach's dream girl, and waved to him in the parks every time she went past on her bicycle.

So Riach swung the rasping blade against the corn stalks, falling in the swath for Nancy to gather in her arms and bind together with a wisp from the sheaf, sometimes with a pair of old stockings on her bare arms to save the skin getting inflamed.

When Kirsteen came home from flower selling after dinner, Craig took another scythe and broadstraik from the gig-shed, and the two of them would join Riach and Nancy, slashing round the field, Kirsteen with a fag in her lip-sticked mouth and gold rings in her ears that matched her corn-ripe hair, tied up with a ribbon like a pony tail.

In midafternoon Rachael sent Helen with a flagon of hot tea and buttered scones for the harvesters, and while they all sat round a stook Hamish went up the road with his shelt and empty float, back from Brochan where he had sold a few hunderweights of early potatoes and carrots, and

was on his way home to Burrowend on the hillside. If the
MacKinnons were near the roadside Hamish would stop
his shelt and pass the time of day with them, and if he came
near enough you could feel the smell of whisky in his breath.
And Riach would taunt him that the grocer had stayed a
long time with his van at Burrowend, where he had seen it
standing at the gable, and if Cora wasn't buying all that
was in it surely she must be taking up with the grocer; a
thing that wasn't possible while her mother was about the
place, but now that she had gotten a house in Brochan and
left the quine on her own, there was no saying what she
could be up to. So Hamish hiccoughed and lit another fag
and said Riach was just bloody jealous he wasn't in the
grocer's shoes, but he turned these things over in his mind
and wondered, and maybe the drink had some influence on
his thinking, and he said he'd away home and skelp Cora's
arse for her trouble. By this time the bairns were coming up
the road from the school: Janet, Meston and Ruth, shelling
peas they had stolen from somebody's park; and they got
a ride on the float with Hamish to the end of the avenue to
Bogmyrtle.

But Hamish was always skelping Cora's bare hips or
threatening to take her knickers off, even in front of the
folk at Bogmyrtle, so they thought nothing of it and never
believed he would try it. He had teased her like this from
the earliest days of their courting and the folk at Bogmyrtle
had become used to it. When Cora sat between Riach and
Hamish on the deas they sometimes had her skirling with
laughter, tickling her in the most vulnerable places, but she
was an open-minded quine who liked a bit of fun and she
played tricks on the men when she had the chance. But
since they got the croft Hamish sometimes came down to
Bogmyrtle on his own, mostly in the evening when Cora
was milking the cow, and Rachael would haver with Hamish
about how many dozen eggs she had sold that week to the
grocer, or how much butter she had churned from one cow,
and the cheese she had curded, and the scones and bannocks
she had baked, and the oat-cakes she had turned on the
girdle; and when Hamish compared this with Cora's puny

output it wasn't long or Rachael had them at loggerheads. And next day at the scything, or maybe cleaning out a ditch by the roadside, when Hamish drew up with his shelt, Riach said it was the postie who had stayed a long time with Cora, and that it was time he had her bairned or someone else would maybe do it for him.

Things like that irked Hamish, and the drink spurred him on, until the day he went home and chased Cora with a turnip slicer, and the poor innocent quine had to run to a neighbour for safety, until Hamish was sober, and the folk thought it was safe for her to go back to him, the neighbour lad taking Cora over the park to the croft, just to make sure. And Hamish now sobered up and filling tatties into bags for his next day in Brochan, wondering what the hell had come of Cora, that she wasn't there to help him; and when she reminded him about the turnip slicer he denied it and said he couldn't remember a thing about it. So the drink was having a bad effect on Hamish; and going to Brochan gave him a chance to buy it from ready cash in his money bag, that Cora took good care of when he got home, or what was left of it. But the silly stories that Riach and his mother told fair irked Hamish, and the drink worked him into a passion almost, and he tried hard to nick Cora to prove himself a man, but as the weeks wore on and nothing happened, and Riach started calling her a dry coo, Hamish consoled himself with more and more drink.

On damp mornings, when it was too wet for Nancy to gather the sheaves of corn, Riach yoked Meg into the cart and drove up the slopes of the Mattock Hill for peat turf. Craig had dug it during the summer and spread it on the heather to dry, and dewy mornings in harvest time was a fine chance to drive it home for winter burning. On one of these mornings Riach took Ruth along with him, sitting in the bottom of the cart, while he sat on the fore shelvin, with his cork leg in the cart, the other foot on the shaft. They followed the old cart track up the hill as far as the feet of the white stone deer, and while Riach loaded the cart Ruth rambled over the white stone dykes that formed the shape of a stag, and when she stood on his antlers he was as big as a farmyard. Far below she could see Bogmyrtle among the trees, and the Laird's castle in Lachbeg Woods, and even the Myre Loch on the coast and ships at sea. The sea captains sometimes took their bearings from the white stone deer on the Mattock Hill, and farmers could foretell the weather by the clouds that obscured it; whether it would be fair or foul, and they planned their work accordingly. But nobody could tell Ruth who had formed the great white stag on the hillside, or where they had found all the white stones to shape him out, though you could hardly make head or tail of him at close quarters.

When the cart was full Riach called to Ruth and they set off again down the hillside, Riach leading Meg by the bridle, Ruth running behind in the new laced boots Rachael had bought for her. Helen promised to pay her back when things improved for her. Ruth was also wearing some of Janet's cast-offs, a long-sleeved frock and a jumper, a shade big for her but decent enough to go to school with, for the summer holidays were over and she was back at her old school with Janet and Meston, passing Sauchieburn every day, but with little thought in her young mind of what had happened there, when memory is short; and only occasionally did she think about her father, until another object replaced him with another thought.

Ruth thought the great cart would be toppled over on the way down, bouncing over the giant boulders fixed in the track, Meg's white fetlocks swinging under the axle, the iron rings on the wheels grating over the stones. But Meg knew the way and chose her footing well, while Riach hirpled along beside her on his cork leg, hanging on to the bridle for support, depending more on Meg than she on him. When they reached the main road at Hillfoot, near the Fairies' Cairn, Riach stopped Meg and lifted Ruth on to the loaded turf, took the reins in his hand and climbed up himself from the shaft and sat beside her, joggling down the brae to Bogmyrtle. It was a thrilling ride for Ruth, high up on the cart, looking down on Meg's broad, mobile back, her grey tail swinging between the shafts, her white fetlocks bobbing under the cart. There were giant foxgloves by the roadside, with bumble bees busy on the stigmas of their purple-red flowers, like fat old housewives sweeping out their doorsteps.

Nowadays it was a privilege for Ruth to carry a peat ember round to Riach on the tongs, careful not to trip over his cork leg, and sometimes he would take her on his knee and give her beardie when he needed a shave, rubbing the hard stubble on his chin against her soft velvet cheeks, until her eyes watered and she skirled with laughter and squirmed in his arms until he had to let her go. She was even more trusted than Janet to stoke the boiler fire in the greenhouses in the colder evenings, where the great vines clung to the walls and tomato plants were tied up to the roofing struts. She wasn't able to lift Riach's watering-can with the long spout, which was for reaching the pots on the backmost shelves, but she carried water from the spootie and poured it into the can for him. She helped Janet and Meston to pluck gooseberries for sale in Brochan, besides plums and brambles, and even went to town on Saturdays with Riach on the spring-cart, when she got a few odd pennies from the housewives to buy Fred's Candy, the most famous sweetie in Brochan, or even in all of the Bogside.

Riach even trusted Ruth in his closet, where very few others were allowed to enter, rich with the smell of shaving soap and hair cream, and he showed her all the trophies he had won at the flower shows, and the framed certificates of merit from the various seedsmen that hung on the walls, and all the knick-knacks he kept locked in his kist, and she was allowed to look at his gardening books with the lovely coloured pictures of all the flowers and shrubs. Ruth couldn't yet read properly but the pictures enthralled her and she wanted to draw them if Helen would give her a drawing book and a box of crayons.

Riach spent long evenings practising on the pipe-chanter, a book of bagpipe music propped up in front of him on his dressing table; and sometimes he took the silver-mounted, ivory-droned bagpipes out of the polished wooden case in his closet and played them outside at the kitchen gable. He swung the white drones over his shoulder, tucked the tartan bag under his arm, blew in the mouthpiece, punched the bag with his elbow, till it squealed like a young pig, fingered the chanter with his flat-nailed fingers, so long used to weeding flowers, leaned forward and twisted the drones if they were out of tune, settled them on his shoulder again, like a stag newly antlered, and the wail of his pibroch went far up the Mattock Hill, so that Cora Swapp could hear it at her fireside at Burrowend, and the Laird listened from his mansion deep in Lachbeg Woods, while 'The Flowers of the Forest' brought tears to the eyes of the widows and those bereaved in Flanders. Riach's heart-searching music died with the twilight, and after tea and a smoke he went to bed, when Ruth was privileged to stand on the lid of his kist to unfasten the leather straps on his shoulders that held his cork leg in position, though he waited till she was back in the kitchen and the door shut before he sat down on his bed and took off his leg and propped it up in a corner. Rachael or Nancy usually fastened the straps for him in the morning, though he said it was time Meston was trying it when Ruth could unfasten them. When Hamish was in the house at bedtime, which wasn't often nowadays since he got married, Riach would cry out to him from his closet, 'Come and tak' aff my leg, man!' as if he were a patient in great pain, and Hamish a doctor about to perform surgery.

Now that the corn was fully ripe the harvest got under way in earnest. Craig yoked Meg and Bell to the drap-pole of the old back-delivery reaper and began slashing down the crop. He worked on one side, guiding the horse team with the reins from his iron seat on the reaper, going back empty to the other end again to cut another swath, waiting till the gatherers had cleared the one he had just cut, some-times gathering a few sheaves himself to aid them. He had to give the gatherers time to bind the sheaves that had been swathed off the reaper springboard from the cutting bar, swept on to the stubble by the tilting lever, a windmill contraption on four revolving spokes, with a spiked rake on one of the spars that delivered the loose sheaf. And while the gatherers trussed and bound the sheaves Riach forked them aside to make a stubble road for the reaper going back empty.

It was a Saturday and the bairns were in the park as well, gathering strabs or making bands for the gatherers, Nancy and Kirsteen and three or four hired helpers, now that Moira and Nora were gone, and even Hamish. It was a hot afternoon and the gatherers were thirsty, so Riach told Ruth to go home for water from the spootie, or a flagon of buttermilk if she could get it. Rachael and Helen were in the kitchen but they didn't hear the soft-footed Ruth come in, where she stood in the lobby when she heard her father's name mentioned. Rachael was ironing clothes with a goose iron on the table and Helen was folding them into a basket on the deas. The door was wide open and Ruth had walked straight in, but now she stood with her finger in her mouth, listening to the women.

'If he doesna tak' me back I'll droon masel'!'

It was Helen who said this and Ruth thought of the mill-dam behind the steading, where the dark peaty water came down from the Mattock Hill and was gathered behind the deep sluice for driving the paddle wheel on threshing days. Or perhaps her mother was thinking of the deep wide lake in Lachbeg Woods, where the Laird's daughter had drowned herself, because she was with a baby to her brother, or so Janet had told her, though Ruth couldn't grasp exactly what it meant. But maybe her mother would go there at night when it was dark, and the fairies that hid among the rhododendron bushes would push her into the lake.

'Dinna speak sic daft nonsense, lassie,' Rachael said, 'I'll write tae Audie Foubister and he'll tak' ye back a' richt. He'll be glad tae hae ye back, lass, tae get a hame for himsel' again. A gie drizzen life he'll be havin' in a chaumer. We could offer him a croft tae bide on.'

But Helen wasn't so sure. 'And how do ye think he wad answer your letters when he doesna answer mine? I've written twice tae him and he's never answered. I've waited on the postie tae hand me a letter till I'm heartsick o' waitin'. And Audie canna read nor write onywye; he can hardly sign his name, and he wad have tae get somebody else tae write the letter for him – his mither maybe, or his half-sister, and ye ken what they think o' me!'

'Then write tae his lawyer, lass, and see what he has tae say.'

'I could do that,' Helen answered, 'but why doesn't Audie come and see me? I wad go doon on my knees tae ask him tae tak' me back but he never comes. Seein' that he canna write he could come and tell me what he thinks.'

'Could ye no go and see him instead?' Rachael asked.

'I hinna the strength or the courage tae go among his folk in my condition. I wad brak' doon a' thegether.'

'But ye say ye wad droon yersel'; surely it wad be easier than that!'

'I dinna ken what tae do. I'm demented,' and Helen began to sob.

'Ah weel, lassie; ye'll juist have tae wait. Maybe yer man will come and see ye in his ain good time – maybe when ye're least expectin' him. And think on Ruth afore ye do onything rash, and the bairn ye're carryin'; it's nae only yersel' ye have tae think on, mind that!'

But Riach would be impatient for the buttermilk and Ruth was afraid to listen any longer; not that she fully understood all of what was being said, but to hear her mother say she would drown herself frightened her, and the mention of her father's name intrigued her, and she just couldn't help eavesdropping. But she couldn't afford to linger any longer, so she made a noise with her feet and hurried into the kitchen, as if she had just hastened from the harvest field. The women stared at her in surprise, Helen with a tear on her cheek, which she quickly brushed aside; but Ruth showed no concern and calmly asked for the buttermilk, though big folk were still a bit of a puzzle for her young mind.

Day by day as the harvest progressed Helen still looked for Audie on his bicycle. But he didn't come and she consoled herself with the thought that he would also be busy harvesting, but he would come to see her when it was all finished. Or maybe his mother or Susan were putting him up to it to stay away? Maybe his lawyer insisted that Helen make the first move? Well, she had written; surely that was something, and she 'had come to her senses', as Audie would have it.

Every morning when Ruth awoke she half expected that her mother would be gone from her side, gone to join the fairies. But everything went on much as usual, except that Hamish had got reeling drunk and thrashed poor Cora, skelped her arse this time, folk said, so that nobody would see the marks. She had flown to Sourrockden again, in her slippers and nightgown, and the bairns had even heard about it at school. Ruth heard Janet telling Rachael about it in the milkhouse, and simply said that Hamish her brother had slapped Cora's backside.

Then Ruth noticed that her mother had started knitting again with the blue wool, something she hadn't seen her doing since they came home from the south.

But the long hot summer broke at last and the white stag on the Mattock Hill was shrouded in mist. For nearly a week he was wrapped in his curtain of fog and a fine drizzle seeped across the harvest fields. The fog-horn on the coast at Battery Head moaned for days and the spiders cast their fine webs across the broom and whins. And then the rain fell and the wind rose, lashing across the fields from the Moray Firth, flattening the corn yet to cut and soaking the stooks on the stubble. There was even a crack of thunder, ripping across the sky at nightfall, while the lightning blobbed over the darkened landscape in white blinding flashes.

When it thundered Rachael covered up all the clear shining things in the house with towels and dusters and odd bits of cloth, from the milking pails to the fire-irons and even the mirrors, believing they attracted the lightning, while anybody outside never ventured near a wire fence or handled a scythe or a fork or a bicycle or anything made of steel for fear of getting hit. Even Hamish who had been in the war didn't like the thunder and said it reminded him

241

of the shellfire. It was God in His anger, they said, and folk that had done an ill turn were at His mercy. The folk in the Bogside sat in their kitchens with bowed heads when it thundered, and the dog growled from under the table.

It had caught the menfolk in the Bogside with their trousers down, half finished with a job that was vital for their survival. For two whole weeks Craig and Riach hadn't cut a stalk of corn nor bound a sheaf, but stood whiles in the stable door watching the puddles growing in the close, the hens in the cartshed taking shelter, where all summer they had fluttered in the dust under the cartwheels; now they stood on one leg in the mud and cocked their heads to one side and then the other, watching the steady drops that fell from the roof tiles and were spattered on the stones at their feet. But the ducks were in their element, waddling over the mud and gobbling up the worms that came to the surface to drink, gabbling over their meal, wagging their short tails and swilling their bills in the rain pools.

But the wind blew away the fog and the stag on the hill-side lay bleached in the rain. When the sun came out at last he was polished white against the purple heather, while the wind chased the drifting clouds over the Mattock Hill. When the wind fell the heather slopes steamed in the sun, the white wisps curling up the hillside like veils of cotton-wool. Folk began to reappear in the parks again, resetting their stooks that had been blown down and soaked on the stubble. Scythes were whetted and backs were bent to cut the lying corn, waiting for a drying wind to get the binders yoked.

It was three weeks from their last cutting when Craig yoked the reaper again, and this time even Rachael was in the field, a white sun-bonnet on her head and a thin jersey to protect her arms, trying to humour Craig with her help when he was so anxious to have the cutting done. Helen was left alone in the house to wash the dinner dishes and fill the piece basket and boil the tea, and the bairns would take it to the park as soon as they came from school.

It was the day that Hamish went to Brochan with his Arran Chief tatties and some early cabbages and cauliflower on the float; the day after Riach had been with his spring-cart. Hamish was late in coming back and Rachael looked up several times watching for him on the road. She could even see Cora's peat reek at the foot of the hill, with a stunted tree or two bent over the barn, their roots fixed in the rock that the wind couldn't move them, but had shaped their growing bodies over the years. But the peat soil was mixed with a fine sand that took potatoes well, and even a corn crop if you gave it muck or herring guts, and Rachael saw no reason why her son shouldn't do well enough in Cora Swapp's croft, if only he'd keep off the drink.

But he was later that day than ever she'd known him to be, for the bairns were coming through the stooks with the tea basket and still no sign of him. It was long past closing time with the pubs and nobody had seen Hamish on the road with his empty float. The four o'clock train was past and still no sign of him; she could hear it rumbling over the bridge on the Leary road. Surely he would be fell drunk Rachael thought, and heaven help poor Cora when he got home in that state. At first she had resented Cora for taking away her son (for that was the way Rachael looked at it) but when she remembered the croft and all its benefits she forgave the quine and bore her no ill will; in fact she was beginning to concern herself about their married life, especially when Hamish was drinking so much, though she didn't believe all she heard about him skelping her back-side, for she had never seen her son angered in her life. She had never known Hamish to lift his hand to anyone; fun was all he was after and Cora must be taking him too seriously. She would get used to him in time and Rachael felt that if she stopped running, Hamish would take her in his arms and kiss and hug her, and that he meant no harm to her at all. Maybe a bairn would help matters between them; if only Cora could have a bairn she was sure Hamish would take more interest in her and settle down. Maybe it was the effects of the war that troubled Hamish, Rachael thought, and some men never got over it at all.

It was after four and they had finished their piece when

Hamish appeared. Rachael was greatly relieved. She had straightened her back making a band for her sheaf when she saw him, and she stood with the wisp of corn stalks in her hand, watching for nearly a minute as Hamish came nearer the gate. He was stretched out on the float, apparently asleep, while the shelt found its own way home, the reins among his feet and like to trip him up, but still he plodded on, head down, nodding up the brae.

What Rachael didn't see, until the last moment, was the traction engine coming in the opposite direction, with a threshing mill in tow, hoasting out black smoke as it rumbled down the brae. Rachael knew that the shelt didn't like traction engines or puffing-billies, or anything on wheels with a rumble of pinions in its insides, and a great many other horse beasts were like minded. A motor car or a lorry they could abide with, or even a train at a safe distance – but a traction engine, never! So far Hamish had never had much bother with the beast, flat-eared and ringle-eyed though he was, and when they met an engine and the shelt began to prance, Hamish got out of the float and led him past the noisy monster; and usually the drivers would shut off steam and stop or slow the engine until the frightened beast was safely on its way again.

But today Hamish was in a stupor of drink and never heard or saw the approaching engine. Rachael was watching from the hairst rigs but Hamish still lay on the float. Fear clutched at Rachael's thoughts and she ran forward, dreading what would happen, crying to Craig to stop Hamish's shelt. But the reaper was noisy and everybody was busy and nobody heard Rachael's panting cries; not even the bairns playing hide-and-seek and crawling under the stooks. The gatherers were hard at work with their heads down; not until they saw Rachael running and heard her cries did they look towards the road.

Hamish still slept on the cart, almost to the spot where Muriel Spark fell off her bicycle so many years before, where the shelt neighed loudly and rose in the air, toppling the sleeping Hamish out of the float. They were about ten yards from the engine and the driver stopped it, shutting off steam and braking the fly-wheel, while the fireman watched over his shoulder from the coal tender. Hamish rolled on the road like a ball, relaxed and unhurt, half sobered by the fall, and as quickly grasped the situation. Drunk as he was he staggered forward to the frenzied shelt and seized the bridle. He led the beast forward until they were almost abreast of the engine, smelling of coal smoke, and hot oil, when the shelt nickered and shied and refused to budge further, rising on his hind legs and pawing the air with his front hooves. Hamish was fourteen stone, and while he clung to the bridle with his iron grasp the animal lifted him clean off his feet. But he lost his hold on the leather strap and a forehoof caught him a crushing blow on the head. Hamish went down in a heap at the animal's prancing hooves, while the frightened beast danced with his iron-shod hooves on his crumpled body. The shelt neighed in terror, foam at his bitted mouth, while he trampled and bludgeoned Hamish to a bleeding pulp. Then he bolted, writhing in his harness, past the engine in a wild dash for home, the cart bouncing behind him, dropping empty crates and boxes on the road.

The engine men were on the road by now but they could do nothing to stop the frantic shelt. But they ran towards Hamish, moaning in his agony, and dragged him to the side of the road. The MacKinnons came running from the harvest field, all except Meston, who was left with Meg and Bell, while all the others raced for the gate, Rachael first, because she had a running start, then Kirsteen and Nancy, Craig and the hired hands, and Riach hopping forward on his game leg. Rachael scrambled through the fence and reached Hamish first, moaning piteously and bleeding through his torn clothes. Blood was streaming from his mouth and ears while he wriggled in pain and tore at the grass by the roadside.

Rachael fell beside him and took him in her arms. 'Hamish,' she cried, 'Oh Hamish, speak to me Hamish!' But Hamish merely rolled the whites of his eyes and thumped at his breast with his fist. He looked at them all as they came closer, licked his blood-swollen lips and murmured, 'I doot, mither, this'll be the end o' me!' Then he closed his bloodshot eyes and turned his gashed head on one side. 'Oh Kirsteen, my quine, get the doctor quick,' Rachael cried. Then she fainted, and Craig and Nancy dragged her away from the bleeding Hamish.

Kirsteen ran home for her bicycle and swept past them for the doctor. Nancy and Janet ran home for blankets and told Helen what had happened. They covered their brother with the blankets while he plucked the grass in his agony, tore it out of the green sod in lush hopeless handfuls. Helen brought whisky from the kitchen press, but Craig thought it dangerous to give it to Hamish, in case he choked, so Helen merely dabbed his lips with the wet cork. Rachael revived, and when she opened her eyes Nancy gave her a teaspoonful of whisky. Then Nancy had to hold her to keep her away from Hamish. The doctor arrived and gave him an injection of morphia to kill the pain and he seemed to sink into a coma. Rachael whimpered and struggled with Nancy to get nearer her son, then broke loose and fell beside him. 'Will he live, doctor?' she cried. 'Oh Daw, they canna let him die. Oh my Hamish!'

But nothing could save Hamish; not even blood transfusion or surgery. After he examined Hamish the doctor took Craig aside and told him so; told him that his son's rib cage was broken, smashed into his lungs, and that he believed his intestines were a quagmire; he would send for an ambulance to have him X-rayed, but he didn't think Hamish would survive that long.

Hamish was quiet now and still breathing while they waited for the ambulance. Rachael was on her knees, his head on her lap, his body twitching unconsciously, everybody waiting anxiously. Hamish vomited his life blood in his mother's lap, rich spurting mouthfuls that slowed with his dying heartbeat, and Rachael fainted a second time at the sight of it.

The ambulance arrived seconds later, and when the doctor had examined Hamish they laid him on a stretcher and motored him up the brae to Bogmyrtle, where they laid him on the floor in Riach's closet.

Cora Swapp was weeding in the garden when the shelt came charging into the back close. He had fire in his eyes and bloody foam at his mouth, his ears working furtively, where he stopped at the barn door in a tremble, sweat steaming from his back, his ribs working like a blacksmith's bellows. Cora looked around the cart for Hamish, while the shelt nickered and champed his bit, apologizing it seemed for the absence of his master. Cora tied the shelt to a gatepost, grabbed the money-bag from the float and threw it into the porch, locked the door and put the key in the rone-pipe, then ran down the road to Bogmyrtle.

She met the engine men at the head of the avenue. 'What has happened?' she cried at them, scarcely stopping for their reply.

'A man was killed when his horse took fricht at the engine and trampled him to death,' said one of the men.

'Oh my man,' cried Cora, 'whaur is he noo?'

'They took him tae the fairmhoose,' the man replied, 'ye'll see the ambulance in the close.'

Cora ran down the avenue and it seemed to her that even the spootie was running blood that day at Bogmyrtle. The hens flew over her head as she ran into the close, scarcely glancing at the ambulance that was just leaving, while she barged in at the door. She fell upon the floor in Riach's closet and wept her heart out for Hamish her man. The doctor had Nancy take her away, for she was frantic in her grief, and it was hard to believe that Hamish had ever laid an ungentle hand on this woman.

Two policemen came on their bicycles and measured the road and questioned the mill men and most of the Mac-Kinnons and one of them wrote their answers in his note-book.

Later in the evening Sherran Begg came with another undertaker and they cut off Hamish's torn clothes, washed and shaved him and clothed him in a white robe and carried him through to Joyce's room, where they laid him in an oak coffin under her picture. They set the polished coffin up on trestles and propped the lid against the marble fireplace. There was a brass plate on the lid which read:

HAMISH MACKINNON: AGED 29 YEARS. So Hamish was with his grandmother: Rachael's first child in Holy Wedlock, as Joyce had seen it, while Helen, being older, was the child of their sin.

Next morning, just after breakfast, Helen was scrubbing the stone step at the back kitchen door, getting things tidy for the funeral. Rachael was distracted in the kitchen and wanted another last fond look at her mangled son. Craig took her arm and led her gently along the passage, quiet on the rugs and linoleum from the noisy scrape of the bare cement floor in the kitchen. Craig opened the panelled door to his mother's room, a room where Rachael seldom entered, even to polish the furniture, but left it to her daughters, and even they were reluctant to be left alone with their grandmother, while she stared down at them in ominous silence. But Helen could stay for hours in Joyce's room, where she could dust and polish till her heart's content and Joyce gave her peace of mind beyond price in her troubles. Helen would dust it again for the funeral, but in the meantime it smelled strongly of eau-de-Cologne or white lilies that nearly overcame Rachael. She lifted the cold stiff hand of her son and touched it with her pale lips, pressed the cold fingers against her cheek, then gently replaced his hand upon the other on his breast. She leaned forward and kissed his cheek while Craig supported her in his strong arms, and the memory of his birth came to both of them. Craig glanced up at his mother's picture and saw the resemblance in his son, for Hamish took after his grandmother in likeness, more than the MacKinnons, or the Bissett family.

Craig took his wife back to the kitchen, where she lay on the box-bed, and when he stepped over Helen at the door a hot tear from his eye landed on the back of her hand. Helen straightened her back, the dripping scrubber still in her grasp, when the words of her old grandmother flashed into her mind: 'Soap and watter will never wash the sin frae your father's door!' Helen remembered that day in her girlhood when Craig had thrown the pail of dirty water over his mother in the passage, a deed which kept her spirit still alive in the house, prevailing strongly where her weak body had endured so much.

Helen rose stiffly to her feet, poured the pail of brown dirty water into the brander and laid the scrubber on Riach's window-sill. She untied her apron and laid it aside in the kitchen, where her mother still lay fully clothed in the box-bed, staring into space, apparently unaware of Helen's presence. Helen slipped quietly into the passage, past the foot of the stairs and the grandfather clock, which had never kept the time since it fell on Joyce. She opened the door to her grandmother's room and crept inside, closing the door with a soft click behind her. She looked at Joyce in her picture and crossed herself like a Catholic, something she had learned long ago in the chapel, then knelt by the side of the coffin and prayed for the soul of Hamish her brother. She prayed earnestly for several minutes, devoutly, as Joyce had taught her to pray, though she had nearly forgotten, and as she rose to her feet another of her grandmother's sayings came to her memory: 'The mills of God grind slowly, but they grind exceeding small.' In her childhood, when Joyce said this, she imagined that God was a miller, and that he had a water-wheel, like the one under the lade for driving the barn mill at Bogmyrtle.

Helen climbed the stairs to her attic bedroom, ever so slowly, one step at a time, holding on to the wooden rail with one hand and holding up her long skirt with the other, lest she should trip on it. By the time she reached the top her head was in a whirl, the bed a white blur in the light from the storm window. She groped her way across the room to the white blur and fell upon the soft bed, where she wept and writhed in the sharp spasms of pain that brought her knees up to her navel, where the bairn was moving in her womb and kicking at her ribs. For twenty minutes she endured, while hot irons pierced her stomach and stirred her intestines, and the hot sweat beaded her brow; then she lay calm and blissful and fell sound asleep.

Janet had gone up to live with Cora Swapp or the funeral was by, or at least or Cora's mother could be brought back from Brochan. Poor Cora was glad of Janet's company, as she stood quietly beside her while Cora milked the cow and fed the calves: things that had to be done even in the midst of death.

A lot of the neighbours came to see Hamish for the last time and to try and console Craig and Rachael. The flowers and wreaths they brought were overflowing in the room, while Nancy and Kirsteen took it in turns to show their brother to the mourners. Nancy was the most composed at the head of the coffin, refusing to give way to the grief that nearly choked her. Kirsteen bit her lip to stem the tears, but they glistened on her fair cheeks and shook her fine frame in spite of herself.

On the day before the funeral Helen took Ruth through to the room and lifted her up to see her uncle. Poor Ruth cried, because she remembered the time when uncle Hamish had sewn up her father's trousers. Maybe God had forgiven him, for Ruth recalled her father saying that uncle Hamish would pay for this yet; that a High Power above would see to that. And Ruth had heard Meldrum Spark telling her mother that Audie her father was one of God's bairns, and most likely He would send His angels to look after him. Ruth cried so bitterly that Helen had to set her down, wondering why the bairn felt so sorry for her uncle for they had never been all that friendly when Hamish was alive.

There was no controlling Rachael on the day of the funeral. Nancy and Kirsteen held her in Riach's closet, for she was no sight for the neighbours to see; her eyes swollen and red from weeping and her grey hair turned almost white overnight. Moira did her best to console her and even Nora came up from the south with her man for the burial. Sherran Begg took the flowers from the folk at the door and took them through to see Hamish if they wished. Craig and Riach gave everybody a glass of whisky, port wine for the women if they wanted it, and Cora helped Helen go round with cups of tea most of the morning.

How long he had been there Ruth couldn't tell. There was such a press of people in the old kitchen, and so many going along the passage to see Hamish, that from where

Ruth stood with Janet and Meston she couldn't make everybody out; people she had never seen before, others that she didn't recognize in their best clothes, and what with the hub-bub of noise, everybody talking at the same time, it was a wonder she managed to spare a glance for her father. But it was him all right, shaking hands with her grandfather and then with Riach, and they offering him a dram, and him drinking the whisky, and then disappearing with Sherran Begg to look at Hamish.

But Ruth was waiting for him by the passage door when he came back, where he grabbed her by the arms and she laid her head against his waistcoat and cried with tears of joy. He lifted her up in his arms and jabbed at her soft cheeks with his moustache, tears forming in his eyes while he held his quine close.

Helen wasn't to be seen, until Ruth remembered she would be making her bed, so she took her father by the hand and led him up the stairs and knocked on the door. When Helen opened it she jumped in her surprise, scarcely grasping the truth, until Audie wiped his nose on the palm of his hand, and she came to him between tears and laughter. Audie held her for a moment and stroked her hair, his little heart filled with pity for his bonnie wee crater, and he petted her heaving shoulders while she sobbed on his breast. 'It'll be a' richt noo,' he said, consoling her, 'a' richt noo. The farmer's wife read it out from the papers about Hamish and I thocht it was a fine excuse tae come and see ye. She also read your letters but said I had tae mak' up my ain mind aboot havin' ye back; so noo I'm here, wuman!' The three of them sat on the bed and talked and smiled and dried their tears and Helen said, 'I've come tae my senses, ye see – I've learned my lesson.' Audie said he would see about getting a flat in the toon 'cause it would be difficult getting a house in the country until the next May term. Then Sherran Begg cried up the stair that the minister had arrived and that he would have to screw down the lid on Hamish's coffin for the service. So all three went down and stood on the bottom step to listen to the minister, because there was such a jam of people in the passage.

Among other things the minister spoke about the short-
ness of life, its uncertainties and pitfalls and its lowly end,
and after the ceremony Hamish was carried outside in his
gleaming coffin and laid upon the long cart. Nora's man
and Kirsteen's lad took one end of the coffin and two of
Hamish's pals took the other. Nancy and Kirsteen and
Janet carried out the flowers while Sherran Begg placed
them around the coffin on the long cart. Rachael stood in
the door of Riach's closet, almost mummified with grief,
Moira supporting her, and the doctor had advised that she
shouldn't attend the burial. Hamish's shelt couldn't be
entrusted with his cortege, so old Meg had the honour of
pulling the long cart, clad in her best harness, and when all
was ready Craig took her by the bridle and led her slowly
up the avenue, now rich in snowberry, by the water spootie
and the mill lade, in the shade of the great privet and laurel
hedges that sheltered the gardens, while the first brown
leaves fell from the trees and the song of birds had died.
Craig walked canny with his son, curbing Meg slightly
in her eagerness, so that Riach could keep up, hirpling
behind the coffin, the bag-pipes on his shoulder, while the
wailing notes of 'The Land O' the Leal' went far across the
listening fields.

By the time Craig reached the main road the last of the
mourners had joined the procession from the close, and
when all were clear of the avenue, Riach stopped piping
and got on the long cart among the flowers, the pipes in his
oxter, while the long trail of folk walked the two miles to
Lachbeg churchyard, where the gravedigger was waiting at
the gate.

There was another long service at the graveside, and then
Hamish was lowered to his last resting place. Audie had a
cord with the rest of the male members of the family,
including Nora's husband and Kirsteen's boyfriend, and
when they threw in their cords the minister raised his hand
and said, 'In the name of the Lord, I am the Resurrection
and the Life: he that believeth in me, though he were dead,
yet shall he live.' The sexton sprinkled some loose earth on
the coffin, and the minister raised his hand once more and

said, 'Earth to earth, ashes to ashes, dust to dust,' and Riach took his pipes again and played a last requiem over the grave of his brother.

Audie spent the night at Bogmyrtle, sleeping with his wife in the upstairs bedroom, while Ruth slept with Janet and Kirsteen next door. When he left in the morning Ruth thought he could take her with him on the bar of his bicycle. Helen had to explain to her that this wasn't possible yet, not until her father found a house for them, and then they could all go and live together again and maybe they would be as happy as they had been before. So Ruth gave way and managed not to cry, though the bairn was homesick for her father once she had seen him again, and the image of Meldrum Spark was fading fast from her young mind.

They went with Audie to the head of the avenue, early in the morning, while the barn cocks were still crowing and the white deer on the hillside was gradually taking shape. The air was sweet with faded honeysuckle and the mint of stubble fields, peat smoke and midden sharn, while dew beaded the grass and birds fluttered silently in the growing daylight. Audie said good-bye on the main road, then got on his bicycle and sped down the brae. Helen was smiling and waving and Ruth joined her, forgetting her homesickness in the smiling face of her mother.

Craig and Riach finished the harvest, with Nancy and Kirsteen to help when they could be spared; mostly forking and loading the sheaves in the parks, while Craig himself built the corn stacks. Then they took in the rakings and thatched some of the ricks for winter. By then it was time for lifting the main-crop tatties, and Ruth managed to give a hand at this, gathering into a little pail she had found in the close.

After the first corn milling Craig brought back sids from the miller and Rachael made sowens for the Meal and Ale, or Harvest Thanksgiving celebrations; not that Rachael had much to be thankful for that year, or anything to celebrate, but she did it for the rest of the family, and to keep her mind occupied, away from her grief. Audie liked sowens, especially

Rachael's brewing, the finest he ever tasted, he said, and he biked all the way from Scotstoun to sample them. Most of the MacKinnons were at Bogmyrtle for the Meal and Ale party, including Ruth's cousins, the bairns of Sherran Begg and Aunt Moira. Ruth detested the sowens and only supped them for the sixpence Rachael had promised might be at the bottom of her bowl, and told her to be careful not to swallow it. But Ruth was disappointed, for Meston got the sixpence, biting into it sharply then holding it aloft for everybody to see.

It was about this time also that Craig emptied the beehives of their honey, a white mask on his face and special gloves on his hands, while the bees crawled all over him. Craig didn't keep a lot of bees, and he hived them to pollinate his flowers more than for the honey, though it was fine on a home-baked scone in winter and a spoonful sometimes cleared your throat when you had the cold. But meantime the huge combs were dripping over the basins on the kitchen dresser and the bairns got a broken comb to suck, the sweetest syrup Ruth had ever tasted.

Cora Swapp couldn't abide the killer horse about her croft, and even though her mother was back to bide with her for a while she couldn't stand the sight of the beast from the kitchen window. This beast had made her a widow, a very young widow, and she couldn't forgive him; every time she looked at him his eyes seemed wild and he cocked his ears wickedly at the slightest sound, or so Cora imagined, and maybe he would kill again in his fright. That was why Cora wouldn't hear of him being sold, because he might widow some other poor woman or make some poor bairn an orphan, and though the shelt still actually belonged to Craig, Cora had objected strongly when Riach spoke of selling the shelt to a horse dealer. So he was kept prisoner at Burrowend, at least for the present, an idle criminal, for Rachael wouldn't let Craig or Riach go near him, especially Riach with his artificial leg. But he ate up all the grass on Cora's croft, so that there was hardly anything left for the cow and the stirks, so Craig said he would halter the shelt and take him down to Bogmyrtle, where there was always a bite to spare. Cora was relieved to see him go, his long tail nearly touching the ground and his ears working wickedly when Craig took him out at the gate.

But now the beast haunted Craig and was a sore torment to Rachael. If she had been a younger woman she would have taken a fork and stabbed him through (like she used to prick poor Meg and Bell when they didn't deserve it) but now she merely stared at the beast from the kitchen door and thought of the mangled body of her son. Riach argued that the poor beast had killed in fear, not out of intent like a human body, and that he was a quiet friendly brute most of the time. But Rachael still hated him and lay in the box-bed thinking of ways she might put him out of the way, maybe with poison in his bruised corn when the winter came on.

Craig too had his feelings; especially when he thought of the scoundrel who had sold him the shelt, and the trouble and scandal he had brought on his household by waylaying his daughter. Maybe if he hadn't bought the shelt it wouldn't have happened, and his son would have been alive today? The more he thought about it the more he hated the shelt; thinking on ways and means whereby he might avenge himself on fate. He even had wild thoughts of shooting the shelt, or killing him with a fencing mallet, though he never revealed his thoughts to Rachael, nor she to him.

Rachael looked haggard and thin after Hamish died. It was easy to make her weep nowadays. And not for a fortune would she enter Joyce's room. Joyce looked at her so accusingly from her picture that Rachael wouldn't go further than the end of the passage, even though the best of her furniture stood there, her best rugs on the linoleumed floor, her finest curtains on the window. Rachael was afraid of Joyce, especially on windy nights when she tapped her foot in the ben-room, and Rachael would lie listening to it at Craig's back in the kitchen bed.

'That knockin' in the room,' she cried: 'Oh Daw, I'm fear't. Yer mither's restless the nicht.'

'Lie doon and sleep, wuman; it's only a loose stane in the lum.'

Rachael lay trembling in the dark, until Craig screwed up the lamp and tried to console her. Maybe it was only a loose stone in the chimney, rattling in the draft from the flue – nobody had taken the trouble to find out – but it kept the spirit of old Joyce alive at Bogmyrtle; alive in Rachael's guilty mind, fretting her conscience as she grew older. The 'wee angels' that Joyce had fondled at birth she was now taking to her bosom in death: that was what Rachael believed, and that Hamish had been the first to go. So Joyce's room became a sanctuary; her portrait that of a martyr, triumphant in death . . .

It wasn't long or Audie's mother found a small flat for him in Scotstoun. Audie would have preferred a country cottage, but this was well nigh impossible until the Whitsun Term, when the cottars would be on the move again, and it was too long to wait. He cycled down to Bogmyrtle on the Sunday morning to give Helen the good news: that he had found a room for her in the toon, until something better should turn up, and they could all be together again.

Towards the end of the following week Craig yoked old Meg into the long cart again, and with Riach and the bairns to help him they loaded Helen's furniture out of the barn, where it had been stored since the May Term. Helen and Nancy polished it all with dusters and Mansion Polish, to clear away the dust and give it a fresh smell, even the huge carved sideboard that had once been the pride of Helen's ben-room. Ruth came across her mouth-organ in one of the drawers and started playing again, some of the tunes that Riach played on the bagpipes, and he was fair taken with the quine for this and loth to let her go. Something they had in common had been discovered too late, or sure enough Riach would have had her playing the bagpipes in no time, dressed in a kilt and tunic and stravaging round the close at Bogmyrtle. As things turned out he had to let her go, but they parted far better friends than they met, and he no longer called her 'a sulky little bitch'. Riach's good rela-

tions with his little niece had also softened his feelings towards her mother, especially since Hamish died, and
nowadays Helen had some of Riach's sympathies in the
problems she faced, though he never said as much openly.
But he was less cutting in his remarks and showed more
understanding towards her than a body would have looked
for from Riach MacKinnon, even though she was his oldest
sister.

Helen got up on the cart with her father, Ruth beside her,
and as they all gathered round the kitchen door to see them
off Craig clicked his tongue to Meg and the great cart
creaked and crunched on the gravel as it lumbered out of the
farmyard. Ruth felt a little sad at parting from Janet and
Meston, at the thought of leaving her old school and all her
chums, and even her teacher; but the pull of home was
stronger, a new home in the big toon where everything was
exciting and she would meet lots of new chums at the big
academy.

But it was farewell to the purple heather on the Mattock
Hill, and the white deer on its slopes, sniffing the peat reek
with his slender nostrils, the wail of Riach's pipes in the
Lachbeg Woods; farewell to the Fairy Palace where the
Laird lived, the clang of the Kirk bells on Sunday mornings
(to remind you where uncle Hamish was sleeping), Leary
station with its busy trains, and the far Myreloch where the
snipe called from the sea. Good-bye also to Brochan with its
tree-lined streets, where Ruth sat on the cart while Riach
weighed out carrots to the housewives. All these things Ruth
had come to love and enjoy, but must now pull herself
away to something quite different in Scotstoun, where
granny Barbour lived in her grand house up on Toddlebrae.

Helen's new abode was little better than a dungeon,
though bang in the middle of the toon. When Craig and
Audie had carried in the furniture they went up to Toddlebrae for Audie's share, which had been stored with his
mother, and she gave them a dram and had a good laugh
with Craig, while he smoked his pipe and talked of what they
called 'the good old days before the war', and then they
spoke of sadder things, on the loss of her son Frank on the

battlefield, and the sad death of Hamish that she had read about in the papers. Because Audie was present they couldn't say anything about the broken marriage though it was uppermost in their minds all the time. Craig parted with Mrs Barbour on a promise to meet again sometime, a promise that neither intended to keep, but found it a convenient note to part on.

There wasn't much space in the house after all the furniture was brought in; only one room and a boxroom, what some folk called a glory hole, sub-let from the woman who leased the ground floor from the miser up the street, but Audie was glad to have it, and the rent was reasonable.

Old Meg was impatient to be off home again, even though Craig had a sackful of hay for her that he shook out at her feet. She was champing at the bit and would hardly wait or Craig was ready to go. Some of the town bairns came to look at her broad white fetlocks and fine pleasant eyes, to admire the glitter on her polished harness, or to marvel at the huge cart that stood behind her, like a tumbril from the French Revolution. Craig gave the bairns a ride out to the suburbs, and when they returned Ruth wanted to show off and tell them that Craig MacKinnon was her grandfather and that old Meg was his mare.

Helen's flat was on the ground floor of a two-storey tenement with its gable end to the street. It was a dark grimy hole with only one window that looked out on the gaunt harled wall of a huge warehouse. When the furniture had been placed against the papered walls there wasn't much space left in the middle of the floor, where Helen had laid a bit of linoleum to cover the cement. The window was at the furthest end from the close mouth, next to the wash houses and the water closets, standing parallel with the warehouse to form the pend.

Across the street there was a brewery, where the carters' horses reversed their iron-wheeled lorries into the causeway entrance to load and empty bottle crates for the shops and pubs around the town. Further up the street there was a fashionable drapery establishment with a pillared arcade over the pavement and wax ladies in the huge glass windows.

Behind the brewery there was a smokestack, and the bare Gothic spire of the Parish Kirk could be seen over the roof-tops from the middle of the street.

Ruth slept with her father and mother in the recess bed, which was just a fancy town name for a box-bed, the same as they had in the cottar houses, and some of them even had chaff mattresses. The Landlady and the neighbours were decent kindly folk and Ruth found a playmate in the girl upstairs. Barbara Holmes was about the same age as little Janet, with round blue eyes and soft dark hair that hung in ringlets to her shoulders, and she always wore brown worsted frocks with black stockings and high-laced boots fastened with a button hook. Her father had been killed in the war and she lived with her widowed mother in the little attic at the top of the tenement. Ruth would sit with Barbara in the little gable window overlooking the street, watching the horse-carts and lorries and motor cars, and sometimes they got out their dolls and picture books, or played housies in a corner while their mothers gossiped over the fire.

After dark, when the street lamps were lit, the girls clattered down the bare wooden stair to swing round the lamp posts or stot a ball on the pavement, under the glare of the gas, or they would stand for a long time under the drapery arcade, their hands behind their backs, admiring the wax ladies in the lighted windows, their long silk dresses reaching to the window-sills, fancy hats on their heads and bangles on their arms, their skin as pure as peach and their eyes shining in the gaslight. Their dresses were changed as the richer customers bought them, and some of them wore their dresses for such a long time that the girls tired of looking at them.

Further down the street, opposite the Muckle Kirk, there was an Italian ice-cream shop, where the girls spent a lot of time admiring the pictures of King George V and Queen Mary and the Prince of Wales on the chocolate boxes, the King and the Prince in their shining gold braid and the Queen wearing her crown and all her sparkling jewellery. It was seldom they had a penny for a cone or a poke of chips from the frier next door, unless they rummaged in the ash-bins at the head of their close, where they sometimes found a few coppers, and Barbara said the miser lost them when he was counting the rent over the fire because he wouldn't pay a penny for the gas meter. Ruth had seen the miser once or twice, a thin old man with a wizened face, in rag-bag coat and sandals, clasping a penny bundle of kindling sticks, never speaking to anyone, nor looking to right nor left, but waddling through his dingy doorway out of sight as fast as his spindly legs would carry him. Barbara said he was very rich and owned half the street, all the best houses with granite walls and polished doors and Venetian blinds on the windows, yet the miser's own house was hung with cobwebs and coated with dust: her mother had seen it, she said, when she fell behind with the rent and went to see the miser, and he opened the door with a candle in his hand. Down at the corner grocer's the girls could get a penny for a jam jar or two jars for a bagful of broken biscuits, and the day they picked up a florin on the pavement their mothers had a picnic.

Ruth went to the Central School, because they said she wasn't old enough for the academy. Here she learned to read properly and she loved the history lessons; all about Joan of Arc and Thomas Becket, William Wallace and Robert the Bruce; but unfortunately she stuck her head in the school railing and the Headmaster had to get a hacksaw to release her.

Audie was still working in the country and Helen found it difficult making ends meet living in the town, especially when they had a rent to pay, which was something they weren't accustomed to in the country, and Helen missed the perquisites; coal, meal, milk and tatties, besides the hens and what could be got from the garden. She hadn't been well either, and several times, on returning from school Ruth had found her weeping over the coal fire. Apart from the Landlady and the neighbours she had no friends and nobody looked near her. Washing days in the wash-house out back, when she had to light a fire in the boiler, was about the only time she saw the neighbours, mostly watching her from the windows while she hung her washing on the clothes line. A trip to the shops was her only outing and most of her time she spent alone in the flat.

One Sunday evening, just as the folk were leaving the kirk, Susan Barbour knocked on the outside door of the tenement and gave Helen such a tinking as scarcely left her with the chastity of the vilest whore in Christendom, while the kirk-folk gathered round the close mouth and the neighbours listened from their open windows.

'You little MacKinnon whore,' Susan cried, 'Ye should hide yer head in shame; awa' whoring with a tinker while ye'd more need to be at hame like a decent woman lookin' after yer man and yer bairn. You're not fit to lick Audie's boots let alone sew a button on his shirt or wash his clothes or cook him a decent meal. The poor man hasna had a chance wi' a bitch like you. Think shame o' yersel, woman; ye should go inside and hide yer guilt frae the neighbours!'

You would have thought she was sticking up for Audie in front of the neighbours, but Audie didn't want her sympathy and took his wife inside, big with child and tears on her cheeks, and shut the door on his half-sister. As a farmer's daughter Helen had been a sore disappointment to Susan's town pride, all fur coat and no drawers as they say; and she went down the close with her head in the air and through the kirk-folk like she was a paragon of virtue – most likely mad with the thought that she couldn't get a lad of her ain, taking her spite out on Helen who had had her share of lusting.

Helen's first thought after this outburst was to save enough money to buy another marriage ring. It would please Audie, besides being a pretence that she was as good and respectable as the next woman, among strangers anyway, and would help to keep the likes of Susan Barbour in her place. No doubt some of the neighbours knew Helen's history, and what they didn't know before, Susan Barbour had filled in the gaps. But Helen was too sick at heart already to concern herself any more and steeled herself to face them.

After about two months in the basement flat Meldrum

Spark's child was born. Helen had been sick in the morning when Ruth left for school, walking the floor with a pain in her back. At dinner time the Landlady merely allowed Ruth to peep into the dungeon, then took her through to dinner in her own apartment. Helen was lying with a scarlet face on the white pillow. She ventured a painful smile at Ruth and turned her face away when another spasm of pain twisted her body. It was ill enough to bear for your own man but hell for a stranger, for besides the pain in your guts you had the guilt in your mind, and you couldn't look for sympathy. Ruth wanted to stay and held on to the doorknob. What did they know about her mother anyway? Inwardly they probably despised her, especially after what Aunt Susan had yelled at her in the close. But how could they really know what she and her mother had been through? Those town women who had never washed their linen in the river or slept under the open sky, or sold besoms at the cottage doors. But her mother would manage; she was as hardy as any of them. All the same, it was good of them to help. But the Landlady was firm with Ruth, stubborn though she was, clinging to the doorknob and crying for her mother; but the woman wrenched her away and took her through to dinner with Emma, the fat dress-maker who was always sewing at the gable window when Ruth came home from school.

By supper-time the baby was born and Ruth was allowed inside. 'You've got a brother,' the Landlady said, and Helen thought she meant it in the full meaning of the term, in spite of what Susan had said. But for a brother he was the most crab-faced, pink-skinned creature Ruth had ever looked at. She could hardly believe that boys began like this, well not pretty boys anyway. Ruth put her thumb in the creature's fist and it held on tight, like a limpet on a rock, with skin as pink as shell-fish and less hair on his head than her grandfathers, old Craig or Mr Barbour. When Ruth took her thumb away the creature twisted its face and whimpered, then looked sadly at her with its blue eyes that were really pretty.

This was something her dad should hear about and Ruth

wanted to be the first to tell him. She knew where to meet her father coming in from the farm and she ran out to the suburbs to catch him. He walked into town every evening after supper and Ruth met him on the Toddlebrae, out among the toffs where the Barbours lived, though you could hardly call the Barbours gentry. It was getting dark in the suburbs and Ruth overtook the lamplighter on the brae. When she saw her father coming there was a terrific flash of lightning, and but for the sight of him Ruth would have been afraid. She never called him Dad: somehow it made her feel embarrassed; so they just talked without names and she said she was waiting for the thunder because it was so far away. Then Ruth said, 'I've got a brother,' trying to keep up with his big strides.

'Oh aye,' says her father, never dachling, 'but he's nae mine, lassie . . . he's nae mine!'

Ruth thought he said it rather spitefully, as if he was angry, and she said no more, just kept up with his rapid step back to the dungeon.

Audie opened the door and went thumping into the basement flat in his usual clumsiness, clumsy for a smaller man who should have been more nimble on his feet. The gas was burning on a mantel bracket over the fireplace and the air was rank with the smell of lysol and baby powder. When Audie saw the Landlady and the midwife he took off his cap and stood awkwardly in the middle of the floor. 'Aye, though,' says he, almost apologizing, 'there's been a gie steer here, I doot,' then wiped his nose on the palm of his hand and waited for an answer.

The women nodded their heads and the Landlady made some excuse and went through to her parlour. Audie went nearer the box-bed and looked at his wife and asked, 'Are ye a' richt noo, wuman?' Helen blinked at him from the pillow. 'Aye,' she said, sighing slightly, 'I'm nae sae bad.' Then to the midwife, 'Has the lassie got her supper?'

'Aye, she's gettin' it frae the Landlady.'

Audie washed himself at the washstand. When the midwife had gone he went over to the bedside, just as Ruth came back from the Landlady's room. Audie leaned over his wife and took the coverlet away from the baby's face. 'Faith he's like 'im, though,' says he, 'aye fegs he is, wuman.'

Ruth supposed that he meant Meldrum Spark: she didn't know why, she just guessed; and her dad must be a fool to suggest such a thing. That crab-faced creature like Meldrum Spark: surely he must be silly to think that. And why should the baby be like Meldrum Spark anyway?

'But he'll have tae pay for it, though,' says Audie, beginning to colour up in the white glare of the gas. 'Surely he canna expect me tae bring up his bairn and him go scot free!'

His face hardened with the thought and tears bulged yet again under Helen's eyelids. Now that she was down maybe he wanted to kick her. Maybe this was where he wanted her so that he could teach her a lesson. If he didn't it wasn't that Susan hadn't put him up to it, and even his mother and Doris too, though perhaps a little more discreetly.

'Have nae mercy on the bitch,' Susan had said, 'especially when she comes tae bed doon!'

'Mak' her lick yer boots, Audie,' Doris added smugly, diddling her own bairn in her arms and dipping its dumb-teat in her mother's jam jar.

But Audie Foubister was a soft-hearted man: 'ane o' God's bairns', as uncle Riach said of him, full of compassion and human pity, and he wouldn't punish his wife. Maybe he would have a short childish outburst of temper but it wouldn't last. Soon he would be stroking her jet-black hair again and calling her his bonnie crater; bonnie wifie though.

'He'll pay for his bairn,' Helen said, wiping away a tear with the coverlet, 'can ye no see I'm heartbroken as it is, withoot worryin' me aboot siller.'

This was like a day of sunshine to a snowman and Audie went to smush at the sight of her.

'Dinna fash yersel', wuman,' says he, his small eyes enlarging in sympathy. 'Dinna fash yersel'. I wunna be hard on ye, lass. Ye ken yersel' I'm nae hard-hearted. It's juist that I thocht it a bit hard the wye things have turned oot for me. Juist put yersel' in my boots, wuman – wad ye be as lenient if I was in your place? And mind ye've had a bairn tae that devil but ye wadna hae ane tae me!'

The bairn was fretting and Helen uncovered a nipple to give it suck. 'But ye'll register the bairn in your ain name, will ye no?' she asked, 'then folk canna say lawfully that the bairn's nae yours.'

'I'll register the bairn, wuman, tae please ye; and sae lang as he pays a sma' thing for't I wunna say a word tae vex ye.'

Helen looked up at him with those eyes of hers that were like blue summer skies after rain. 'But ye'll hae tae look for anither hoose; we canna a' bide here noo: there wadna be room for us.'

'Aye, wuman, I'll try and get a cottar hoose somewye, and meantime I can sleep in the chaumer at the fairm so that Ruthie can sleep in the bed wi' ye; at least till ye get a cradle for the bairn. I dinna like sleepin' in a bothy when I've got a hame o' my ain again, but it'll do for a time.'

'Ruth can sleep on a rug on the fleer.'

'Na na, wuman, the lassie will get her bed; she's mebbe sleepit in some gie queer places as it is but she'll get her ain bed noo. And besides that, it'll save me walkin' oot and in frae the fairm ilka day.'

'Maybe ye could get a job in the toon, drivin' a carter's horse, or maybe a scaffie's job.'

'Na na, wuman, I dinna want a toon's job. I wadna get ane onywye; there's owre mony lads lookin' for jobs already. And besides, I dinna like this toon life; it's owre expensive.'

So they called the bairn James, because Helen liked that name, and she took Audie's hand in hers over the table and taught him how to sign his name on the Register of Births, because he had hardly written a word since he signed it last time, and Ruth was nearly nine years old.

On the night the bairn was born there had been a terrible freak thunderstorm in the Bogside. Helen read about it in the Landlady's newspaper, of how cattle still out in the parks had been killed by the lightning and barns set on fire. Folk had never seen a thunderstorm so late in the year, now into November, and reports said the sky was red by morning and the air warm and smelling of sulphur. Two days later Helen had a letter from Rachael, written on the back of a tea bag, because she never bought writing paper, and the letter said that Cora Swapp's shelt had been killed in the park, where they had intended leaving it out all winter to save the hay for the other beasts, and that there was a brown scar on the grass where the lightning had left the wire fencing and gone across to the shelt, and it was still warm when Craig found it in the morning. Another flash had split the room chimney and a stone fell down the lum and landed on the room fleer ... all in Rachael's own spelling; and the letter brought some strange thoughts into Helen's mind, of how her mother would maybe get peace now at Bogmyrtle, because she remembered another of her grandmother's sayings: 'The Lord moves in mysterious ways, His wonders to perform!' And when she said that, Helen used to imagine God crawling about amongst the great white clouds, watching everybody in the Bogside.

About a month after Meldrum's child was born, Audie plucked up courage and went to see a doctor about his rupture. He was encouraged by the thought that if it could be cured he would maybe get his own way with Helen and make another bairn; after all she was his wife and he was entitled to try. But the doctor told Audie that his rupture had been neglected too long and couldn't be put back because tissue had grown into the cavity. He got a belt to wear from the Insurance Society but it gave him hell and he had to throw it aside. The hernia had never given him pain before and he wasn't going to aggravate it now; Helen would just have to put up with him as he was, and though she didn't like his fumbling ways he would make damned sure this time that Meldrum Spark didn't get near her.

Shortly after the New Year Audie got the chance of a hovel for his family in the country, not far from the farm where he worked. They moved out of the basement flat on a day of pouring rain. When they reached the hovel it leaked under the thatch and there was a hole in the gable that almost served as a door.

There was a box-bed in the kitchen where an old man had

just died. Helen set fire to the straw he had lain on and scrubbed the bottom boards with hot water and lysol before she laid down her own mattresses and bedding. The but-and-ben clay biggin' had become vacant at the old man's death. Some of his calendars for years back still hung on the damp walls. Ruth wanted to look at them but Helen tore them from their rusty nails and threw them on the fire. She got busy with the sweeping brush in every hole and corner. Cobwebs were dislodged in handfuls and spiders and cockroaches were running everywhere. Ruth stood on a chair, holding up her skirt nearly to her knickers, sure that there was mice in the stinking presses. The condition of the old cottage angered Helen and the cleaning of it put mettle in her spirits. She could hardly believe that Audie would have brought them to such a place, unless it was the nearness to the farm where he worked. When he came home at dinner time Helen gave him the sharp edge of her tongue: Bringing them to such a place, she stormed, where the bairns might catch cold or even pneumonia; and didn't he know there was a hole in the gable would nearly let in a horse and cart?

But Audie stood in the middle of the floor and said it was the best he could do. No, he didn't know there was a hole in the room gable. It was dark when he looked at the house and he never noticed it. The farmer's wife told him about the house being empty and he just took it on lease from the farmer it belonged to. It was nearer his work and surely he was entitled to some consideration. Most likely the farmer would sort it in the summertime.

Helen swore that she wouldn't stay in the place or the summertime; that she was going back to town in a day or two, and that he could get the farmer's wife to stay in it herself if he liked, but it wouldn't be her. Some folk thought anything would do with a cottar body but she wasn't putting up with this.

Audie flared up at last, frustrated and angered and hardly knowing which way to turn. 'Ye wad a done it for yon ither lad, though,' he hissed, 'ye had some gie queer shak' doons wi' him, nae doot, and nae word aboot it either; nae a hoose at all, juist a tent tae sleep in, but mebbe it didna leak, or ye was juist lucky tae get fine dry weather when ye was awa' sooth. But mebbe I'm nae worth sae muckle tae ye. Is that it, wuman?'

This was the first time since the birth of Meldrum's child that Audie had openly reproached his wife. He had been patient and kind and forgiving, almost childishly so, with a woman who had wronged him so cruelly. It was not in his simple nature to be anything else; not that he really understood his wife's feelings, but the exasperation of the moment had sharpened his wit to a very fine pitch. Even now Helen's heart still bled for her lover. Audie never guessed it but he had used the most lethal weapon in his armoury at the most opportune moment, and he had wounded his wife where it hurt her most.

Helen made no attempt to answer him. She thought him a heartless brute to ask such a question, even though he had every right to do so. Her heart was still tender in her love for Meldrum Spark and she winced under the taunt. She was silenced at last but there was a breath of defiance in her final jibe at Audie: 'I wunna bide a week in a tattie pit like this!'

'Weel weel, wuman, I'm affa disappointed that ye canna sattle yersel'.'

'Sattle masel', here, in a place like this? Dinna be daft man. Tak' a day aff the morn and go tae the toon and see what ye can get for us.'

'And what am I tae tell the fairmer's wife? She tel't ma aboot the hoose.'

'Tell 'er tae come and bide here hersel'.'

All night long the wind whistled through the hole in the gable and the old discoloured wallpaper flapped and bulged out on the damp clay walls. It rained for days on end and Helen was nearly out of her mind with rage and disappointment. Had she known of this she would have stayed with Meldrum Spark, and if it didn't improve she would return to him. Worst of all the brown sooty drops trickled down the walls and dropped from the ceiling on to the table at mealtimes.

Before the week was out baby James threatened pneumonia and the local doctor ordered Audie to move his family out at once, or as soon as possible. Audie was thrawn, but he took the next day off from work and cycled into the toon to see what he could find. He went back to his old Landlady but the basement flat was already occupied. But she knew of another room just down the street, and when he went there he got it; a room and a closet over the Kirkgate Bar, bang opposite the Muckle Kirk and the jam factory, with a view of the sea from the window. The rent was a bit high but Audie was glad to have it and didn't argue. He hired a horse and lorry from the nearest contractor and when the rain ceased they loaded up the furniture again and headed back for the town.

The new Landlady was a crusty little busybody who made it quite plain that she would stand no nonsense about the rent. Pay up or get out was her policy and Helen would do well to remember it. Audie explained matters to the farmer and he got a few shillings more to his pay and it helped. Helen bought a second-hand pram for baby James, and Barbara Holmes came down the street occasionally to take him out, sharing the pram with Ruth, who wasn't yet to be trusted on her own with the baby in the pram. Barbara sometimes brought her dolls and they played housies in the back close, especially on washing days when Helen was up to her elbows in soap suds.

Baby James wouldn't take the breast any more; every time Helen tried it, even though he was hungry, he screwed up his little face in a greet and turned his lips away from the nipple. He got thinner every day until Helen put him on to bottle-feed with cows' milk, adding a little sugar and hot water, and with this he settled down contentedly. But Helen's breasts grew hard and sore and she sent Ruth to the chemist's shop for a breast reliever, a rubber-and-glass contrivance that was supposed to drain away the milk and ease Helen's discomfort. But the suction wasn't strong enough and Helen endured days and nights of agony with inflamed nipples and swollen breasts. The pain was so intense that Helen made Ruth suck her, leaning over the bed, spitting the sweet watery milk into a basin. Ruth detested this and tried to get away, while Helen in her agony held her by the wrist, forcing her daughter's lips to her nipples, the human milk mixing with the tears that Ruth spat into the basin. Ruth was greatly relieved when the Landlady told Helen to dose herself with Epsom salts and to rub her breasts with vinegar; an old wives' cure, as they say, but it was effective; and when her periods started again the milk left her and her breasts grew soft and spongy, while her hunger for intercourse returned.

The Whitsun Term came and went but Helen wouldn't budge a second time. Audie got a job on another farm about a mile nearer the town and he was content for the time being. Helen was easily upset these days and even Ruth seemed to get on her nerves sometimes. She still pined for Meldrum Spark and the least thing was an excuse for her little outbursts of lovesickness. She knew that the game was up; that even Audie was not to be trifled with a second time, and yet the wildest little schemes exercised her imagination, whereby she might meet her lover.

She still had a letter from him occasionally, sometimes with a ten-shilling note tucked inside. In the evening she would show it to Audie.

'Look what I got the day,' she said, a little sparkle of mischief in her eyes, as much as to say: 'I told you I was on your side.'

Audie was flattered. He took the ten-shilling note and held it up to the light, as if he suspected its legality.

'Fine, though,' he said, 'as lang as he pays a sma' thing noo and than I hae nae ill feelin's, wuman.'

He pretended to read the letter and to censor its contents, but he hadn't seen the row of kisses at the foot of the page where Helen had torn them off. It was easy to deceive him. You could have shown him the same letter several times and he wouldn't have known the difference. But apparently he was pleased and that was all that mattered.

'He'll nae get a foot in here again – I'll see tae that,' was all he said. Audie was now in full control of the situation.

Sometimes Helen got impatient for Meldrum's letters. Several times she sent Ruth up town to the post-office to have them rummage the mail bags, and if Ruth was lucky she could have almost anything for the asking.

Meldrum had asked in a letter to see his bairn; perhaps just an excuse to meet Helen again. But Audie refused. 'Na na,' says he, 'lat him see his bairn and that wad gie him a start again. He's nae comin' here!'

But it is just possible that Helen may have contrived a secret meeting with Meldrum Spark in some out of the way side-street. If she did, Ruth nor Audie never knew about it; but Audie was at work and Ruth at school, and there's no saying what Helen got up to in their absence, even with the pram, to show Meldrum his child.

She never slept with Audie again. He lay in the closet bed and nursed his big hernia, though it had never given him pain again since he removed the rupture belt.

Helen lay with Ruth and the baby and dreamed of her life with Meldrum, his letters under her pillow. Ruth was content because 'The Real Angel of Mons' was hung up on the wall again, where she could see it from the bed, and 'King George and the VC Heroes' beside it, so she felt secure. She had developed a great notion for pictures and music, and now that she could read properly books were an added interest. Sometimes when she was reading her book her father would give a big snore and waken himself up in his chair, then he would sit staring at her as if he had nothing else in his mind. Suddenly he'd say, 'But you are mine, lassie; you've got my nose and my lugs. I mind the nicht ye was made; ye're made o' good stuff, ma bonnie quinie!' Everything he liked was bonnie. Maybe he thought she should have been a loon, and that if he had been bigger it mightn't have happened. Certainly Ruth had his thin straight nose and his protruding ears; but she had Helen's nature too, whatever that meant to him. Ruth had his sloping shoulders and his egg-shaped head, though she managed to hide it with her hair; you could see it in her school photographs. Audie should have had plenty of brains in a head like that, but Mrs. Barbour once told Helen that he fell off a dyke when he was a bairn and hurt his head. He was unconscious for days, she said, and maybe damaged some of his brain cells.

'What are ye readin', ma bonnie quinie?'

'Robin Hood.'

'I dinna ken what ye see in books. I couldna read a book tae save ma life. I left the school when I was twal tae work on the grun.'

Ruth well knew it. He couldn't even read the newspapers; just looked at the pictures and threw them aside. He couldn't even sign his name. Helen had to forge it for him; nor count his wages without Helen being aside.

He never asked Ruth about their life with Meldrum Spark: where they went or how he had treated her. He seemed content that they were back and that things were much as they had always been; especially when Ruth played the gramophone and he sat and smoked and listened. All the old tunes again, because he couldn't afford to buy new records. But he still liked them, the old pipe tunes and the melodeon and fiddle; and Harry Lauder was his favourite vocalist. On Saturday nights you could hardly hear anything for the hubbub in the pub downstairs, though Audie never went down for a dram.

'Na, faith ye,' he would mutter suddenly, 'he wunna get a foot in here again,' just like that. It was still on his mind and he still felt humiliated; his manhood insulted, brooding, fretting over his misfortune. Other men were strong: why did it happen to him? Or perhaps it was just his way of reassuring himself, by saying it aloud, 'He wunna get a foot in here again; I'll see tae that!'

The local flower show was held annually in the Music Hall. Craig MacKinnon had been preparing for it all summer. He had won the silver cup the year before and he was out to repeat his triumph. If he could win the cup three years in succession it would be his for keeps. Scotstoun was out of his reach as a market for his vegetables, so that the prize was of little use to him as an advertisement. But Craig said it was fresh vegetables that impressed his customers, not diplomas, though the vase-like thing looked fine on the kitchen dresser.

But he yoked old Meg into the long cart and loaded up with his most luxuriant pot plants, the most luscious vegetables, and the best cut flowers Kirsteen could find in the gardens. He had leeks as thick as your forearm, parsnips as big as a drainpipe, tapered to a root of horse-hair thinness; turnips that looked like giant apples, and potatoes that were polished with butter and displayed in sphagnum moss. He had an impeccable selection of strawberries, gooseberries, blackcurrants, plums, tomatoes and cucumbers that had kept Nancy and Janet and Meston busy for a week; and Craig's greatest anxiety now was the autumn breeze that threatened his hydrangeas and pelargoniums and fuschias in the swing of the cart. He took Riach and Sherran Begg along with him to Scotstoun, and he promised them that if he won the cup again he would give them the time of their lives.

Craig set out in the afternoon, so that everything could be arranged for the judging in the evening before the day of the show. The Music Hall had been cleared of its forms and whist tables and the flowers and fruit and vegetables were arranged on boards set up on trestles. Craig then stabled Meg at the Palace Hotel and went round to Helen's place with Riach and Sherran Begg. He was in tearing spirits, and now that Helen lived above the Kirkgate Bar he promised everybody a roaring time if he won the silver cup again. Helen gave them supper, and Craig returned with Riach and Sherran Begg to watch the judging in the Music Hall.

The prize list was published the following morning, and Craig had won the cup. To save them expense at the hotel Helen had managed to bed them all down on the floor, so after breakfast the three worthies returned to the flower show. They returned about teatime, just about the time that Audie came home from work, and after supper all four of them went downstairs to the pub. Craig was in triumphant mood and took the Kirkgate Bar by storm, so to speak, lashing the drink about him as if it had been sea-water.

Half the locals were drunk by closing time, and were wildly acclaiming him as the town hero, while a host of ruffians fought each other for admission to the bar.

When the pub closed, Craig came staggering up the stone stair at the back with all the drink he could carry, Sherran Begg supporting him from behind, while Riach pulled him self up by the railing, trailing his cork leg behind him. There was a great hubbub at the mouth of the close, where women were trying to get their menfolk home, pulling each other's hair to get at their husbands. Blows were exchanged among the men and some false teeth were trampled on the pavement. The noise was a bedlam until the police arrived with their batons and stunned some of the worst offenders.

Audie was missing and Sherran Beg had to go downstairs again to look for him. He was staving drunk when Sherran Begg brought him up the stair and he smashed some of the Landlady's crockery that she had stanced on the landing. He grabbed Helen in his fury and was like to wring her neck for deserting him, laying forth about what he would do to Meldrum Spark right now if he could lay hands on him. Sherran Begg got him away from Helen but it looked for a while as if the MacKinnons had created a monster they couldn't control. Ruth had never seen her father like this before and she hid herself under the table. Audie wanted more 'Fireflacht', as he called it, and before Craig could pour him a glass he had hold of the axe from the fireside and was like to tear up the linoleum to get it. Riach got hold of him from the back but Audie threw him aside like a sack of straw. He was no match for Audie in his present mood and it took Craig and Sherran Begg to hold him down, foaming at the mouth he was and his eyes rolling. He wasn't accustomed to drinking and with a few friendly glasses of Highland Firefly the MacKinnons had turned the gentle Audie into a rip-snorting tearaway maniac.

Craig took the axe away from Audie and somehow they managed to get him into an armchair. Meanwhile the Landlady came hammering on the door, demanding compensation for her broken crockery. She said she wasn't going

274

to have her rooms turned into a drunkards' brothel (whatever that was supposed to mean) and that if her damaged crockery wasn't paid for she would have them all out on the street. Helen couldn't reason with the woman; for it was only an old flower pot that had been broken, and a kiln-cracked vase that had been knocked down, and the rugs had saved them from worse harm. It was the earth that had been scattered on the floor that angered the woman, and Helen got the brush and shovel and started clearing it up. Meanwhile Craig put a crumpled pound note in the Landlady's fist and she soon backed out, closing the door behind her.

Sherran Begg still sat on top of Audie, and when Helen returned she made strong tea and Craig made Audie drink it to sober himself. Audie spluttered and choked himself back to sobriety, then sprawled himself on the chair, where he lay with parched lips and rolling eyes.

'I want tae spew,' he gurgled.

Sherran Begg took Audie through to the sink, and when he tottered back to the chair he was white and shaky, clean washed out.

When things had quietened down a bit Ruth came out from under the table and sat on the fender, where her mother gave her tea and a biscuit.

'Audie man,' says Craig, all of a sudden, 'I have a proposition for ye afore I gyang awa'.'

But Audie merely slumped forward out of the chair and lurched over the table, where the bottles and glasses sparkled in the gaslight. He fell on the nearest chair and sprawled his elbows on the table, where he lay with his head on his hands, staring at the glassware and licking his parched lips.

Craig sat down beside him. 'Audie man,' he said again, 'foo wad ye like tae be a fairmer? Lat Helen there be what she likes she could be a good wife for ye yet, a fairmer's wife at that. Mind ye, she's still a fairmer's dother, and efter all ye've been through I could put the two o' ye back on yer feet again. Foo wad ye like a craft, Audie?'

Long years ago something of the sort had been suggested to Audie. Some memory of it came into his fuddled brain but he had lost interest. He gesticulated with his hands and shook his head. 'Tae hell wi' yer craft,' he mumbled, 'I dinna want it!'

'But, Audie,' Craig insisted, 'I'm in dead earnest. Cora Swapp's gettin' married again and she wants tae sell her craft; if ye want it, Audie, I'll let Helen there get her share o' what siller she's entitled tae and ye could tak' the craft at Whitsunday.'

It was a generous offer, and coming from Craig Mac-Kinnon it showed what respect he still had for the little man who was his oldest son-in-law. In his sober senses Audie wouldn't have had the courage to refuse such an offer, even though he had wanted to, but the drink bucked him up to say what he wanted to say. 'Na na,' he groaned, 'I dinna ken naething aboot buyin' stirks and sellin' corn; I could be swicket richt and left and a'thing wad gyang tae hell. I wad rather work tae somebody else than hae a fairm o' my ain. And besides, I hinna the siller onywye.'

'But I'm tellin' ye, Audie, we wad gie ye the bawbees, and lend ye mair if ye wanted it. Ye could pay us back later on. Mind, ye wunna get anither chance like this in yer life again.'

'Ye should think it owre and tak' the craft,' Riach urged; 'we wad keep ye richt wi' the buyin' and sellin'.'

But Audie cocked his eye at the glassware, licked his lips, shook his head, and slumped into a heap over the table-cloth. 'Tae hell wi' yer craft, tae hell wi' Cora Swapp; gie's anither dram – d'ye hear!'

'Man,' says Craig, 'gin ye wasna my gweed-son I wad shak' the life oot o' ye. It's a damned insult, that's what it is; me offerin' tae set ye on yer feet again and ye turn it doon. Tae hell and buggery. Open anither bottle, Riach, and fill the bugger drunk again!'

Riach whipped out the cork from another bottle of Scotch and poured several glasses on the table. 'If ye had ony spunk in ye, ava man, ye wad try it,' he said to Audie, 'ye wad be yer ain maister for ae thing.'

But Audie was silent. He merely stretched out his thin arm for the nearest glass and drank it down at a gulp.

Maybe he had his own ideas of being his own master, with the MacKinnons as his overlords. After what had happened in his life he may have wanted to put as much distance between the MacKinnons and his own household as he possibly could. He may have learned from bitter experience that there was more lasting kindness and understanding to be had from strangers than he had ever had from his in-laws.

Helen was silent. She hadn't said a word all evening since Audie charged her with desertion and was like to grip her throat. She sat there and drank hot toddy she had prepared for herself from her father's whisky bottle.

'Drink it doon, lass,' Craig said to her, 'we a man like that ye'll never be naething but a cottar wife onywye.' And then he turned to Ruth, still sitting on the fender, her chin on her knees almost, her hands clasped round her legs. 'And you, quine, you'll never be a fairmer's dother, dammit no, quine.' He never had much to say to Ruth at any time but he had to acknowledge her existence.

He took a brimming glass of whisky from the table and swilled it under his red moustache. His hand trembled and the glass rattled against his tobacco-stained teeth. His eyebrows bushed out and rage and resentment glared in his eyes. 'It's a damned insult,' he said, 'tae hell and buggery,' and banged the empty glass on the table.

Baby James had slept through it all, but now he awoke and cried from the recess bed. Ruth went over from the fireside and picked him up, still in his shawl of white wool, almost all that Ruth could carry, warping his little mouth for food and looking about him with his clear brown eyes. Craig eyed the bairn thoughtfully, though he didn't oxter it, but took a half-crown from his pocket and put it in his grip, telling Ruth not to let him swallow it (for he put it straight to his mouth) and Craig gave Ruth a shilling also for her pains. Riach and Sherran Begg both eyed the bairn from where they sat, though they passed no remarks about his looks; but each left a piece of silver for him on the mantelpiece when they stood up to leave.

The town was dark and quiet when they left the flat.

Audie was in a stupor of drink and never raised his head to see them go. Craig went down the back stair in a dangerous swagger, Sherran Begg supporting him, while Riach took it one step at a time, holding on to the rail. They said good-bye to Helen and Ruth at the close mouth, then up the street to the Palace Hotel to yoke Meg and light the candle lanterns for the long journey back to Bogmyrtle.

Next day was Sunday and the pub downstairs went on fire. A cigarette stub had been swept up with the sawdust on the Saturday evening and had smouldered all night in a wooden box. The bar was thick with smoke and bursting into flame in the morning. The milkman saw the flames through the windows and ran to get a policeman. Ruth watched the fire-engine from the upstairs window, the firemen spewing water through the pub door from their leaping hoses. A policeman came upstairs and said they would maybe have to get out, but everything was soon under control and they didn't have to move.

Audie was almost himself again but a bit light in the head. After breakfast, when the fire-engine had gone, he washed and shaved himself and put on his best 'go-ashore' suit, as he called it and took Ruth with him for his usual Sunday morning stroll around the harbours to look at the boats.

As time went on Helen ran into debt and fell behind with the rent. Ruth couldn't even wheedle the price of her schoolbooks out of her mother. Audie was now thoroughly convinced that it was well-nigh impossible to live in the town and pay the rent of a flat on a farm worker's wages. By the end of the week Helen was sometimes without a morsel of bread in the house or a lump of coal in the grate. Even a penny for the gas meter was sometimes hard to come by. Helen had only recently paid the contractor for their last removal, and to get it he had to threaten her with a solicitor. Meldrum Spark still paid a small sum for his child, but it was like a drop in the ocean to what he required. Audie took well to the bairn and treated him like he was his own son, though he never liked folk wondering where the bairn got his brown eyes or who he looked like.

When the fee-ing time came round again Helen consented that Audie should look for a cottar place, with a proper house this time, and they could all move out at the May Term. Audie got a place about three miles out of Scotstoun, a good slated house to live in and a job as cattleman. He took Ruth on the bar of his bicycle to help him plant the garden in the spring evenings, after his day's work in the fields.

But Helen was too far behind with the rent and the Landlady wouldn't let them budge until they paid up. Every evening before the Term it was the same story and Audie would say, 'Whaur will we get the money, wuman, tae pay the rent? I dinna like tae ask it frae your folk efter I refused the craft; and besides, we michtna manage tae pay it back.'

'And I suppose the fairmer will fee somebody else if the Landlady doesna let us oot o' here by the Term.'

'Oh aye, wuman, I'll hae tae lat the fairmer ken afore that, so that he can look oot for anither man. I juist wonder wha wad lend us a fiver?'

A fiver. Five pounds owing to the Landlady and Audie was stuck for the money. Two weeks to go and they still hadn't found it. Ruth remembered the miser up the street. Perhaps he would lend them the money. Helen didn't think he would and Ruth had to think again. Her next brainwave was that her father should approach the farmer for a month's pay in advance, which was five pounds; this would pay the rent and the farmer could deduct a pound from Audie's wages every month for five months to pay it back.

It was Ruth's suggestion and her father was tickled with the idea.

'D'ye think it wad work, wuman? D'ye think the fairmer wad gie me a five-pound-note into my hand afore I'd done a stroke o' wark tae earn it? Fegs, wuman, it's worth a try. I think I'll jump on my bike this verra nicht and gyang oot tae the fairmer and hear what he has tae say aboot it. Gweed sake, quine, ye're learnin' something at that school efter a'; I wadna hae thocht on't.'

'But ye'll hae tae tell the fairmer what ye want the money for,' Helen reminded him.

'Aye, I'll dae that, wuman.'

The scheme worked. The farmer gave Audie five pounds on the conditions Ruth had suggested, and Audie went home smiling and brandishing a brand new five-pound note. He held it up against the gaslight on the mantelshelf, then folded it lovingly and gave it to Helen, and she slipped it under the pendulum clock to await the eve of the Term.

On the eve of departure Audie stepped across the passage and rapped on the Landlady's door. When she appeared he thrust the brand new fiver into her hand and addressed her with his forefinger, 'Now, wuman,' says he, proudly, 'there's yer money and we can leave when we please!'

'Oh that's all right, Mr Foubister,' said the busybody, 'but how did ye manage tae raise the money?'

'Never ye mind that, wuman; it's good clean honest money and ye have nae business whaur we got it.' And with that he shoved the Landlady inside her room and shut the door. Then he took down a glass case with a boat in it that she had on a table in the lobby, and set it on the floor, while Ruth swept up with a bunch of dried asters she had in a vase at her door.

On the day of the Term the horse-carts arrived from the farm and were backed into the tenement close. Audie and the foreman carried the furniture down the stone steps and loaded it on to the carts, while Barbara Holmes came down the street to say good-bye to Ruth and baby James. Then they were up the Kirktoon and out to the country, just like old times, Helen sitting on top of the second cart with baby James and Ruth, Audie plodding on behind the foreman, the reins from the second beast in one hand and holding on to the cart with the other – back on top of his little world again, a bit shaken but wiser, and determined to make a fresh start. And what with his 'bonnie wee wifie' beside him again he felt equal to the task.

And as they climbed the hill to Windslap, high above the howe and the toon, where the sun beetled down on the sea,

Helen got her first glimpse of the new world about her, with the far Mattock Hill hardly seen on the horizon; little more than a molehill, so that you couldn't even pin-point the stone deer above Bogmyrtle. Folk were strangers here and wouldn't know her character, unless it came after her like the slime of a snail; for you couldn't stop folk from talking, whatever you did, and she would just have to thole the gossip of smearing tongues. It wasn't Meldrum Spark country either, so far from Stronach, and he wasn't likely to come round this way with his box. Even if he did, most likely Audie would see to it that he didn't get a foot in the door. He hadn't been paying for his bairn these last few months, but it didn't matter; she would manage without it in the country and Audie would never know. Meldrum could keep his money to buy fags; it was all she could offer him now. What she valued more was the infant loon in her arms, a keepsake always reminding her of the one great love in her life.

The End

Epilogue

Helen wrote to her mother, giving her new address, and with all the particulars of the flitting and the countryside they had moved into; asking Rachael to come and visit them, now that Riach had a motor bike and side-car. Not since their years at Millbrae had Rachael been to see her daughter. Rachael had never seen baby James, nor had Helen ever mentioned him in her letters; it was as if he didn't exist, feeling perhaps it was something she ought not to brag about, but should keep it as quiet as possible, even with her own mother. Helen got a scribble back, so badly written that she could hardly make it out, but promising a visit during the summer, between Aikey Fair and the hairst, when folk weren't so busy for a while.

Rachael told in her letter how the Laird had died, without a proper heir, and that maybe Bogmyrtle would be sold with the rest of the estates, and she hoped that Craig had enough money saved to buy it. Riach had played the pipes at the Laird's funeral, and they had set a new gravestone up on Hamish in Lachbeg kirkyard – you must come and see it sometime, quine, a braw stone with his name in gold letters. Kirsteen was getting married this year and Moira had gotten another bairn, but there was no word of any family for Nora yet and poor Nancy was still at home. Janet and Meston send their love and their best wishes for Ruth and Audie. I'm going blind, Helen quine, and can hardly see to write your letter, but I'll manage it before the postie comes from Leary . . . And your father has a bad shake in his hands and can hardly lift a pail of water or put a spoon to his mouth; it's a terrible business when you are growing old and you remember the good days of your youth when you was young and swack . . . But here the letter was so completely jumbled that neither Helen nor Ruth could make head or tail of it, except for the crosses that stood for kisses at the end.

Nowadays nobody could tell you when the MacKinnons came to Lachbeg. All that is forgotten, and with the dying of the railway the MacKinnons are going too, with no male heir to carry their name at Bogmyrtle, for Meston died in his youth. There were only grandchildren now at Bogmyrtle, born of in-laws with a different name and they didn't remember the old folk. Most of the farm had been sold to land speculators and the old gardens gone to weeds. And now that the last Farquhar Laird has died nobody plays the bagpipes at the kitchen gable, for Riach sleeps quietly with his folks in the green churchyard at Lachbeg.

And you can hardly see the handsome deer on the Mattock slopes, overgrown with scree and rank heather; and that radar screen above his head, tilting in the wind like a windmill, supposed to be an early-warning system for hydrogen bombs in the Bogside; and the dungeons the Military have dug in the hillside, to hold their machinery and their press-button controls, shaking the deer with their drills and their blasting, and not a creature allowed on the hill nowadays beyond his antlers.

The folk in the howe have changed too: long-haired loons and mini-skirted quines, the likes of whom you never saw when you was at Leary School; and everybody flying about in motor cars and watching television, their parks overgrown with thistles and tanzies and their cattle beasts starving in winter for want of a decent byre or somebody to look after them. Not a peat cut in the moss nowadays, nor a cole of hay to be seen, or a stook, and the fine shaved rucks of the Bogside are a thing of the past. Cottar houses standing empty and ditches choked with weeds; dairy byres deserted and the cows all slaughtered, stone dykes a shambles and nobody to repair a fence. Your old school at Leary has been turned into a drying kiln for farmers' barley after it comes off the combine-harvesters; and the kirk is a garage for contractors' plant, diggers and earth removers, shaking the dead in their graves that got little peace in their lifetime.

They even tried to scare the snipe from the Myreloch,

piping ashore their maritime gas, but for the good folk of the Bogside who said Na, faith ye! Gang further sooth, ayont the Battery Head wi' yer gas pipes; and the navvies laid them across the bents where the farming billies used to get the shell grit for their hens.

North Sea oil has replaced the whale oil at Scotstoun, and hardly a herring curer left in the toon, though the place has got sae big that the Toddlebrae is noo halfway from the suburbs to the Broadgate. But Brochan is much the same, with its fine trees in the streets and its Toolworks, and of coorse the gut factory, turning out fish meal for the pig farmers.

Lachbeg Woods have even got a thinning, and the Big Hoose filled with broiler chickens. Not a whiff of peat reek in the howe, nor the scent of natural sharn newly carted out on the golden stubble, though the stench of sludge sprayed on the grun would sicken the minister from his manse, though God knows where they'd find another to take his place.

But with all their poisonous weed-killers they haven't killed the bird song in the howe, and you can still hear the whirr of a grouse on the Mattock, or the wheeble of a teuchat in the parks at Millbrae, where the thackit hoose where Ruth was born is now lived in by the gentry, sold as a week-end cottage to some swank from Aberdeen, with a new roof on the place, and double-glazed windows as wide as the turnip shed, where you could back in a horse and cart, if such a thing were to be found in the Bogside.

But neither have they stopped the showers of willow-herb and burr thickening in the sunbeam and blowing across the howe; insecticide has failed in this as much as the hoe, and even worse when you look at the parks, where the blown seed has landed.

Glossary

bawbees money
beetle to shine or polish
ben-room end or best room of a but-and-ben household
bents or **links** seashore, mostly in rough spinegrass
besom switch or broomstick made from heather or broom
biggin building, mostly one-storeyed
bink shelf or ledge, mostly of brick at either side of fireplace
braw grand, bright, gaudy
bree stock, sauce or gravy
breeks breeches, trousers
breet timid; one deserving of sympathy
breid oatcakes
briest breast or bosom
brose oatmeal mixed with boiling water, salt and pepper
bubblie-jock turkey-cock
buckie sea-shell

chaumer sleeping quarters for single farm workers
chauve struggle, fight, tussle
cheil or **chiel** man
claes clothes
cottar married farm worker living in a tied house
coup-the-ladle see-saw on a board over a rail, swingboard
craft croft
creel fish- or herring-basket
crook bent hook like the letter S

dam-brod black and white squares, draught-board
dander or **daunder** walk, stroll, amble or wander
deas or **deece** wooden bench with back support
dominie schoolmaster
dother daughter
doup buttocks
dreep drip; down at heel, miserable
drizzen dull, colourless, cheerless
dubs mud

fash fuss, worry
fee-ed to employ; engaged for work on a farm
ferlie a rarity, a wonder or unusual sight
fleer floor
fleg to frighten, scare
fule soiled, dirty

gaun going
gelding young castrated horse
gie steer a big stir, commotion

gipe fool or silly ass

girdle flat pan for baking pancakes, scones or oatcakes

girnal cabinet for holding oatmeal

greep floor of byre or stable, sometimes laid with cobblestones

greet to cry, weep

grieve foreman in charge, gaffer

gumption stamina, courage, initiative

gyang go

hame-ower home-loving, domesticated

hippen baby's nappy, napkin

hirple to limp; cripple

hoast cough

hooch to shout from the throat while dancing

howe valley

ilka every one

kaim comb

kebbock rounded cheese from the drying press

kirn assorted, mixed

kist trunk or chest, mostly of wood

kitchiedeem kitchen maid

kye cows

lames broken porcelain

libbed castrated

loon boy

lug ear

lum chimney

maun must

merrite married

neeps turnips

nick to impregnate, pregnant

nowt cattle

onywye anywhere

oxter armpits, bosom

pech gasp, pant

perquisites provisions in lieu of wages, a form of barter

phaeton four-wheeled horse carriage or brake with hood

pirn cotton reel

pishen saturated with urine

ploo or **pleuch** plough

press kitchen cupboard

queets ankles

quile peat cinder

quine girl

rax to stretch

ruck corn stack

ruggit pulled
runt stem or stalk

sair sore
scunner to upset, to put off; loss of appetite, disgust
sech sigh
sharn cow dung
shaws haulms or leaves
shelt light work horse, large pony
shelvin shelf on horse cart
siller sterling, money
skelp slap, wallop
skirl scream, shrill shout
sleekit on the sly; cunning, clandestine
sober frail, spiritless, thin
somewye somewhere
sotter mess
spaver trouser flap
spootie spout for running water
spunk light, spark, fire
squile squeal
stang tongue or stem of instrument
stite nonsense
swack swift
swick to cheat
swye swey, or swivelled gantry over the fireplace
syne then or since

teuchat lapwing
trauchle weary struggle
trump jews' harp

vricht joiner, carpenter

wall-tams leather straps with buckles worn under the
knees by farm workers; same as Nicky-Tams
wecht weight
whaup snipe or curlew, sometimes pea-pod
wunna will not

Thomas Cowden
47 Gilberdson Road
Lerwick